The Soul Winner

by John Burbridge

PublishAmerica
Baltimore

ISBN: 1-4137-7381-8
PUBLISHED BY PUBLISHAMERICA, LLLP
www.publishamerica.com
Baltimore

Printed in the United States of America

Dedicated to my mother and father

I would like to acknowledge the people at PublishAmerica, who I am grateful to for giving this work a chance.

Chapter One

May First landed on Tuesday, and Tuesday was laundry day.

Nick spotted him immediately after they lumbered through the laundromat's glass double doors. It was late afternoon, or early evening—depending how you separate the two—after the day's classes. They each toted their own loads, collectively enough during the preceding months for an excuse to stick around well after sunset. Yet with the days getting longer and the clock already sprung forward, there would be plenty of sunlight for the return.

The routine started during the first semester. It was agreed to have Alyce and Pedro work the tavern next to the laundromat amid the half-gutted strip mall. Nick, more marked by youth, always stayed to transfer the loads from the washers to the dryers, and worked the laundromat—though Nick never considered it work; that was Pedro's terminology.

Work or not, Nick believed in careful observation before engagement. Nick took sly glances at him while he and Pedro separated the loads into their proper groups and stuffed them into the machines. Alyce did all the mixing of detergent and bleach and fed the machines quarters from her margarine cup with a yellow smiley face for a lid. All three contributed quarters to the margarine cup, but never kept tabs.

He looked up and caught Nick staring. That was a reoccurring problem for Nick: always catching the attention of people he was observing as if his gaze emitted heat or some sort of vibrations whenever it focused. Once their eyes were aligned, Nick quickly adverted and fiddled with the multi-coin slot of one of the machines as if it were jammed.

He was the only other customer at the laundromat.

"Looks like we just beat the rush hour," said Pedro, gesturing with his head toward that other customer. The lone employee, a frail but menacing time-worn Arabic woman, looked up with piercing eyes at the trio from her seat behind the counter.

Alyce smiled at Nick. Her look also pierced, but in a good way. Alyce was gifted in appearance, even in uniform, which consisted of a light-blue overall dress that descended an inch or two above her small black platform shoes, over a white short-sleeved shirt. Alyce's eyes matched her dress, and that smile complimented with her cheeks—one part rose, two parts luminance—always prompted a ticklish feeling in Nick's chest, emanating, no doubt, from the heart and since sanctified for his guiltless enjoyment. As for the unsanctified feelings Alyce's bewitching aura—bountiful flow of golden hair, compact hourglass shape (like a timepiece that measured slow motion whenever she walked)— conjured up in other men, Nick understood and forgave them.

Indicated by her heart-shaped pendant with the engraved image of the Virgin Mary and Baby Jesus resting on her bosom, Alyce no doubt understood them, too.

"Little distractions make better interactions," Alyce quipped with plumped lips that complimented her cheeks – except being two parts rose.

After the lids had been shut, making the machines whirl in unison, Pedro said to Nick, "I guess you can hold down the fort."

Once again his eyes were aligned with Nick's. They stayed locked much longer than the first time—two, three, four seconds. Nick had to act fast. The washers were in motion. Fiddling with a coin slot could no longer be a deft deflection.

Alyce and Pedro said their goodbyes as they made for the double doors, giving Nick a chance to somewhat gracefully break from the stare to acknowledge the exit. Through the picture glass, Alyce and Pedro leaned back and smiled at Nick before stepping out of view. Their expressions were radiant. The open air enlivened Alyce's bountiful flow.

Now he was observing Nick. He was most likely in his 30s, Nick surmised, and probably single or divorced—it appeared that it was his only laundry that tumbled in three of the jumbo dryers. He had an athletic build, but looked to be fighting off the extra weight that creeps up side-by-side with middle age. He had short curly black hair, the type that could remain uncombed and still pass for acceptable in some circles. The lower part of his long face was unblemished and boyish, but the skin around the eyelids and along his forehead was squinted and wrinkled. His eyes were probably brown—that's usually the case with dark-haired people—but even though Nick twice looked into them, he didn't take note of their color. What Nick did take note of was his serious countenance. Terminally serious.

Nick sought a hidden vantage point. The rows of washers were separated by back-walled benches which, when one would sit on them, would lower one's head below the tall washers. Seated between the middle rows, Nick was effectively hidden from the two other people in the laundromat.

As for the other customer, he was a row over standing behind a waist-high table and in front of his three dryers along the opposite wall. Nick estimated he was midway through his drying cycle.

Though it was early spring, the temperatures managed to break into the 80s for the second straight day. It was a dramatic turnaround from the surprising snowstorm just several weeks before. Such sporadic transitions, even during the course of a day, left a lot of people guessing in the morning before trying to choose appropriate clothes. Nick had left his dark sports coat in Pedro's car after having worn it during the school hours of another warm day.

The other customer wore a blue T-shirt and (originally) black jeans that had faded well past gray and closer to a dirty shade of white. After his dryers rolled to a stop, he, as Nick had anticipated, used the table-attached hanging rod visible from Nick's seated view. This was good for helpful info.

It was odd, yet refreshing, Nick thought, that the bright and solid-colored T-shirts that dominated his load were sans of bold advertisements and stupid juvenile script. Nick continued to watch and became more relaxed as the time went by. He went through possible exchanges in his head while imagining counterpoints—though Nick knew dialogue usually never took a predictable course.

Nick had decided to wait until he finished hanging and folding his laundry and left through the double doors. It was only going to be one trip out. He had stacked his only two baskets with the hangered shirts placed in between. He put on a pair of wrap-around sunglasses, which reflected like a mirror, and made for the doors as several of the trio's machines concluded their final cycles. When he passed, Nick felt his stare from behind the mirror. After he left the building, Nick got up but didn't want to follow him immediately; rather wait until he got to his car, which was parked deeper in the lot away from the building. He must not have beaten the rush hour.

Nick watched as he clumsily dropped the stacked baskets, spilling the top contents onto the parking lot. "God damn it!" he shouted with such force that it was audible from inside. Nick thought he might be sending a signal, yet took a deep breath and walked out the doors.

"Excuse me, sir," Nick said as he gingerly approached him with his outward palm raised. "Excuse me, sir, excuse me. May I ask you a question?"

His mouth straightened on the brink of a frown. He seemed to suspect the type of question Nick would ask. In the wrap-around mirror, Nick saw himself staring back at him, and was re-introduced slight figure, dressed in a white shirt, thin dark-blue tie, dark blue slacks and black dress shoes all topped with a thin freckled face and closely-cropped red hair. Nick appeared timid looking up with his diluted blue eyes at a higher level.

"If you were to die today, where would you go?"

He looked slightly away. Now his sunglasses were reflecting the sun.

"Technically speaking, energy never dies," he matter-of-factly answered before bending over to collect his wayward laundry and then opening up his trunk to deposit it. "As for consciousness energy, mine that is, I can't assure you where it's going to go, but I know personally it's here right now and I plan to use it accordingly, knowing that this might be my only chance to do so." With that, he closed the trunk with a punctuating slam.

Nick smiled and said, "I'm sorry. I forgot to introduce myself. My name is Nick. What's yours?" Such was a taught academy tactic: Always pretend to forget to introduce yourself before asking the opening question.

"John. I'm sorry. I'm kind of in a hurry. I have no time to pray with you."

"John—such a good name. No, I don't want you to pray with me," said Nick, who rarely prayed himself. At the academy, the power of prayer was vigorously scrutinized, especially when petitioning for a favorable outcome. "John, you know if you accept God in your life you'll bask in the grace of His kingdom in your afterlife? And all you have to do is accept Him, to invite Him into your life and He'll invite you into his afterlife, which will be your afterlife … and mine—all of ours. Now tell me, John, are you willing to exchange invitations?"

John pinched his long chin with his index finger and thumb and said, "What about Jesus? Aren't you Christian guys into Jesus?"

"Of course we are," Nick said with a deliberate laugh, but he knew that he and his brethren didn't classify themselves as Christians. After a contentious encounter with another stranger who claimed that it was preposterous to acknowledge Christ as savior yet not consider oneself a Christian, Nick usually did his best to sidestep the issue.

"Yeah, but which one?" John said.

Nick was confused by the question. "Which one? You mean God or Jesus?"

"Okay," said John, looking back at and reflecting the sun, "we could start with which god, but I don't even know if you guys are sure on that subject. Let's see, there are Jesus, God and this Holy Ghost, or Holy Spirit or whatever. Like tell me, who the hell is this Holy Spirit? Is it something you borrowed from the Hindus, or they borrowed from you? Is this Holy Spirit similar to the Brahma or atman? I get the two confused, or the three confused for that matter."

Nick had come to learn of the flawed triangle and wanted to clarify his beliefs, but John was quicker with the tongue.

"You guys may want to investigate that further," he said. "But to keep it simple, let's just start with Jesus. So which Jesus?"

"The one who wants to lead you to God, John," Nick said. "He wants us to join him in heaven with his Father, John. I want you to join us."

"I know, I know," John said. "But which one? Which Messiah?"

"Jesus our savior, that's the one," Nick said. "But like I was saying —"

"And like I was saying," John interrupted, "which one? I hope you are aware that there were more than one person claiming to be the Messiah during that time in the so-called Holy Land. There are still people around claiming the same thing today. What do they call it? You may be more familiar about this than me, or maybe not—Jerusalem syndrome—that's it. You know what I'm talking about, don't you? People running around claiming they are prophets or Messiahs, or avatars or whatever. Still happens today. So how do I pick the right one? Are we sure only the Constantine-endorsed one is the Man—or as you people put it ambivalently, the Man-God?"

"That's why I'm here to help you," said Nick, who was well-versed in the dubious history of Jesus. At the academy, there were several multi-class packages students had to take, and all the classes had to be taken to get credit for any of them singularly. One package consisted of a class entitled "Real Jesus I," which brazenly told of Jesus' obscure siblings, openly questioned his virgin birth, and even seemingly suggested that Jesus didn't rise from the dead nor was the son of God, nor had been the a person at all—rather an amalgamation from a series of imposters and magicians. It was a bewildering experience for then freshman Nick, who wondered why such a class was offered.

But its companion class, "Real Jesus II," set the record straight as far as Nick was concerned. Two academy elders and a heavy-set jolly woman, who was a director of theology at a major university, taught it. The woman wasn't part of the all-male faculty at the academy. She wore layers of golden-cast necklaces and bracelets, and more than enough earrings and rings considering there are just so many places on the body to appropriately put them. Most of her jewelry was weighted with multi-colored stones—if she were a Negro and not a red-head with pasty skin, she could have been mistaken as a voodoo shaman.

About once or twice a week, she brought her Scripture clips, which she would display on a projector screen while combing out their significant treasures. It was rare that direct passages from the Bible were ever displayed or used as teaching tools at the academy. But they were effective teaching tools for Nick, whose faith in the pervasive presence of God, Jesus and even the devil was reinforced.

"Really, there's only one savior," Nick said. "His life is the greatest proof of God's existence."

"His life?" John said. "Or do you mean what is written about him?"

"I mean his life," answered Nick, who while looking at himself in the mirror glasses appeared, this time, to be more confident. He knew where to take this from here. "John, let me tell you about Jesus' most trying times —"

"Okay," John interrupted again, "so Jesus is living proof that God exists. And there is only one real Jesus. What happens if I don't accept this legit savior, or even God for that matter?"

Slightly disappointed about being turned away from a common driving point, Nick chose to answer the question with hopes of eventually getting back on track. "If you don't accept God, you're doomed to suffer eternal damnation," Nick said. John's head and wrap-around mirror remained still. "Do you know what eternal damnation is, John? Can you even imagine it? Have you ever had a toothache that paralyzed the side of your face in pain? If you did, the pain probably went away. But imagine suffering pain forever. Pain much worse than a toothache. And having it never go away. But that's not even half of it. The real pain is the terrible realization of what could have been, what path could have been taken but refused, and how a simple choice, a simple course of action could have resulted in the kingdom of God rather than never-ending torment. But you don't have to suffer, John. You don't have to be left behind. All you have to do is make that simple choice. That's all you have to do."

John chuckled and shook his head before saying, "It's all about fear, isn't it?"

Nick squinted from the glare reflected off John's sunglasses.

"It's fear that makes this religion thing run on all cylinders," John said.

"Now I'm all for fear. I see these kids today, jocks or wannabe jocks, and they have this 'No Fear' boast printed on their shirts. [Nick was reminded of John's unscripted wardrobe] No Fear? Tell me, how can one reach their potential and truly succeed if they don't have a fear of failure? Talk about writhing about what could have been. That's why we need fear."

"And that's why we need God. Fear, like hate, is a weak force. God, like love, is a strong force," Nick said. "And a strong force can always overcome a—"

"Wait, wait, hold on for a second," John said. "Fear, weak force or not, no doubt begot religion, or make that mythology. Now I like mythology, even religion, which, of course is mythology. And I firmly believe we need religion—civil religion that is. As for the superstitious variety, I believe — now I may be in the minority here—it sustains too much of its reptilian-complex nature and indignation toward other religions that it undermines any of its redeeming qualities.

"Now when do you think was the first time that our ancestors experienced fear? I mean real primal fear. Yeah, you can expect them to fear wild animals, especially when they didn't develop weapons yet. And they may have feared other tribes that were bigger and stronger than them. And, of course, they probably feared death. But aside from that, wouldn't the unexplained, the supernatural as some would refer to it, really scare the hell—excuse me—out of them?"

"But John, with God—"

"Nick," John said while cocking his head upward in a manner that he was able to peer at Nick from under his shades; he did have brown eyes. "Nick, that's your name, right?"

Nick nodded.

"Well, Nick, I think the most terrifying thing our ancestors ever experienced was a total eclipse of the sun."

Nick had never witnessed a total eclipse of the sun, just partial eclipses. One day during a partial eclipse, Nick observed blotches of sunlight that filtered through some trees overhead and onto a sidewalk. The blotches were all shaped like miniature partial eclipses. To this day, Nick couldn't figure out how that was possible.

"Now imagine, our ancestors probably had a lot of respect for the weather, and things like thunderstorms and overwhelming winds were forces that played on their minds," John continued. "But to have the sun disappear completely in the middle of the day, especially if they had a sense of the order of things, that must have really shook them up. It shook them up to a point, no doubt, that they needed God, or gods, to deal with their anxieties and the unpredictability of their lives."

"John, man did not create God—"

"Yeah, yeah, " John interrupted again. It reminded Nick of the way his father would breach him in mid-sentence. "Now it may seem I'm getting off the subject, but bear with me here. Take a look at this piece."

John was referring to his car, an ancient Honda Accord. There was rust around the gas cap door and its keyed lock. Apparently corrosion had either frozen the lock, or made it more difficult to work, as the cap door was not fully closed with the inside latches no longer complimenting each other. There was also rust around the wheel wells. The car's formerly red interior was fading, especially the backseat headrests.

"When I say 'piece' I mean as in 'piece of.' I can't count how many times it has left me stranded in places I didn't want to be. And they say this model is still the crown jewel for car thieves." Nick cocked his head and wondered why. "It's the parts, that's why. They're interchangeable with other editions. But they could have it as far as I'm concerned. But really, I do plan to keep it until it passes 200,000 miles. If you change your oil, get regular tune-ups and keep up on general maintenance, your vehicle should reach 200,000 miles."

John paused. Nick initially decided not to reply, certain he would be stopped in mid-sentence again. But after a substantial wait, Nick snuck in, "I don't know much about cars. I don't own one."

"Unfortunately you will have to. They're like personal computers and cell phones. You almost need them to be self-sufficient, unless you make money doing this."

"Believe me, I don't do this for money. I'm doing this for you, John. I want you to—"

"Back to the piece," John broke in. "Now 200,000 miles is what you would call a car's full life. Now I'm not too sure about the scientific term half-lives. I think it applies to the atomic world, or the sub-atomic world or whatever. But you could apply this term, in a way, that is, to things like cars and even humans."

John cleared his throat, and like a used-car salesman, turned to his car with hand outward, "This car has about 120,000 miles on it. Or at least that's what the odometer says. I didn't buy it off the showroom floor, so I don't know for sure. Anyway, taking that a car's full life is 200,000 miles, this car is past its half-life. Of course, like I said, don't confuse me with an atomic scientist. Now you can look at it this way: the car should give me another 80,000 miles. Or you can look at it this way: because it's past its half-life…"John raised up peace-sign fingers on each side of his face when he said "half-life" "… most anything can go wrong. The timing belt could snap, the head gasket may blow, the transmission may drop in the middle of the street—if any of those things happen, it's getting towed straight to the junkyard." John pointed to the junkyard conveniently located across "The Great Highway". "Then it could be gutted for parts with no resistance from me.

"Now, you were talking about death when you first came up to me. On that subject, I say, with the advancements in medicine and the better living conditions, at least for you and I, that living 100 years should be fairly common this new century. But even with that thought in our back pockets, we had better watch out once we get to 50, or even 40, or heck, I know of some people who have had fatal heart attacks when they were still in their 30s."

I thought he was in a hurry, thought Nick, who was at least glad John was the evasive taciturn type.

"Now, if that doesn't get you, think of this," John said as he moved closer to Nick. "You probably know that our sun is a star. According to what I've heard, our sun, or make that our star, is a type of star that lives for about nine billion years. Now I read—of course you shouldn't believe all that you read—but anyway, I read that our star is over four and a half billion years old."

John stopped as if he waited for Nick to respond, probably just to interrupt him again.

"Don't you see?" John continued, pointing to the sun, again reflecting off his glasses. "This star is past its half-life. Yeah, you can take the optimistic view and sleep well at night with the assumption that we have about another four and a half billion years of sunlight. But man, like my car and like a middle-age man eating potato chips in front of his TV, this sun, or star, can go at any minute."

On its way down and peering through a tissue-thin cloud cover that ascended along the horizon, the sun's white-bright brilliance had been refracted into a shade of red-orange, or orange-red depending how you separate the two. All this seemed to bolster John's claim.

"You don't have to worry about the dilemma of being sucked into a black hole, if that is in fact the consequence of a dying star. We'll be long gone before that happens, burnt to a crisp that is. You see, before this star says sayonara, it will fan out—super nova-like—taking out every planet in the solar system."

John moved even closer to Nick to softly say, "Now, what would happen if some group of scientists found out that this was going to take place within, let's say, a couple of millennia, or even sooner?"

"Believe me," Nick said emphatically, "I, or we, would have a lot easier time getting people to accept God's invitation."

"I'm sure you would," John said with a grin.

"Of course we would," Nick said. "You see, John, this life is only temporary and—"

"Temporary?" John shouted, startling Nick. "I'm sick and tired hearing you people talk of our temporary life on Earth, as well as the ill-conceived belief that there has to be an afterlife because—and I still don't understand how such idiocy has taken root—life here wouldn't mean anything if there weren't. Stop and think about that for a while, I mean really stop and think about it, and you should arrive at its polar opposite: if there were an afterlife, life here wouldn't mean anything. What? We're just living out some sort of pre-heaven tryout? Ridiculous! And..." Nick opened his mouth to interrupt, but John signaled with his hand to let him finish "...why do we have to depend on God and Jesus to save us? Can't we save ourselves? We might be the only true sentient life form in the universe, and we're not willing to save ourselves."

Nick felt this discourse was turning his way. "John, we need God. We need Him because we are helpless without Him. Your theoretical situation proves my point."

"But we can save ourselves," John said.

"How? What are we going to do? Build spaceships? And even if we can build enough of them, where are we going to go?"

"We don't have to go anywhere," John answered, and then while pumping his index to the ground with each one-syllable word, continued, "We...can...stay...right...here." Then he pointed at the reddening sun. "You see, remember when I was talking about solar eclipses, and how they most likely scared the shit—sorry again—out of our ancestors? Yet ironically, this terrifying phenomenon, at least troubling back then, could actually be the key to us surviving the enviable fate of our star dying."

Nick folded his arms. He wasn't going to try to talk this time.

"You see, one thing that these eclipses have taught us, or more like showed us, is that the moon and the sun tend to appear to be the same size in the sky, though the Earth revolves around the sun and the moon, you see, revolves around the Earth..."

Nick was slightly offended by John's condescending lesson on moon and Earth orbits. He assumed that John assumed that his scientific knowledge was poor because he obviously prepped at a religious institution. Nick wanted to inform him otherwise, but he was more curious about the pending explanation.

"I've heard theories that we can build a giant biosphere around the planet that may maintain green-house effect warmth even without a sun. But like I said before, in the event of our dying star we need to get the fuck out of Dodge because that biosphere will be burned off like wax off an apple thrown into a camp fire. But we can still stay here, and this how we do it.

"We send a bunch of astronauts, cosmonauts—of course this needs to be a worldwide project—as well as bunch of engineers, rocket scientists, and even a bunch of ditch diggers because obviously there needs to be a lot of work done to the moon. Once there, now there may be different ways to do this, we build some jet propulsion system on the surface of the moon or inside the moon, whatever works best. This is just a theory of mine, or theory I've heard of, mind you. If I had all the specifics mapped out, I probably wouldn't be driving this piece of shit."

Nick, he would have to admit, was starting to get entertained.

"Now with this system, we can conceivably nudge the moon off of its original orbit. If we can do that, you see, the moon in turn should pull the Earth out of its original orbit."

Something didn't sound right, thought Nick, who still listened intently.

"This could set off a cosmic dance, between the Earth and the moon. They would engage in intertwining orbits, like they were waltzing across a dance floor. And if the dance could be started in time, we, the Earth and our moon that is, could be well out of our solar system before the sun blows. Of course, we had better plot a safe course. We don't want to run into a comet or something like that. But that shouldn't be that much of a problem during an age that has already developed eon-reaching telescopes."

Though entertained, Nick was far from convinced. "But what good would that do?" he said. "And I'm not too sure about the moon being able to tug us across the universe to safety after we alter its course. You see, this is a fine-tuned universe—"

John was now laughing out loud, which irked Nick more than the previous interruptions.

"Huh, huh, yeah, laugh if you want!" Nick's angry voice vibrated in his own ears. "But don't you people get it? If the Earth's distance to the sun were just a wee bit different, we would never be here. Life would not be possible."

"Fine-tuned?" John mocked while elevating his shoulders and waving his hands near his ears. "Fine-tuned? If everything is so fined-tuned, why is the sun ready to blow at any millennium?"

"And I'm not too sure about that, either," Nick said. "I can assure you that the coming of the Lord and His son will have happened long before our sun will have a chance to expire. But back to that civilization-saving remedy of yours— what good would waltzing out of our presumably doomed solar system do if we don't have a sun anymore? Unless you say building a giant hemisphere is now practical."

John nearly laughed. "Biosphere, you mean or I meant, but there's a better way than that. Like I was telling you, a solar eclipse sheds light for our survival by showing that the moon in the sky is often the same size as the sun. All we have to do is cover the facing side of the moon with superduper panels that radiate light and heat. And think about this, a moon-orbit heat and light source could very well be much more efficient that a sun-orbit — eh, excuse me — an Earth orbit, or make that a spinning-Earth orbit around the sun, when it comes to ideal weather for better world-wide crop harvests."

John cleared his throat again. "Yeah, making these panels and tacking them onto the moon is going to be a heck of a project. Likewise for moving the moon and tracking a safe course. Such a plan may be beyond our capabilities right now, and, of course for those heat panels, we would have to develop or discover a much more efficient and abundant energy source than what we have right now. But jeez, if we found out today that something like that had to be attempted in the immediate future, we just might be able to pull it off."

John took a moment to inhale, and then capped his point. "All we have to do is face our fears. Hiding our heads in superstition will not get it done."

Nick admired John's fervor, especially at the end. Then Nick made his final attempt.

"John, I'm glad I had this talk with you. I know you're in a hurry as you say, so I'll let you go," Nick said while extending his hand. John was cordial enough to offer his hand, and Nick seized it with a firm grip and put his other hand on John's elbow to gain even greater control.

"John, I'm just going to ask you one last time to accept God Who wants you to join Him in heaven, because He loves you. I want you to join me in heaven, John. We can all be with God and Jesus."

Nick was speaking fast. And, as taught to him by his older brother, whose previous "work" was greatly revered at the academy, Nick had his right index and middle fingers extended along the big veins under John's palm. Whenever Nick said "God" or "Jesus," he pressed on the veins like he was performing spiritual CPR.

Just as that moment, Alyce and Pedro emerged from the bar with a pair of work-clothes patrons. All four were laughing heartedly. The second the commotion caught Nick's attention, John slipped his hand and arm free and quickly entered his car and closed the door. The window was already down, so he was able to say, "Nice talking to you." Then John turned the ignition, which let out a chi-chi-chi-chi-chi under the hood before catching and coughing up a cloud of deep-purple exhaust from the tailpipe.

John then drove off into the sun with the deep-purple cloud turning to black upon ascending to the red-orange background.

Chapter Two

The two patrons belched most of the laughter. They both could have been any age between 24 and 52, and they definitely were having a jolly time, probably even before Alyce and Pedro arrived. They dressed differently, but the same. The half-foot taller of the two wore a flannel and jeans; the shorter a leather vest over a T-shirt and jeans—a trucker and a biker, perhaps.

"Haughrrh, haughrrh, haughrrh," the taller chortled as if he was throwing up mangled words. "Pardon the expression, but that was goddamn funny."

Nick stepped over to the spot vacated by John's car to observe from a distance, and inadvertently stepped in a fresh oil deposit. Though neither were smoking, the tobacco stench the patrons brought out from the bar had reached Nick. Maybe they chewed.

"That's sure a Top Tenner," taller continued. "But ya know, I normally would have been offended. What made it so funny, I guess, is that someone like you told it." Then he playfully yet forcefully pushed his shorter companion. "But if you would have told it, I may have given you a head slap."

"Haaeelll," tongue-drawled the shorter, who in addition of being six inches shy of his friend, appeared to be a drink or two less tolerant. "I t-t-thing I'm going to tell that to my m-mother, w-w-who's likely going to tell it to your momma."

"Wait a minute here," taller said. "We have some Christian folk here. We don't need to be talking about our mommas' social life."

More laughter—from all four.

The partially obscured T-shirt underneath shorter's vest was scripted. Something about burning flags and asses.

Alyce and Pedro, nonetheless, naturally blended in. Pedro was also in

20

uniform—sort of. Pedro always refused to wear a tie. "It cuts the circulation of blood and oxygen to the brain," his reason among others. Freed from any constraints, Pedro's collar was opened two or three buttons, just low enough to reveal hair in the cleavage—still sexily in style in Pedro's case. Pedro was average height on the tall side, and angular and nearly filled out. Pedro was not Hispanic, though he did have dark skin for a Caucasian, even during the dead of winter. And his black hair, long enough for a center part—again retroactively sexy—gave his complexion a smoky quality.

His real name was Peter, but he insisted on being called Pedro.

Although handsome and doing most of the talking, Pedro commanding presence was, as usual, partially usurped by Alyce, who could blend in with any group of men. The patrons couldn't keep their eyes trained away from Alyce. She had one of her heels lifted, which enhanced the contoured lines of her quads and calves in both legs, further making her lower body a work of art.

It was part of the grand plan, marveled Nick, who, from where he was standing, saw Alyce's heart-shaped pendant flicker in the sunlight.

"Freakin' wicked," taller said. "Is freakin' cool with you guys?"

"These are C-C-Christian folks as you say," shorter said. "So freakin' is uncouth."

"Don't worry," Alyce said. "I sometimes use freakin' myself."

"Heh, heh, heh. A pretty girl like yous ought to watch what she says, especially if you knows the meaning of freakin'," the shorter patron said.

"Okay, let's get an consensus here," the taller patron said. "And simply refer to the joke as wicked?"

"Wicked it is," Pedro confirmed.

"What you said before, though," the taller man said while casting his eye to the sky. "Ya, know, the more I think about it, the more sense it makes."

"That's right," shorter said.

"That's right? You don't have a clue."

"S-s-sure I do," shorter countered. "Yous should give my intellect more credit."

"Not with your attention span, and the way you were riding her elevator."

"Heh, heh, heh," the shorter man chuckled—he knew he was caught. "May you then cast the first stone, that's-s-s if you qualify."

"Regardless," taller said, trying to regain a serious tone. "It seems so simple, but the way you told it, it's greater than genius. It's, ah, majestic."

And Pedro was best at telling this majestic tale.

"Do you believe in miracles?" he would begin. A yes or no answer always led to "Do you believe Jesus was confronted by the devil on this world?"

Yes. "Why did the devil ask Jesus to turn stones into bread?"

No. "So you don't believe the devil asked Jesus …"

Why did the devil ask Jesus to jump from his mountain perch?

Why did the devil ask Jesus to join him in uniting the world?

And why did Jesus refuse on all occasions?"

"Why? Why? W-H-Why?" Pedro patiently expounded. "Because if he didn't, to any one, we wouldn't have been provided the opportunity to decide between good and evil with the knowledge of good and evil. Without that opportunity, yeah, things may seem to be better off—never go hungry because he and his Father would always provide us food; no fits of doubt, because their mystery and magic would be eyewitness accounts; and maybe most important or most beneficial with such an arrangement, no wars and no killing. We'd be one big happy family, but as soulless as a heap of ants.

"Just think about how profound that confrontation was. Think it was conjured up by some scribe? Some philosopher? Some group of scribe and philosophers? No! Not on their best days! Just to think of such temptations indicates deceptive cleverness to the infinite power, but the wisdom to refuse them supercedes infinity. No, the devil's three temptations to Christ are not a work of fiction. They couldn't come from paper or papyrus alone. They really happened.

"So yes, Virginia, there is a devil, but there's also a Jesus, who is the son of God. And yes, Virginia, there is a God."

"Don't listen to him," shorter said. "I p-p-perfectly understand it. Like, like, if J-Jesus or God or any supernatural being came into this bar—really, Jesus and God are the only supernatural beings…am I right about that?"

"Don't forget the devil," taller added.

"Yeah, how can I forget him?" shorter continued. "But anyway, Jesus or God comes in an picks up a stick and hits all the bars in on a break, or turns beer into whiskey, or floats in the air in front of our eyes, I mean real high not like that David…w-w-what the f-fuck's his name?…B-B-Blaine bullshit, or I mean doesn't do typical magician shit, but what I mean is what he does is real, real amazing shit, like turn day into night and back again, and just freaks the shit out of us."

Pedro and Alyce were smiling and nodding in synch.

"…I mean what would I or wes do after seeing shit like that? We would have no f-freakin' choice but to bow down and worship. We'd be damn fools if we didn't because He proved without a doubt that He is the Man."

"Point well taken, " taller said. "But on that subject, get to the point."

"I am getting to the point," shorter countered. "If yous understood it as well as yous s-says yous do, you would know where I was going. Anyway, how could you not worship the guy? From that point forward, we'd better get our asses to the church and start praying like a motherfucker because—damn!— God is real because He showed us that He can turn day into night and kick everyone's ass in pool with just one shot. But really, and I'm more or less speaking for myself, the hero that I am, we would be scared shitless of crossing this Guy or God because he could crush us like … like … like stepping on that heap of ants you were talking about. But those people already at church, those who weren't around for that crazy shit but still worship the Dude anyway, now those people are going to get the best VIP rooms in the big mansions in the sky."

Pedro's mirthful grin widened

"One thing," taller said, "though you shouldn't be drawn in by miracles and mystery alone—if you do or are, that's where you get your piss-poor faith— but all throughout the Bible, and you could correct me if I'm wrong, but isn't there all kinds of magic and miracle shit going on from cover to cover?"

"The Bible is a book of great knowledge," Pedro said. "But like any book, its knowledge is frozen."

The two patrons arched back slightly before the shorter man opined, "Then again, maybe you need to throw a bone to the dogs and do a miracle here and there. If not, what's going to distinguish our God or religion from the Muslims?"

"Or even Islam," the taller man added. Pedro had to chuckle at bit at that.

"We have get-togethers every Sunday," Alyce said. "This should be our first outdoor one of the season if the weather stays this way. Why don't you be our guests?"

"And come as we are," the shorter man asked.

"And come as you are," Alyce answered.

"If you come as you are right now—" the taller man gestured to Alyce "— then you can count me in."

Laughter, then the shorter man asked, "Is there going to be alcohol. If not, mays wes bring our own?"

Chapter Three

As expected, the sun remained for the return—but the day's warmth had departed. Chilled currents brought the subtle stench of Northern industry, sweeping away the season's fresh scent. Nick was glad he brought his sports coat, especially while sitting in the back seat with the windows rolled down as Pedro's dark blue muscled Malibu engaged in a needless race against time.

The academy's outdoor setting was nearing its peak as aesthetics go, although that surprising last-strike snowstorm painted a masterpiece of its own. Then, artistic strokes came early during the heralding sleet shower that fastened itsy-bitsy icicles to the trees' branches and newly-sprouted buds.

Now, in a setting so different that it didn't account for the short span of time, the orchards lining the road just outside the academy blossomed with pink petals, still weeks away from summer green. The weeping willows that dominated the academy's landscape and formerly wore the icicles most fashionably now had miniature leaves on their whip branches. Along the banks of the academy's man-made lake, many willows were double exposed in inner-Earth.

The fountain was on, springing from a single spout just off the middle of the lake. The water fanned out like the back of a shellfish. The lowering sun peeked its way around the weeping willows while concentrating a beam aimed through the shell. A projected spectrum in slits of color reached out to the aligned sight of Nick, who was looking into the shell from the passenger's side of Pedro's car as it traveled southbound toward the academy's main entrance. The water shell rose about 50 feet. Nick thought of its height and laughed a little inside.

"I know Oral Roberts was lying when he said he saw a giant Jesus," claimed someone, who Nick had targeted.

"Maybe he wasn't lying," Nick responded.

"No, he was flat out lying. I won't even give him the benefit of the doubt that he may have been hallucinating…too much herbal tea, or whatnot. And you know how I can tell? You know how I can tell? He said he saw a 47-foot tall Jesus. Forty-seven-foot tall. Now Oral, you sure he wasn't 50-foot tall?"

Out on the lake about 20 feet in front of the fountain out on the lake was a wooden island. It had just enough room to hold a picnic table. A wooden bridge with rope rails led to the platform. Weather permitting, it was favorite gathering place for Elders and students—usually not together.

The platform and bridge were built after the fountain, and it wasn't long before a flaw was revealed, especially to those who planned to read or do any type of paperwork there. The fountain was too close, and even on the stillest days a persistent mist would descend on the occupants. There was no such foresight to account for the dilemma.

Already set and too expensive for readjustment, they decided to put a big umbrella through the picnic table. The umbrella was opened and closed through a hand crank on the metal shaft. The shaft could be adjusted and angled to fend off the sun, the mist from the fountain, or both.

However, this posed another problem. The umbrella, when opened at the right—or wrong—angle, would sometimes shield the occupants from those approaching via the northbound bridge. Students would sometimes venture toward the platform only to find out midway there that several elders occupied it. Thus, uncomfortable retreats were common. Yet, there was one elder most students felt comfortable with, even in the case of unscheduled encounters— Elder Steven.

His arrival in the fall enriched the academy. Young, tall and lean, Elder Steven sported a stylish Van Dyke beard and mustache. Like his thick hair, all dark, all handsome. Like many under-class requisite courses, Nick and Alyce both had him for "Parables and Possibilities."

And so did Pedro, though he was a first-year advanced student. Apparently, though Pedro would never confirm or deny, he had either failed or didn't complete the course the year before, but was still allowed to graduate contingent on taking two full semesters again. It was through the class that Nick and Alyce formed a kinship with him. Nick and Alyce were already close.

During the first day of the first semester, it didn't take long before a rather humiliated Pedro to act out his brewing frustration. Being almost late, or as he would say, "on time," Pedro—with a weapons-grade scowl—seated himself just seconds ahead of Elder Steven's entrance. The teacher had waited outside the classroom's doorway greeting students with his Van Dyke-outlined smile. He appeared ready to write something on the chalkboard, like his name or something. Instead, he faced the class and said, "I recently heard the most funniest joke."

Oh no … not another stand-up wannabe who thinks he's reverent enough for unconditional laughter.

"Jesus and Moses were up in heaven, and Jesus goes to Moses, 'You remember when we were down on Earth when you hit Egypt with all those plagues and I turned water into wine and did all that stuff, you remember that?' 'Sure do,' Moses said. 'Those were the good old days.' Jesus said. 'Say, let's go back down to Earth and relive some past glories.' 'Sounds good to me,' Moses said."

Elder Steven was fighting back his own laughter. Some students giggled. Most remained silent.

"So they're back on Earth and they take a raft out onto the Red Sea, then Jesus goes to Moses, 'You wait here, I'm going to walk out on the water.' So Jesus steps out of the raft and starts walking on the water, but he sinks to the bottom. Moses splits the Red Sea, revives Jesus, and Jesus goes, 'Man! I must be getting rusty. Let's go out a little further and try again.' So they go out a little further, and Jesus gets out and starts walking on the water again, but sinks to the bottom again. Moses splits the Red Sea again, revives Jesus again, and Jesus goes, 'Damn! This used to be so easy. Let's go out further and try again.' So they're really out there, and Jesus gets out of the raft, starts walking on the water, but sinks again. Moses splits the Red Sea and saves Jesus, and Jesus goes, 'I must have gotten really soft from all those years up there. I've really lost it.' But then Moses looks at Jesus and says, 'I've been watching you and I think I know what your problem is.

"'When you did that before, you didn't have those holes in your feet.'"

Some of the students let out sudden laughs before immediately halting themselves. Nick thought the joke to be shockingly funny, and felt that he was about to burst out uncontrollably, but feared disdain. But soon most of the class was laughing freely and loudly, like they all understood the punch line in a simultaneous delayed reaction.

However, Pedro wasn't laughing. "That's terrible," he said while leaping out of his chair and throwing his No. 2 pencil to the floor. That's about the only idem Pedro brought to that particular class: a No. 2 pencil.

"That's bullshit!" Pedro continued while glaring at Elder Steven, who managed to maintain his stylish smile. "Excuse my French if you may, but that was fuckin' offensive."

Pedro kicked the unattached seat from his desk, upending it with a loud crash, took several long aggressive strides toward the door which he flung open violently, breaking the door jam and putting a hole in the wall with the doorknob, and stormed out of the room and out of the building.

Pedro's violent bolt left the classroom stunned. Even Elder Steven seemed embarrassed by all this, and an apology seemed forthcoming. Instead, Elder Steven shrugged his shoulders and said, "Good thing I didn't tell him about the Three Nuns who had Three Wishes."

Within the week, Pedro returned. He made peace with Elder Steven and lifted the joke to aide his own sermons.

Chapter Four

As for the class "Parables and Possibilities," it was the epitome of the academy's unconventionality.

"All kinds of crap," Pedro related shortly after befriending Nick and Alyce in late summer. "It's a jigsaw puzzle with unfitting pieces from 30 different boxes, that's what the class is. Okay, some grass seeds will get trampled, some seeds will get washed away, some will be shaded from sunlight, some will grow. We've got it already. And just wait until we go through the paradox of irrational numbers."

Eventually, Pedro conceded that Elder Steven's class was an improvement. Nick found it interesting and revealing, especially when he was used as an unwitting assistant to a sight experiment.

"Are you color blind?" Elder Steven asked Nick one day.

"No," Nick answered.

"So you can recognize an object's color, right?"

"Of course I can. I think."

Nick wasn't too sure. Midway through the long road trips to and from the academy, Nick, Dom and his father would insist that a stretch of highway lighting had a dark yellow or beige tint (depending how you separate the two). But Nick's mother claimed they were light pink. She also referred to others familiar with the lights who supported her claim—all of whom were women.

Do women see things differently?

"You think?" Elder Steven said. "We'd better find out for sure."

Elder Steven collected three hardback books that were visible fixtures on his desk. One had a red cover: *The Scarlet Letter* by Nathaniel Hawthorne. Another had a black cover: The Bible. The third was a dictionary wrapped in a prominently yellow sleeve with some white and red script. The books varied in thickness, but their two-dimensional shapes were about the same.

"Make a dictionary your first option over a thesaurus," Elder Steven said before walking to the side of Nick, who was seated in the second desk of the first row, right behind Alyce. Elder Steven crouched down catcher's style about three feet away from Nick's side while leaning his back against the wall to steady himself.

"Now look straight ahead," instructed Elder Steven, whose eyes were level with Nick's. "You see me in the corner of your eye? No, no. Look straight ahead, but keep me in the edges of your peripheral vision. You still see me?"

Nick nodded.

"Good." Elder Steven picked up a book and placed it in front of his face. "Now tell me what color this is? And don't guess."

The Fisher's Academy was not accredited. Its standard classes had grades concurrent with standard high school—freshman to senior, though its advanced classed varied from the typical college timeline. There, you could graduate in three years, or maybe less, or maybe more—it was contingent on Elder Bingham's final evaluation.

The academy reputation for educational excellence often preceded itself. Students would consistently score well above the state and national averages on SATs—even when taking them as sophomores. The local press took notice whenever they wanted scrutinize the state of public education.

At the academy, the Theory of Evolution and Creationism were thoroughly addressed side-by-side—you won't find that at too many public schools.

The academy wasn't affiliated, and the New Testament was embraced on the academy's terms. There were no crucifixes, no images of Christ nor of any other Biblical characters on the grounds.

When Dom came home for Christmas during his freshman year, Nick noted that he never crossed himself during grace. Nick decided to do—or not to do—the same. The rebuke from his father was harsh and swift.

"What? You in such in a hurry to eat?" his father said while reaching over to slap Nick's plate of meatloaf and mash potatoes all over Nick's shirt and lap, and onto the white-tiled floor.

Nick's father's had an abusive history. It reached its apex when Nick was in fifth grade and Dom was in his final year of junior high. Dom was spared of most grief—he was older and less vulnerable at the time. Nick's father also would batter Nick's mother on occasion. But sometimes she deserved it.

Once when she discovered that Dom—still short of his 15th birthday—had already had sex with at least three different girls, lashed out though Dom wasn't present at the time.

"I hate you kids," she screamed at Nick. And then to Nick's father, "And I hate you. It's your fault."

Bad move, especially because Nick's father had been drinking, "So you hate me, do ya? In that case, I'll just give you a real reason to hate me."

He then back-handed Nick's mother. The action didn't shock Nick because he had seen his father backhand his mother before, and he even silently supported the action—he was also unfairly slighted by his mother. But then Nick's father decked her with a right cross. Then came more punches, and more with Nick's father straddling on top. Nick was tempted to intervene, but didn't.

Eventually, consciousness was lost. Nick's father stepped back, his face writhing. Nick thought his mother was dead. His father must have, too, as he trembled while retreating to the corner of the room. After a minute and of no movement, Nick said with a crackle in his voice, "Should we call an ambulance?"

"We don't need to call a fuckin' ambulance!" Nick's father shouted, now dangerous again.

The next day a mission from the Fisher's Academy came knocking. Nick's father answered the door—he had to swallow hard even to do that.

"Hello," said a tall, clean-cut young man accompanied by another clean-cut young man, but not as tall. "We're visitors from the Fisher's Academy, and we just so happened to be in your neighborhood. If you don't mind us taking up your time, may I ask you a question?"

Nick's father was saved. Thereafter, he conducted himself in a saintly manner, though he did rescind gradually in the proceeding months. Nonetheless, he did vow to send Dom to the academy the coming fall with Nick to follow upon eligibility. Yet Nick's parents didn't pose much of an inquiry about the school, located a whole state away. Its history, the credentials of its faculty, its learning atmosphere, its general discipline, its placement of graduated—all this seemed unimportant. The inexpensive tuition, though, was a point of interest. The alleviation of feeding the boys for most of the year almost had the academy paying for itself.

The paths were set, though Nick and Dom's parents rarely crossed them. They never visited the academy other than dropping and picking the boys up. Even then, they never stuck around to learn more about the place, hence Nick's father's ignorance of the crossless grace policy.

Aside from the attention garnered from SAT scores, the academy occasionally got some unwanted press. Whenever cult exploits would become the news of the day, the Fisher's Academy's social order became the local angle. And once a protest made the front page, and it was drummed up by the missionary who altered the course of Nick's family. He was an unwelcome alumni who crashed a Sunday "picnic" during Nick's sophomore year. No longer clean cut, he now had a full beard and a little more weight to throw around. He was leading a small group carrying placards stating "Don't block out the Son" and…this was really original "…Know Jesus, Know Peace, No Jesus, No Peace." (Reversed statement, that's what makes it original)

He wasn't toting a placard, but wore one of those scripted T-shirts. Though Nick could never forget the man—beard or no beard—he could never completely recall remember the T-shirt's message. It went something like "God does not equal (+/-) times something, something" – an equation of some sorts that never fully rooted in Nick's memory.

"Back away from stepping back!" the former missionary shouted repeatedly through his megaphone at the casual gathering of elders, students and their guests.

"Free yourself! Return to Jesus!"

The rants disturbed Nick. Step back away from stepping back? Return to Jesus? When did we ever leave him other than discarding his archaic cross?

The police soon arrived, and the former missionary was the first to greet them.

"Boy, am I glad to see you guys. What is happening here is a crime of abominable proportions."

Chapter Five

Although Elder Steven's class was a marked improvement, it did tread on old ground—much to the chagrin of Pedro.

"How many of you remember the game show *Let's Make a Deal*?" Elder Steven queried. Pedro sighed audibly. The rest of the class was silent.

"Gee, you people sure know how to make a guy feel old."

Here was the hypothetical setup: A contestant is informed that behind one of three doors is a Mercedes Benz; behind the other two are billygoats. The contestant chooses one door. Then one of the other two is opened revealing a billygoat. The host then asks the contestant if he or she wants to change his or her decision.

As a repeat student, Pedro knew the "correct" answer but he still refused to accept it.

"According to them, or whoever came up with this, the contestant should always change his pick," Pedro said later that laundry day as he paced in spirited agitation around Alyce's dorm room, where the trio regularly studied together.

Like most seniors and advanced students, Alyce had a single dorm. Likewise during her underclass years, which was the growing norm among females. Although enrollment remained steady, there was (somehow) an increasing discrepancy between male and female students, which had grown beyond three to one. Alyce's room had an aura of warmth and comfort, and was much more ordered than either Nick's or Pedro's, who also had single dorms. And as one might expect, Alyce's room was much cleaner. Several times Nick challenged himself to make his room just as appealing. But even after hours of cleaning and reorganization, Nick's room at best was merely antiseptic, like a doctor's office.

The walls in Alyce's room were painted light pink. Students were allowed to paint the walls of their own rooms, and Alyce, with help from several other students on her floor, painted the color over a dark shade of blue—the academy often switched genders of the dorms from year to year, but due to the aforementioned discrepancy, fewer dorms made the change.

Nick once saw a study suggesting that pink walls in prison cells tend to subdue inmate aggression. The color of the prison walls looked to be the same as Alyce's, but Nick saw this documentary on the student commons' big-screen TV that had seen better days and displayed inaccurate colors.

Thick dark-red drapes adorned the sides and along the top of the room's second-story window. Covering the window was a white sheet. Under the window was black wooden oriental table about a foot and a half high with a small lamp on it. The lamp's shade had a bigger opening at the top. When the lamp was on, light splashed onto the white sheet, creating an illusion of daytime even during the darkest of nights.

Pedro continued while chopping his left palm with his right hand. "And it makes no sense, no sense whatsoever."

Nick and Alyce were seated on Alyce's bed, neatly covered with a Christmas-themed blanket that seemed always in season, and a large pillow that matched the walls and drapes – light pink on one side, dark red on the other. Nick and Alyce tracked Pedro's pacing.

"You know, he could be right," Alyce said.

"What do you mean 'he could be right'?" Pedro harshly retorted as if a sore spot was bumped. "Elder Steven? No freakin' way…that's assuming he truly subscribes to this nonsense and is not just following the syllabus, which I might add he has apparently and thankfully spared us from. What I'm saying though is that the whole philosophy of it doesn't hold any weight…any logic."

"But the reason I think it could be the best thing to change your decision in such a situation, and maybe I'm not too sure about this, is because I believe that there is some mathematic or algebraic formula that supports the notion," Alyce said. "I just can't remember what it is. I'm a girl, so I'm no good at numbers. But I think there's some science or numerology of some sort that supports this."

Pedro peered at the night's hidden darkness through a gap on the side of the drapes, then turned to say, "Well I know enough about numbers to know statistics lie…or liars use statistics. Whatever. But the reason why you shouldn't change your original answer is because you should have faith in your original pick."

Was Pedro's ongoing issue with this seemingly irrelevant game-show scenario the prime reason he was forced to retake the course?

"Faith in your original pick?" Alyce asked. "What kind of faith is that?"

"What kind of faith is that? I'm surprised you asked that," Pedro said. "This is a major affront to faith. A major affront! A MAJOR AFFRONT!"

Alyce giggled in amusement at the hyperbolic rant.

"Just listen," Pedro continued with a little more composure. "Let's say I die and I'm at the gates of heaven, and then some Art Linkletter—or make that Monte Hall—or whoever comes out and asks me what god I believe in and I say the God of Abraham, our God. And let's say there were three choices: my God, or make that our God, some tribal god and some, let's say, uh, some mythological diety, like Zeus or whatever."

"Now did you pick your god, or make that our God before you were showed the choices?" Nick asked.

"Of course I did!" Pedro barked lividly. "Just work with me for a second, please. Now if this guy informs me that it's not Zeus, that, no, lightning does not get tossed to the ground like it's a javelin, I'm supposed to change my pick to the Aztec god?"

"You mean the tribal god?" Nick asked.

"Work with me, I said," Pedro shot back. "The Aztec god is a tribal god."

"So is our God," Alyce added.

"Our God is universal, it's not tribal. He's grown...or check that...we've grown from that point," Pedro said. "Anyway, that's a debate for another day. But the reason I'm right in this debate because I know the dangers of second guessing. Haven't you heard about that? You talk about statistics and mathematical formulas. Waste your life second guessing yourself and see where it gets you. They shouldn't be teaching us to do that."

Nick offered a compromise. "Couldn't we when we get a chance to change the answer after one of the two wrong options is revealed to us choose our same choice over again? I mean, I don't know if I'm explaining this right, but our first choice was one of three and our second choice is now one of two. If we still think that the prize among the two is the same one we picked among the three—I mean, can't we just play along and make two separate choices that just so happen to be the same?"

Nick wasn't sure he clarified himself properly, but Pedro replied in complete understanding, "Yeah, that's what I thought. I was willing to compromise as you say. I mean, okay, if you want to give me a chance to change my answer after increasing my odds, that's all right with me. But I shouldn't have to change it. But they say you should always change it. Always. And that's just wrong. I won't question my faith in my original answer."

Alyce rose from the bed. She walked over to her well-preserved cherry-wooded armoire that was a family heirloom dating back to the late 19th century. She opened up a top drawer and fumbled through several letters, papers and other objects while searching for something.

"I don't think the term 'faith' should be applied to this test," Alyce said with her back to Pedro and Nick while still fumbling through the top drawer. "We're not talking God here, we're talking about when playing for Mercedes Benzes while utilizing odds best to our advantage."

"But guesses are made from faith," Pedro said.

"I don't know about that," Alyce said. "The game-show scenario and your God-choice scenario may not differ entirely like apples and oranges, but they are distinct from each other. Your belief in God should not be a guess, it should be a testament of faith."

"My point exactly," Pedro said.

"But you have to realize that when you pick door No. 1 or door No. 2 while hoping to win a Mercedes, those are guesses. Faith is not a guess. In fact, there's even a God gene that humans have that you may have heard about that spurs our mystical beliefs, that sets us apart from the other species. Yeah, if you go against that, there's the danger of second guessing."

"God gene?" Pedro said incredulously. "I've heard it all. But if there is a so-called God gene, couldn't there be a 'Gut' gene, I mean something that guides our gut feelings. You've had those before."

Alyce grinned devilishly. "Oh, I had some gut feelings before."

Pedro seemed to be caught off-guard by the nature of the reply. He then slumped down into the wooden chair he formerly was using.

"It seems we've gotten a little off track, or have yet addressed the glaring fallacy of this," Pedro said. "How does systematically changing your original decision give you better odds when a non-choice is revealed?"

"I don't know," Alyce said. "Like I said before, I think there's an equation that explains it. But we can find out for sure by using these."

Alyce showed a pack of limited edition Bicycle cards she retrieved from the armoire. Then in a show of athleticism that made Nick's blood jump, Alyce dropped down to her knees and quickly motioned to produce the matching oriental table from under her bed. While doing this, the side of her body brushed up gently against Nick's leg, making his blood jump some more. Alyce seated herself Indian style in front of the table—Nick never knew the table under the window had a twin—and began shuffling the cards rather clumsily with her small hands.

"What I'm going to do is draw three cards and place them face down, and one of them is going to be an ace," Alyce said looking up to Pedro, whose body was stretch reclined in the chair and looking away from the table. "Now, after you choose what you think is the ace, I'm going to show you one of the cards that is not an ace. Of course, as you said you would do, you'll stay with your original choice.

"But you…" she looked at Nick, "…will change your original choice when I do it to you. And we'll see who comes out ahead."

Nick was up for the game. Pedro, still looking away and now had his arms folded, didn't seem interested enough to cooperate. Yet when Alyce drew the cards for the first run, he responded and made a pick. Pedro's first two picks were true. Nick's first two picks were also true, but were spoiled by the changes. Although a race to a certain number wasn't determined before the experiment, score was kept through about 10 rounds with Pedro's first-and-only-choice strategy maintaining a two-win advantage.

Eventually, Nick caught up, prompting Pedro to ditch his lackluster gamesmanship and turn to face the table. Soon, Nick took a two-win lead and Pedro leaped out of his chair.

"This is bullshit," he exclaimed. "You're fuckin' cheating."

Nick was startled. He had gotten into disagreements with Pedro before, but never to a point where the language was mean-spirited.

"Come on, Pedro," Alyce said. "How can he be cheating?"

Nick was cheating. Just before he rallied to take the lead, Nick was tipped to the way Alyce dealt the cards on the table. After shuffling the pack, with no hesitation Alyce would place the two non-aces on the table but would noticeably search for one of the four aces in the pack before placing it on the table. Nick had no initial motives to participate dishonestly. It wasn't like he was in support of either option—to change or not to change—but somehow from the experiment emerged a competition between him and Pedro, a competition that he had to win.

Nick's defense was lame. "How can I know which card she's going to reveal?" As the words left his mouth, Nick realized his explanation could be easily proven wrong.

"That doesn't fuckin' matter," Pedro snapped back, not fooled at all. Pedro then got up went to the side of the window to get another peek at the darkness.

Nick grew nervous as Pedro continued to brood silently.

"I'm too tired for this," Pedro finally said. "I'm going home. I'll see you people tomorrow."

Pedro left, and Alyce followed him out the door. They were out of Nick's sight and Nick could hear them talking in the hallway. They talked for a while before Alyce returned.

It was still an hour before the 10 p.m. curfew, and Nick, not wanting to leave, offered to continue the experiment between himself and Alyce, this time Nick would participate honestly for the sake of discovery. Alyce looked at the door from which Pedro just departed with an unfocused stare. She was initially oblivious to Nick's request.

"Oh, I'm sorry. What did you say?" Alyce said while still looking foggily at the door.

"We can still see if the theory works, we'll just take turns dealing —

"Nah," Alyce interrupted. "It wouldn't be the same."

Nick was in love with Alyce. He was naturally attracted to her well before they befriended each other as sophomores. The relationship became even greater after Dom died that same year. Alyce helped Nick recover from something he thought would haunt him forever. Thus a bond was forged between the two—surely unbreakable.

The physical status was platonic, which was all right with Nick. It was best this way. Everything would be pure until the most-ideal wedding night. It would be a union blessed by God and free of the corruption that runs rampant in typical unblessed unions. He was thankful the academy prohibited coeds from kissing, even on the cheek, unless it was between immediate relatives. This was perfect for preserving the pending future between the two, a future with loving offspring and guided by a loving God.

"I'm getting a little tired, too," Alyce said while breaking her stare before putting the cards back in their box and rising from the floor. Funny, she seemed so full of energy not too long ago. "It's going to be a long day tomorrow."

When Alyce bid Nick good night, she flashed her familiar brilliant smile. It stirred the non-purged passions in Nick who, nonetheless, was confident that the greatest rewards come to those who wait.

Chapter Six

Elder Bingham wasn't a big person.

Granted, his height was just a shade under six foot. Yet in girth, he was rail thin and couldn't have tipped the scales at more than 140 pounds. But he was as intimidating as bull mastiff with a bear-killing attitude.

And like a hard-ass coach, Bingham relished at the opportunity to single out an often unsuspecting student for a major helping of bile in the name of discipline. Today just so happened to be Nick's day.

"So, you believe that the sun has reached its 'half-life', at least the sort of 'half-life' defined by you and your friend, and it's going to blow at any minute?" Elder Bingham questioned with quick, pounding syllables.

"I said that 'he said' that the sun may blow at any minute," Nick responded while trying to stay composed. "I didn't say that I believed it."

"Oh," Elder Bingham said while lifting his index finger parallel to his thin and crooked beak-like nose. Then he stepped closer to Nick's desk to hunch over his student, "but you do believe it." Even when Elder Bingham's voice wasn't loud, his beak-like nose added an exclamation point to everything he said.

There was no use in denying the accusation. In the process of being torched by Elder Bingham, several harried students claimed that Elder Bingham was putting thoughts in their heads and/or words in their mouths. Elder Bingham's replies were on the lines that those thoughts and/or words were already in their heads—they just weren't fully articulated. Nick thought such logic was that of a tyrant.

Unlike other organizations, only the administrators and teachers were referred to as elders at the academy. The title never carried any prefixes or suffixes indicating a sort of hierarchy. Yet Elder Bingham was the institution's undisputed foremost authority. And when there was an issue with student conduct, the culprit or culprits had to deal with Elder Bingham, and Elder Bingham dealt with them.

Elder Bingham wasn't the oldest elder at the academy. There were several others at least 10 to 15 years his senior. Yet he had the most prominent head of silver hair that shined so much it seemed colored, as if silver-hair coloring sold on the market. Even though there were no priests or ministers at the academy, Elder Bingham's general apparel made look like one, or an alternative version of one. All of Elder Bingham's button vests had a custom-made gap at the collar that exposed the white garment underneath which together went up to his Adam's apple. It resembled a priest's collar, except for most of Elder Bingham's vests were red-color dominated.

Every Sunday morning, before the indoor or outdoor social picnics, Elder Bingham would lead a sermon at the academy's convention center, which was never referred to as a chapel. Attendance, of course, was mandatory and students would get there early not to be the first to fill up the front row of fold-up chairs carefully set up in a series of semi-circles, but rather to seize the seats furthest back. Like iron filaments slowly attracting to a powerful magnet, the congregation would reluctantly creep up the podium—not an altar—where Elder Bingham made his weekly addresses.

The same podium was used for the morning class, as evident by the marks over the edge of the top made by Elder Bingham's long fingernails when he would firmly grip and dig into the podium's aged wood. Elder Bingham didn't always address the masses standing behind his personal mobile podium. During commencements, a raised and decorated platform would be placed over the picnic table on the small wooden island in the middle of the lake. Elder Bingham, with his special white sports coat, his special white pants, his special white dress shoes and his reddest of vests would conduct the ceremonies from that perch standing alone without any rails. While watching Elder Bingham during both of his brother's graduations, Nick marveled by the way Elder Bingham never seemed to lose balance on what couldn't be a very stable platform, and would speak theatrically with aid of his arms and hands for nearly an hour and a half without the use of written words.

Perhaps the most amazing feat of Elder Bingham's commencement addresses came when he announced the memorized names of the graduates in alphabetical order to receive their ribbon-tied scrolls of paper.

For commencements, Elder Bingham used a custom-made wireless microphone that was placed near the top of his vest. It resembled a cross between an over-sized button and an under-sized medallion. Ironically, although Elder Bingham's voice over the public address system had a metallic tone to it, it was far more personable than his actual voice.

Commencement ceremonies at the Fisher's Academy utilized the oval man-made lake to its fullest, and even for quite some time, the fountain. Facing Elder Bingham's platform from the lake's east bank was the sectioned-off picnic area. The pending graduates and their families and guests would converse together just before Elder Bingham took his post. How he got up there with no ladder visible no one seemed to know. Apparently, no one ever saw him climb up there, nor did they see him climb down afterwards. It was a mystery that several students year to year were determined to solve in anticipation of the coming commencements, but somehow universal distractions or lapses in attention would emerge at the right times at both times.

The pending graduates would move to a section on the north bank while lining themselves in the order from which they would receive their diplomas. After the speech's conclusion, students, upon having their names called, would approach a pair of elders stationed on the west bank, directly behind Elder Bingham, to receive their diplomas.

The fountain, which was in between Elder Bingham and the diploma station, would obscure the view from the picnic area of the students receiving their diplomas. This was by design, symbolizing a sort of baptism from the picnic area's vantage point with the graduates emerging from the other side of fountain before completing the circle around the lake and returning to the picnic area to rejoin their families and guests. Several parents complained that they couldn't see the students when they actually received their diplomas, and were unable to photograph the event—it would have taken a very long and expensive lens to photograph it anyway because nearly 250 feet of water separated the east bank from the west bank with Elder Bingham and his pretentious platform in the middle.

But the fountain remained a part of the ceremony until after Dom's second graduation, which took place on an unseasonably cold spring day coupled with gusty winds. During Elder Bingham's speech, it was apparent that the mist that trickled onto him continuously was unbearable, although he initially tried to hide his displeasure. But when a gust directed a showerful of water onto him, making him visibly soaked, Elder Bingham shouted, "Turn that God damn thing off!"

The fountain was never used for commencement again, even during ideal weather.

"So, what was your reaction to this—this means of human survival?" Elder Bingham grilled while still hovering over Nick.

Nick felt too fatigued to call up much memory, even from the day before. The class, which had no official name but was referred to by students as "Soul Winning," started ridiculously early at 6:30 a.m. The earliest any other class at the academy started was 8:30. On good days, Elder Bingham would wrap things up within an hour, giving some students a chance to return to their dorms for much sought for naps. But on other days, Elder Bingham would keep them there exceeding long, making them tardy for their next classes. And if Elder Bingham made you tardy, there was no excuse.

"He really didn't give me a chance to respond. He was in a hurry," Nick said.

"In a hurry?" Elder Bingham exclaimed. "Why, he was able to take his sweet time to sell you on this incredibly ambitious scheme, and he was in a hurry?"

Nick was the only underclassman in the "Soul Winning" class, which was huge because it included all of the advanced students. He was promoted to the class due to his fraternal association with Dom, who was revered at the academy for his soul-winning accomplishments the way most other schools pay homage to their outstanding athletes. Nick thought such an association made things even tougher for him in the eyes of Elder Bingham, although Elder Bingham at least did not to bring Dom's name up or compare Nick to him whenever he was haranguing Nick.

"So he was doing all the talking, and you were doing all the listening?" Elder Bingham said. "You sure would make a good wife." There was a break of laughter among the male-dominated class.

"I implored him with great effort to accept God into his life," Nick said.

"And what was his response?"

"'Which one?'"

"So he had multiple responses?"

"No," Nick said while feeling the sweat build under his armpits. "He said 'Which one?', as in which God and Jesus. He brought up the Holy Spirit…" there were several sighs heard in the classroom at this point "…and that there were other people during Jesus' time masquerading as the Messiah."

"So you believed that, too?"

"No!" Nick responded in a frazzled manner. "I don't believe that."

Elder Bingham turned away from his position over Nick and returned to his podium. But he wasn't done with Nick, yet.

"As for people masquerading as the Messiah during that time, you should believe that," Elder Bingham said. "Just like there are people masquerading as servants of the Lord today."

Elder Bingham then called on Bryan from the back of the class. Bryan was amid his final year at the academy, and someone Nick always felt he received bad vibes from. Nick, who usually sat in the first two rows of all his classes, often turned to the back of the class to discover Bryan staring at him. It happened too frequently to be a coincidence, Nick thought. Nick also believed Bryan was jealous of him due to Nick's close association with Alyce. Bryan, like many of the more bold males at the academy, would seemingly go out of his way to chat up Alyce, even when Nick was present. Nick knew his ambitions were wicked—yet he "understood" them—but he was confident nothing could come between him and Alyce.

God wouldn't have it any other way.

"Tell me and, more importantly, tell him what you would have asked this scientist of sorts who believes his plan can save the world from eminent peril."

Bryan leaned back in his chair and addressed Nick with his head cocked to one side. "Where do you guys expect to get such power? Didn't you guys take in account the energy needed to fire up all those—what are they called?—panels on the side of the moon?"

Bryan didn't follow Elder Bingham's directions to a tee. He was asked what he would ask Nick's "target," but he phrased his question to also include Nick, supporting Elder Bingham's assumption that the two were in concert. This infuriated Nick.

"He said that he wasn't sure," Nick said after turning to face Bryan. Then Nick turned back, not to face Elder Bingham, but to continue his answer while staring ahead unfocused. "He said that we would probably find and create an abundant energy source while the project was going on, especially faced with the dire need to pull it off."

"Oh, well I guess that explains everything," Elder Bingham chimed. "I'm glad to know that you two place so much faith in mankind and its ingenuity under duress. Why, who needs to call on God when you have such confidence in necessity? Taylor, my man, what question would you pose to these heroes?"

Although there was no tabulated class rank at the academy, Taylor was the Elder Bingham's prized pupil. He was only two years ahead of Nick, but talk was that he was going to graduate early from advanced studies at the upcoming commencement and was being groomed for an Elder position at the academy.

Grooming top students to become elders — a decent-paying teaching position that provided room and board if needed or wanted — may have been one of the original grand plans at the academy. But fewer and fewer students who went through the whole program opted to stay on as elders. Dom, for one, was groomed to be an elder, but had other plans. New elders usually came from the outside, like in the case of Elder Steven.

Unlike Bryan, Nick felt more at ease in the company of Taylor, who was seated at the other side of class and in the front row. One time during a Sunday picnic, Nick overheard an interesting discussion between Taylor and one of the invited guests. The guest apparently was willing to accept the invitation, but wasn't shy about taking issue on things.

"How do you explain the lungfish?" the guest asked Taylor, who was always the most social academy representative at these social picnics — interestingly, Elder Bingham never attended picnics. "The lung fish possesses a breathing apparatus that has no purpose in its current environment."

"So what's your point?" Taylor asked.

"My point is that it's obvious that the ancestors of this fish had to come up and adapt to land life after their water habitat was depleted. When the water returned, they returned, lungs and all. Now if God did have a role in all this, how do you expect me to place much faith in such an inefficient engineer of life?"

Without missing a beat, Taylor countered, "So the fish returned to the sea after developing lungs on the land? Why, I could use that as a related example on why we have developed faith in God. Like you said this fish's lungs have no apparent reason for living in the sea, but received them from their brief stay on land. Likewise, our faith in God has no apparent reason for base survival if you take in account the other creatures in the world. But we have it anyway. Where did we get it? Well, like your lungfish being fitted with lungs, our species was blessed with faith when we ventured outside our surroundings and ourselves when the primal meaning of our existence was depleted. That's when we caught a glimpse of God, a sight that has prevailed to this day and has continued to uplift the human race."

The guest, also without missing a beat, curtly replied, "You think you're so smart." He then stepped up close to Taylor as if he was about to physically challenge him. "Let me just solve a little black-box mystery for you. Eyes…" he pointed at his own, "… come from bubbles in the sea."

Taylor, who remained steady as a ship firmly anchored in a still harbor, smiled and said, "Water is life."

Taylor always greeted Nick with a friendly hello when they would cross paths, and was the first to congratulate him when Elder Bingham announced that Nick was being promoted to the class during the first day of the school year. But the two never had engaged in an extended conversation.

"Let's see," Taylor said while turning slightly to face Nick. "You know that our moon already has a crucial purpose other than affecting our tides and enhancing our imagination. Its orbit helps keep the Earth tilted and rotating at its current axis. If the axis was slightly altered, the results could be catastrophic, sun or no sun. The tides would be affected. Mass floodings would occur. The general cycle of things would be warped forever.

"My question is if you push the moon off its obit in effort to move the Earth to safety, how would it affect the Earth's axis?"

Nick was silent for a moment to comb his mind for an answer before realizing again that it really wasn't his idea to support.

"He didn't mention that," Nick said while looking at the floor. "And I, uh, didn't know enough to ask him about that."

"Another thing," Taylor said. "It's a good thing winters counteract summers. That's how viruses get killed."

Nick slowly mumbled, "I … or he didn't, eh, mention that either."

"Let me just suggest this," Elder Bingham said while clawing his podium. "Until you and your friend learn a little bit more about the laws of nature, why don't you just leave the task of saving the world in more reliable hands.

"Now on to the subject of the spring break mission. Unfortunately for those involved, as I already stated what could happen last week, it has been called off due to lack of funds."

There was a murmur of disappointment rumbling through the class before a distinguishable "What the fuck?" emerged from the back row. There was little doubt where it came from.

It was ironic that "Soul Winning" and "Parables and Probabilities" were the only two classes Nick and Pedro had together, with Nick being a year ahead in one and Pedro being held a year back in the other. Although Pedro had his problems with the latter class, in the former is where he appeared most at ease. And he had an enviable relationship with Elder Bingham, who always had time to banter with Pedro. Elder Bingham often prodded Pedro with slight critical jabs, but it was cordial and somewhat respectful, and Pedro had enough nerve and suave manner to return some jabs.

In addition to being the only male student at the academy to never wear a tie, Pedro enjoyed other freedoms, like gratuitous use of profanity in the presence of elders. Before Elder Bingham's class, Pedro would congregate with several other students in back of the cavernous classroom and speak with little regard of his tongue. Nick never was compelled to join the group, nor could pick up what they were saying from a distance, but bits of "fuckin' this" and "fuckin' that" with an "ass" or "prick" or "shit" randomly thrown in often emerged audibly from the group complements of Pedro.

Elder Bingham never confronted Pedro about his language, but this time it was, in a way, directed at him.

"I'm sorry, Pedro, but what did you say?"

There was a hush that overcame the over-sized class. Pedro looked at Elder Bingham and calmly replied, "You heard what I said."

Due to his success in reeling in prospects to join the academy for its social picnics—Alyce, of course, helped—Pedro was chosen to be a part of a 20- to 25-student mission to head down South during late spring break. The timing was designed to reach conventional college students who had just finished their school years and are more likely—especially if they just graduated—concerned about the real world than revelry. For those chosen, the mission was something to look forward to. Of course, spring break down South would naturally be a sought-after adventure. But Pedro may have wanted to be a part of the mission due to his adversarial stance toward missions from other churches and schools, as if he wanted to set the record straight in other parts of the land.

Earlier in the year, Pedro, Nick and Alyce bumped into a mission from the Church of Latter Day Saints, which just so happened to be working the laundromat and tavern area, but outside. They instantly were attracted to each other, but meeting soon started to become uneasy due to Pedro's growing irritation with the mission and its beliefs. First, Pedro was surprised due to his unfamiliarity with the Church of Latter Day Saints that the mission consisted entirely of "elders," even though it was apparent that most were barely out of high school and some still may have been in high school. But what made Pedro blow his top was the mission's and church's claim that Jesus also lived and taught in the New World.

"That's bullshit," Pedro said with his favorite exclamation. Members of the missions visibly recoiled at the abrupt remark. "The reason Jesus is so great and is without a doubt the son of God is because he traveled a radius of no more than 35 miles during his ministry and lifetime, yet he managed to reach all corners of the world.

"But no. I guess that's not good enough for you people. You have to put him here, like others put him in the south part of France or Africa or wherever, to make him your own personal, provincial Jesus. That just undermines his greatness."

Elder Bingham stepped out from behind his podium.

"Pedro, I've been meaning to tell you this for some time. When you say 'fuck' and 'shit' and 'piss' and, oh whatever, but mainly 'fuck,' you're engaging in cathartic behavior. Now catharsis can be beneficial, if used in moderation. But when it's abused the way you abuse it, it can be addicting— an addiction that becomes consuming.

"A man who is mentally deficient will reply to a problem or complex situation then by saying 'fuck' or 'shit' all the time because that's the only way he knows how to express himself. If you can't control this addiction of yours, that's the only way you will know how to express yourself in such situations. And that would be shameful, because you're a lot smarter than that.

"Now, I know that you and probably the other people involved are disappointed by this turn of events, something I was careful enough to prepare you for. But I'm sure that you, as well as the others, can somehow find away to take advantage of it, to turn a negative into a positive."

Pedro looked at Elder Bingham as if he was in the process of contemplating all that he had said. Then finally Pedro displayed an upright thumb. Everything was cool—at least between those two.

Chapter Seven

Nick had several days and sleep-deprived nights to shake the ill effects of Elder Bingham's wrath. Still they lingered. The scornful edict "just like some people are masquerading as servants of the Lord" scarred more in recollection than when first absorbed. Subsequent "Soul Winning" classes went without incident—at least for Nick—but he sensed collective disapproval from his classmates, especially from Bryan, whose unnerving stare from behind emitted a distinctive heat of its own.

Maybe I was brought up too soon, Nick came to think.

Eventually, Nick's depression dissipated and he anxiously waited for the next laundry day. He longed for another encounter with John, where he could hopefully encourage him to retell about the convenient coincidence of the sun and the moon being about the same size in the sky, and then maybe throw the axis dilemma out there to add a wrinkle to the dialogue. Nick saw in the pending re-meeting an opportunity to fully regain his confidence after being tempered with a crushing setback. The next laundry day, Nick determined, was going to be a major turning point for him, a passage to the next plateau.

Things would be different from that day forward.

But as they pulled up to the strip-mall parking lot that next laundry day, Nick was disappointed in not seeing John's Accord. Though he had never seen John until the week before, Nick somehow had expected him to be there again, like he was a Tuesday regular.

Still, the day shined like brand new penny. From different points in the distance, lawnmowers could be heard. Spring had definitely taken hold. And, as Nick sensed in a strange way, there was something special in the air. There would be other chances.

The double doors of the laundry mat were opened wide with wooden triangle door jams. The back door was also open, allowing the pleasant draft to slip through the place the like a gentle stream. For once, Nick thought Pedro and Alyce got the raw end of the deal, having to work the tavern next door which—probably due to an ordinance—seemingly always kept its doors shut and, presumably, much of the sunlight out with its smoked windows.

After Pedro and Alyce left, Nick noticed that the laundromat was deserted except for himself and the Arabic lady employee. The laundromat had become increasingly less busy since the fall, but there was usually at least one other customer. Nick assumed that people probably opted to blow off their indoor chores on such a picture-perfect day.

Nick hoped that someone would show up. He had his heart set on immediate redemption. Any further delay could slip him back into the pit of despair.

Time went by…no opportunities. But shortly after Nick transferred the loads from the washers to the dryers, a man with graying hair and a full beard appeared out of nowhere. Nick didn't see him come in; usually he was tipped off of incoming customers by a string of activated miniature bells that hung from the top of one of the double doors, but the steam-like breeze caressed them continuously for constant yet pleasant chimes. The man didn't come in with a load. Nick thought maybe he was picking up a dry-cleaning job—he talked momentarily with the lady at the counter. Yet that wasn't the case as the man began walking around with a look of aggravation, as if he were looking for something, like his keys.

Eventually, he went into the washroom located near the back door and within seconds re-emerged as if he finally found what he was looking for. The man was making a bee-line toward the exit when Nick decided to intercept him.

"Excuse me sir, but do you mind if I ask you a question?"

The man looked sternly at Nick and said, "I'm a Jew."

"I just want to—"

"I'm a Jew!" the man said again with more force before departing in an obvious rush.

Soon, it was suggested that he wasn't a Jew after all.

"I shouldn't even bother to tell you this, but you ought know it," said the lady employee, whom Nick never particularly liked and suspected yet didn't care that the feeling was probably mutual. It irked Nick that her portable radio was always tuned to Rush Limbaugh's mean-spirited right-wing rant, but what irritated Nick the most was her expounded ignorance. Once, Nick heard her talk to another customer about how certain things should be left in God's hands—or make that Allah's hands (gee, Rush is really sympathetic to Muslims)—but later during that same conversation railed on about how a local convicted murderer should get the death penalty as soon as humanly possible.

"That guy isn't a Jew," she said. "I know a Jew when I see one."

Nick was dumbfounded.

"The only reason he said that was to get you out of his face," she said while revealing her yellow teeth.

Nick approached the counter, and the lady turned away, taking a couple of steps back before turning to face him again. "It really pisses me off that you peoples come in here preaching about this and that while you peoples are really nothing but a bunch of hypocrites," she said as bits of spit, which also appeared to be yellow, flew from her lips. "Hypocrites, all of you! I've been letting it go too long. I minded my own business. But it is my business. It is business that we're losing because of you peoples, because other peoples are fed up with you."

Nick didn't buy it, or more like he didn't want to buy it. "What do you mean?" he said in a whining defense. "We've never been told they felt that way."

"Open your eyes," the lady said. "How many peoples do you see here? None. How many peoples have you forced yourself on and have never seen again?"

Nick tried to think of an example of at least one repeat "peoples" before the lady again answered her own question.

"None! I've about had it with you peoples. This used to be one of our busiest days of the week. Now look at it. Either you keep your beliefs to yourselves, or I'm going to run you all out of here for good!"

Nick turned and walked away. This was one argument the customer was doomed to lose. "Hypocrites!" the lady barked again with a parting blow. Although in retreat, one of the lady's bits of spit was able to take flight on the draft and land on Nick's neck.

Nick decided to go next door to discuss the grief with Pedro and Alyce.

Before he was to enter the tavern, Nick wanted to see where Pedro and Alyce were stationed within the place so he could join them immediately before being hassled for an ID. But looking through the smoked windows, Nick couldn't spot neither of them, only an obscured figure behind the bar. Nick continued to look waiting for them to emerge into view. Nothing…no one.

How strange, Nick thought.

Nick turned his attention to the parking lot and saw that Pedro's car wasn't there. Nick wondered momentarily before reasoning that they probably returned to the academy to retrieve something left behind—like Alyce's bed dressings. Similar situations had happened before.

Nick returned to the laundromat where the lady glared at him more viciously than before as if she mulled over her disposition to attain greater vindication. Nick decided to go stand by the open back door to gain more distance while waiting for the tumbling to cease.

Good thing it was such a brilliant day. Nick spied the blossoming back yards of the subdivision located beyond the building's back alley, and took a deep breath. The air tasted fresh enough to lift any floundering spirit. Then he looked back at the lady. Sure enough, still fuming.

Nick took a step outside for even greater distance. He gazed down at his dress shoes and gently moved some small rocks along the gravel alley to give him something to do. Nick looked up to his left and saw Pedro's Malibu.

How strange, Nick thought.

The car was parked about 35 feet away with its raised backend facing Nick, and at first glance appeared to be unattended. No one was in the driver's seat, nor the front passenger seat. As Nick approached, he was able to see that though the engine was off, the car was not completely idle—it was like an inert beast who had swallowed something still alive and kicking in its bowels. The struggle made its shocks squeak, and then when the struggle became more feverous, squeal. It emanated from the back seat, and that's where they were at.

Alice was on top bouncing up and down like she was riding one of those old-fashioned, coin-operated pony ride machines that used to grace the front of drug stores. Nick moved closer and closer as if he was being magnetically pulled toward the action. He still couldn't see Pedro, but he saw Alice like he never had before.

Her overall skirt was pulled up and pushed down, forming a blue crumpled ring around her belly. Alice's panties were removed revealing her firm, snow-white bottom that would come into rear-window view when it was at the top of its up-and-down thrusts. Alice was semi-perpendicular to her prone partner as the Malibu only gave her so much headroom. Nick could see her buttoned shirt slightly opened, but her breasts were still kept concealed by her bra. But then during a brief break in the action, Alyce removed her shirt and bra, displaying her full bounty accentuated with erect nipples.

Then she went back to work as her hips swiveled like the little girls Nick would benignly watch back in his hometown having hula-hoop contests. Who could keep it up the longest, that was the object.

Oh my God! Nick thought as his palms began to sweat while he still was being slowly drawn in, now close enough to hear the carnal cries muffled by the closed windows.

Oh My God! Nick's bodily fluids began to pour into his groin area—but no sanctified tingling in his chest, though.

Suddenly, Nick stifled his approach when he found himself 10 feet from the car. He was mystified. *How can this be happening?* he thought, and then drew closer to the car.

For a brief second or two, Nick was urged to jump in to join in on the action. *But no! How dare I think such sinful thoughts!* Yet the impulse shimmied his addled consciousness. Nick now was inches from the bumper.

This should not be happening, Nick almost said out loud. *They have no right to do this to me, or to each other. This is a sin! This should not be happening!* The vehicle began to squeal more wildly.

Just northwest of the action, a housewife was mowing her chain-linked-fenced backyard. She mowed in pattern parallel to her house, and Nick noticed her when she and her mower made a turn toward him and the lovers. Nick wanted her to see what was going on. Nick wanted her to drop everything and run inside to call the police or something. But even as she kept getting closer, she remained oblivious.

Why can't she see this? They can't get away with this!

Eventually, the woman did notice something—that Nick was staring at her. She gave him an irritating glance as if to say, "What are you looking at?" and Nick was alarmed, as was being exposed as an accomplice to this Godless act.

Nick quickly retreated back into the laundromat were the tumbling had ceased. Nick couldn't control the shaking of his hands as he tried to fold the clothes and almost jumped at the sight of Pedro and Alyce when they returned to the laundromat about 10 minutes after Nick left the scene of the crime. And there was evidence of the crime as Alyce's hair was slightly out of place and Pedro's shirt was unbuttoned one button lower than normal.

"There wasn't much going on next door," Alyce said. Her nipples were still erect as shown through her repositioned bra and shirt.

Nick didn't know what to say. Then he caught a look from the lady at the counter who, since his hasty return, Nick managed to ignore.

"Hypocrites! All of you!"

Nick shook during the trip home, although he tried his best to hide and contain them. He felt the warmth of the seat where the fornication had taken place. He also noticed that the car had a different scent—familiar, but from where? He would glance at Pedro and Alyce to see how they now looked at each other, to see if anything would be different as now surely things were.

After being dropped off at his dorm, Nick noticed that his almost painful erection was, like Alyce's nipples, probably evident to anyone who looked in the right spot. After Nick removed his laundry baskets from the truck, he left them in the parking lot and said to Pedro, who was returning to the car after opening and closing the truck and was about to drive Alyce to her dorm, "I'll be back for this." Then Nick quickly jogged into his dorm building and into its ground-floor washroom. Please God, let no one be in there, Nick wished. There wasn't.

Nick went into a toilet stall. *Now this is the scent I was reminded of*, then shut the latch door and, in a manic pace, flung off his belt, un-zipped his pants and nearly ripped off his underwear to get his hands on his penis. Nick was amazed how big it was. He always considered himself "less endowed" from unwitting caparisons he would make at a line of urinals with other pissers present. If it were in any other circumstance, he would have been proud of his piece. But there was no time for self-admiration as Nick sat on the toilet and began masturbating to the pace he remembered Alyce riding Pedro.

"Why isn't it me, why isn't it me?" Nick said out loud between moans as worked his member. "Why, why, waaaaaahy?

In less than 20 seconds, semen shout out with the second thrust splashing Nick in the chin. It was a major load, as it continued to pour out of his penis and onto his hand like foam from a bottle of soda previously shaken up before its cap was opened. It had been a long time since Nick had masturbated, nearly a year and a half, believe it or not. Ironically, the reason he refrained from the act was his visionary, non-corrupted future with Alyce. Now as the semen dripped into the toilet, Nick knew he was soiled again. That fact came even more apparent when Nick tried to clean himself with toilet paper, which its thinness was no match for the sticky substance as it began to dry on his skin.

His innocent thoughts of Alice were also soiled, but oh my God, what a woman!

When Nick finally got himself clean enough to go back outside, he was dismayed to see that Pedro and Alice were still there serving as sentry guards for Nick's abandoned laundry. They both looked at him as if they expected an explanation.

Like I should give them one, Nick angrily mumbled to himself before offering, "I'm sorry, I just had to come—or I just had to go."

Chapter Eight

Habitual wasn't the word. More like chronic.

During the following week, Nick masturbated seven … eight … nine … even more than ten times a day depending on how you separated the night from the morning. If he hadn't performed the successive feats himself, Nick would have never believed such an output was humanly possible. Once during a fleeting moment after reaching double figures in orgasms, Nick had a smack sense of pride, similar to when he whipped out his enlarged member in the student commons washroom. Yet shame quickly prevailed as Nick knew he was overcome with sin while continuing to covet what he couldn't have but should have had in a more perfect world.

Perfect world, huh? Long before witnessing Alyce's torrid ride of Pedro in Pedro's car behind the alley of the laundromat, a ride that took place on such a perfect day for a ride further enhanced by such a perfect rider—*Oh my God! What a woman*—Nick thought he had conquered the urge to copulate. When he first came to the academy, Nick, as he later thought shortly after he passed the phase, was at his peak in giving in to self-fulfillment. But even back then, Nick wasn't graced with many opportunities to carry out his urge. Like all underclassmen, Nick had a roommate, a likable chap a class ahead of Nick. For Nick to jack off, it would have to be during a span of time when he knew for sure that his roommate wasn't going to be home. Nick was afraid to attempt it at night with their beds, although at opposite ends of the room, being fairly close together.

Once however, when he heard his roommate snore which Nick assumed he did in the throes of deep sleep, Nick decided to chance it and began to tug on himself as quietly as he could. But as Nick quickened the pace to reach that brief moment in time, the increased noise must have woke up his roommate because shortly after that brief moment in time, Nick, to his horror, realized his roommate was no longer snoring. Nick then, while trying to stifle the panting of his breath, started to snore himself in efforts to fake his roommate into believing that he was asleep and had been for quite sometime.

Nick longed for his privacy during that first year. He longed for the ability to relieve himself whenever he pleased. Back then, Nick's lusts were usually never inspired by fellow classmates. Although there were a couple of girls at the academy Nick found attractive, he considered them forbidden fruit, as if fantasizing about coeds at the academy only compounded the evil. Instead, Nick would masturbate to the fantasies of the celebrity women he would see on T.V., especially the ones on cable.

But by the time Nick got his own room his junior year, there was no longer a need for such privacy. His lust was curtailed by the true love he now harbored for Alyce, a love that he thanked God for, and a love he would not sully in His honor.

The perfect world. *But oh my God! What a woman!*

Now when Nick went at it, his fantasy was never well thought out beforehand, and even remained fairly lucid during the act itself. At first, he would imagine that Alyce was fucking him, then Pedro—usually, Nick would shoot his wad when the scene more realistically switched to Pedro. *Is it the creepy voyeurism that gets me off?* Nick thought.

Once Nick had a orgasm while imagining Alyce with Elder Steven, and was taken aback on how lurid his fantasies had become.

"God, forgive me," Nick pleaded as his semen spilled onto his knuckles.

God never gave an audible answer, but Nick heard voices from the past. "Hypocrites, all of you ... like some people are masquerading as servants of the Lord ... What is happening here is a crime of abominable proportions."

That first night after Nick witnessed the perfect fuck on the perfect day, Nick didn't get an ounce of sleep (but sure spilled multiple ounces). The following morning, Nick, without the slightest hunger for food, skipped breakfast before attending Elder Bingham's class. Nick's stream of conscience was skittish and half dry, but his nerves were charged with twice as much voltage.

"I said, 'How does order come from chaos!'" Elder Bingham shouted at Nick while looming over him, making Nick nearly jump out of his chair as a portion of the class snickered.

"Uh, uh, I'm sorry. I didn't here you," Nick said. Nick was tuned out as

THE SOUL WINNER

visions of Alyce and Pedro were again humping in his head and enlarging his groin. When Elder Bingham disrupted the trance, Nick's initial split-second fear was that he was caught self-fulfilling in the middle of class. Even immediately afterward, Nick felt that he was exposed.

"You didn't hear me? I'm standing right in front of you," Elder Bingham said before leaning down closer to Nick to where his beak and Nick's shell-shocked face were only an erection apart. "Do you hear me, now?"

Nick decided to take the following day off to spend more time, well, masturbating. The academy allowed students to call off sick two times a year without a required evaluation from its infirmary. Nick had one more day at his disposal, so he decided to take advantage of it. He wondered if his growing habit would force him to call off another day. But what could he tell the resident physicians? That he had a masturbation sickness?

Funny thing, Nick thought, *there was some truth to that.*

He even passed on studying with Alyce and Pedro, which they scheduled to do that night. Nick figured that they probably figured that he wasn't going to make it after seeing that he wasn't present during their classes that day. They obviously wouldn't be disappointed, because it would be just them two alone in Alyce's pink and red room. The thought of what they were doing in that pink and red room gave an extra boost to Nick's sickness.

"Oh, Why? Why? Why?" Nick lamented out loud after another climax. His penis and right hand were glazed with dried semen that, combined with his sweat-worked groin, emitted the foulest of stenches, and his mattress seemed to sink lower with the imagined extra weight on top of it.

The weather for the next laundry day was furious and wet. The wind-swept rain made the day seem harsher than any endured during the winter. The three raced to the double doors with their loads with their heads bowed to shield the effects of the pelting chilled water. Upon entering, Nick noticed the counter lady's hateful eyes focused on them, particularly him. Nick paid little attention. There were other things on his mind, other problems that plagued him.

One thing Nick was little relieved of was the laundromat once again had a decent crowd. Maybe it was the weather. Maybe the counter lady was just full of shit.

Another thing that put Nick at ease was the terrible weather, the type that, with its low clouds and high winds, usually gives people fears of pending tornadoes. But at least Alyce and Pedro wouldn't resort to any shenanigans, or so surmised Nick who somehow thought the conditions would discourage them. After all, it wasn't a perfect day.

Some time after Alyce and Pedro left to supposedly "work next door," Nick went to the washroom at the back of the building to urinate. As Nick was accustomed to do, he would sit on the stool while taking a piss. It was a way he liked to relax while mulling over various thoughts in his head. Over the toilet was a grilled air vent with a free-spinning fan inside. During the cold months, a cardboard slab was placed inside the grill which trapped the stench after well-scented bowel movements, but blocked the cold. Now the cardboard slab was gone allowing violent wind to pour into the washroom while whistling through the rapid spinning fan.

And there was more sounds from outside—the sounds of Alyce and Pedro going at it again.

The week before when Nick witnessed them at close range, their sounds were muffled by the car's rolled up windows. Now in a return to the scene of the crime and apparently confident that no one would be outdoors to hear their cries, the windows were rolled down.

Nick could hear Alyce's sweet voice yelp out intermittent "Uhhmmm baby, uhhmmm baby!" but it was Pedro's voice that made Nick's blood race. Pedro continuously repeated a sentence that sounded like it was suppose to say, "Oh my god." But really it went like this: "Ooooohh my gaaaaa! Ooooohh my gaaaaaaaaaa!"

Nick grabbed his penis while still sitting on the stool. He was going to join in following the rhythm of their cries. He could tell that they were both soon heading for that brief moment in time, and he was going to reach it with them. It would be a big, gigantic simultaneous orgasm.

But just before they all got there, Nick noticed someone was pounding on the washroom door. The pounding was violently hard, indicating that the knocking may have been going on for a while. Nick hastily zipped up his pants and opened the door where the counter lady greeted him with another raging look with a customer and her pre-school-aged child at her side.

"You know that there are other people here who need to use this washroom."

The back seat of Pedro car still had droplets of water on it for the ride home. Nick was unable to fully tuck his erection in his underwear when he was interrupted, and couldn't find a way to gracefully right it in the presence of others. And as he sat on the seat, the rain droplets were able to seep through his pants and tickle his misplaced balls. That just made things harder.

Nick felt compelled to pull it out start jacking off in the car. Yeah, they would be shocked, but so was Nick when he first saw them a week ago. What comes around goes around.

Just then, Alyce turned to look at Nick. Nick hoped that she would notice his erection that continued to edge down the side of his leg. Nick had his legs spread open to make it more obvious.

"Nick, you look cold back there," she said. Her window was shut, but the driver's side was almost half down—even today.

"No, actually I'm hot," Nick said while trying to speak a sultry voice. He wanted to add, "I'm hot for you" but he still maintained enough control of his fleeting common sense.

"What?" Alyce said with a quizzical look on her face before turning away. "You looked cold to me."

Nick felt that the way Alyce turned away before saying the last sentence had a smack of indifference, and it delivered a pang of hurt to Nick. When the affair first came to light, Nick did feel slightly victimized by betrayal. Now the feeling was starting to take greater hold. Nick thought the way Alyce and Pedro were hiding their blooming sexual relationship from him made the situation even more wrong.

Immediately after returning to his dorm, Nick masturbated and unleashed a spectacular load. The semen launched about three feet in the air and fanned out, similar to that of the fountain in the lake. Nick then masturbated some more, and some more, but obviously couldn't get the same type of ejaculation. But amazingly on his 11th round an hour shy of bedtime, Nick got a decent shot off. Just when he got it off, Alyce was fucking Dom.

Nick jumped out of his bed after over four straight hours of lying on his back, and went to the mirror over his mid-sized drawer. Nick saw that his eyes were sunken and his face was a shade paler than normal.

"I will not jack off again," Nick said pointing to himself with his soiled finger. "If I do, may I be sent straight to hell!"

Nick was determined to keep his vow and was serious about the self-imposed penalty. He even decided to adopt a better attitude while addressing Alyce and Pedro. He would now converse with them exuberantly with the confidence in himself to accept the situation and move on. This too would pass.

The next day, Nick, Alyce and Pedro were having lunch in the middle of the lake. Nick, while trying to exhibit an air of undeterred self-confidence, asked Alyce and Pedro what their plans were for spring break. Neither gave a definitive answer, yet Nick disclosed his plans

"I was thinking for the break to go out to the woods or something, to literally rough it for a while," Nick said. "It will be a good way to get closer to God. You know, sometimes we take things for granted and get away from God, and allow ourselves to stray toward false pleasures."

Nick thought he may have been too obvious with his "false pleasures" remark. But Alyce and Pedro didn't seem to catch it, or even hear it.

"But you guys don't have to come with me or anything," Nick said. "I was going to go by myself. You know, it's good to have some quality time all by yourself every once in a while. You know, to get closer with God."

During the academy's spring break, many students went home to their families, as Dom used to do. Nick, on the other hand, never went home during spring break—except during his only year with Dom—and stayed at the academy, which was usually half occupied.

"When you think about it, getting to experience the outdoors more this time of the year seems like a good idea," Pedro said as he looked unfocusedly among the surrounding treeline of the weeping willows.

"When is your family coming to pick you up?" Nick asked Alyce, who always went home during the breaks.

"Nah, I decided to stick around here this time around," she said. "I guess I just can't get enough of this place."

During spring break, Nick did break off from the outside world. But not the way he announced. Instead of venturing out into the wilderness, Nick decide to hole himself in his dorm room for the duration of the week and stocked his mini refrigerator with a bowl of egg salad, a bowl of tuna salad, and another bowl of a combination of the two, two loafs of wheat bread and two gallons of milk. He didn't want Alyce or Pedro or anyone else to see him outside his dorm, or even inside as he had his window shades pulled down.

To relieve himself—in the necessary way—and to clean himself, Nick would go to the dorm's community washroom and shower down the hallway from his room during three or four o'clock in the morning so not to be detected. When nature didn't comply to the altered schedule, Nick did his best to hold it as long as he could, or he would try to sneak to the washroom during conventional hours when he felt the coast was clear.

Aside from that dilemma, things didn't go as quite as planned for Nick. For some reason, Nick consumed the gallons of milk at a glutton's pace and was out in less than two days. That forced more ventures to the washroom to fill the empty plastic jugs with water. But Nick was able to preserve his sandwich supplies, although the taste was getting staler by the day.

In the mean time, Nick tried to bide his time by reading. But Nick was never much of a reader, and felt fortunate that the academy didn't include much required reading for its classes. And when Nick did read for leisure, it was more out of obligation than pleasure.

After failing to remember much of what he just spent two hours reading, Nick wondered what Alyce and Pedro were up to. But his imagination tugged at his groin forcing Nick to repeatedly shake off the urge to break his vow.

On the fourth night after Nick defecated at 3 a.m. after holding the contents inside for nearly five hours, Nick fell back in his bed but was far from going asleep. A day earlier he had opened up his window to air out his room with fresh spring air, but was careful not to lift the shades and moved his desk drawer under his window to trap the bottom of the shade so the wind wouldn't move it noticeably. The morning before, Nick woke to singing of the birds which returned in droves. He was tempted to go outside for a walk, but he refrained.

Outside in the distance, Nick thought he heard something.

It couldn't be, Nick said to himself when he seemed to recognize the sounds Alyce and Pedro made on that rainy afternoon with the windows rolled down. But the cries seemed more muffled, or self muffled, as if the sources were half-willing to let the world hear and see what they were doing, and half-reluctant of being caught in the act. Nick tried to hone in on the sound and estimated that is was coming from the lake, more precisely, on the picnic table on the island in the middle of the lake.

Nick reached for his penis. "Oh, no," he audibly said to himself while starting to fuck his fist. "Here we go again."

But suddenly the sounds in the distance stopped as if they were never there in the first place. Nick tried to listen for more, but couldn't pick anything up. Maybe he was just imagining things, he surmised. Surely they wouldn't fuck in the open in the middle of the lake.

Nick then thought he heard other voices; voices from a group of people, not just from two lovers. The curfew around the academy was usually lax during the break. There were probably some underclass students out after curfew.

Nick put his penis away. No orgasm, no foul.

On Sunday morning, Nick decided to leave his room and to check up on his friends. He could tell of how his experience in the wilderness was greatly beneficial and actually did bring him closer to God. But he noticed that Pedro's car wasn't in it usual spot in the academy's parking lot. And when he went to Alyce's room and knocked on her door, there was no answer. Nick thought maybe that they were inspired by his quest to get away that they themselves took to the outdoors, and camped out somewhere, or went somewhere out of town.

But the next morning, when classes resumed, Pedro's car still wasn't there. And when Nick took his seat in Elder Bingham's class, he noticed that Pedro wasn't among the familiar pre-class social congregation. But the congregation was still active without him, except the voices consisted of quieter whispers.

Elder Bingham soon arrived rolling in a truck of stacked cardboard boxes. He then pulled out stacks of thick, spiral-bound books and, after counting them, gave them to the students seated in front of each of the rows and instructed them to take one and pass the others back.

They were the academy's student handbooks. Each family of a student was given one upon enrolling.

"Now I'm not one to speak on the virtue of the written and frozen word," Elder Bingham said. "But some rules need to be clearly defined. Turn to the chapter regarding proper student conduct, and read the first passage."

It simply stated, "Fornication among students is strictly forbidden, and is subject to immediate expulsion."

Nick knew right then that Alyce and Pedro got kicked out of the academy for fucking on Elder Bingham's stage.

Chapter Nine

Nick thought he would have missed Alyce and Pedro more, especially Alyce. Other than the day he ditched all classes and the subsequent study session to masturbate, and the stretch of time during spring break when he isolated himself in his room, Nick had conversed with Alyce to some extent every day for over two years. It was almost the same way for Pedro during the current school year.

Now they were gone, two of the only students other than, of course, Dom he had really opened up to during his four years there. But somehow Nick didn't feel that lonely, or as lonely as he felt before. During the final weeks leading up to Alyce and Pedro's expulsion, that's when Nick experienced his greatest loneliness. Then, Alyce and Pedro were still in the picture, but Nick was in the process of being pushed out.

He wondered where they were. Did they go back home to their families? Nick knew nothing of Pedro's family, and even very little of Alyce's, although Alyce was quite familiar with Nick's due to the comforting role she played during Nick's grieving process. Basically the only presence Nick saw from Alyce's and Pedro's families was that both of them always had money despite not holding jobs. Nick's family never sent him money. Nick worked two Sunday mornings a month cleaning up the academy's cafeteria for $30 a pop. It was good enough for laundry money, random fast food breaks and little else.

It was funny, but it seemed that Elder Bingham missed Pedro more than Nick did, although Elder Bingham no doubt was the one who sealed the young lovers' fates. After issuing the refresher course on the academy's policies in the wake of the now infamous fuck on the lake, Elder Bingham conducted the rest of the class in a somber tone before dismissing the class an hour earlier than normal. Nick had an urge to take advantage of that extra time by going up to his room to reenact that infamous fuck on the lake, but fought it back.

Once during a class discussion on the factors that may or may not go into effect when a self-destructing soul suddenly becomes "reborn" or "saved"— a discussion that was uncharacteristically light-hearted for the class—Elder Bingham remarked out loud that he wished Pedro was still around since his "two cents" on the subject would have surely been worthwhile and amusing.

Elder Steven seemed to miss Alyce somewhat in the same way, but not entirely. Once during one of his classes, Elder Steven mistakenly called on Alyce before realizing again that her desk was terminally vacated.

"Oh, my. Excuse me," Elder Steven said with detected embarrassment. "Out of the corner of my eye, I thought I saw her." Elder Steven's seemed to get more embarrassed after giving the explanation, before gracefully responding, "Sorry Nick, I hope you're not offended for me mistaking you as Alyce."

Nick often passed by Alyce's and Pedro's former dorm rooms. Pedro's dorm was on the other side of campus from Nick's and was a ground-level apartment. There were some disadvantages of having a ground-level room. One of which, of course, was that it made you a more likely to be burglarized. Though crime, despite the accusation made by the former student who saved Nick's father's soul, was for the most part nil at the academy, and had always been so. But one of the advantages, at least if you were social like Pedro, was that people could congregate just outside your glass-sliding doors — which came with most ground-level apartments — to partake in cookouts or other indoor/outdoor activities. Nick rarely visited Pedro at his dorm, mainly because he had a sense he really wasn't welcome there. Nick suspected that Pedro probably stored alcoholic beverages in his mini-fridge and shared them with the predominate upperclassmen at these gatherings. Every once in a while, Nick smelled what he thought was alcohol on Pedro's breath, not just the days when he and Alyce would "work" the tavern.

Nick never drank an ounce of liquor, but he would never rat on Pedro, and Pedro probably knew that too. Still, it was probably best that a non-drinker like Nick should avoid such gatherings to prevent possible tension among those who may not trust him as much.

More often Nick passed by Alyce's room and looked up at the window. For nearly a week after the fact, the white sheet in the window remained. Nick remembered when he would walk by window while returning to his dorm at night after many study sessions. With the lamp light coupled with the inverted reflection off the pink walls, the sheet from the outside had the color of a strawberry milkshake, one part strawberry and two parts vanilla. Sometimes he could make out vague shadows of Alyce on the sheet.

Nick imagined that Alyce and Pedro made love in that room—How could they be in love?—and he imagined that the act was transmitted on the sheet.

The sheet was eventually removed and pink walls could be seen due to the incoming daylight. Upon first viewing the exposed walls while walking by, Nick experienced a melancholy feeling. The room was no doubt cleared out by then, punctuating the indefiniteness of the loss.

Once late in the afternoon, Nick passed by the wooden-roped walkway leading to the lake's wooden island. Evil feelings started to boil up inside him again. Like the way he was attracted to Pedro's Malibu that day in the back of the laundromat, Nick felt drawn to the island. He took a couple of steps on the walkway before stopping and asking himself, "Just what am I going to do once I get there?" The thought made him shiver, and he quickly turned back and encountered a couple of elders who were also heading toward the island.

"Why, you don't have to leave to just because of us," one of them asked Nick in an inviting tone.

Yet Nick took that first step. How often he was reminded how a slight step here or a quick decision there could alter one's life in dramatic fashion.

Later that night, Nick knew it was slipping away. The setting was a near-copy of the night Alyce and Pedro's heeded to the call. It was threeish in the morning, just like it was that night when Nick heard them in the near distance. Nick was prone in his bed, trying to battle the temptation. Finally, he got up and hastily dressed. He was erect.

The guard at his Nick's building's counter was usually an upperclassmen who checked the times residents came in and came out as well as for their visitors. And the guard usually was semi-responsible. Be it to go to the bathroom, or to grab a snack to eat at the building's commissary room which had vending machines and a complementing microwave at the other end of the ground floor, or just to walk off boredom, the post was more often vacated than occupied, especially after midnight. And sometimes when the post was occupied, the guard was asleep while either eased back in his chair or with his nose and face in a book he was trying to read. Nick knew of these lapses in security because, on occasion, he would use the ground floor washroom instead of the one on his floor because his room was located near the stairwell and it was a shorter distance than walking down the hallway to use the washroom on his floor.

This played into Nick's plan of escape. If the guard wasn't at his post, Nick would make a run for the doors—or at least a fast-paced walk. If the guard was at his post, Nick would retreat to the washroom and emerge after some time to see if the coast was clear. If the guard was still there, Nick would return to his room before replaying the ploy 15 to 30 minutes later. If such returns would catch the guard's eye, Nick's excuse would be on the lines of him experiencing intestinal problems or other "sicknesses."

Plus, most of the guards were familiar with Nick's choice of washroom and the habit of using it in the middle of the night, so it shouldn't raise much suspicion.

When Nick came down, to his delight the guard was away from his post. He felt his erection grow another half inch as he quickly and quietly slipped through the doors. The cool, sweet air hit Nick, who hastily dressed himself in sweat pants, T-shirt and sneakers without socks, with a dose of reality. *What will happen if I come back with the guard back at his post?* Nick thought. But he realized his concern was virtually irrelevant. Nick was going to that wooden island and jack off in full view of God and anyone else who just so happened to take notice at that hour of the day. It didn't matter if he got caught the same way Alyce and Pedro did. Nothing was holding him back. The first step was taken. Nick was following through.

The academy grounds were partially illuminated by a single willow-obscured lighting standard in the parking lot north of the lake. Other than that, it was the clear night sky. When Nick reached the wooden walkway, he saw that the still reflection of the stars and moon in the lake—the fountain was off, like it was after every sunset—created another beautiful night sky.

Nick was reminded of another beautiful night that took place during the winter. But to Nick, it was more intriguing than beautiful. Nick, Alyce and Pedro returned from the laundromat on a very cold night. Light snowflakes fell from the sky, and Nick noticed that every light that was activated on the academy grounds—even the ones emitting from building windows—produced beacons that went straight up and down. Why did they do that? Nick wondered. He then asked Pedro what he thought about the phenomenon.

"I don't know what you're talking about," Pedro answered.

Nick couldn't believe what he was about to do. But the hesitation couldn't hold. "Screw it all," Nick said out loud before briskly walking toward his destination. Nick didn't care about the consequences. It was almost like he was dreaming. The situation was so surreal. While halfway to the table, Nick felt he was walking in outer space with the constellations above and below him.

But as Nick neared the island and picnic table, Nick saw that someone was already on the island. It was Elder Steven. He was shielded from Nick's view from the angled and opened umbrella.

Elder Steven didn't live on campus. Rather, he rented an apartment about a mile from the academy. It was unusual to see Elder Steven on academy grounds during non-daylight hours, let alone in the middle of the lake at three o'clock in the morning. Obviously, Nick was shocked to discover him there. And it seemed to be the same for Elder Steven toward Nick, or sort of.

The surprised look on Elder Steven's face seemed rather subdued in comparison to how Nick was taken aback. It was like Elder Steven initially may have been more surprised than he showed that he was, as if he had detected Nick's approach before revealing himself, which was probable since Nick's steps on the walkway echoed softly in the still night just before he audibly said, "Screw it all."

"Why Nick?" Elder Steven said with an exuberant greeting before noticeably lowering his voice. "What brings you out here at such a, ah, a strange time?" Elder Steven had that same embarrassed look he had when he mistakenly called on Alyce during his class.

Nick himself was embarrassed. There was no way he was going to give a true explanation. Unlike Elder Steven, who was appropriately dressed with a buttoned-to-the-chin wind-breaker. Nick, with his sweats and T-shirt, felt that he looked really out of place. And he saw that his hard-on noticeably poked out from his sweats.

"Gee, uh, I was going to ask you the same question."

Elder Steven smiled and looked up at the sky, "I guess I just needed to get away for a while. It's weird, but you want to get away from something and you end up going to where you originally want to get away from. I don't know if that makes any sense to you. It doesn't really make much sense to me."

Nick nodded his head in approval, but it was an instinctual response.

"Plus, it's such a beautiful night," Elder Steven said. "And I just couldn't get any sleep. I don't know why."

Although Elder Steven lived close by, Nick couldn't figure out why he would come all the way out to the academy to relieve insomnia while taking in some night air.

"Yeah, uh, I couldn't any sleep, either," Nick said. Technically, he was telling the truth.

"Ah, I bet your excited about graduation?" Elder Steven said.

"Yeah, but uh … " Nick trailed off. He was about to mention that he felt bad Alyce wasn't going to be there, but he didn't want the conversation to go there. ..." I don't know. Maybe I'll appreciate it better after I do graduate."

Elder Steven looked at Nick for a second before returning his attention to the sky. "Well, I guess that's one constant—we treat things in greater reverence when we look back at them. It's kind of like the stars in the sky. Or make that, oh I don't know what I'm saying is pertinent, but you know that isn't it kind of amazing that when we look at the stars that we're in a sense traveling back in time?"

Nick heard of that thought before.

"You could look at it this way, we're looking at stars that are no longer there, but the stars, in a way, are, or were looking at us before we even existed," Elder Steven said.

Nick squinted his eyes. "But that's impossible. In order to be looking at each other, we and the stars would have to exist at the same time."

"But we're looking at the stars now, and they're not there."

Nick scanned the constellation. He wondered who would be looking at the Earth's star in the future, long after it was gone.

"You know," Elder Steven said, "they just sent up a balloon photo-taking telescope with a special lens over the North Pole that can focus all the way back to the so-called Big Bang, or Big Expansion, or whatever they call it these days. One theory is that the universe is expanding to a point that is flat, or is flat already, or flat in a theoretical sense. Isn't it ironic? It took mankind ages before it realized that the Earth wasn't flat. Now we may be discovering that the universe is flat.

"And you say we can't look into the future the same way those stars up there could have looked into our future. Yet by gazing at events of the past, we could really be uncovering our fate. It is going to be fire or ice? We may find out."

"Really though?" Nick said while folding his arms to give his underdressed body some warmth. "How can this space camera take photographs of the past while uncovering our future? I mean, I understand why we can see stars that no longer exist. But how can we see the so-called Big Bang, that is if it ever existed? I mean, what are we looking for? Do we know what the Big Bang looks like? No one I know was around when it happened, that is—again—if it ever did happen."

"From what I know, it's going to try to photograph, or record and decipher light photons from that time," Elder Steven said.

"Light? Funny, but I thought you said that there was light at the beginning."

"Yes, there was. And remnants of that initial light have survived as light photons," Elder Steven said.

"Just what are light photons?" Nick said as he unfolded his arms while leaning on the picnic table with his off arm.

"Light photons are strange," Elder Steven said. "Like I said, they're particles of light, but they're particles that violate laws of nature, or the laws we have set for nature. There was a recent experiment that split a single light photon into two independent entities and sent them in different directions. But, according to those conducting the experiment, if you measure the state of one of these entities, it immediately affects the other half, even at a great distance."

"But how?" Nick asked.

"Somehow the two halves, though both are claimed to be independent, are entangled. And the entanglement serves as a conduit of sorts that exchanges information or states faster than the speed of light. Or faster than anything, since when once one half gets altered, the consequence to the other is instantaneous. Isn't that amazing?"

Nick was trying to follow along. "Yeah, that is kind of amazing," he said, though not quite knowing what he was agreeing to.

"Oh, it is. And there is a lot more amazing stuff that is going to discovered," Elder Steven. "You watch, science is going to take a major turn."

"But science is always revolutionary," Nick said. "It always changes."

"No," Elder Steven said. "It doesn't really change. More like more things get discovered that force long-lasting beliefs to change. For example, there was a theory that traveling faster than the speed of light was impossible. But the light photon theory, if its not a sham, debunks that."

"That is if it's not a sham," Nick was quick to point out.

Elder Steven widened his smile and looked at the stars, this time from the reflection in the lake. "There's so much to learn," he said. "And I'm speaking from a civilization stand-point. The same could be said about us, or anyone else."

Nick and Elder Steven continued to talk. For a while, Nick hoped that Elder Steven would eventually "call it a night" and head back home so Nick could complete the task he intended to do. But sometime during the conversation, Nick's hard-on dissolved. Soon after, Nick and Elder Steven walked off the island together.

Nick returned to his dorm (the guard still wasn't at his post) and began to reassess his situation from an untormented perspective while looking up at the darkness from his bed. Alyce fucked Pedro because Pedro was a man and she was woman. Nick felt he was still a boy. The realization didn't hurt that bad, yet it heightened his resolve. Nick decided that the only way that he could attain true manhood was to take more steps in that direction.

Indeed, there was much to learn.

Chapter Ten

Nick was beginning to fully realize difference between walking to the laundromat/tavern mini-mall and being propelled there by Pedro's speed limit-violating Malibu.

A little more than two miles separated the academy from the mini-mall. Going to and from there with Pedro and Alyce usually never allowed much time for conversation. The wind pouring through Pedro's driver-side window further discouraged talk, even small talk, at least with Nick participating as the few words he would say were often blown back in his face and barely audible to those in front. The rough and chuckling sound of the Malibu's pedal-pushed engine didn't help, either.

But a serene walk to the mini-mall provided plenty of time and space and silence for talk, especially for Nick to talk to himself.

Nick left the academy some time after seven o'clock. He had imagined the trip would take about 20 minutes. But after what had to be at least 45 minutes of brisk walking while working up a sweat which reared up shiny blotches on the front and back of his white shirt, Nick was still a half mile from his destination.

Like always before, possible scenarios went through Nick's head about who he would encounter and how they would respond to him. The walk's underestimated time of arrival, Nick thought, was a blessing in disguise—the extra time would no doubt pave way to a successful mission.

Nick wondered what kind of makeup was at the tavern at this time of the day. He thought he got a fairly good read on the pair Alyce and Pedro engaged the day he met John, as well as the few who attended picnics from Alyce and Pedro's invitations. They all seemed like nice people. Reckless, but nice.

Though the sun was still well above the horizon, Nick noticed how his shadow cast from behind had grown longer since he first started walking eastbound. Shadows had helped primitive men and ancient civilizations tell time, Nick reminded himself as his thoughts began to drift. Nick didn't have a watch. The few he ever owned were usually lost for good within weeks after receiving them. He had never bought himself a watch; they were always gifts. One Christmas his father gave him a LED digital watch, which was the rage back then and fairly expensive. Before afternoon, Nick had lost it, presumably during church where, while seated in a pew, he played with its small steel buttons to get repeated numeral displays of the time, stop-watch seconds and the month/day/year date after unfastening the wristband for two-handed handling. This was well before religion became prominent in Nick's family's life, as church-going for them was only practiced during the major Christian holidays.

When they returned home, Nick's father asked where his watch was. It was a Christmas Nick would never forget.

After reaching the top of the highway bridge where Nick walked along a slim path on the bridge's shoulder not designed for pedestrians as oncoming traffic whizzed dangerously close by, Nick could see the mini-mall parking lot from a good distance. It was filled to the brim with cars and pickup trucks. They couldn't mainly be from laundromat customers since the laundromat couldn't nearly accommodate a score of customers at one time. Also, this time during the day—whatever time is was—couldn't be ideal for doing laundry. Could it? It also couldn't be the time for bar revelers to congregate in such mass. Could it? Nick was far from being an authority on either subject, especially the latter

After a while Nick reached the edge of the jam-packed parking lot. He saw that the tavern was the prime source of the crowded parking lot. If there was a closed-door ordinance, it was not acknowledged today as the tavern was wide open, exposing its insides for those passing by to take notice. As Nick had guessed before, the brightness from inside was greatly obscured by the smoked windows. The electric light blazed through the open doors indenting the approaching dusk. The electric light bulging outside had an amber tone. An illusion? Nick could see that it was a nearly a standing-room-only setting inside. But for some reason the crowd wasn't festive as Nick had imagined a tavern crowd of even a third that size would be. Nick could hear no laughter. He expected some, maybe not as boisterous as the patrons Alyce and Nick recently targeted, but at least enough to indicate levity.

Instead, the atmosphere seemed serious. Not trading-floor or court-room serious, yet serious enough to emit a sense of tension. Barks of "Oh, no!" "Jesus Christ!" "God dammit!" "Jesus Christ, just shoot me, god dammit!" were heard by Nick as he neared the doors. Not all noises inside were little fits of anger. There was a momentary applause and brief cheer. There was a quick and distinctive sound of two palms colliding together for a high five, or a low five. And there was the hard-clicking sound of billiard balls coming in contact with each other.

Then Nick took notice of the white banner that hung over the tavern's open doors. A cash-prize pool tournament was in progress.

As Nick neared the opened doors and the attractive electric light which grew brighter and less amber as he approached, he felt his heart shift up a gear. He stopped short of the threshold, as if he was waiting for someone to invite him inside. Nick noticed the tavern's nine, ten or eleven pool tables were all being used and were surrounded by men—and even by some fairly attractive women—of a span of ages, yet united in stereotypical "tavern-class" wardrobe. Many of the tables were lined perpendicular to the tavern's long bar that stretched from about 15 feet inside the open doors to the back of the building. Low-hanging lamps hovered over each table, and trapped and highlighted clouds of tobacco smoke under them. Nick could smell the smoke, and the alcohol, and the leather as well as a hint of body odor. Most of those seated at the bar had their stools turned to face the tables. They probably didn't smell a thing.

The tables look familiar. The academy had a table that was a near spitting image of those in the tavern. Except the academy's pool table's felt was worn to a light aqua after, presumably, being the kelly green that adorned the ones at the tavern. The academy's table arrived at the academy during the winter of Nick's freshmen year. Who knows? Perhaps it was donated by the tavern. That would have been nice of them.

Upon its arrival, the table was a hit among students, and even a few elders. It was altered not to require coins to play as pocketed balls would bypass the rack collector inside and get deposited in an open shelf at the bottom of one side of the table. At the tavern, Nick noticed these collectors were released by the coin slots — similar to those on the laundromat machines — making whole racks of balls come crashing down loudly at once into the shelves. At the free-pool academy, players had to put their names on a chalkboard waiting list due to table's initial popularity. At times, arguments and even slight skirmishes would break out among those waiting players who thought they were cheated from their spots on the board, or from the results of the games. General rule was that winners got to stay on the table. Losers, if they wanted to play again, had put their names at the bottom of the list.

When threats from academy authorities of removing the table from the student commons area if people didn't start acting more like "servants of God," the conflicts ceased. But they probably would have ceased anyway. By the end of the school year, the table's popularity waned dramatically. Now, the table's use was virtually nil, except as an extra table for food and drink for various social functions. Students and elders at the academy just got bored with pool.

Obviously, that wasn't the case for those at the tavern. Along the wall separating the two businesses, there were five cue racks all with sets of dark wooden cues. None of them were being used. The poolplayers instead used their own slicks and glossy cues which could be unscrewed into two pieces and placed in handsome carrying cases. Nick caught a glimpse of a couple of these cases placed up against the bar and along the separating wall. One had a menacing dragon embroidered on it. Others had scripted names of their owners, and a few even boasted of their owner's accomplishments at other tournaments.

Maybe the best players in the world don't "hustle" anymore, just intimidate, Nick thought.

Nick assumed that most every customer present was either playing or was waiting to play. He sensed that interrupting them during their games would not be wise, so Nick was unsure what to do.

Then Nick saw him.

One customer appeared not at all involved in the tournament. He was seated at the far end of the bar. He didn't have a cue carrying case in sight. And he was facing forward, that is away from the action and looking up at the TV placed overhead behind the bar. He was a slight man with narrow shoulders. He was balding and sported a scruffy and graying goatee. He seemed immersed with what was on the tube, only looking away to take a sip of his beer, which was in glass and next to the half-full bottle it was poured from. While watching the TV, it looked as if the man was in deep concentration, like he was reading. Nick thought he could have been mistaken as a professor, or some sort of out-of-place intellectual, if it weren't for the subject he was watching: professional wrestling.

That was Nick's target he decided, as he finally breached the threshold. To get to him, Nick had to pass a gauntlet of sorts as the thin passage between the pool tables and bar stools was constantly opening and closing with players maneuvering around to the bar side of their tables before bending over to draw their cues for a shot. Nick thought of using the path on the other side of the table before approaching his target from behind. But that offered even less room for error as the separating wall was closer to the table than the bar, and along the wall were more stools with more players. After standing in place while feeling eyes starting to descend upon him, Nick saw a opening and quickly made his way to his target.

He never got close.

"Hey! What the fuck is you problem?"

Nick, though careful to plan his move while no one was lining up a shot on the bar side of their tables, failed to negotiate a spilled drink near the first table in the row and slipped clumsily when his hard shoes took the surface like ice on a sidewalk, and fell rather hard into a player. It screw up the player's shot and probably his game.

"I'm sorry," Nick said while feeling himself blush, "I…I…I tried—"

"I…I…I…What? You got shit in your mouth?" the man said. He wasn't a big man. Probably a good two inches shorter than Nick. And he had a rather wiry frame, but wiry in a fearsome way, like he could be capable of unleashing quick bolts of violence like a lightweight boxer with an impressive knockout ratio. The man had a tanned-baked face, perhaps from doing outdoor work. His blonde hair was combed back, and he had a thin, sharpie mustache that descended to the edges of his jaw. His eyes were blue, pretty blue if they weren't so menacing.

"You don't even look like you're even fucking old enough to be in here. What the fuck you trying to hump me for?"

"I…I…I wasn't trying to—I just slipped."

"I said what the hell are you doing here?" the man demanded, though not really repeating the question.

"I…I…I—"

"I…I…I…I…I… you got some sort of stuttering problem, motherfucker?" the man said while moving close enough to almost have his face touching Nick's. Others began to notice the brewing conflict as Nick could hear the playing cease and the crowd starting to gather around. Nick took a quick glance at the man at the end of the bar. He was still fixed on the TV.

Seeing that he attracted an audience, Nick thought his best shot was to take a leap of faith.

"Okay, I'll tell you why I'm here," Nick said as he felt himself tremble. He hoped no one could see him tremble. "Let me ask you a question."

The man tilted his head opposite the way it was and backed off a couple of inches as if to indicate he was willing to listen to Nick's question. He still had a raging mien.

"If you died today, where would you go?"

The man took a second as if he was actually contemplating a civil response. But then his eyes widened, and he appeared madder than ever.

"Are you saying I'm going to hell?" the man said while jumping right back in Nick's face, this time actually brushing up against it. Nick now noticed the smell of his cheap cologne.

"No, no! I…I…I…didn't say that," Nick said while quickly backing away.

"You telling me to go to hell, motherfucker?" the man said while closing ground on a cowering Nick. For a moment, Nick thought the man may have trouble comprehending simple conversation. But it was becoming all too apparent that the man had already decided he was going to physically assault Nick, and there was nothing Nick could say to prevent it. But he tried, anyway.

"I…I…I…I—" Just then the man caught Nick in the jaw with his thrusting palm. Nick's upper bridge sunk into a tongue, creating a searing pain throughout his mouth and skull. Nick fell back and into a poolplayer from one of the tables off to the side. The player had a cue in one hand and a mixed drink in a tall glass in the other, or until Nick bounced off him, causing him to drop the glass for another spillage on the floor. This player, tall and lean with tatoos on his arms and probably other places on his body, was noticeably pissed about losing his drink. For a second, Nick was relieved at this assuming that he may take action against Nick's attacker. He did respond, but against Nick.

"Hey, watch where you're going, asshole!" he said before in the spirit of a Roman soldier took his cue and rammed it's "butt" into Nick's groin. Now Nick had taken some groin shots before, and they had inconsistent effects. Once his father went downstairs with a full-force bolo punch, but somehow Nick didn't feel much pain, although he did double over on the ground in hopes to discourage further blows. But then once playing catch with a baseball with Dom, Nick misplayed an in-between hop allowing the ball to barely graze the head of his penis as it passed through his legs. Now that was painful.

The pain inflicted by the cue was in the latter category, except much worse, as Nick immediately felt that he might be injured for life as he involuntary stumbled over to his original attacker. Nick was bent over holding his mouth with one hand and shielding his midsection with the other. Then Nick took a raised knee from the initial attacker that caught his cheekbone and sent him reeling to the floor. Nick felt the sickening vibrations rattle in his head. He could taste the blood in his mouth that leaked from his damaged tongue. Nick was on his back and sensed people overhead looking down on him, but he couldn't really see them as his vision was plagued with little blue dots which, of course, were another illusion.

Then somebody gave a swift kick to Nick's side causing him to roll over on his stomach. Though the kick was hard, Nick didn't really feel it—probably because his nervous system was too busy sorting out so much other pain. Nick stayed on his stomach hoping nothing more would happen. After five motionless seconds, Nick thought it was over, that the beating had stopped for good and he was going to be left alone in the middle of the floor to leave on his own volition while the pool players resumed to their tournament. But soon after, Nick, like he had grown wings that had a mind of their own, was lifted up and spirited out the doors by a pair of men which, as Nick was able to determine, were not the original attackers. After reaching the parking lot, Nick was set free with a "helpful" lift into the air. Nick would have came down flat on his face if he somehow didn't get a leg under him to make contact with the asphalt first. Upon contact, Nick turned his ankle and, before he could get his second foot on the ground, his shoulder bounded into one of those pick-up trucks.

"Hey, mind my god damn truck," someone shouted.

Nick rolled to the ground and felt the small pebbles freed from the asphalt on his cheek. The vibrations in his head now had an audible sound. Though he was looking away from the tavern and was not about to look back out of pure shame, Nick knew that a group of patrons were outside the tavern taking in the spectacle by the shadow they and the amber electric light cast against the vehicles deep in the parking lot. He could hear them talk, but couldn't lock in on a full sentence. But he heard the word "hypocrite" more than once.

And Nick could hear them laugh. Now they're laughing.

Nick had to flee and fast as possible. He didn't fear more physical assaults. That was done for the day. But he feared exposure, as if he was being exposed in his pathetic situation. "Jackoff" was another word said more than once.

Eventually, Nick was able to get on his feet, but his balance was fleeting. He tried to walk, but a strange form of gravity seemed to tug him back toward the ground. His struggle prompted more laughter. Nick was able to regain enough of his faculties to move himself in the direction from which he thought he came. But he swayed from one side to the other while trying to go forward.

The trip back was definitely going to be greater in time and distance, that is if Nick could make it back.

Chapter Eleven

How Nick made it back was a mystery, even to Nick.

Nick remembered nil after his ascent up the bridge's narrow shoulder, this time with traffic. With his rattled equilibrium, Nick repeatedly fell onto the highway while stumbling up the slight grade. Once an 18-wheeler sounded its horn before Nick lunged out its way, a split second ahead of graphic death. The horn exacerbated the ringing in Nick's ears. Nick contemplated deliberately swaying onto the highway again to alleviate himself of his existence.

After that brief thought...nothing. That's why when Nick woke up in the during the early-morning darkness, he at first was relieved, thinking the whole ordeal was just a nightmare. But when he felt the fresh scab on his tongue and a sharp pain in his ribs—now he was feeling it—it confirmed the real world experience. He could also taste the blood in his throat.

Further confirmation came in the morning when Nick, still plagued with ringing ears, surveyed the facial damage in the mirror. There was deep purple swelling around the cheekbone reaching all the way up to his left eye's socket. Nick didn't want to go to classes, but he had already used his last unconditional sick day. Fortunately, Nick had a vial of makeup he kept hidden under his socks and underwear in his top dresser drawer. It was there to counter intermittent bouts with acne.

Despite Nick's makeover effort, which was discomforting upon touch, the bruise still peeked through. "Why did I waste that day to jack off?" Nick said out loud to his pathetic reflection.

And could he still jack off? Not that Nick had thoughts of breaking his vow. Though the pain in his ribs demanded the most attention, Nick was cognizant of his groin's condition. When he peaked with one fretful eye into his underwear, he saw it was still there, thank God, but it was retracted to toddler size (shouldn't it be swelled up?). Nick feared that he might piss blood. He had yet had to urinate despite it usually being a morning requirement. Nick was at least optimistic knowing that the groin is the most resilient part of the male body.

But ribs were not as resilient. Nick thought about going to the academy's infirmary to get them checked up, but he didn't want to reveal what happened to the physicians, who no doubt would attempt to extract as much information as they could to aide the treatment.

During breakfast, Nick could barely get small bites of food past his lacerated and swollen tongue. Nick knew eating would be painful, likewise for drinking orange juice. But Nick was determined to eat and drink a full meal like a glutton for punishment.

Before Elder Bingham's class, Nick prayed to God that his condition would not be discovered and further exposed. His prayers were almost answered, until several minutes before dismissal.

"Good God! What happened to you?" Bingham boomed for all to hear after he finally took note of Nick.

"I…I, eh, fell down some stairs," Nick said.

Elder Bingham took a more studious gander with the sides of his eyes crinkled with condescending pity. "That must have been one hell of a fall."

The breezy weather on the way to Elder Steven's class woke the stench of tobacco, alcohol and other stale aromas Nick brought back from the beating. Nick didn't shower, though he did bother to change clothes.

Nick was bitter, but not toward the prime perpetrators. Instead, Nick's anger focused on that malicious laundromat lady. He didn't actually see her that night, but Nick placed her among that "peanut gallery" that thought necessary to add to Nick's painful humiliation. Likely that "hypocrite" piled-on to the cheap shots was compliments of her. The voice may have been more masculine than feminine, but what the hell, that lady is none of the above, rather a wicked blur of something in between, only capable of procreating bile.

Oooh, that probably made that bitch's day to see me like that. Nick never hated anyone worse.

During Elder Steven's class, Nick was fortunate that his savaged profile was sided toward the wall. No one seemed to notice. Upon dismissal, Nick attempted to be the first out the door, but that was foiled when he lost control of his books just as he sprung up from his chair. Keeping his head down, Nick gathered his books while allowing the rest of the class to exit ahead of him. Elder Steven addressed him while he finally made his way to the door.

"Nick, may we talk?"

Nick's next class was a study hall which had degenerated to a social hour with lax attendance policies. Thus, Nick did have time to talk, just no ambition to do so. Nonetheless, Nick seated himself in Alyce's vacated desk. Elder Steven sat in the first seat in the next row and gently leaned over to Nick, "I heard you had a little problem last night."

This caught Nick off-guard. He expected his condition may attract suspicions, but Elder Steven indicated that he already knew the whole situation.

"Who told you?" Nick evasively asked.

Elder Steven smiled. "Some things tend to come my way whether I want them to or not." There was an uneasy pause before Elder Steven continued, "Do you want to talk about it?"

The situation was similar to their "chance" meeting in the middle of the lake. Like then, Nick didn't know of anything to say other than what was on his mind, and what was on his mind he didn't want to reveal.

"Ah … I…I don't know," Nick stammered. "It's really nothing."

Elder Steven reached over to put his hand on Nick's shoulder, causing Nick to wince upon contact—it was the first time in a while that another person's touch was intended to soothe. "It's hard to discuss things like this, but keeping it inside can be cancerous."

Nick took a deep breath and then exhaled. "It's just, eh, just why are people so evil?" When Nick said "evil," the vision of the laundry lady amid the peanut gallery popped in his head. *Yeah, just what I thought – she was there.*

"No one sets out to be evil, even those deplorable demagogues we've been told hate in the name of nationalism," Elder Steven said. "But people also don't set out to be afraid, to be fearful. And when they do become afraid, they try to cover up their fear and lash out against those who remind them of it.

"You see," Elder Steven continued, "it isn't like those people don't believe in God or don't want to go to heaven. Everlasting life in paradise is a common hope for all. It's the thought of the alternative that makes many question their lifestyles, and that's where the fear kicks in."

"And that's where my face gets kicked in," Nick interjected. "Is that going to make their fates any better? Is that a way to face one's fears?"

"Of course not," Elder Steven said. "But the thing people fear almost as much as hell is change…change of their slovenly spiritual ways. That's where most of the grass seeds, unfortunately, get washed away. But that's why people like you are so invaluable."

"Invaluable?" Nick said as his scarred tongue made the word difficult to say. "Well, they sure have a unique way in showing their gratitude."

Elder Steven got up from his chair and paced a bit before addressing Nick again. "You never know who you might reach through your suffering."

Nick was tempted to roll his eyes.

"Easy for me to say," Elder Steven said with a smile. "But for now let's go down to the infirmary and get some ice for that beauty mark of yours."

Nick gave in to the suggestion. Maybe they could also check his ribs.

The following laundry day, Nick threw a large canvas bag with a retractable loop-rope handle over his shoulder, and headed toward the laundry mat. Like the previous trip, underestimation plagued Nick. This time the weight of the load he was humping. Nick couldn't go much more than 300 yards without relieving his back. At the bridge's top and winded from the climb, Nick rested while watching the on-coming vehicles zoom by, taking note how close they continually came to the narrow shoulder. It was a miracle he didn't get killed that night.

Nick surveyed the mall from the perch. There was only a couple of cars in the parking lot. Still, Nick wondered if he would encounter his assailants again—a possibility he dreaded but had to chance.

Yet whether he would meet them, John or anyone else, there was one person he would cross for sure: that laundromat lady. Nick had shed his vengeful aspirations and decided to greet her with a cheerful "Hello" or "Good afternoon" at first sight. Who knows? Maybe it could be a start of a lasting friendship.

When Nick entered the laundromat, the lady contemptuously looked him over from behind the counter. Nick's intended pleasantries stuck in his throat and his hatred boiled up again. That settles it—she was no doubt part of that peanut gallery.

After getting his load going, Nick went next door.

Though he put the lady there that night without actually seeing her, there was someone Nick actually did see that night but didn't remember until seeing him again. Now more than ever before, Nick had a habit of upgrading his memory by filling in the gaps with subsequent information. And when Nick first entered the tavern and got a good look at the bartender, he was reminded of his presence.

He was a burly man, 6-5, 6-6 … 250, 260 pounds. Probably played football or basketball during his younger years, maybe still does now. He had a square face outlined with bushy-black eyebrows that matched his military-cut hair. His short-sleeved red shirt tightly packaged his upper-body bulk. Still filling in some gaps, maybe he was one of the two who propelled Nick. Or maybe he was the only one—he looked more than capable.

The bartender sized up Nick with narrow eyes as if two had quarreled before. Except for a figure at the pay phone located near the back, Nick was the only other customer. Nick grew uneasy after he seated himself on a stool and the bartender, whose eyes were still narrow, didn't bother to ask something like "What can I get you?" or "Can I help you?" After couple of more seconds of uneasiness, Nick finally asked, "May I have a Coke, or Pepsi?"

The bartender remained inert, as if contemplating the request. He then reached down into a cooler and produced a can of Royal Crown Cola. "Two dollars," he said an octave or two too high while he placed the can in front of Nick in the manner of a judge striking down with his gavel.

Two dollars? When the soda machine in the student commons area raised its price from 50 cents to 75 cents, it created a stir and a boycott from the students. But then again, the machine didn't supply such "personable" service. Nick fumbled for a handful of quarters—that's all the currency he carried for this laundry day (by the way, whatever became of that smiley-face container?) — and placed them on the bar. The bartender quickly snatched them without counting – there were probably nine or 10, but definitely not less than eight – and put them in his pocket instead of the cash register.

Nick then opened his can and was immediately sprayed. The gavel-like service agitated the contents inside, and cola foam soaked Nick's hands and forearms, and spilled onto the bar. Nick looked for some napkins to rectify the situation, but the napkin holder near him was empty. The bartender responded, though he wasn't very pleased about it.

"Lift it up," he said to Nick.

"What?" Nick said, not quite catching on.

"Lift it up, the can," the bartender said, nearly scolding.

Nick lifted the now half-full can and the bartender wiped the surface below it with a bar rag, which he was at least civil enough to give to Nick to clean himself with. The bartender then slapped a coaster in front of Nick like he was slapping down a trump card to take away someone's home, and walked away shaking his head.

A couple of seats down to Nick's right the man at the phone returned to his stool.

"Bitches. A day like today makes me glad that O.J. got acquitted," the man said over Nick while addressing the bartender.

"Ya know," the bartender said, "if I were a smart business man, I would rip out that pay phone in favor of an ATM and tell ya people without cell phones to get with the 21st century. But you have a cell phone."

"Well, they make good beepers," the man said while placing his phone on the bar. "The way they jack up the roaming charges, that's the only use I have for them."

"With the company you keep, roaming charges were probably conceived with you in mind."

"Yeah…bitches I say."

The man was short and old, but probably not as old as he looked. His snow-white hair was thinning yet reached out wildly from his skull like a strong field of static electricity affected it. His white and bushy mustache looked as if were affected the same way, or more like an overused flayed cotton base to a Velcro fly. He wore another one of those buttoned leather vests designed like a tank top, but with no shirt underneath as a myriad of tattoos were displayed on his saggy arms. The tattoos were old and their fading color meshed almost naturally with prominent veins along his arms and forearms. The man wore horn-rimmed glasses with lenses so thick that it magnified his blue eyes twice their normal size.

Aside from his cell phone, on the bar in front of the man were a half-full clear bottle of beer, a short glass of clear alcohol and a hard Marlboro pack. The man took a swig out of the bottle, and chased it with a sip from the glass. He then lit a cigarette and took a deep drag before discharging much of the body-filtered smoke through his inflamed red-pocked nose. Nick marveled by the man produced a couple of perfect rings with the remaining smoke—one of which wafted over his head like a halo. Nick decided to engage him.

"Excuse me sir," Nick said, changing stools get up close. "May I ask you a question?"

With his magnified eyes, the man surveyed Nick from head to toe and back to head. He took another drag of his cigarette and sipped from his glass. "What can I do for you?"

"First of all, let's see, um, I got a funny joke. Do you want to hear it?"

Smoke again poured from the man's nostrils. "I thought you were going to ask me a question."

"I did, I mean I do, but, eh, but first let me tell you this joke. I think you'll like it."

From the man's stoic look, Nick took that as a cue to get on.

"Okay … Jesus and Moses were in heaven and they were kind of bored, you know, and Moses goes to — or make that Jesus goes to Moses, 'Why don't we go down to Earth and, eh, you know, do the stuff we used to do.' So they go down to Earth, and, you see, they take this raft, or boat out onto the Red Sea. And they're in the boat, and Jesus goes, 'You wait here, I'm going to walk on the water.' So Jesus starts walking on the water, but he sinks. So anyway, Moses sees this and he saves Jesus by splitting the Red Sea in half and revives Jesus.

"Jesus is pretty shaken up by this, but decides he wants to try it again. So they go out further, and Jesus gets out of the boat and he sinks to the bottom again. Moses splits the water and saves Jesus again. So Jesus, thinking that he's rusty or something, tries it again only to sink after a couple of steps. Moses comes to the rescue. But Jesus goes, 'Let me try it one more time.' "

The man took another drag in a sighing manner. But Nick was still confident that the punch line would carry the effort.

"So the same thing happens, and Jesus is mystified. He doesn't know what's going on. But then Moses says to him, now get this, he says, 'You have holes in your feet, and when you did that before, you didn't have holes in your feet.' "

The man eye's narrowed, similar to the bartender's, and his flayed Velcro eyebrows curled at the ends. He spat his smoke at Nick. "So, what's the joke?"

Nick was taken aback that the man wasn't busting a gut, but sensed he may have butchered the punch line. "Well, that is the joke."

"So that's the joke, huh?" the man said. "That's supposed to be funny? And I'm supposed to laugh at that?"

"It's just a joke," Nick said.

"And it's a pretty disgusting joke at that?" the man said before taking another deep drag and then crushing his cigarette violently into a nearby ashtray, causing tobacco embers to land and self-extinguish on the bar

"To tell you the truth, I don't like the joke myself, it's just—"

"Then why the fuck did you tell it?" the man said loudly with smoke coming out of his nose, mouth and even his ears.

"I…I…I…" Nick was stuttering again, and wondered about another brutal battery. "…I just wanted to break the ice a little."

"Break the ice? What the hell for?"

"To ask you a question."

"Then ask it, and get out of my face."

"Okay," Nick said before taking a deep breath. "If you were to die today, where would you go?"

The man remained scornful for several seconds. Then, rather unexpected to Nick, he displayed a tobacco-stained smile, as if it was prompted by a question he loved to answer, if only more people asked him it.

"If I were to die today, where would I go?" he said as his magnified eyes gleamed. "For your information, son, I've already died."

"Here we go again," said the bartender from the end of the bar. "Now look what you've started."

The man reached for his Marlboro box and opened it, revealing legal cigarettes and illegal cigarettes. With a subtle upward jerk of the pack, man popped up one of the latter and coolly put it in his mouth and lit it. He took a long hit that, unlike his legal drags, seemed more like a swallow than an inhale, then held the joint out for Nick to take.

"You'll need this," the man said as smoke seeped out of several orifices in his head, "to open up your mind."

Nick stared at the offering, unsure if he wanted to accept. Once years ago he split a joint with five fellow freshmen. He didn't really feel the effects, probably because he only took a couple of timid hits. Eventually, Nick reached for the joint, or attempted to—like the same poles from different magnets, Nick's index finger and thumb shook more and more uncontrollably the closer they got from touching the joint, which in contrast the man held with the steadiness of a surgeon. Nick dropped it the instant the transfer was made, causing it to lose its cherry when it fell to the floor.

"It's not going to make you lose your mind," the man said while retrieving it. "Then again, losing your mind is not always a bad thing."

For some reason, Nick was able to handle the joint better with no cherry burning. Nick was able to taste the sweet leaves on his lips. The man lifted his lighter.

"Now when I light it, take a good, deep hit," he said. The flame on the end of his lighter danced like it had an epileptic mind of its own due to an air current that came from the open back door. Nick's hand still shook as he tried to keep the joint in his mouth while trying to align the other end with the flickering flame. Finally he got it on the fire, but a little up from the tip. The man sighed, probably savoring the couple of hits lost due to the clumsy re-lighting. Nick inhaled a healthy portion, which expanded and tickled his lungs.

"Now hold it," the man said just as Nick had a hacking attack. "Good … if you don't cough, you don't get off. Now I can tell you my story.

"Now I always say, 'Say No to Drugs,' best advice to give anyone," the man said while seemingly not aware of the joint in his hand. Maybe he didn't classify it as a drug. "But if you ever find yourself doing heroin—or smack if that's what they're calling it now—don't get me wrong, stay away from the shit, but like I was saying, if you ever find yourself doing it, take my advice, shoot it up yourself."

"Hey," said the bartender sneaking up on the pair, "have you forgotten about our bar tax, or should I inform the authorities?"

"You run a shady business," the man said, passing the joint.

"With shady customers to boot," the bartender said, taking the joint.

"Where was I?" the man said. "Oh, like I said, shoot up yourself. If you're too fucked up to shoot up yourself, then you shouldn't be shooting."

The bartender tried to hand the joint back to the man. "Give it to him," the man said gesturing at Nick. The bartender, instead, put it in the ashtray.

"Go on," the man said to Nick. "Take another hit."

This time, Nick handled the joint with better dexterity. He sucked in another chest full of smoke, determined to hold it in for at least five seconds without coughing, but failed to while exhaling.

"Anyway—where was I? I keep wandering," the man continued. "Yeah, don't have someone shoot up for you. No matter what." The man took a swallow from each poisons, the joint first, the beer second and his chaser third. Nick took note of the way bubbles materialized in the middle of the remaining portions of the man's beer when he would put the bottle back on the bar, and Nick instantly was reminded of Taylor's proclamation, "Bubbles are life."

After the man swallowed his chaser, he exhaled what remained from his first swallow as the smoke seemed unaffected. "Now that's what I did. I let this bitch—bitches I tell you…" the man was talking to the bartender "…all of them—but I let this bitch fix me up because I was afraid I was going to break the needle in my arm. But you see, she didn't do it the way I do it, or did it because I'm off that stuff now. When I did it, I did it at a nice, slow injection, in a way which I could fully feel it entering my system. It's like I had my own style of doing it. But this bitch, she just squirts the whole dosage in me in a split second, way too fast."

The man passed the joint to the bartender after the bartender accused him of "Bogarting it."

"So that got me fucked up. Next thing I know, I'm being carted to the hospital. And while they were taking me down the hall, I noticed that I wasn't inside of me but hovering over my body as it was going down the hall."

Nick leaned forward as his interest grew stronger. The bartender took his hit and almost passed the joint to Nick, before correcting his actions to again place it in the ashtray.

"I was floating above my body. I was watching the doctors and nurses, or whoever they were, trying to save me. I knew right there that I was dead."

The man grabbed the joint and took another hit. He passed it to Nick, which altered the original sequence.

"So there I was, dead. So what do you do while you're dead?" the man asked Nick, who was trying to avoid coughing for a third time.

"Get a load of this," the bartender said to Nick while taking the joint from him. The bartender seemed jovial while addressing Nick, like he was the third man in a trio of close friends, which relieved Nick, who was convinced that the bartender had it out for him. But the bartender's scowl resurfaced, as if he caught himself being friendly with someone he didn't want to be friendly with.

"Yeah, yeah, get a load of this," the man said in an angry tone. "Tell me, why is this so far-fetched to you?"

"Because it's a freakin' fairy tale," the bartender said, this time with smoke coming out of his mouth, nose and perhaps ears.

"It's a fairy tale huh? How do you know it's a fairy tale when it didn't happen to you?" the man said, still angry sounding. "I know it's true because it happened to me."

"Well, go on. Finish your story," the bartender said. "Tell him about your phone message. Now that's a good one."

"I was getting there," the man said before leaning closer to Nick. "Like I was saying, what do you do when you're dead and you know it? Well, I decided that I should at least leave a message to notify my friends or anyone else trying to get a hold of me." The man started laughing as the bartender shook his downward head. "So, you see I was floating above my body and I began to realize that I could wander freely away from my body, like we were in the process of severing our relationship. So I floated down to a nearby pay phone at the hospital, called my answering machine and changed the message to, now listen to this, 'Hello. I'm sorry you can't reach me anymore because I'm dead.' Hee, hee, hee."

Nick was amused but far from sold. Although while listening to the story, Nick became aware of the state he was now in, and, in a way, it was like he was floating outside himself. Nick was relaxed to a point where it was like he was experiencing a lucid dream. Nick used to commonly have lucid dreams when he was much younger, but somehow rarely experienced them since he became of academy age.

"Tell me this," the bartender while leaning over the bar. "How did you make the phone call? I know you sure in the hell didn't use your cell phone with those out-of-body roaming charges. It was a pay phone, right? You even said that before. So did you carry any loose change or a phone card in your phantom presence?"

"I just made the call, and it went through."

"Two words: Bull Shit," the bartender said.

"I'm telling you, I made that call and made that recording," the man said while leaning closer to the bartender to where their mugs were less than a foot across. Though Nick didn't fully believe what he was hearing, the way the bartender's doubts fired the man up indicated to Nick that the man may actually believe he was telling the truth, or at least convinced himself to believe himself.

"And I got proof."

The bartender broke away from the close stare, and let out a short laugh. "That proves nothing."

"That proves nothing?" the man said, then turned his attention back to Nick.

"When I came back and went home my message was on the recorder. How 'bout that?" The bartender shook his head again. "And I have friends who called me and have confirmed that they also heard that message. They even come here every once in a while so they can tell him and rest of the people who don't believe me. But they still don't want to believe it." The man leaned even closer to Nick and said in whisper, "It's like they're scared of believing it."

"That proves nothing," the bartender repeated. "Of course they may have heard this recording, but you obviously made it when you got back."

"They called while I was in the hospital."

"Then you could have recorded the message while you were in the hospital. While you were no longer dead." When the bartender said dead, he displayed two fingers from both hands to indicate quote marks. Must be a fad, Nick thought of the increasingly familiar form of sign language.

The man took a deep drag from the joint, which was now diminished to a half inch. He held it in for a much longer time than previous, before exhaling and responding calmly, "The only call I made was when I was dead."

"I'm going to tell ya," the bartender said. "The reason why I don't put much stock in these after-death or near-death experiences is because they have long since been explained scientifically. I don't know about that call and message, which I don't believe, but I do believe that you probably did see yourself float above yourself."

"You're damn right I did."

"Yeah, that happens to a lot of people."

"Further proof for the putting."

"Yeah, but that also happens to jet pilots when they get G-force tested," the bartender said. "You've seen those contraptions that these pilots get in and they spin them around and around at god awful speeds until they pass out?"

"Like a particle accelerator?" the man said.

"Yeah, like a particle—no, not quite like that."

"Like a particle accelerator," the man repeated.

"No! I was watching this program on these after-death, or near-death—it's really near-death experiences if you ask me—and these people talk about going down a tunnel and floating over their bodies just like you said you did."

"Like I said, just like a particle accelerator."

"What the hell are you getting at?" the bartender said. "Now put that out. I think I just saw someone pull up."

Someone did pull up, but it was a laundromat customer. Nick looked out to parking lot and saw who he thought was the man who claimed he was a Jew. But he couldn't tell for sure.

"It's not like a particle accelerator," the bartender said. "Yeah, both make things go round and round, but they are very different from one another. A particle accelerator has a track that about five miles around. This thing they put these pilots in you can almost fit in this building if you tear a wall down. And this thing doesn't accelerate particles, it accelerates human beings."

"And in both cases, they give us glimpses of the unknown," the man said.

"Yeah, glimpses of the scientific unknown. But scientific, not supernatural."

"It's all the same," the man said while reaching for his pack, this time for a legal cigarette. "It's all the same. You say because these pilots experience tunnel vision and float above their bodies after being spun around rapidly disproves there's life after death just because it was simulated in a scientific setting. But just look what was taking place. The pilot was accelerated at such a rate that his conscienceless, now listen closely here, was pried from his body because his body was moving too fast to stay with the space-time field."

"What the fuck? Space-time field?" the bartender squawked.

"Yeah, space-time field. Really. They were pried from it, and that proves that we can exist outside the present field we live in."

The bartender was silent, as if he was stumped for a response. Nick was also silent, and just noticed he had been that way ever since he started hitting the joint. But now he was content in just being a listener.

"And about those particle accelerators—what the hell do you think they are trying to do? I mean, hell, these particles they're working on are so freaking small, but they need a build a laboratory about as big as most towns—like you just said—and even as big as a few counties, so they can drive these particles at incredible speeds into protons. For what? Because they want to see what's inside of them when they explode. But they have to keep shooting these particles at faster and faster speeds to make the explosion bigger and, most importantly, longer so they get a better chance to track the debris from the protons."

"And what the hell does this have to do what we've been talking about?" the bartender said as he walked over to the cash register.

"Because the debris from these protons quickly snaps back together in a microsecond. It's like the stuff that makes up protons is held together by some sort of super small rubber bands."

"Like I said, what the fuck are you getting at?" the bartender said while waving his big hands over his big head.

"Because the same thing happened to me when I came back from the dead," the man said in a proud tone. "I was snapped back in my body like my soul was attached to a rubber band."

"Like this?" the bartender said while taking one of several rubber bands, presumably to bound paper money, and shooting it like a schoolboy. The shot hit Nick exactly in the spot he took the lifted knee. Nick couldn't have been the intended target, but the way the man and the bartender were laughing, and the way Nick was feeling, it didn't matter.

Just then the man's cell belted out an obnoxious phone company-composed tune.

"Bitches," the man said. "Well, it's been nice talking to ya, but I've got to get going." Then the man took a gulp from both of his drinks, finishing them both off, and lit his legal cigarette.

Nick shook the man's hand, but didn't bother to use his brother's favorite trick. Nick stayed at the bar to finish his drink, and didn't mind when the bartender continued to sneak peeks at him with a hairy eye. Such conflicts now seemed petty to Nick as he smiled to himself while reviewing other things that have plagued him recently. Nick even let a tip of five or six quarters, and issued a cordial good-bye to the bartender when he left his stool. The bartender didn't respond. It didn't matter.

The walk back was much more pleasant, and seemed to take up far less time. Nick found considerable enjoyment in thinking about the man's alleged experience as he walked, and even wished he could have been more active in the debate with the bartender. Then again, you learn a lot by listening. Before

Nick knew it, the academy was in his sights. But just then Nick realized that he left his load at the laundromat.

Smoking pot will do that to you.

Chapter Twelve

The following Saturday morning, Nick had a meeting in Elder Bingham's office.

Nick got the message for the meeting from the student working the check-in counter Friday afternoon, when Nick strolled in with light and happy steps after the day's classes. Nick was feeling good at the time, not quite as "high" as he felt after he smoked that illegal cigarette with the man at the tavern— *Why didn't I get his name?*—but with only one week left in the school year, Nick was set to cruise down the home stretch.

Nick and the other primary and secondary graduates would officially get their pieces of paper the following weekend during the official commencement around the lake. There was only one week left in regards to actual school work, including finals. It was a long road for Nick, who saw himself ready for the next plateau.

Still, Nick wondered why he was summoned to Elder Bingham's office. During Elder Bingham's Friday morning class, and even, while looking back, during most of the week, Nick sensed that he was shielded by some sort of benevolent force field from Elder Bingham's ire. It wasn't that the teacher was any less mean-spirited than normal. Rather, Elder Bingham seemed to have burr up his backside during that entire week, especially during the end, haranguing students more vehemently and more unpredictably than normal. But for some reason, Elder Bingham never tormented Nick. Even during several brief moments when Nick was aligned with Elder Bingham's beak-pointed stare, he seemed to look through him, like he was trying to peer through a window while squinting past his own reflection. Nick didn't think much about it, nor took it much for granted. He knew that Elder Bingham could spring his rapacious anger on him in a micro-second.

For his meeting with Elder Bingham, Nick prepared himself for the worst, or what he imagined the worst would be, which really wasn't that bad. Only "Soul Winning" students, with the exception of a paired-up Alyce, were allowed to engage outsiders outside the academy in the matters of the Lord. Nick thought that maybe, because of his age and, maybe, because of his shaky recent performances, he may be taken off mission status during summer break. No doubt it would be a wrenching demotion, but Nick planned to take it like a man. After all, Nick would now just be par with other graduating primary students.

Also, Nick thought it would probably be better to have the time off. It would give him a chance to learn more about himself, something Nick conceded he needed to do.

However, Nick was a little irked by the time of the appointment—six o'clock. Nick liked to sleep in on Saturdays, though sleeping to noon or even eleven or ten o'clock was not an option, at least if you didn't want to be disturbed. Every Saturday, one of the lady custodians from Nick's dorm would come through at nine o'clock to collect bed sheets, coverings and pillow cases for cleaning while dropping off a fresh set. For some reason, the academy insisted on cleaning its own bed dressings. Thus, Nick had to be up before she came because he never wanted to be awakened by her arrival. She would always enter without a knock while using a master key. Yet one could almost set a watch by her arrivals, and Nick knew he could sleep as long as 8:30, or 8:45, and he was grateful for every extra minute.

Despite the time of the appointment, Nick made sure he was at least 15 minutes early. In the gothic and ivy-covered administrative building and outside Elder Bingham's office, Nick was greeted by a frail and steely-faced female secretary who told Nick to go inside and to wait for Elder Bingham. He apparently hadn't arrived yet. Nick was hoping that he would get some sort of indication of what this appointment was about by the secretary's diction or manner. But her general indifference didn't reveal anything—yet why was he asked to wait inside instead of outside?

Although Nick had never been called on to meet Elder Bingham one-on-one, he did meet with him in his office just before he enrolled as a student. Then, Nick's parents accompanied him. Dom wasn't present, but the conversation between Elder Bingham and Nick's parents frequently repeated his name. Then, Nick was considered the second coming.

Much had changed since then—in the office, that is. Before, a giant painted portrait of Elder Carson, the academy's founder, hung on the back wall looking over Elder Bingham's massive mahogany desk. The painting portrayed Elder Carson as a serious man with a dark full face and strong brown eyes that beamed through his thin-wired glasses. Elder Carson's hair was jet black with a thin streak of bright silver running through one side of it.

With his upper torso squared in a dark blue business suit, Elder Carson looked like a banker who was graced by the sight of God, and he was—a banker at least. He was also a financial advisor, and apparently gave his best advice to himself. Thirty years ago, Elder Carson founded the academy with his riches. Five years later, Elder Carson died of a massive heart attack at a relatively young age of 55.

Elder Carson's portrait still hung in the office, but it with paired side by side with another portrait—that of Elder Bingham. In that portrait, Elder Bingham's gaze was angled toward Elder Carson's portrait on the left and down at the chair that faced the desk, the chair that Nick was now seated in. Depending on perspective and interpretation, Elder Bingham could either be looking at Elder Carson, at the person seated in front of the desk, or both. Elder Carson's portrait, on the other hand, looked straight ahead.

To note, Elder Bingham's portrait was not entirely accurate. It portrayed him as full-fleshed and as almost as dark and, dressed in a similar suit except in a lighter shade of blue, as handsome as Elder Carson.

Could Elder Carson's portrait also be inaccurate?

Ironically, there was one similarity between the two men that Elder Bingham, if he in fact wanted to mirror his predecessor, could have genuinely added to his own portrait—eye glasses. Elder Bingham wore contact lenses, and most students, like Nick, knew that out from harrowing up-close confrontations.

The pairing of the portraits suggested another inaccuracy—Elder Bingham did not succeed Elder Carson. Shortly after Elder Carson's death, Elder Brady, Elder Carson's top aide, took over the academy's administrative duties, thus occupied the office and was the unofficial head of the academy. That unofficial title only lasted a couple of years before Elder Bingham took over. How and why?—another academy mystery.

The office was as big as most of the academy's classrooms. Yet with massive book shelves closing in on all sides, except for the strip of wall designated for the portraits, the office didn't have the same spatial feel to it. And the contents of the book shelves seemed to portray Elder Bingham's character more so than the portrait. When Nick first cast a studious eye along the shelves, he had hoped to see titles of various literary works, or even books and novels that Nick was familiar with. But all the books, and there were hundreds of them, all had thick dark blue or black hardcovers with different combinations of Roman numerals on the spines, as if they were a massive opus of rules and regulations. None from this volume had any script on the spine. For all Nick knew, these books may not of had any words inside.

There was a set of *New Oxford Review* magazines placed amid the hardcovers. The periodicals were also often placed, seemingly strategically, on several end tables in the student commons. Several times Nick perused some issues. Would God and Jesus approve of such mean-spirited literature?

There was no Bible in Elder Bingham's office.

In the middle of the office was a brown wooden table about the size and shape of a bed, except a little higher. On top of it was a hand-held lamp attached to a long extension cord. There were no chairs around the table.

There was a single folding chair in front of Elder Bingham's desk, which Nick placed himself in. It sure didn't match the chair on the other side—that of Elder Bingham. His was an over-plush swivel model with dark, leather-like skin that was a shade darker than maroon. It resembled a cross between an oversized Lazy-Boy and an undersized throne.

The top of Elder Bingham's desk was almost as characterless as the bookshelves if it wasn't for the oversized gold-plated nameplate that was too shiny for its own purpose. Depending how the office's fluorescent lighting reflected off it, you could barely read the name, although the big etched script was intended to be bold.

Also on the desk was clock. Other than the pair of imposing portraits, the clock was the most interesting item in the office. It was about the size of a mini-football, and its exoskeleton design revealed its precision mechanisms in action. The mechanisms were also gold, or at least gold colored, and Nick watched them churn in solid increments that indicated the seconds. There was no second hand on the white-base, black-Roman numeral display. Obviously, there were minute and hour hands, both gold and with artsy, curly-designed shafts tipped with dagger-like points. The clock was encased in a glass cylinder that fitted into a indented circle at the clock's base that resembled a giant coaster. The cylinder didn't have a handle on it, and Nick assumed that it was never to be removed, as if the clock was meant to function in a vacuum that could never be corrupted.

The clock chimed every quarter of an hour. The notes would get longer and more complete leading up to the top of the hour. Then the entire musical movement was completed and followed by repeated single-note chimes that indicated the hour of the day. The chimes seemed audible enough to be heard outside the office, but apparently were muffled by the glass cylinder. By studying the flickering florescent-light reflection on the cylinder, Nick was able to estimate the degree of vibration caused by the chimes.

Nick naturally became preoccupied with the clock because several hours passed without any signs of Elder Bingham. Nick wondered if somehow Elder Bingham forgot about the meeting, but he didn't dare to venture outside the office, or even out of his chair, although his comfort level was decreasing rapidly, and he could feel droplets of sweat creeping down his back. After the clock chimed eight times, Nick imagined that this could be some sort of test Elder Bingham was giving him. Nick had heard about various tactics to test one's commitment by making them wait for hours on end with no explanation. But whether Nick would get an explanation or not, he was confident at least that Elder Bingham would eventually show up for work, and Nick would still be around when he came.

That should impress him even more.

Around the 8:45 mark, the time Nick would usually wake up Saturdays, Nick heard some voices just outside the office. One of the voices sounded like Elder Bingham. The other voices also sounded familiar, but Nick couldn't quite make them out. Then just after the clock chimed for the ninth time, Elder Bingham walked through the door.

According to his plans, he was probably right on time.

Just before Elder Bingham closed the door, he signaled to someone outside the office with his raised index finger, as if he was indicating he would be with them in a moment. Maybe this meeting would not be very long, although Nick had already been sitting in place for over three hours.

Elder Bingham paused after walking a few steps toward Nick. Nick twisted in his chair to face him. Nick didn't know if he should stand up, like for a judge entering a courtroom. But Nick stayed planted. Elder Bingham had a sterile expression, and his mouth was rigidly straight, as if he was refraining from smiling or frowning.

"There's a friend here to see you," Elder Bingham said while peering down on Nick about the same way his portrait was at another angle.

Who could this friend be? Nick thought as Elder Bingham stared a little longer at him, probably to tease his curiosity. Finally, Elder Bingham turned back to the door and opened it to signaling someone to come inside. Nick saw a huge shadow approach from the side before its huge person appeared in the doorway. It was the bartender. And by the way he peered at Nick with the same scowl as days before, Nick knew that he was no friend. Both men approached Nick in unison before stopping about at the same place Elder Bingham paused before. This time Nick was more compelled to stand up, but again remained seated. Then Elder Bingham spoke.

"This gentleman says that you have been smoking pot at his establishment," Elder Bingham said in a way that he had already confirmed the accusation, and just wanted to see Nick squirm to come up with his best, yet ultimately feeble, response.

Nick was shocked. He couldn't fathom a motive for the implication, other than bartender disliked him. Nick looked at the bartender, as if he deserved an explanation. Yet the way the bartender stared back at him, Nick knew that he would only get one on the bartender's terms.

"Well, is this true?" Elder Bingham said. The bartender turned to Elder Bingham with a slightly perturbed look on his face—he seemed offended that Elder Bingham seemed to question his word, which Nick knew he didn't.

"I...I...I..." Nick was stuttering again. At first, Nick wanted to say that the bartender also smoked the joint. But what good would that do? Nick was able to halt his stuttering, but slumped silently in his chair not knowing what to say. Then the bartender gave his explanation—on his terms.

"I'm no saint myself," the bartender said while trading eye contact with Nick and Elder Bingham and back to Nick. "I don't contend to be one. But I'm sick and tired of you people disrupting my business by causing all kinds of trouble when you're really no better than the rest of us. We don't need your preaching."

Nick could smell the tavern on the bartender. An occupational hazard, no doubt.

"I don't want to see you, or anyone else from this place in my place again," the bartender said. "If you ask me, you're all a bunch of hypocrites."

That word again. That didn't seem to bother Elder Bingham, though.

"I will make sure your business will be not be bothered by anyone from this establishment, as you have a right to be upset," Elder Bingham calmly said while issuing an apology that, to Nick, seemed more like a rebuke directed at him. Elder Bingham then led the bartender out the door. Before the bartender receded from Nick's view, he focused a final scowl at Nick. Then Elder Bingham signaled someone else with his index finger before closing the door and addressing Nick again.

"You also have more people to see you," Elder Bingham said. Now a grin reared from his straight face as he appeared to be enjoying this.

Now who could these 'friends' be? Nick wondered while slumped in his chair with the weight of his impending doom, as Elder Bingham retreated to the door. When it was revealed who these people were, Nick thought his heart was going to stop dead.

They were his father and his mother.

Nick's mother was sniveling with a sickening sound that comes from the regurgitating snot with tears. Nick thought he may have heard her crying earlier outside the door, but again he was filling in the gaps. Nick's father had a ashen face that Nick learned to associate with his violent temper. When Nick's father was red-faced, Nick knew his father was still shy of the danger zone. Yet now Nick's father appeared to be in a state of shame, as he looked down at the floor with slumped shoulders, about the same demeanor he had before he was saved by the academy's missionary.

Neither wanted to look Nick in the eye, and Nick didn't want to face them as he looked straight ahead. Nick also didn't dare to look at the portraits overhead.

Soon, Elder Bingham seated himself in his Lazy throne and naturally became aligned in Nick's sight. Now Elder Bingham's stare wasn't like someone looking through a window. Nick wanted to look down or away, but couldn't find a way to gracefully do so. While still looking straight at Elder Bingham, whose grin could now could pass for maniacal, Nick could see through the black-and-white vision in the corners of his eyes that his father and mother stepped up to the desk to flank him on both sides, yet at a good arm's length distance.

Elder Bingham eased back in his chair while dictating an excruciating span of silence, albeit the sniveling from Nick's mother. Both Binghams cast their countenances on Nick and his parents.

"Your son has been smoking marijuana," Elder Bingham said while still eased back in his chair. Nick's parents must have known the reason they had been called to the academy a week before graduation. But when Elder Bingham voiced the accusation, the sniveling from Nick's mother suddenly upgraded to a louder and more sickening sound.

"Now drugs, and drugs and alcohol have always been a concern for us here," Elder Bingham said, while easing up a bit from his stern tone. "We're not blind. We know that some of our best students have tried one or both at one time, or even several times while being enrolled here. I guess we could issue drug tests, and really crack down on this problem that seems to fester from generation to generation. But that wouldn't really solve the problem, now would it?"

Elder Bingham paused before continuing. "Let's face it, children and young adults are going to be confronted with drugs, confronted with the devil. You can't hide from them or him. He's going to find you. And when these children and young adults get confronted by this devil, even the best of them may give in for a while, and maybe that's a good thing. I mean, we've all acted irresponsible at times. All of us. Me, you and the people that came before us."

Elder Bingham then made a slight head gesture over his shoulder to Elder Carson's portrait.

"But it's how we respond to these personal pratfalls, our resiliency in the light of our sins that will determine the type of person we are," Elder Bingham said while regaining his former tone. "I've always said, 'People don't change, they emerge.' And that's as true as anything on this Earth. That's why I tell my students that they shouldn't try to change the people you're trying to save, but help them be more of themselves, a best possible version of themselves through the faith of the Lord.

"And faith," Elder Bingham raised his voice to emphasize 'Faith,' "is what enables us to emerge stronger and more tempered from such confrontations."

Elder Bingham paused again before reaching to open his desk's lower drawer. He then produced a duffel bag before walking around the desk.

"But apparently some people don't possess that faith," Elder Bingham said while approaching the table in the middle of the office. Nick tracked his path until it aligned his sight with his sniveling mother. He then looked straight ahead in his chair, although his black-and-white vision told him that his parents retreated to the table.

"Nick," Elder Bingham said, "why don't you join us."

Nick got out of his chair and approached the table while trying not to look at anyone. Then Elder Bingham, who produced a pair of latex gloves which he snapped on his hands before unzipping the duffel bag and reaching for the contents inside. Nick was obviously curious about what was inside and why it pertained to the situation. When he got a sight of the cloth inside, Nick was still mystified. But as Elder Bingham pulled the first folded stack out and began to place it on the table, Nick was horrified of where this was going.

These were Nick's bed sheets.

"Now this is from three weeks ago," Elder Bingham said after activating the utra-violet lamp and waving it over the sheet. Blotches of dried cum stains were drawn out like an archipelago of orange islands in a deep-blue ocean. Is this why the academy insisted on collecting and cleaning its bed dressings?

"Now if that wasn't bad enough, look at the next week," Elder Bingham said while producing another sheet more stained and more disgusting than the former. Usually after spilling his seed, Nick would try to clean up with a towel he kept under his bed in a bucket. During that time, the towel tended to become more stiff at it got more soiled until laundry day. But when Nick got on a roll, he would ejaculate repeatedly without bothering to clean up in between orgasms. Now that was coming back to haunt him.

"You see, drugs are the tools of the devil," Elder Bingham said. "And this is what happens when you let them consume your soul. We've been told, often by people who say they worship the same god as we do, that we should forgive such sullied souls. But when it gets this bad, it's our duty for the sake of others to eradicate the afflicted from our system."

Chapter Thirteen

Aside from Nick's mother's sniveling which showed no sign of ending soon, Nick's parents remained mum as they drove him the short but seemingly long distance from the administration building to Nick's dorm. Nick's father's face was still ashen, and like Nick's mother, he avoided direct eye contact with Nick. But when Nick took his seat in the back of his parent's cop-car-like Caprice, Nick could see his father's eyes, bloodshot from either pent up anger or lack of sleep from getting up early to make the long journey, or both, peer at him through the rearview mirror. Nick could only guess what was going on behind them, although he should have had a good idea.

When Nick left the vehicle to fetch his belongings, tears began to well up in his eyes. The gravity of the situation was being fully realized. Although Nick was a week away from graduating from primary studies, the expulsion had a retroactive effect—all of Nick's previous grades and credits were going to be purged from the academy's files, if they weren't already. It would be like he had never enrolled there and, in essence, was merely an eighth-grade dropout. All students and their families knew of the academy's grave penalties when it came to expulsion.

While gathering his belongings, which was a rather light load made up mostly of his wardrobe—no bed dressings, of course, and no furniture or TV— Nick began to feel shameful in not giving much thought to the fates of Alyce and Pedro. Their academic records were also purged completely, even though Pedro had already graduated from primary studies.

Nick's parents didn't help him pack his bags, and that was probably a good thing. Instead, they waited in the car with the engine running. When Nick came down to complete the first of what would be three trips, the Caprice's truck popped open, activated from a lever under the driver's seat. Nick could see his father conversing with his mother. But with the car's windows being rolled up, Nick couldn't hear what was being said. As he approached the car, Nick again caught his father's eyes staring at him through the rearview mirror. His father's eyes must have noticed Nick's eyes through the reflection his father saw at his end, as he quickly looked away and continued his talk with Nick's mother.

As Nick turned away for another trip to his room, he could feel his father staring at him again. Perhaps the phenomenon still applies even when mirrors are involved.

While trying to hold back the tears that became more pressing, Nick started to snivel in about the same vein of his mother. There were several other students milling in and out of their rooms on Nick's floor. Nick tried to be inconspicuous and looked away and downward in efforts to hide his watering eyes, and tried to bite down on his sniveling. Yet the students had to take notice that Nick was moving out a week early. Several of them were upperclassmen, and were fellow students in Elder Bingham's class. Nick dreadfully wondered what kind of lecture Elder Bingham would deliver to the class the following Monday morning. Would he bring out the academy handbooks again?

When Nick re-entered the car after completing his third round—*Should I turn in my key? Ah, what the hell* — Nick could see by the fuel gauge near the full mark that it would be a non-stop trip. They must have filled up just before coming to the academy. As the Caprice pulled out of the academy gates, Nick's mother resumed her sniveling, which was probably halted by the conversation she had with Nick's father while Nick was packing. Other than that, no words were spoken as the Caprice headed west into the sunless horizon.

Then when the academy grounds were well out of sight of Nick, who couldn't help but look back, Nick's father blurted through clenched teeth, "It's like we don't have a son anymore." Nick's mother's sniveling upgraded again to sobbing.

"All this time," Nick's father continued while glaring at Nick through the rearview mirror before altering his complaint, "all this damn money we invested into you and this, and all in the name of God. And what do you do? What do you do?" For the repeat question Nick's father turned to face Nick before turning back to the road and up at the rearview mirror again. "You smoke dope and jack off all over the god damn place!"

Nick's mother's sobbing reached its crescendo, and Nick began to cry, too.

"Shut the fuck up, both of you!" Nick's father said. Nick was able to fight back his tears, but his mother continued to cry and then snivel for about another mile.

As the Caprice continued its journey, it ran into a major storm. Bright white bolts of lightning accompanied by heart-thumping repercussions descended around the highway. The Caprice seemed like a moving target, and maybe it was. The torrential rains managed to keep most of Nick's father's attention on the road and not in the rearview mirror. Nick began to get sleepy from watching the rapid motion of the windshield wipers, as well as from his depressing malaise. Soon, Nick decided to take a nap to somehow escape this nightmare. But that re-ignited the ire of his father when he took another glance in the rearview mirror.

"Don't you lay down!" Nick's father said with a voice almost as loud as the thunder, immediately bringing Nick to upright attention. "Before we know it, you'll be jacking off back there like you did—like you did back there!"

But as the miles compiled westward, Nick was too lifeless to stay seated and eventually lowered himself in the prone position. He didn't care anymore. How much more angry could he make his father? Funny thing though, the moment Nick did lay down he did have an urge to masturbate.

Nick didn't dream. Nick didn't fall asleep. But as he looked up at the driving rain roll down the door windows of the car, blurring the electric-charged outside world with a thin layer of water, Nick traveled back in time, back when his parents had a "real" son. He remembered that spring break, that final spring break in which his family had actually bothered to come and get him despite having to bring him all the way back. But the trip back to the academy was far more depressing than the current one back to the house.

There was so much promise that spring break. There was so much indication that God had touched the family's life in such a generous manner. Whenever Nick looked back at that idyllic moment, it just made the subsequent horror that much more disturbing. Then, Dom accompanied Nick's father and mother while coming to pick up Nick for spring break. Nick remembered how the two conversed in the back of the same Caprice, then brand new, and speculated about the future, which was as bright as a fair morning's sunlight reflecting off the academy's man-made lake, or any God-made lake for that matter. The previous year at the academy, Nick's first and Dom's last, the brothers often palled up during their free times, except when Dom was with his girlfriend. Though Dom was more robust version of Nick with the same color of hair, when people first befriended or got to know them better, they were usually taken aback of the fact that they were brothers. The first names probably threw them off more than anything else. Dom and Nick both usually derived from Dominick. But Dominick wasn't on neither birth certificate, rather just Dom and Nick. Why? Who knows? Other than their father, who named both of them.

As stated before, Dom had been groomed to be an elder at the academy. It was a major disappointment when Dom opted not to go that route, not only for Elder Bingham and other academy faculty, but for Nick as well. Nick would not have his brother around during his sophomore year. That's what made that spring break something Nick looked especially forward to. He could be with his older brother again, for a whole week, like he was during the entire previous school year, and during the previous Christmas break. He could catch up on Dom's plans to start his own congregation in their hometown, something Dom had said he always had dreams of doing.

"It's going great," Dom told Nick on the way back home that spring break. "We've already raised most of the money to get started. And you wouldn't believe how many people are interested, and the type of people we got interested. Real civic leaders. People who remembered me as a little kid, even before you were born, if you can believe that."

Nick did believe many people would be interested. People were always drawn toward Dom, even when he wasn't trying to save their souls. But Dom still had some obstacles to negotiate. One was securing a place. During Christmas break, Nick learned that Dom and his staff—he even assembled a staff—were having trouble renting out a gym at the local high school for the fledgling church which was due to start sometime that summer. It was a public school, and school council members were concerned about compromising separation mandates.

"Do you have a place yet?" Nick asked.

"Oh yeah," Dom said. "A temporary place for now."

"You do? At the school?"

"Oh yeah." 'Oh Yeah 'was a common phrase of Dom's. "We got that all taken care of. Most of it, anyway. Like I've always said, wisdom will always prevail over vices if you have faith to let it to do so."

"You also have to have faith in God," Nick's father chimed in from behind the wheel. Nick's mother nodded in agreement.

"It's really the same thing," Dom said.

When they came to get Nick that spring break, it was late in the afternoon. With a midway stop at a restaurant for dinner, the trip back home didn't conclude until after ten o'clock. Nick was anxious to see the site of where Dom's church would be built once enough funds were raised. But that would have to wait for morning. The long drive took a lot out of the family. The brothers immediately went to bed in the room they shared since they were toddlers.

In the middle of the night, Nick found himself awake. Dom was awake, too. And when Dom apparently suspected that Nick wasn't asleep, he called his name from the other side of the room.

"Nick, Nick. Are you awake?"

"Yes," Nick immediately acknowledged. "I guess I can't wait to I see where your church is going to be."

"It's right by the forest preserve," Dom said. "Beautiful setting. Couldn't be better for what we're going to achieve. You're going to love it. But anyway, this is weird, but I just woke up from this strange dream."

"All dreams are strange," Nick said. "I mean if they're not strange, they're probably real." There was a pause before Nick asked, "What was it about?"

"It's not really what it was about, but I've had these types of dreams many times before, and you've probably had them, too. Its—maybe I should ask you. Do you ever have a dream where you had a memory of what happened before the dream?"

"Of course I do," Nick answered.

"I don't mean that type of memory," Dom said. "Or I don't know if you know what I mean. But, yeah, you naturally take some of you real-life experiences into your dreams. And you naturally apply them to the dream setting, if they're needed, I guess. But what I'm saying is when you dream a setting, a setting and situation totally different from what you experienced in the real world, although there is probably some sort of deep-seeded relation, but anyway, while existing in this setting and situation you somehow have a memory that pertains to that setting and situation, but that memory is independent of any real-life memory. It's like you're another person with that other person's memory. But where does that memory come from? Do you ever have dreams like that?"

Nick thought for awhile. "Yeah, I do sometimes have dreams like that."

"Isn't that strange?"

"Yeah," Nick said, now fully grasping his brother's observation. "That is strange."

That was the last night the brothers shared a room together.

The following morning was draped with a wet fog when Nick and Dom headed out to the site, which was within a healthy walking distance from the house. After feeling the chill and moisture in the air while opening the door, Nick suggested that they should wear jackets.

"Nah," Dom said. "This is going to be a beautiful day. Just you watch."

Sure enough, by the time the two had reached the forest preserve the temperature had reached an ideal mark and the bed sheet-like fog was lifted when the sun ascended above tree level. The colors of the season seemed to stand out much more vividly than normal, as if there was a light source shining from within the budding leaves and reborn grass, like a green light not signaling go, but one offering an illusion of doing so from the daylight traveling through it and being reflected back out.

Nick would later compare that morning to the swan song of the old wooden-cabinet-cased color TV set that used to dominate the family living room. The set was on its last leg as indicated by its snowy display of images that were compressed from the top and bottom of the picture tube like it was transmitting a wide-screen movie not formatted for television. But one day the TV displayed full images with colors more bright and vivid than ever before, even when it was spanking new. Nick and the rest of the family were amazed when they saw what had happened. It was like the TV fixed itself—a miracle of sorts. But the following day when Nick's mother turned it on, the picture tube flickered and went out, leaving a white dot in the middle that soon shrunk into oblivion.

The brothers entered a trail at the base of the forest preserve. The trail consisted of brown wooden chips and tree bark softened by a previous rain. Even the brownness of the trail shined aided by the sun that trickled through the trees that still were not at full foliage. The brothers had walked the trail before, usually in the summer when the thickness of the trees overhead blocked out most of the sun and made the forest gloomy along some stretches. All was familiar to Nick, until Dom directed them to a path that branched from the main trail.

This path was unlike the walker-friendly main trail. It was a simple dirt trail, muddy in several places, and its narrowness made it impossible for the brothers to walk side by side like they did on the main trail. It cut through a thicket of dead stick-like trees that apparently never had ample room to grow.

Dom led about two meters ahead of Nick. The distance between the two grew before Dom, obviously anxious to show off the site, turned to his brother lagging behind and urged, "Come on. I'm the one who's supposed to be the old man."

"It's these shoes," said Nick, who was wearing his black dress shoes, yet were the same type worn by his brother. "How much farther do we got to go?"

"Not too far," Dom said. Either he was fibbing or the remaining distance was short in Dom's mind, as it took another five minutes of brisk walking before they reached their destination.

"Here it is," Dom said just before leading his brother out of the forest and into a wide-open prairie graced with standing water in several places which, from a long view, made it appear that diamonds were growing in the grass by the shimmering reflection made by the sun facing the brothers from overhead. "It's going to over there," Dom said while pointing to the flickering diamonds. Dom took a couple of steps closer, but standing water nearby stopped his approach.

Nick stared at where Dom was pointing and tried to imagine the structure that would stand in the future. He tried to get a better indication by the glimmer in his brother's eyes, which were fixed on the site, like in trance.

"Only one thing, Dom—Dom," Nick said while trying to get the attention of his brother, who finally broke his trance. "The only thing is, well, maybe it's more than one thing, but for one, how are people going to come to this place?" There was no road within at least a mile from all sides of the site.

"The same way we did," answered Dom, who apparently paid little mind to the long and narrow path that had to be negotiated.

"You mean you think people are going to be willing to walk all that way through the woods? And where would they park before going into the woods? Are the forest preserve people going to put up with extra cars in their parking lot?"

When seeing Dom's cheerful expression turn sour, Nick feared that he may have hurt his feelings with his scrutinizing inquiries. But a smile soon returned to his face.

"Oh yeah they will," said Dom while answering the first question. "You'd be surprised how far people will walk to be saved, even in the cold of winter, even in the heat of summer, even in the insect-infested fall…" Dom sounded like he was giving his first sermon "…and the park director is on my staff."

Nick wondered if having the park director on Dom's staff would create another snag, the same type that accompanied the proposed school-gym rental. But he didn't ask that question, instead, "How are we…:" Nick used WE for the first time while discussing this project. That widened Dom's smile immediately upon hearing it "… to get all the building material here? It's one thing to walk here, but to drag all the wood, bricks, concrete—whatever it takes all that way is next to—next to…" Nick initially wanted to say impossible, but he thought it might sour Dom's demeanor again. "… I mean, it's going to be a pretty tough task."

Dom put his hand on Nick's shoulder and said, "Don't worry. With God, all things are possible." It was an old cliché, yet Dom was never afraid of using old clichés as he always seemed to breathe new life into them. Even though Nick knew it would be a "pretty tough task" and probably wouldn't have taken the project seriously if it was proposed by anyone else, he had faith that Dom would follow through, like he always did whenever he took on a task, or whenever he reached out to the most un-savable soul.

Nick turned and stared at the diamonds in the grass. The vision of the church became more real. It would be solid, solid as diamonds.

Eventually, the brothers went back into the woods.

Once again, Nick lagged behind while trying to keep up with his brother. Dom had a distinctive hop in his step, even when he wasn't in a hurry, and that day offered no reason to be in a hurry. What the brothers would actually do with themselves for the remainder of that day had yet to be decided. The big event had already passed, but Dom seemed he couldn't wait to get home.

Even while trying to keep up with Dom, Nick came to believe the thin and muddy offshoot wasn't as long as he thought it was while recalling the trip to the site. He could already see where the main trail started again, and where the alive trees overtook the dead ones slightly beyond Dom's lead.

About 15 yards from the wooden-chipped path, Dom came to a sudden halt. Nick stopped in his tracks, too, before walking slowly to catch up with his brother, whose eyes were fixed on a spot the same way he stared at the pending vision of his church. Just as Nick reached Dom, Dom patted his hand toward the ground, signaling Nick to either stop or to be as quiet as possible. Nick tried to aim his sight to where he thought Dom was looking, which appeared to be pool of dirt-black water amid the standing sticks several yards from the path. Nick concentrated to see what his brother saw, and just when he whispered, "What is it?" ripples in the water indicated something was moving.

Nick only caught a glimpse of what it was before losing sight of it. It had color, but because Nick only saw it in the corner of his eye, its color wasn't revealed to him. Yet Dom was able to track it to near a patch of grass that somehow emerged from the mud.

"I've never seen one that big," whispered Dom, now fixed on the grass. Nick still couldn't see what Dom saw. But after a long look at the grass, Nick finally made it out. It was a snake of some sort. It looked as if it had some chameleon-like qualities, as if its skin wanted to blend with the grass. But Nick didn't know of any snake of that kind, and its color didn't quite match its background. The snake's color actually resembled a green light signaling go, which brought out its three-foot long body from its background.

"What kind is it?" Nick asked, although he didn't suspect Dom of being an authority on the subject.

"I dunno," Dom said. "It looks like it could be a gardener snake, but like I said, I've never seen one that big."

Dom started inching closer to the snake.

"You think you should get near it?" Nick said. "Don't you think it could be poisonous?"

"Around here?" Dom said while still moving closer. "For one thing, it sure isn't a diamondback."

"But still—" Nick's plea of caution was cut short as Dom patted down toward the ground again. The snake was coiled back and was locked in its position, like it was petrified. Dom inched closer and closer. The snake still didn't move. And then, just as Dom got close enough to reach out to perhaps snatch it just under its head, the snake, in a micro-second flash that seemed to violate the laws of nature, sprung at him with a wide-open mouth that made its head appear four times as large and bit Dom on the hand just above the wrist.

"AAHHHH!" Dom shouted in a decibel that Nick never thought Dom would ever have to use. Nick saw the snake then scurry away while covering more ground than a brisk jog on its way toward the main trail before disappearing from sight.

"That thing had fangs," Dom said as he tried to show Nick his wound before covering it with his other hand. "My God, does it hurt!"

Nick issued a stock response, "You think you're going to be all right?"

Dom shook his head approvingly. But then he tilted his head with a troubled expression, as if he could feel something inside of him going wrong.

"I should be OK," Dom said, but he didn't sound too sure. "I think we should get it looked at now, though like real fast."

"Let me see it," Nick asked, a request that had no real purpose other than curiosity.

Dom tried to comply, but once he revealed the wound, he pulled it back as if exposing it made it hurt more.

"We got to get going, I mean, I don't want to scare you, but I'm not feeling good right now," Dom said. "Maybe its just nerves but …" he then tried to take a deep breath, "… I'm having trouble breathing right now."

"Just stay calm," Nick said while trying to comfort his brother. "I've always heard that the snakes in this country are not as dangerous as people think."

"But this snake had fangs!" Dom said with considerable panic in his voice. Seeing Dom in such a state alarmed Nick even further.

"I'm sure we can find someone to drive you to the hospital," Nick said. "Let's just get to the parking lot."

When Dom tried to move forward, things got even more desperate.

"It's like I can't move this side of my body," Dom said on the verge of tears as he lowered himself to be seated on the mud path and leaned back against several dead trees which bent back under his weight. "No, no. You better go and get help. I gotta of stay here. I'll be right here. I can't move. Hurry, please hurry."

Nick's eyes widened. This couldn't be a serious as if appeared. Nonetheless, he turned and ran down the bark path as fast as he ever did for that distance, even with his black shoes. When he reached the parking lot at the base of the preserve, to Nick's dismay, he saw that there were no parked cars.

"Damn!" Nick cursed out loud. "Why did it have to be so far away from everything?"

Nick ran out toward the road, which was a good quarter mile from the parking lot. When he got there, Nick signaled passing motorists to pull over. When none complied, Nick ventured out onto the road and put his life in front of an approaching SUV. Luckily, it came to a screeching halt not more than a foot from Nick's trembling stance.

"What the hell — "the driver shouted before Nick interrupted.

"My brother, he has been bitten by some sort of snake."

The driver was equipped with a cell phone and was able to contact an ambulance. Within five minutes, one arrived accompanied by a pair of squad cars. Nick frantically directed them toward the site while often looking over his shoulder as the EMT's, similar to the way Nick lagged behind Dom, tried to keep up while hauling their equipment.

When they got to Dom, Nick saw that he moved from where he left him, and was leaning against a live tree about 30 feet inside the wooden-chip trail. Dom was motionless and in a fetal position. Yet the position had a grosteque twist to it, as Dom's lower body was slightly corkscrewed from his upper torso, and his writhing eye-shut face seemed to be locked in agony. Dom's bitten hand, which he still clutched with his other, had ballooned to twice its size.

"What kind of snake around here can do this?" one of the EMTs asked Nick.

"It was a green snake," Nick said while realizing the situation was growing graver by the second. "It looked harmless until it bit him. Dom, tell them what it—Dom? —Dom?…"

Dom wasn't moving. Nick moved closer to Dom and the EMT crouched by him, but the two officers who ventured into the woods intercepted him and, gently as they could, pulled him back. Nick didn't want to leave. He wanted to see Dom at least show signs of life from his fixed position. Eventually, Dom did move, but it was an act that sparked terror rather than a relief. Dom's upper body suddenly shook for several seconds like he was suffering a seizure.

The police officers convinced Nick that it would be best to wait back at the parking lot. Nick, not knowing if he could witness much more, complied. Nick waited and waited, and even prayed. But when one of the EMTs finally emerged from the woods, his body language told Nick that Dom was lost.

Nick never saw them remove the body, though his parent, who were called to the scene, did. Prior to the wake, it began to hit Nick that the last time he saw his brother was with that terrible grimace on his face. He had hoped at the wake, even though from past experience that people in a casket looked distinctively different from when they were alive, that he would see Dom's face in a more peaceful state. But when Nick went to the wake, he was disturbed to see that Dom was encased in a closed casket.

Oh yeah, Nick had to bear some of the blame. When his father sternly asked why he didn't try to suck the poison out, a quirk in Nick's conscious provoked him to let out a slight laugh. He was reminded of dirty joke he heard in grade school, which told of a guy getting bit in the groin by a deadly snake and informing his friend to seek advice from a nearby snake expert. The friend asked the expert what he should do, and he was told to simply suck the poison out.

"What did the expert say?" the bitten victim asked.

"He said that you're going die."

"What's so funny?" Nick's father demanded. There was no way Nick was going to respond truthfully. "You've just lost a brother, and you think it's funny."

Eventually Nick's parents found the real culprit, or the real culprit found them. After the news of Dom's demise hit the paper, amazingly the owner of the snake was willing to come forward. He admitted that his pet, a South American green mamba, got loose several days earlier but didn't bother to alert authorities, thinking that it would eventually die from the non-tropical conditions of a still cool spring.

Nick's parents wanted justice. They adamantly wanted the snake's owner, a college student who collected exotic pets, to suffer the same fate.

"An eye for an eye—a fang for a fang," Nick's father said out loud more than once. "Just like in the Old Testament."

But the student wasn't going to be executed or even convicted, neither were Nick's family going to get much restitution from him. Instead, they went for the real, REAL culprit: the company that legally sold the student the snake.

"Oh, my God! Oh my God! Oh my God!" Nick's mother said a week after the incident while looking at her computer screen. She had logged on to the company's Web site to see what they were dealing against. "Come look at this," she pleaded to Nick and Nick's father, who were within earshot of her. The site was framed with gothic curls, and featured a menacing dragon flanked by an array of reptiles.

"Just as I suspected," Nick's father said. "Agents of the devil."

Eventually, Nick's parents cut a deal with these agents and settled out of court to a tune of $30,000. Not much, really, but the family's lawyer suggested they should take it because winning the case in court was due to be cumbersome.

Nick's parents told local newspapers that they were going to put the money, as well as the funds raised for Dom's church, into a separate bank account under Nick's name. Nick would fulfill Dom's dream of a church in the forest.

After Dom's funeral, Nick never returned to the grave site which could only remind him of Dom's closed-casket corpse. Instead, Nick opted to visit the site of his death: the tree where he last saw Dom leaned up against. While Nick was back at the academy, his family decorated the tree with a huge red cross, and flowers, a wreath and ribbons. On each side of the shrine there were case-enclosed weather-proof candles. Inside the wreath was a card-folded eulogy authored by his mother and edited by his father. It said, "With all the sin around us, you have found a way to escape it."

It was a disgusting effort. Nick's mother signed the names of the three surviving family members. With love, of course.

When Nick returned to the site, it was during the apex of summer. The increased leaf growth darkened the forest as gloom prevailed even during the sunny midday. That allowed the candles to produce an ambient shroud—like the one that graced the tavern—during all times of the day. While kneeling down to replace the withered flowers Nick's parents had placed there when

Nick was back in school, Nick turned to the dirt path and dead sticks that basked in the sunshine.

That summer night in the room he now had to himself, Nick reflected on the scene. He remembered the dead sticks. *Why did they never get enough room to grow?* Nick asked himself. He remembered the light around them, except now he remembered the light being the same type tone of light emitted from the candles. And the light, as he remembered it, seemed to come from the ground. Nick didn't sleep that night as troublesome thoughts began to torment his mind.

"Those lights are pink, I'm telling you," Nick's mother said. They reached that point in the trip. The rain was now a drizzle, but the cloudy skies kept the street lights on. Nick looked up. Sure enough, the lights were yellow.

"Now don't you think—"

"Fuck the lights," Nick's father said. That was the end of that.

When they arrived at home, Nick's father decided to help Nick unpack— well, sort of. He aggressively grabbed articles of clothing out of the trunk, once even seizing a handful from Nick, and threw them onto the driveway. Once the trunk was emptied, Nick's father slammed it shut in one of his typical forceful gestures.

While Nick unpacked in his room, he could hear his father interject through his closed door. He couldn't quite make out all that he said, but Nick did catch something to the effect, "He's 18 years old! He's no longer our god damn responsibility!"

Nick's mother started crying again. He could also hear that through the door. Damn! For most of the trip, she didn't cry at all. How could she start up again almost on cue?

Nick was always irritated by his mother's crying and sniveling. All it did was magnify trying situations. But as he listened to his mother cry, Nick began to sense there was more to it than just sorrow. He imagined that she was calling him out, calling him out to be comforted and to comfort her with the binding faith that this too will pass.

Tears began to roll down Nick's face. He then opened the door, and walked toward his sobbing mother with open arms. He wanted to tell her that he was sorry. He wanted to tell her that he loved her. Then, hopefully, she could tell him that she loved him too, no matter what.

"Don't you touch me!" Nick mother said as she slapped Nick across the face. It was about the same spot where he took that lifted knee, except it hurt much more. "You disgust me."

Nick retreated into his bedroom. Soon, he decided that he would leave for good in the middle of the night.

Chapter Fourteen

The door remained shut for the rest of the evening and into the morning.

Every now and then Nick heard his father spew more bits of rage at the door, several times at close range as Nick could feel him standing just outside the barrier.

The rants ceased by prime time. Nick's parents eventually retreated to the evening news on their big-screen TV, which always displayed vivid images. Then they had dinner. Beforehand, Nick could faintly hear his mother work in the kitchen as well as smell what she was cooking. It was spaghetti with meatballs, something Nick thought his mother made better than anyone else, and, consequently, was his favorite home-cooked meal. It seemed to be a tradition to have spaghetti with meatballs every time Nick or Dom or both came home for the summer or any other break. The academy never served spaghetti with meatballs. They did serve a spaghetti-like soup, but it was terrible according to Nick's tastes. Nick wondered is this could be a ploy to get him out of his room. But Nick thought about the resounding slap to the face.

No way. If they did want him out of his room it would only be for more abuse.

After dinner, Nick's parents returned to the big-screen TV. They watched various real-life game shows and several real-life sitcoms before the real-real-life evening news. Every once in a while, the volume of the TV was turned up considerably louder than the household standard. Whenever the program would transmit breaks of silence in spite of the amplification, Nick could hear his parents whisper among themselves, as if they were conspiring. Nick feared that they were on the verge of bursting into his room and demand that he leave at once.

Nick had already made up his mind about leaving. Yet he wanted to do it on his terms.

Nick's parents continued to watch TV well past the evening news, which was unusual for them. They watched a variety of late night programs and talk shows, still at high volume, until 3 o'clock in the morning. Nick had planned to be long gone by then. After an ear-stabbing beeeeeeeeep — volume still on high — heralded the test pattern on the channel they were watching, the set was turned off. The annoying beeeeeeeeep seemed to recharge Nick's father's disposition as he immediately began bitching in a similar volume.

"If it ain't one thing, it's another," Nick's father said. "What do we got to do? What do I got to do? I mean, damn! It's not fair! It's just not god damn fair."

Nick didn't know exactly where his father's grievance was directed. At him, probably, but maybe the academy, or Elder Bingham, or God Himself.

"It's not fair. I mean we have done everything. It's not fair."

"I'm sure there's a reason for this," Nick's mother gently opined.

"There ain't no fuckin' reason for this," Nick's father responded. "If there is a reason, it's a god damn curse. You hear that, a god damn curse."

Finally, after about another hour, they went to sleep. That's when Nick started to gather what he needed for his long trip. He planned to travel light— toting only three sets of clothes with three pairs of socks, three extra underwear briefs, a sleeping bag, and a gray wool parka that was given to him by one of his targets at the laundromat.

That target Nick approached like any other, asking him about where he thought he was going when he died. He was an elderly man, and—looking back—maybe it wasn't very tactful to pose such a question to someone of that age. But it soon came apparent to Nick that he didn't have much of his hearing or other senses as his responses didn't match up with Nick's questions. Eventually Nick, in an apologetic tone, said that it was nice talking to him and he was going to leave him alone to do his laundry. Later, the man approached Nick and gave him the parka just before he left.

"Go find the man who stole your shoes and give him your coat," he said to Nick.

Nick planned to use the same over-the-shoulder sack he used to tote his laundry when he was on foot. He only had one pair of black shoes. He had two other pairs, but he must have left them in his dorm room, or in the trunk of the Caprice. Didn't matter, he wasn't going back to either place.

Nick planned to leave through his bedroom window. There was no way he was going to leave through the front door for fear of waking his parents. Even

114

opening his bedroom door would probably alert them.

Back when Dom and Nick shared the bedroom, Dom would sometimes leave through the window in the middle of the night and come back several hours later through the same means. Nick surmised that Dom was carousing with his girlfriend at the time, but he never confronted Dom for verification.

After Nick got all his stuff together, he waited for about 30 minutes before he made his break. Initially, it got off to a bad start when Nick twisted his ankle upon landing awkwardly on the ground outside the window. Nick didn't prepare himself for the drop as the distance from the window to the ground was about two feet higher than his bedroom floor. The pain was excruciating. Nick tried not to expound the pain he was in, although it would have been doubtful that his parents could have heard him since their bedroom was on the other side of the house, as he clutched his ankle with his back to the ground. From past experience, Nick knew that excruciating pain was a good thing when it came to ankles—it signaled that it was likely not broken, yet would definitely be swollen for a couple days.

Nick thought of calling the whole thing off. But while looking up at the window, he saw that the self-closing latch was locked in place after the lower half slithered down. Dom had always put a folded pair of socks in place to prevent the latch from locking. Nick had no such plans because he had no such plans of returning. Now he wanted to return, but how?

The front door of the house was locked, as always, and Nick didn't have a key. In fact, Nick never was furnished a key. No need to, his parents thought. It wasn't that Nick had a habit of returning home during odd hours of the night and morning. But Nick still had the key to his dorm room. A lot of good that would do.

Nick eventually was able to get to his feet. A faint teal glow from the east indicated that daylight was not far behind. Still, the night stars had yet given up the clear sky.

Nick knew where he was going, but he couldn't quite start going there for at least another day. There was a problem in leaving on the eve of a Sunday, or on Sunday for that matter—Nick couldn't go to his bank to draw money from his savings account for travel and living expenses. Nick didn't have an ATM card. Never wanted one. He actually wanted to save his money, the little he made from odd jobs during the summer. Now he needed all of it, but it was out of his reach until Monday morning. Monday would have been the ideal day to make his break. But Nick came to his decision by the slap of mother's hand. He was not going to endure another day of humiliation, and if that meant sleeping and living in the woods for a day before catching the first Monday morning bus out of town, so be it.

For the next couple of hours, Nick sat half asleep on a park bench a stone's throw from his family church. Nick was wearing the gray parka, and had the hood draped over his head. He wanted to see if his parents were going to church, that is if they still went to church. There was only one mass, that at 9 a.m.

As 9 a.m. passed and the church's organ heralded the start of mass which Nick could hear from his bench, Nick figured that his parents were not going to show up. But wait! Nick saw the cop-car-like Caprice enter the parking lot. Nick's parents emerged and walked into the church with mass already underway. They didn't seem affected by Nick's absence, that is if they even knew Nick was gone. Nick trained his eyes them as they made their way through the church's wood-carved double doors. Nick's was doubtful that his parents would recognize him if they looked his way. But Nick didn't care if they did or not as he seethed in anger.

For years, Nick's parents had blamed him, and sometimes even Dom, for making them terminally late for mass. It was an embarrassment, they were told, in showing up late for church. It indicated that they didn't care.

Nick didn't stick around for the end of mass. Instead, he went to the local YMCA about three blocks from the church. Nick had decided that he wasn't going to spend rest of the day and the following night outdoors before leaving town. After all, sheltering the homeless was one of the YMCA's early functions, Nick thought, even though he never saw anyone who appeared to be homeless hanging around the place during the times he and Dom would go there for exercise and recreational activities.

The YMCA opened its doors at 9 a.m. every day, even Sundays. When Nick walked in, he was immediately recognized by the Y's roundish and jovial director who had been at the Y as long as Nick could remember.

"What brings you here?" the director said. "I haven't seen you around in a long time."

"I think I'm going to walk around the track. I sprained my ankle, and I need to loosen it up," Nick said while feeling a little relieved that he didn't have to tell a lie. Yet he was worried that the sack over his shoulder might inspire an inquiry.

"You hurt your ankle? How did you do that?"

"I fell from my window," Nick said, still telling the truth.

"You fell from your window?" the director said. "What made you do that?"

Now Nick had to lie. "Oh, I was painting."

116

"Painting? Did your brother help you?"

Nick paused before bluntly reminding the director that his brother was dead.

"Oh, Jesus to Betsy," the director said, clearly embarrassed by the reddening of his roundish face. "Gee, I'm sorry. I just forgot. No, no—I knew, but—for so long I've seen you two together that—you just remind me so much of him and I just naturally brought him up. I'm sorry, really I am. But anyway, use the track to your content to get that ankle better. And if you need anything, just give me a holler."

Nick wasn't offended about the director's gaff, rather relieved that it hastened his departure and he didn't have to endure any more pressing small talk. After putting his sack in a unlocked locker, Nick went on to walk around the oval track, which was elevated around the basketball court. There was no one on the court, but there were a few people jogging and walking around the track. Nick looked for people who could possibly be vagrants, but he was the only one around who could remotely fit that description.

After about a 100 laps around the track, which did more to kill time than loosening up his ankle, Nick descended to the row of un-folded bleachers which were adjacent to the court. When he and brother did come to Y, Dom would sometimes play pickup basketball when there were enough players to run full-court. Nick sometimes played, but he was never really athletically inclined and he was often bettered by the opposition and even on occasion hectored by his teammates. Usually, Nick would jog around the track before taking time to watch his brother play from the bleachers.

Dom was an exceptional athlete and basketball was his favorite sport. At times Nick thought it to be unfortunate that Dom was enrolled at the academy, which didn't have organized sports. Dom could have definitely gotten a scholarship, maybe even to a big-time university, if he had the opportunity to shine in a normal scholastic setting. Yet shine he did at the Y.

To note, Dom wasn't exactly a humble player. During the course of these "call-your-own" contests, Dom tended to call touch fouls whenever he missed a shot in traffic. And when he did hit a shot, it was usually a banker prompting Dom to say, "Caroms always have better eyes."

Later in the day, Nick took in some television in at the Y's TV room. Nick watched an array of PBS programming, which the activated TV was set to when Nick entered the room. Nick never got inspired to turn the channel as he didn't pay much attention to what was on the screen. He was just killing time.

At about 6 p.m., Nick could see through the room's big-glass windows and the opening in doorway some of the Y's workers leaving for the day. A little bit later he saw the Y director leave. Maybe they still cater to the homeless, Nick thought as he felt the building get more empty while no one was paying much attention that he was sticking around.

At about 10 p.m., a young Negro custodian entered the room. Nick thought he might ask what he was doing there but, instead, simply asked to change the channel for a recap of the day's sporting events. After the custodian apparently got the information he needed, he left but didn't change back the channel. After watching a series of sports highlights that bored him, Nick decided to leave the room rather than change the channel and possibly irk the custodian if he decided to return.

Nick went back the gym, which now was only illuminated by a couple of fluorescent lights positioned above half court. Nick saw a man sleeping between the lower rows of the bleachers. This relieved Nick now knowing that he wasn't the only homeless person being sheltered at the Y. But the man, not as dirty as one might expect, wasn't relieved to see Nick, whose black shoes made enough noise while lightly treading on the wooden floor to wake him from his slumber. Apparently alarmed, the man picked up his backpack and cursed, "Why can't you damned people leave me alone?" while quickly shuffling out of the gym.

Nick was a little hurt by the hasty response, but understood the reaction. Nick went to the spot where the man was sleeping and saw an open package of soft chocolate-chip cookies with three of the four still left. On the package was a cute, smiling bear, which made Nick sigh to himself. Even the most benign cartoon character could no longer deflect the rigors of the real world.

Nick was hungry. He had been hungry for the whole day. At times, he had wished he had taken advantage of those spaghetti and meatballs. But that didn't happen. The cookies were probably those of the homeless man, and he was also probably hungry, or will be in the morning. Nick took a cookie out of the package, and by his touch he could tell that it was still fresh. Nick popped it in his mouth, all of it even though it was big enough for at least three bites. Nick could feel the brown sugar and chocolate mesh together between his teeth. Once all that got down his throat, Nick popped in another. It tasted good, but Nick was incapable of fully enjoying its taste. And bear was still cute and benign, making things even more bittersweet.

Nick slept in the spot vacated by the homeless man. Nick did remember dreaming of waking up and finding himself back in his room at home. He wasn't that disappointed when he woke up to find himself back in the gym again. But when Nick fell asleep again, he dreamt of waking up back in at his dorm room. He was disappointed when he woke from that.

If the chocolate-chip cookies didn't appease Nick's hunger, they at least energized his morning. Nick was out the doors before the Y's morning personnel arrived. Very rapidly, Nick walked about mile and a half to his bank only to get there before its morning personnel arrived. It wasn't yet 8:30, the bank opened at 9. Needing to kill even more time, Nick walked around town while sensing that this may be the last time he would see the place again. Nick managed to conjure up more bitterness toward his parents, and was drafting a vow in his head never to return to the town unless they moved away or died—both of them. Nick even doubted if he would bother to come to their funerals.

Yet it wasn't until shortly after the bank had opened that Nick's bitterness had reached it apex. Nick managed to save $720 in his bank account, not including the $30,000-plus from the settlement that was supposedly added. Nick had planned to withdraw all of the former amount, plus maybe a thousand or two from what was added. But when asked about his balance, Nick found that not only it wasn't the $30,000-plus there, but he only had $240 to his name. Now Nick's situation was really desperate.

Nick started walking, and walking fast. Inspired by Pedro's claim that Jesus only covered a span of 35 miles in his lifetime, Nick was going to cover twice that much, or make that thrice as much by nightfall, and even more into the next morning. Knowing that he needed to budget his $240 until he found a means of income, Nick thought that he could walk the whole way without stopping to rest, thus not needing to stay at a hotel. Nick imagined he would stop off at a McDonalds or something like that here and there. But all meals would be to on the go, and Nick was confident he could go at least the first day on foot without stopping.

But like his first trip on foot to the laundromat, Nick overestimated time and distance that could be attained with just dress shoes. The approaching sun was now overhead and on the verge of becoming a leaving sun, and Nick was just at the outskirts of his hometown and not even over the border. Repeatedly, Nick had to remove gravel and stones from the inside of the dress shoes, and the shoulder of the highway that would take him almost straight to his destination was treacherous and muddy in many spots.

Nick kept walking—now walking faster as Nick was focused just on what was ahead, helped a little from the hood over his head and protruding several inches from his face. But what Nick saw directly ahead began to torment his spirits. His shadow kept growing and growing as the departing sun behind him was making much better time. Eventually Nick saw stars appear and get brighter before thick clouds from the north shielded them from his view. The wind also picked up, chilling Nick and making him curse his decision in not taking along something heavier than his gift parka. Nick folded his arms with his right hand, his good hand, gripping the retractable string, moving the bulk of the sack to rest mostly on his shoulder and neck. This made Nick very uncomfortable, yet it made him forget about his bum ankle.

Nick was walking with traffic, which is never a good idea, but Nick was now a habitual offender. The ambiance behind Nick became too weak to grant him a shadow that could stand out from the general dimness ahead of him. Thus, Nick could now better tell when a vehicle behind him was approaching when his shadow would reappear and quickly rush toward Nick just before the headlights passed. Earlier in the day, passing vehicles would sometimes surprise Nick after they whizzed by because the pulled-over hood muffled his hearing.

Still, Nick got his rudest jolt at nightfall. A passenger from an approaching car, which Nick sensed by his headlight-spawned shadow, shouted "Hey, asshole!" while passing. Nick saw the driver of the stick out a back-handed middle finger out of his window while not even appearing to look back. Nick initially was startled before casting them off as immature cretins, but Nick became conscientious of why he was called an asshole. *Do they see something in me that I don't see?* he pondered.

Soon after, Nick sensed some other headlights approaching. From past experience, the brightness indicated that they were from an 18-wheeler. Nick moved further from the road, off the shoulder and beyond the lip of the ditch to brace himself for the misplaced air and turbulence. The truck passed, blowing Nick deeper into the ditch, but immediately slowed down with its compression brakes screeching before stopping completely about 100 yards ahead of Nick.

Nick was curious and slightly concerned. He thought about doubling back, or even darting into an adjacent field due to his healthy fear of strangers in the night. But Nick came to think that it to be unlikely that dangerous felons would be employed or self-sufficient truck drivers, especially ones who were given the responsibility to operate or own a fancy rig like the one in front of him. The illuminating red and orange lights and reflectors that impressively lined the silver back of the trailer hinted that Santa Claus could be the driver.

As he approached the rig, Nick could see the humorous artwork on the side of the trailer. It was a depiction of a camel, similar to Joe Camel of banned cartoon past, running on its hind legs while arm-pumping with its front legs. The camel's tongue was draped out of its mouth, indicated that it was flapping from exertion. Over the figure was the script "Humping to Please."

Just as Nick passed the trailer and approached the cabin, the passenger door flung open. Nick stopped momentarily, experiencing a little of his former fear, before walking forward. When he got to the open door, he looked inside and saw driver leaning over.

"Where are you going, son?" he asked with a thick, Bible-Belt ascent.

"Over the border," Nick answered.

"Over the border? I think you may be going the wrong way."

"No," Nick said. "The other border."

"The other border? If you mean the one at the end of this road, I could take you about 20 miles from it if you need a ride."

Nick climbed in the cabin, which looked as if it served as a second home for the driver. Nick noticed plenty of room behind the seats, with the floor lined with several blankets. Also back there was a plastic cooler, a big one, like the kind Nick's family would take to picnics when Nick's family still went on picnics. Whatever liquid refreshments inside, there were probably accompanied by items of food that needed to be chilled before being cooked, as a heat plate with its cigarette lighter adapter wrapped around it was on top of the cooler. And leaned up against the cooler was one of the those pool-cue cases ablaze with artwork. This consisted of a snake-like creature with a dragon's head. As Nick remembered it, the dragon's head was similar to that of the figured that adorned that reptile farm's Web site. The snake-dragon's body curved back and forth down the case. The tip of the tail straightened out depicting the tip of a cue freshly covered with blue chalk. There was more than enough room for Nick to put his sack in the back.

Though the driver apparently didn't smoke, as Nick saw that his open ashtray only contained gum and candy wrappers, the cabin had a stench of used tobacco—like someone just lit up. Yet there was another odor, and there was visible proof of its origin. It was of Nacho Cheese Doritos, or more like of Nacho Cheese Doritos breath. On the side of the driver was a half-full jumbo-size bag, with its opening rolled up. Nick, who hadn't eaten since that vagrant fled without his cookies, longed for a handful or two. Yet he was content in waiting for the driver to offer him some first rather than flat out asking.

"There's rain coming," the driver said. "I figured you wouldn't want to get wet."

The driver was a short and stocky man, or seemed short since Nick couldn't really tell with him sitting down. He had closely cropped white hair that drew out his blue eyes. His face was red, as if he just sustained a severe sun burn or had some sort of blood-vessel-based skin condition. If the driver did or ever decided to grow a long beard, he would be Santa Claus.

"Some times I don't know about you people," the driver said in an affable manner. "I mean the way you looked with that hood over your head — you look like you're on the lam, that is for most people. But I knew you're OK."

How the driver knew that Nick was "OK" was beyond Nick's reasoning. An assumption, probably, just like that of the punks who called him an asshole and gave him the finger. Nick undraped the hood from his head.

"If you want some Doritos, help yourself."

When the rain came, Nick felt more indebted to the driver because it came with the same ferocity of the storm that pelted his return home, sans the thunder and lightning. Once again, Nick grew sleepy while watching the wiper blades—these operating from the top and performing in inverted and outverted unison. Nick imagined a vision of the truck from an outside perspective cutting through the wind, and the mist in its wake.

"You know there's a charge to this ride," the driver said, which immediately snapped Nick out of his relaxed state. Wait a minute. The driver said nothing about charging for a ride. But before Nick could wage a protest, the driver explained the terms.

"You gotta say something at least once every hour," the driver said. "If not, I'm liable to fall asleep, just like you are about to."

Nick wondered if he did fall asleep and if an hour did pass. But as for something to say, Nick didn't have much to talk about, especially when it would undoubtedly lead to an exchange of life stories. Nick's life story was not one he felt comfortable about sharing with strangers, or even friends. But while groping for something to say, Nick found a worthy question beaming through the windshield.

"Those lights—you see those lights?" Nick said. There were at that point in the road.

"What about them?"

"What color are they?"

"What color are they?" the driver said with an expression that brought out the wrinkles in his red forehead. "They're yellow, of course, or maybe beige." The driver shook his head.

"Just had to ask," Nick said apologetically.

"Just had to ask? Why, what color do you think they are?"

"The same you do."

The driver shook his head again. "Well then, I guess that makes them officially yellow or beige—or a combination of the two."

There was silence for a few seconds as Nick tried to find something else to say.

"I don't know," the driver said while still shaking his head a little. "You seem like a strange one to me. Tell me, where are you from?"

In his head Nick rummaged for a response. But he didn't want to delay an answer for fear of inducing suspicion.

"I'm from the Fisher's Academy," Nick said.

"The Fisher's Academy," the driver repeated, but not in a tone of a question. "Ah, yes, the Fisher's Academy."

Nick wondered if the driver did know about the Fisher's Academy. His route could have taken him through the area and maybe even routinely past the place. And maybe he could be familiar with it from playing pool nearby at the tavern. Nick didn't remember the driver, or his rig, being at the tavern the night he got roughed up, but maybe he did remember seeing his cue case there. Yeah, Nick did remember that …

"Isn't that a military school?"

… maybe not.

"It's a school that teaches about God," Nick said.

"Ah, a Christian school," the driver incorrectly assumed before re-focusing his attention to the road. Suddenly, he didn't seem as talkative anymore, but Nick had to follow up by asking, "Sir, do you believe in God?"

"Ahhh, hummph," the driver said as he pressed his chin closer to his neck, drawing out the excess flesh. "I knew you were going to ask that. But, hey, I guess I asked for it." The driver paused as Nick sensed that now it was he who was groping for something to say.

"For that, all I can say is that I was born a Christian. Like they say, there's a sucker born again every minute," the driver said before waving his hand at Nick as if to erase what he just said. "Sorry, that wasn't appropriate. It's just that while I'm on the road all the time I come across all these stupid bumper stickers, and I sometimes repeat them for some reason even though I know that they're stupid."

Nick smiled and said, "So you do believe in God?"

The driver pressed his chin again as he still seemed uncomfortable with the question. "Well, like I was saying, I was born in a Christian family, or we called ourselves Christians, and I don't think anyone ever renounced the notion that I was a Christia—I mean the pope has never personally told me that I was excommunicated, or anything like that. So I guess I'm still a Christian, so I guess I still believe in God."

"Do you go to church?"

"I knew you were going to ask that," the driver said, still appearing to Nick that he was evading the issue. But then the truck driver took a deep breath before letting his whole body exhale, and turned from the road to face Nick as if he finally decided to reveal what he formerly wanted to conceal.

"If you need to know, I can say this—I used to go to church every Sunday. And I was on time." When the driver said he was on time, he pointed to Nick with his shift hand.

"It was part of a deal," the driver said while leaning back in his seat and slightly readjusting his seat beat. "My ex-wife—she was my soon-to-be wife at the time—told me that there was no way in hell she was going to marry me if I didn't go to church. I mean she was a real stickler when it came to religion and church and God and all that. So I went to church, and we went to church on time," once again, the driver pointed at Nick, "that's the only way she would have it.

"So I, with my wife, would make it to church every Sunday, and we did that for a very long—ah—make that for quite a while. And it wasn't too bad, I mean it wasn't what I expected from watching it on TV. I mean I thought I would get to hear about all these catastrophic floods and beasts coming out of the Nile to devour the unbelievers. I thought I would get to hear all this wrath of God and the devil is going to burn your ass-like raving and all that. But the church we went to was more subdued. It usually centered around the life of Jesus and his apostles. That was the first part, and there was usually a different story every week."

Nick gathered that the driver went to a Catholic church, the same type Nick's family went to.

"Some of these stories were kind of hard to understand. Yet others I was able to get, or able to get like later during the week or the month from something I experienced outside the church in the real world. But the second half of church was all the same. Don't get me wrong. I didn't have a problem with sitting, standing and kneeling in church—that's one thing that kind of amused me, the way they would make us change positions in unison—it lasted less than an hour, as you may know. But the second half seemed like a lot of—what's the word?—conditioning. And then, near the end after they passed out baskets for contributions, people would go up to eat these wafer-like pieces of bread handed to them by the priest. I mean, and I know you're familiar with this, the priest would place the piece right on your tongue. Some people were a little smart as they would take the piece in their own hands before placing it in their month. But come on, I mean it's one thing to eat peanuts out of a community bowl at a bar with people coming out of the restroom with the toilet flushing just before digging in, but how do I know where those priest's hands were?

"That's where I put my foot down." Just as the driver said that, the speedometer of the truck exceeded legal limits. "I told her that I wasn't going up for—what's that?"

"Communion," Nick answered.

"Yes, communion. No. I wasn't going to participate in that. My wife, or my ex, got pissed off at that. But she was still glad I went. But being on the road all the time, there were Sundays I just wasn't home. And when I was at home on Sunday, I was usually pretty beat. There are times when I don't sleep for over 48 hours. Like now for instance, I've been chuggin' 55 hours strong, that's why I gotta stop off a up the road a bit to get some rest. That's why on Sunday I like to catch up on some sleep, I mean sleep in, allow myself to recover, maybe watch a little football. So I started missing church. My wife, of course, was a real bitch about it at first. But after awhile she stopped busting my balls about it, and she just went without me.

"But some time later, I had—you may know what this is—an epiphany, I think that's what it is, an epiphany of sorts, or something like that where something was telling me that I ought to go to church. So one Sunday I got up early, even before my wife, and start getting ready for church. When my wife woke up and saw that I was in my church clothes, she said, 'Oh, you don't have to go to church. Why not sleep in all day.' Believe me, she said that or something to that effect many times before. But I was usually still in bed at the time, and when she said it, it was in a bitchy and sarcastic tone—'Whaaay not sleep all fuckin' daaay,'" the driver mimicked in an unappealing female impersonation. "But this time it was different, like she really didn't want me to go to church.

"That's what got me to thinking that someone is shitting in Denmark. So the next week I made her believe I was on a route out of town when I really rented a motel and staked out the church in a rental car. And that's when I saw walk hand-in-hand with that sumbitch. And I lost it right there."

The rest of the trip went without incident, except near the tail end. The driver was about to exit the highway to where he was going, but had to abort his path when a quick candy apple-red Neon came out of nowhere to flank the truck on its way to the exit, forcing the truck driver to back off to avoid contact before issuing a stream of obscenities that probably weren't heard by the Neon's driver and a horn that probably was.

"I tell you, if I had it my way I would send all you drivers back to driving school," he said while pointing at Nick as if he part of a car-driving contingency. "And the first thing I would teach you all is this: If you can't see my mirror, I can't see you."

So true.

The near-accident was a blessing to Nick. The driver had to travel another five miles before getting a chance to double back. Back on his feet, Nick didn't know if it was late night or early morning, but it didn't matter. His legs were reinvigorated, his injury was non-existent, and the sack that he slung over his shoulder seemed much lighter. The rain had since stopped, or the journey passed its range, and Nick didn't pull the hood over his head. By the time Nick reached the border, the same morning stars that Nick gazed at after falling out of his bedroom window had returned. By the time Nick had become adjacent from the road with the academy, which from where Nick was walking wasn't visible since the surrounding foliage concealed the buildings and dorms, the teal glow returned to the eastern horizon. Amazing, Nick thought, he had won the race with the sun, or at least tied it.

By the time Nick had reached his destination—an apartment complex that resembled a Swiss hotel resort with the black-and-white wooden-crossed facing on its buildings—the sun had emerged. Nick had imagined that he would have made it here by that evening, but had since come to realize that such a goal was unrealistic.

Nick thought that he should be getting up about now. He saw his car under one of the aluminum carports in the complex's parking lot. Elder Steven also drove a Neon, but his was midnight blue.

Chapter Fifteen

Although it was over two hours before his first class, Elder Steven was up. He was dressed in a T-shirt and shorts, which were matching, gray-based, and the T-shirt had faded red initials "SMU" prominently displayed on it. Was Elder Steven a former student at Southern Methodist University? He never mentioned where he went to school during any of the classes Nick attended. Then again, no one asked.

Elder Steven's eyes widened when he greeted Nick in the second-story hallway of his apartment just outside his door. He probably should have known who it was before opening the door as Nick had stood directly in front of the peephole to reveal himself during such a early time in the day when many people would likely ignore a knock at the door, or not answer it if the person wasn't a recognizable friend. Nick placed his sack off to the side near the stairwell, presumably out of the peephole's sight.

"Why, Nick," Elder Steven said with enthusiasm, although he kept his voice low. Most of his neighbors were probably asleep "What brings you out at such an ungodly hour?"

Nick had been to Elder Steven's apartment once before. One day during the winter, Elder Steven's Neon was in the shop and he requested a ride home from Pedro with Nick and Alyce tagging along. When they arrived at the apartment, Elder Steven invited the trio inside for some hot chocolate. Upon entering, Nick was immediately captivated by Elder Steven's creative interior. An array of celestial-based tin and wire mobiles hung from the ceiling. One depicted a crescent moon in the middle with smaller stars hanging around it.

Another depicted the sun in the middle with planets around it. And a third had the moon, sun, stars and planets, but nothing dominated the middle. A ceiling fan was in the middle of the mobiles with its thin wooden blades just out of the way of the wires. Attached to the ceiling fan's activating chain — it wasn't activated that day — was a leather strap with brown and white feathers sown into it.

Also hanging from the ceiling amid the mobiles and fan were a couple of ceramic frogs with wings, one small, another about three feet long and seemingly destined to fall to the ground after the strain on its thin wire, which descended from one of a series of screwed in hooks in the ceiling, would eventually make it snap.

But the trinkets that caught Nick's attention were those that had American Indian themes. Elder Steven had several paintings depicting Indian chiefs and warriors in various settings. He also had some handsome wood carvings of Indians, a replica totem pole that stood over five feet tall and displayed demonic characters that fixed Nick's gaze after the three had taken a seat that day on Elder Steven's sleeper sofa, which in a one-bedroom apartment must have been intended for guests.

The table in front of the sofa was also interesting. Its base was a thick slice out of a giant and oblong tree trunk of some kind. Its rings numbered in the hundreds, and several knot holes added to the table's character. The base was glazed with a lacquer finish. Elder Steven explained that he got it from a furniture maker who only used fallen timber or driftwood as opposed to anything that was a result of deforestation.

Pedro also took note of the Indian artwork, particularly a painting of an Indian chief standing side by side with a buffalo as if they were brothers.

"I hate to burst your bubble here, but the way that Indian is keeping company with that buffalo isn't very accurate," said Pedro, who was sitting on the opposite side of Nick on the sofa with Alyce in between.

"You don't say?" Elder Steven responded.

"For years we've been hearing on how the Indian and the buffalo lived hand-and-hand before the white man came around and nearly wiped them, the buffalo that is, out," Pedro said before pausing a few seconds. "But really, if it wasn't for the white man—or the Old World settlers—the buffalo would have been long gone well before the 20th century, or even the 19th century."

Elder Steven, who was seated in a recliner across from the tree-truck table, leaned closer as Pedro continued.

"You see, these Indians, or make that Native Americans—wait, that's not even right. We're all Native Americans. Make that—let's see, yeah, that's it—American aborigines, that's what they are, American aborigines. Anyway, these aborigines didn't have such an ecological policy toward the buffalo as we for so long have been led to believe. In fact, and there's proof of this, these aborigines often would drive whole herds of buffalo over cliffs when they only needed to kill a handful. And quite a few tribes would go out of their way to kill every buffalo in sight for fear—get this—that a surviving buffalo would tell other herds to flee the area."

Elder Steven responded, "Don't you think buffalo can communicate with each other?"

"Yeah," Pedro snorted. "And that's a bunch of bullshit—or make that buffalo chips."

The subject soon got off American aborigines and buffalo chips that day, and onto God and Genesis.

A television set was not visible in the apartment, but Nick assumed one was encased in a book-shelve-like cabinet placed in front of the table and sofa. Books, magazines, a clock and several other small wooden and plastic trinkets surrounded on both sides a pair of double-doors in the middle, which appeared big enough to shield a 25-inch-plus television screen. But even if there was a TV behind the doors, the fact that the doors were shut at the time at least indicated that Elder Steven was a selective viewer.

He was also a selected reader. And amid about a scoreful of books—many of which were from the great Russian writers, and one Nick eventually took note of—*Just Six Numbers* from British scientist Martin Rees — and magazines was a Bible, which was the spitting image of the one always on his desk. Elder Steven rose from his chair to get the Bible before sitting back down and opening to the book to Genesis.

"It says here," Elder Steven said while pointing to a passage in the book, "that God made man out of clay. Do you really believe that?"

None of the three responded before Elder Steven directed the question specifically at Nick.

"Do you really believe that, Nick?"

Nick didn't know where Elder Steven was going with this, and hesitated to answer.

"If it says so in the Bible," Nick finally said, "then it must be true."

"Come on, Nick!" Elder Steven said. "Making man out of clay? You mean you haven't heard of DNA?"

"Yes. But I don't know if science is always so exact," Nick said.

"Maybe, but I don't know when it comes to DNA," Elder Steven said. "They got that pretty much mapped out, as you know."

"Okay, so God didn't make man out of clay," Alyce joined in. "Not everything has to be taken literally."

"What do you mean not to be taken literally?" Elder Steven said. "The Bible professes to be the truth, and that's how it should be read as."

"So what's your point?" Pedro said.

"My point is this," Elder Steven said before rising again to place the Bible back on the shelf and, on the other side of the double doors, retrieved one of the magazines—a science magazine.

"The reason DNA is the building block of life is because of its ability to replicate itself," Elder Steven said while thumbing through the magazine before finding the spot he was looking for. When he found it, he folded the magazine back and tossed it to Nick, who was able to maintain the spot when he caught it against his lap. Alyce looked over to see what article Elder Steven singled out and, sure enough, it was an article with illustrations pertaining to DNA, yet Nick didn't feel compelled to read it at that sitting. Instead, he expected Elder Steven to give a summary, which he did.

"There's a theory that suggests that the basic components of DNA, mind you the building blocks of life as we know it, had to somehow learn, or to have an attribute transferred to them, to make copies of themselves. And that, as the article right there says, may have happened when these components fused themselves on a surface that has been known for its replication abilities.

"And do you know what that surface is?" Elder Steven said, now posing the question to all three.

"Clay."

Nick could see that much had changed—or more like replicated—in the apartment since that winter day. There were more mobiles hanging from the ceiling, and yet another ceramic flying frog. The ceiling fan was now activated, making the planets and stars orbit their sun and moon while the other mobiles and frogs swayed back and forth. Several of the new mobiles hung lower which, had Alyce and Pedro accompanied him, would have made it difficult to sit three on the sofa since the people on the ends would have had tin and wire draped on them. There were also more Indian—or make that American aborigine paintings and trinkets, and another totem pole, this one bigger and more demonic than the former and placed next to the book cabinet reaching almost to the ceiling.

"Why don't you come in?"

Nick didn't take his sack in with him. That would have to wait until it was appropriate. He didn't think Elder Steven noticed it.

Elder Steven hadn't yet shaved as indicated by his facial stubble that, in Nick's eyes, enhanced his handsomeness. Elder Steven didn't seem that tired, although he seemed to be in a state of total relaxation. When Nick entered the apartment, he caught a whiff of what seemed to be incense that complemented—or was meant to cover—another smell, that of the type of tobacco Nick had smoked during his latest venture into the tavern. But Nick couldn't see any smoke in the air, although the fan would have probably dissipated it.

Nick couldn't see any ashtray either, but he did notice an open box of a variety of Krispy Kreme donuts on the truck-sliced table.

"Help yourself," Elder Steven said. "You've still got youth on your side, but I got to stop eating like a kid. Each one of those has a day's worth of fat in them and then some. But they had a special—a dozen for $1.99, and I couldn't resist. The only thing is after two days they're stale so I got to eat them in that span. Good thing you showed up."

Nick sat himself on the sofa between the hanging mobiles. He took a bite out of a white-creamed-filled donut, and finished it off the same way he ate the vagrant's cookies. It too was bittersweet.

"So, like I was saying, what brings you out here?" Elder Steven said as he lowered himself into his recliner. He still looked completely relaxed.

"You mean you don't know by now?" said Nick, who had lost track of time. It had seemed that such a long time had passed since the morning he was expelled and later driven in disgrace back home before running away to return to the region. But actually, only one school day had passed, although Elder Steven should have noticed that Nick was absent.

"I don't know what?" Elder Steven said while leaning forward. Nick was a little suspect of Elder Steven at this point. Nick wondered how much he actually didn't know about his expulsion.

"You should have noticed I wasn't in class Monday—yesterday."

Elder Steven took a long look at Nick before finally responding, "Yes, I did notice. But you've missed class before."

"And I'm going to continue to miss classes," Nick said with emotion building up in voice. He noticed that Elder Steven's eyes slightly narrowed, but he didn't appear much more nudged out of his relaxed state.

"I've been..." Nick lowered his head and then looked up again. Elder Steven was still unmoved, "...expelled."

Elder Steven again paused before asking, "For how long?"

"For how long?" Nick said incredulously. Maybe Elder Steven was ignorant about what happened, but he should have known about the academy's indefinite and retroactive expulsion policy. "For good, that's how long. Just like ah—you know. I'm gone. Never to be allowed back. And all my records, all my grades, are gone for good, like I was never there."

Now Elder Steven did appear moved as he leaned even closer to Nick. "Why?" he asked

Nick attempted to get up from his seat to answer on his feet, but he saw that he would have to ungracefully negotiate the mobiles, so he plopped back down deeper into the sofa. "It's—eh—it's from smoking pot."

"Smoking pot?" Elder Steven said while—successfully—rising from his chair. "You've got expelled for that?"

"Well, it's not just that."

Elder Steven sat back in his chair. "Then what was it?"

Nick anticipated that he would eventually have to address that issue at some level, but not now.

"It was other—eh—things."

There was a considerable gap of silence as Nick kept his head lowered and Elder Steven eased back in his chair.

"So why are you not at home? Did your parents kick you out?"

"No," Nick said with his head still lowered. "But they basically disowned me. It was only a matter of time before they kicked me out if I didn't eventually take off myself. But I couldn't take another day there."

"That's a shame," Elder Steven said before uttering the words that Nick longed to hear. "If you need a place to stay, I mean, I could use a roommate."

Nick's heart was fueled with relief. During the entire journey back, Nick was confident that Elder Steven would allow him to stay with him. But he still wasn't completely sure until the invitation came from his mouth.

"Oh thank you, thank you. I owe you so much," Nick said while being tempted to step over the table and give his teacher a hug, but refrained from doing so. "It won't be for too long. I'll make sure of that. It's just I'm in a bind right now, and I—"

"You can stay as long as you like," Elder Steven said, giving Nick another jolt of relief. "And while you're at it, why don't you have another donut?"

Nick graciously accepted the offer. This donut tasted so much better than the first.

"But what were these other things?" Elder Steven asked after allowing Nick to joyfully consume the donut. Nick cringed when the issue was readdressed.

"I...I don't want really want to talk about it," Nick said, giving about the same response he gave Elder Steven when he asked about the beating incident at the tavern.

Elder Steven rose to get his Bible from the bookshelf and then returned to his chair. Nick wondered why he got it this time. Elder Steven held it between his knees with his palms on both covers.

"So you don't want to talk about it?" Elder Steven said.

"No. I don't—I don't," Nick repeated, although he was feeling it being drawn out of him. "It's just that—I don't know—it's just that—that I no longer feel like I'm suited for this."

"Suited for what?"

"Suited to be a servant of the Lord. I mean, it's just that I'm—it's just that I'm such a, eh—a hypocrite."

"A hypocrite?"

"Yes, a hypocrite!" Nick nearly shouted, as he now was agitated at what he thought was a relentless grilling. "That's what I am. I mean I have all these lusts and evil thoughts going through my head and body and probably my soul. I mean, who am I to save someone from the things that torment me, when I can't save myself?"

"Why can't you save yourself?"

"Because I have all these evil lusts and thoughts, like I just said."

"What are these thoughts?"

Nick's agitation was now upgraded to near rage. Elder Steven wouldn't let the issue go.

"Just bad thoughts. I...I don't know how to describe them."

Elder Steven again eased back in his chair and smiled. Maybe he now knew what these evil lusts and thoughts were. "May I ask you another question?"

Elder Steven had taken the liberty to pose the former questions without asking permission, so Nick was apprehensive of what this one was going to be. Nonetheless, he gave his permission.

"Have you ever seen the *Last Temptation of Christ*?"

Nick had seen the movie. During his first year at the academy, one of the students on Nick's dorm floor had a VCR and a tape of the movie. He invited Nick and about ten other students to view the movie one night. Though the movie wasn't listed as forbidden material at the academy, the students were careful to look out for the resident assistant—an upperclassman assigned to check dorm activity—by placing a mirror strategically in the doorway to see if he was coming down the hall. Nick thought the movie was confusing, and he was disturbed to see Jesus portrayed in such a tormented state.

"Yes," Nick answered. "I saw it."

"What did you think of it?"

"Well, what do you think of it? That is if you saw it," Nick said.

"Yes, I've seen it many times," Elder Steven, said. "In fact I have it on video tape."

"You have it on video tape? Do you have other videos?" Nick asked, with his second question serving as an attempt to change the subject.

"Yes, I have several other videos," Elder Steven said as a sheepish grin crept onto his face. "But I don't think those would really interest you. But anyway, what did you think of it?"

"I didn't understand it," Nick said. "I mean Jesus marrying Mary of Magdalene and being tricked by the devil and all that—it's was just another case of revisionist history that is so common nowadays." Just then Nick noticed that the painting of the American aborigine and the buffalo was no longer hanging on the wall.

"Is that what really bothered you about it?" Elder Steven said while maintaining, as Nick was interpreting it, relentless pressure.

"Yes, it bothered me very much," Nick said with emotion returning to his voice. "I mean to portray Jesus in such a way is blasphemy and, like I said, terrible revisionist history."

Elder Steven opened up the Bible to a passage in the New Testament. "Well, in that case maybe we should just refer to history as it is recorded right here. Now, as you well know, Jesus never married Mary of Magdalene, but he did save her from an eminent stoning. You do know that, don't you?"

Nick nodded his head.

"You know how he saved her?" Elder Steven asked, but Nick responded with silence. "He told the crowd that he without sin may be the first the cast a stone. And no one cast a stone. You know what that means, don't you? It means that everyone present was not without sin."

"Except Jesus, of course."

"No!" Elder Steven said with emotion now in his voice. Nick could feel the little hairs on the back of his neck start to tingle and stand up straight. "That's where you're wrong—dead wrong!"

"What do you mean? I…I don't understand," Nick said. "He told that to the people ready to stone her. He wasn't going to stone her."

"And he didn't," Elder Steven said.

"But that didn't mean he wasn't without sin," Nick replied."

"Then why did he say that he without sin may be the first to cast a stone knowing that would qualify him as an able executioner?"

Nick didn't know how to respond, prompting Elder Steven to lean over the table to show him the passage in the book. "You see he says it right here."

Nick shielded the book with his hands and looked away, as if he was offered to gander at an explicit photograph but didn't want his virgin eyes to be corrupted. With Nick being uncooperative, Elder Steven eased back in his chair and stared at Nick who didn't want to stare back. Instead, Nick fixed his eyes on the donut box, although he wasn't hungry for a third.

"Nick," Elder Steven said after a period of silence, "I have a confession to make."

Nick looked up to make eye contact with Elder Steven again. Elder Steven put the Bible next to the box of donuts and eased back in his chair again, this time looking more relaxed than before.

"Do you remember that night when we met in the middle of the lake?" Elder Steven asked.

"Yeah," Nick said. "What about it?"

"Haven't you ever wondered what I was doing out there?"

Nick could feel his hairs stand up again as well as his heartbeat shift into overdrive. He sprung from his sofa while waving a menacing finger at Elder Steven.

"Don't say that about my Jesus! Don't say that about my Jesus!" Nick shouted at the top of his lungs. While waving his finger, Nick's forearm got entangled in one of the mobiles, which in turn got entangled in the ceiling fan. The chaos spurred by the fan immediately included the other mobiles and the large ceramic frog. The frog's wire snapped, and then the frog shattered into an infinite amount of pieces when it crashed loudly onto the table. Some of the fragments and dust ended up in the donut box — now they were really spoiled—and on the Bible.

Elder Steven quickly rose from his chair to shut off the fan. "Jesus, Nick," he said while trying to untangle the mess.

Nick, now facing Elder Steven at closer range, repeated, "Don't say that about my Jesus," but in a much lower voice.

"But Nick, he's my Jesus, too."

Nick went into a rage again. "Don't say that about my Jesus!" he shouted.

Elder Steven, who while still trying to right the mobiles, looked at Nick in what seemed to be fearful concern, as if he suspected that Nick was on the verge of violence.

"Don't say that about my Jesus!" Nick shouted again while stumbling backward toward the door. When he got to the door, he fumbled frantically with the deadbolt before unlatching it, and slammed the door as he departed. Nick momentarily forgot to retrieve his sack as he began to race down the stairs. Realizing this, Nick doubled back up the stairs only to see that the door he slammed was open, as if he slammed it too hard to close. He saw that Elder Steven was approaching the door. Nick grabbed his sack and continued his hasty departure.

While glancing up the stairwell before heading out of the complex's door, Nick was slightly relieved that Elder Steven didn't appear to have followed him out of his apartment. But while race walking away from the scene, he heard Elder Steven call out to him from the landing's window.

"Nick! Come back!"

Nick began to run, a strenuous act with a sack of clothes on his shoulder. The strain made Nick breathe hard, but not quite as hard as Nick deliberately made himself breath in order to drown out Elder Steven's pleas.

Chapter Sixteen

Now Nick was really desperate.

Even when he found out that his bank account was depleted, Nick still was confident Elder Steven would shelter him long enough for the ordeal to pass, or at least until Nick became self-sufficient. Now all bridges were burned, even with Elder Steven beckoning for him to come back.

Nick ran as fast as he could for as long as he could until he was well out of the complex. He was still worried Elder Steven would track him down in his Neon, but Nick was too winded not to stop and rest. Nick let the sack on his shoulder fall to the ground, which was in a convenience store parking lot adjacent to the complex. Pained from the weighted run, Nick was bent over with one hand on his side and the other on his thigh. While looking down, Nick could see through his blurred eyes that his tears were forming a series of droplets on the pavement—big droplets and Nick couldn't stop them. He tried to suck them back, but while doing so he made that sickening sound his mother often made.

When Nick looked at the droplets again, he became alarmed because they seemed to be too numerous to be coming from his eyes only. Nick thought it was starting to rain. After clearing his eyes with the sleeve of his parka, Nick could see it wasn't raining but appeared ready to. It was actually darker than it was when the sun had yet cleared the horizon earlier that morning. A puffy deep-purple canopy covered the sky, and Nick thought he heard thunder in the distance, though at dawn it seemed as if it would be an ideal day.

Nick had to quickly find a place to stay.

Nick didn't have a Plan B, yet figured a worse-case scenario would have him coming into town at an inconvenient hour—like noon, well after midnight or shortly after Elder Steven left for the academy—forcing him to stay at a hotel for a day and night. Nick thought the hotel district about three miles east of Elder Steven's apartment might provide a good place in the interim.

Now there was no interim, but Nick headed that way anyway.

There were some reasonably priced hotels. One that advertised for $26.95 a night caught Nick's attention, and it didn't look that bad from the outside. But when Nick was informed that he would have to drop down a $75 deposit because he didn't have a credit card in his name, he balked at the notion. Nick was leery of placing any money down, especially when he had so little on his person.

Yet all the hotels Nick inquired in that vicinity had about the same policy. Nick wondered if it was the sack that made the management hit him up for such large lump sum up front. After four tries and still no roof over his head with the day making its morning-to-afternoon transition, and with only open space to the east, Nick decided to head up north to where many of the academy's lily-white students referred to as "The Heart of Darkness."

If anyone at the academy seemed undaunted by the predominately black city noted for its dangerous reputation, it was Pedro. Often Pedro ventured into the city to save souls, never with Nick or Alyce, but usually never alone. Pedro bragged heroically about his experiences in "The Heart of Darkness." Once, Pedro got a pair of city dwellers to come to one of the academy's picnics. When they arrived, just like Pedro had heralded they would, most all of the picnic's social talk came to an abrupt halt before being deliberately kick-started again.

Nick headed down the main boulevard toward the city, which boundaries allegedly always spilled deeper into the town according to the town's lily-white populous. But even when Nick approached the city limits, he was relieved by watching the cars go by and several pedestrians that he wasn't the only lily-white person in the area.

But Nick was no longer lily-white, and he knew that when he looked into the washroom mirror of one those hotels. His face was seriously sun-burned from his extended time outdoors on his feet. Nick thought maybe that might help him not stick out if he had to continue to travel north. But who was he kidding?

Eventually, Nick realized the mix had become dominantly more darker and soon he was the only Caucasian around. He thought about pulling the parka's hood over his head, but Nick realized that would probably make him even more conspicuous. Nick sensed people driving by checking him out, perhaps because he was white or perhaps because he was lugging that sack over his shoulder. Maybe they were worried about the element crossing over their border.

Nick was grateful for one thing: there still was a threat of rain. The afternoon heat pushed the deep-purple clouds higher into the air, and they were no longer deep purple anymore, but a dingy shade of gray, like the grimy back of the smelly buses that often passed by up and down the boulevard. Still, it looked as if could rain at any moment. And Nick thought the threat of rain would keep most of the would-be Negro troublemakers indoors, or at least in their cars. After all, Negroes were supposed to have this thing against wet weather, right?

Nick kept walking, and people kept staring. There were even some outdoors—rain be damned—who gave Nick a noticeable gander when he passed. Some were young, dangerously young Nick thought, with black knitted caps and solid-colored FUBU jerseys and baggy jeans with pockets so big that they seemed to be designed to conceal an array of weapons. Some had headphones sticking out from their caps while grooving to the beat of unheard music. Nick could feel the sweat build under his parka. It was too hot for a parka—and perhaps even for a FUBU jersey—but Nick wasn't about to strip down in open, especially not here.

Nick's perseverance soon paid off. Until then, Nick was growing frustrated that no hotels were stationed along the boulevard. There were plenty of boarded-up buildings, many seedy bars and strip joints that were already open for business, several run-down theaters with provocative titles on their marquees', an occasional fried-food restaurant, and a surprising abundance of churches. Nick noticed that a church was located on most every block, even on both sides of the street. That was a hell of a lot more than any lily-white neighborhood Nick was familiar with. But no hotels. That is until Nick nearly got to the end of the road.

There, tucked in between a large daily newspaper building and yet another church, was a two-story brick building with rickety wooden railings in front of the rooms on the second floor. Room rental was dirt cheap—$12.95 a day, and the $20 deposit made it even more reasonable for Nick. And the room wasn't that bad.

Then again, it wasn't that good. It was fairly clean and—would you believe?—there was even a mint placed on the bed's pillow. Yet the room reeked of stale cigarette smoke. The nightstand, the only piece of furniture in room other than a bed and a rabbit-eared TV, had some sort of sticky substance on its surface that trapped what had to be a month's worth of dust that probably could only be removed with a scraper. Covering the window were taped newspapers that dated over a year ago and had since turned yellow. The window was half open, showing through its screen the boulevard's seedy view just over the balcony's rickety rails.

Nick let himself fall backwards onto the bed. He popped back up immediately. A sharp edge of a broken spring was sticking through the mattress and slightly pierced Nick's buttocks through his pants. Nonetheless, Nick positioned his lower body away from the piercing spring and stared up at the ceiling light. Nick could see through the light's white-tinted shield that one of its two bulbs was out. Nick didn't fall asleep, but while in his prone position the hours began to pass quickly. Looking out at the boulevard, he could see that the sun had finally come out as the threatening rain clouds dispersed without producing rain. Nick remained unmoved, even much later when the sun started to set.

After a while, Nick was reminded of his hunger and decided to get something to eat. During his journey, Nick had noted that there was a McDonald's several blocks down from the hotel. It's general cleanliness amid the taverns, strip joints, boarded-up buildings and even churches stood out like in that part of the city. Nick also noted that the restaurant was advertising another one of its two Big Macs for two bucks special. Nick really never acquired a taste for Big Macs, or anything else served at McDonald's, but forced to live frugally, it was a deal that he couldn't pass up.

The only thing was that Nick, despite his hunger, couldn't conjure enough energy to get up from the bed. Instead, he continued to lay there with the confidence that the McDonald's wasn't going anywhere soon. But when the sun descended below the buildings on the other side of the street, Nick dinner plans were foiled. Not too far in the distance Nick heard repeated gun fire and was immediately reminded of where he was at, and that it's dangerous reputation, which rivaled even the more bigger and more notorious cities in the nation, was not a myth. Dinner would have to come to him.

Fortunately, inside the nightstand's drawer was a phone book. And hey, it was only six years old. There was a Bible, too, and that actually looked even newer. Nick ordered a pizza from a pay phone near the balcony's stairwell. With darkness taking greater hold, Nick dialed nervously and got even more nervous when he was put on hold. Eventually, Nick ordered a large pizza with pepperoni. That was a big pie for Nick to devour by himself, but he planned to make it last for two or three days, although his room wasn't equipped with a refrigerator.

Nick was surprised that the pizza delivery man was a Caucasian. When Nick handed the man a twenty-dollar bill to pay for a thirteen-dollar pizza and waited for his change, the delivery man squawked, "You expect me to come out here for nothing?" So Nick paid $20 for a large pepperoni pizza. And he didn't even get any free pop.

Although Nick had planned to make the pizza last for a couple of days, he nearly finished it off in one sitting. He washed it down while drinking directly from the faucet of the bathroom sink. As Nick found out earlier when he washed up while waiting for his pizza, there was no hot water. Now while slurping from the faucet, Nick noticed that there wasn't any cold water, rather luke warm with a hint of sulfur. Nick couldn't figure out how city water could taste like well water. Then again, maybe it wasn't sulfur Nick was tasting.

When Nick decided to activate the rabbit-earred TV, he was surprised that it was a black-and-white one. A black-and-white TV? After determining that its lack of color wasn't from an aged picture tube, Nick marveled that such a model still existed and, thus, could be almost classified as an antique. Nick was slightly amused watching contemporary programming displayed in black-and-white, like the shows were being transmitted back in time.

When Nick was awakened from the TV's test pattern beeeeeeep, he again was pulled from a series of dreams that had him back at home or back at the academy. Nick had been watching TV while sitting on the bed since that was the only place to sit, and later began watching while lying down. When Nick turned the TV off he heard some more gun fire, this time a little closer than before. Nick wondered what could ever influence a person to shoot another. The environment, maybe?

Nick went to the window to close it. Then he turned off the light and dreamed some more of being places he was no longer at.

Nick managed to adjust to his new digs by the following day, and even started to get comfortable with the daylight setting. After an extended period on the move, Nick was relishing the opportunity to settle down in one spot. Yet time and money were not on Nick's side. He thought about getting a nearby job, hopefully during the day. But noticing groups of black men mulling around at the nearby street corners during all times of the day, Nick surmised that regional jobs must be hard to come by, or the jobs available no one wanted to do.

Nick did eventually start taking advantage of the Big Mac special at McDonalds. But he also squandered a chunk of his money on junk food when he went to a convenience store down the street to originally buy shampoo, soap and some milk. For some reason, Nick had a developed a taste for donuts, cookies and Doritos.

While returning to his hotel during the first of these food runs, Nick noticed a ravishing "streetwalker" with rust-colored curly hair gracing the hotel with her presence. Soon after, Nick determined that she was renting out one of the lower rooms. At first, Nick wondered how such a figure could blatantly use the hotel for such business and not be swept away by the owners. But maybe that's why the hotel was there in the first place. That part of the city sure wasn't what you would call a tourist trap.

The first time Nick saw her, she was wearing blood-red elastic top that pushed her bosom high and firm and gripped her middle like a drum. The top had no sleeves, displaying all of the slim and toned contours of her brown arms and shoulders. Her jet-back mini-skirt was also a size or two too tight, accentuating the small and solid shape of her butt as well as her legs which, like her arms, were thin and muscular and molded even more by high-heeled sandals. She didn't wear nylons—didn't need them. But she did wear plenty of makeup, lipstick and nail polish, blood-red nail polish—even on her toes, which shone brightly through her sandals.

Later from his window, Nick couldn't help but notice when cars would pull up to the curve and apparently inquire about the going price. Nick also couldn't help but notice when a customer, wearing a grin and a hard-on that shone through his corduroys, was invited inside for what must have been a business transaction. When that happened, Nick longed to hear between the ceiling and walls.

On the second day, she was wearing something else. The mini-skirt and sandals were probably the same, but the top, though apparently made from the same type of elastic fabric, was decorated in a blue flower-white lily illustrated mix. While approaching her after the second of his McDonald's runs, Nick couldn't determine which top he liked better, yet the flower top indicated a creative variety.

Nick had since planned to approach the woman if she was not conducting business when he returned. It was not to conduct business himself, but to maybe to engage in a meaningful conversation that perhaps could appease some of Nick's sensual desires. Nick noticed that she noticed him as he neared her position just outside her room. She made brief eye contact with Nick, but furtively looked away as if she already knew that Nick was merely window shopping. Nick wasn't going to hit her with his familiar line of where she thought when was going when she died. Nick had decided to avoid all of that. Instead …

"Excuse me, my name is Nick. What is your name?"

She seemed startled by Nick's question, and proceeded to scan him from head to toe with her milk-chocolate eyes.

"Khalid," a husky voice replied.

Nick fled the city the following day.

He had no Plan B, C, D or E at this point. But he had to go back—but back to where? Heading back down south was the only destination Nick had defined in his mind. Nick hoped that something would come to him as he traveled, but his immediate goal was to get out of "The Heart of Darkness."

Unlike the un-beaten trail leading to Dom's dream church, the walk out of the city seemed longer than the walk into it. Though when he finally crossed over to the land of Caucasians, it was still mid-afternoon. But Nick could see by the muscle cars that cruised up and down the boulevard that the kids were getting ready for Friday night. Several times the occupants of these muscle cars would yell something that appeared to be directed to Nick as they drove by. It didn't seem as mean-spirited as verbal abuse Nick endured just outside of his home state, but Nick could tell that they were trying to get a jump out of him. And they succeeded.

Nick could have swore he saw Pedro's Malibu cruising along the boulevard. It was up at a light a few blocks ahead of Nick. Nick didn't notice it until it passed by him. He was very familiar with the back side of that automobile. But if it were Pedro, and probably Alyce, too, why didn't they recognize him when they passed? They may have never seen Nick in his gift parka before and didn't recognize him.

Nick had bypassed the McDonald's in his haste to flee the city. But even with another McDonald's waiting where the boulevard met "The Great Highway," Nick was already tired of the taste that he wasn't too crazy about in the first place. Instead, he ventured into a convenience store. Before entering, Nick dug into his sack for his bill fold. That's when he found out that his shampoo, which he haphazardly threw in his sack before hitting the road again, had spilled onto his dirty clothes and into his bill fold, drenching Nick's money. Nick was sure he could eventually save the bills, but they were probably too slimy and soapy to be used as legal tender at the moment. So Nick decided to do something illegal—he shoplifted a can of overstuffed beef ravioli.

Beforehand, Nick decided to leave his sack outside. Anyone coming into a store with a sack on his shoulders would raise suspicions, Nick thought. When

Nick departed the store with the can under the lower part of his parka with Nick's arm positioned in a way to keep it in place against his body without actually holding it—it was easier than Nick thought, and he already forgave himself in the name of necessity and was sure that God would do the same—Nick thought someone stole his sack, with the cleansed money and all. Nick was in a panic. His instantly thought that is was God getting back at him for blatantly violating one of his commandments. Nick once again came face to face with his sinfulness.

"Hey, is this yours?" a short, round black man said while emerging from the store with Nick's sack in hand. In one hand, that is, as Nick marveled by the way the man was able to hold it out and at shoulder level seemingly without much strain. "You left it outside, and I almost tripped on it coming in," the man lectured. "You're lucky no one stole it, especially with all these thieves around."

Nick had his sack and ravioli, too, but no place to eat it. Nick cursed himself for not packing any utensils, or buying—or stealing—any when he had the chance. Fortunately the can was designed to be opened by a pull ring so a can opener wasn't needed, but Nick figured he would have eat it uncooked and with his fingers. And Nick wanted a little privacy to do that.

But where could Nick go? Thoughts of reconciling with Elder Steven and taking up his generous offer began to crawl back into Nick's head only to have him shake them away, even in a physical sense as Nick noticed a car of curious teenagers gawk at him as Nick realized his shaking head probably made him look like a madman.

When Nick finally reached "The Great Highway," he had a decision to make. *Should I continue to go south or east, into places unknown, or west into places known but have since left behind?* North was already eliminated from the equation. After standing in place for about five minutes, Nick decided to go west. The thoughts of ringing up Elder Steven again persisted as Nick headed toward the apartment complex. It was late afternoon and, depending on Elder Steven's workload, he should be arriving at his apartment by the time Nick got there. Academy graduation was scheduled for the following afternoon, so Elder Steven may have been able to go home early or, then again, later if he was planning to attend some social event after school with the pending graduates.

Nick could wait a few hours or so—but NO! Nick started shaking his head again as he walked. NO! Staying with Elder Steven was out of the question. And once Nick finally reached that definite conclusion, he got an idea of where he was to eat and sleep: the junkyard across from the laundromat and tavern.

Nick never paid much attention to it other than acknowledging the fact it was there. Now it was going to be his residence. About a quarter of mile away from the apartment complex was a bicycle trail that went north and south and extended through five towns. Of course the path veered off when it approached the backlands of "The Heart of Darkness," but it didn't veer away from the expanded back end of the junk yard. Nick knew this from the walks he and Dom often took along this trail. Nick had suggested to Alyce and Pedro back when the fall was still bearable that they should walk the trails together while their laundry was in the wash cycle. But both insisted that there was work to be done.

Yeah, right—work to be done.

The only problem in getting to the bicycle trail on that side was that Nick had to walk through Elder Steven's apartment complex, where it was possible he could run into Elder Steven. He could enter the track by way of a nearby subdivision on the other side, and then cross over by way of the trail's tunnel under the crossroads. But Nick would have to walk an extra several miles to enter the subdivision if he didn't want to climb over fences and trespass through backyards.

Nick decided to go through the complex while avoiding Elder Steven's building. To Nick's relief, no midnight-blue Neon approached him.

Adjacent to the southern-most point of the trail was where the junkyard's chain-link fence with rusted barbed wired at the top came to an end, yet the junkyard itself continued for about 50 yards. Near the back of that open 50 yards was a silver Dodge minivan that, if it wasn't for an ominous indentation in the back that obviously breached the gas tank, it looked as if just came off the showroom floor. Nick only viewed it from the end of the trail, but he already determined that it was his new home.

Yet Nick wasn't going to move in to it in broad daylight. So he decided to walk back and forth along the trail until dusk or until the walkers and cyclists had gone away. When Nick finally was about to move in, he was happy to see that the vehicle's windows were intact, except in the back where the crumpled hatch back was without its window, yet remnants of the glass were not visible to Nick and probably left somewhere else. When opening the driver's-side door to place his sack inside, Nick could see by the back interior that a fire had razed through the van during the accident. The two sets of back seats had their coverings melted away, displaying charred springs. Amid the springs were ashes consisting of the charred remains from the inside of the seats and, perhaps, other things. The van's carpeting was gone, either burned away or removed, but the two bucket seats in the front were somehow unharmed.

Nick had an indication that the driver and a front-seat passenger could have survived the fiery crash. But of course, if there were only two passengers in the van, what was the sense of having a van in the first place?

While sitting in the driver's seat, Nick popped open the can of over-stuffed ravioli and began eating it with his fingers. It didn't taste as bad as Nick thought it would cold, but it was extremely messy. Nick's third white shirt was probably stained for good. After dinner, Nick adjusted the back of the seat to go all the way back and looked up at the stars, an act made easier by the long windshield that accentuated the van's sleek, aerodynamic design. *How long am I going to live like this?* Nick pondered, though again feeling the relief of alleviating his fatigue, didn't bother to dwell too deeply on his situation. To Nick's amazement, the van's power windows still worked. He decided to open the both windows in front to allow air to flow through the van while he rested and slept. One drawback, Nick thought, were going to be the mosquitoes. Since the back window was gone, Nick figured they would come in anyway. But for some reason, Nick had yet to be tormented by any, although he saw a few around the top of the windshield, seemingly trying escape but unaware of the true openings.

The gentle current moved through the van and caressed Nick as he gazed at the stars and grew more relaxed in nearly horizontal bucket seat. And when Nick fell asleep, well before the typical weekend revelers on the boulevard and even back at the academy had called it a night, he didn't dream of being at places he was no longer wanted. Instead, Nick became a spectator to settings and characters he was not familiar with, like he was watching a movie. But the movie had no plot, or at least no beginning, middle or end.

It centered around a blonde hair, pre-school-age girl. Nick watched the girl blow out candles on her fourth birthday—there were four candles on the cake. Nick watched the girl skip out of church ahead of her family. Nick watched the girl cry in her bedroom after being disciplined by her parents. The dream seemed too real to be a dream. In his state, Nick took note of the dream's uncanny details—like the colorful sugar-based sprinkles on the homemade chocolate birthday cake, the pre-school artwork posted on the refrigerator, the Sunday dress the girl wore to church and the barrettes that designed her hair, and the vast Beanie Babies collection that adorned all corners of the girl's bedroom—something he didn't expect his subconscious to create, or recreate.

But who was this girl? Nick never saw her or her family before, or at least he didn't think he did.

Suddenly, Nick woke from the dream after he thought he heard someone whisper in his ear just outside the driver's side door. Nick was startled, and opened up the door to see where this whisper came from but only saw the carcasses of other vehicles. Nick got back into the van and looked up at the stars again. Who was that girl? Nick thought and continued to think until he started to fall back asleep. But just as he was about to go under, that same whisper returned and Nick nearly hit his head on the windshield when his nerves propelled him out of his chair. This time the whisper didn't seem to come from outside, but rather from the back of the van. Nick looked back at the charred springs and ashes but saw no one.

That's when Nick became certain that he was in the little girl's tomb.

Nonetheless, Nick stayed put. He stayed awake until dawn, and then fell back asleep. When he woke again, the sun was well in the sky and Nick estimated it was a little past 10 o'clock. He could now see the full extent of his ravioli-stained shirt, and decided that he needed to do his laundry.

When Nick walked into the laundromat, he noticed that the evil counter lady worked on the weekends. But instead of casting her hateful eyes on Nick, she seemed to pay no attention when he walked through the double doors with his trusty sack over his shoulders. She even paid him little attention when Nick exchanged one of his cleansed bills for quarters. But when Nick went to the washroom after starting his load—he didn't have any detergent, but used the remaining shampoo for soap—he could see that the lady probably didn't recognize him. In fact, Nick barely recognized himself. Nick wore the parka and his cleanest pair of pants with nothing underneath just to prevent him from being naked while washing his limited wardrobe. Though Nick at this stage in his life was incapable of growing a full beard, the accumulation of facial stubble from a long stretch of not shaving had giving him a much different look. The stubble, like his pubic hairs, was a lighter shade of red from the hair on his head. Matched with his now severely sun-burned face, the stubble seemed even lighter and could even be mistaken as gray from a distance.

And Nick did feel like he aged a lot in the last couple of weeks.

Nick decided to view the academy's graduation ceremony while his clothes were being washed. They would probably be done and ready for the drier by the time Nick crossed the bridge, but the laundromat had the same hours during the week and Nick didn't have any other plans for the day, or for really any other day. Plus, it felt good to walk around again without his sack on his shoulder.

Nick got there just in time, and staked out a view from a drainage-ditch bridge south of the academy. Through the spaces between the willows from about 150 yards away, Nick could make out the ceremony but could barely make out individuals. He did see Elder Bingham because, during such events, he was hard not to see. But the grandiose stand from which Elder Bingham was perched from was not on the wooden island. Nick could only imagine that recent events on that wooden island may have corrupted it in such a way that it would never be used by Elder Bingham again, and was probably doomed for demolition.

Now the stand was placed in front of where the graduates received their pieces of paper. If past ceremonies seemed absurd, this one could be perceived as worse. The fountain was in play gain, but from where graduate family members and friends sat, Elder Bingham was behind the fountain and probably could only be seen through a thick film of sprayed water. But Nick could see him from his angle and was determined to catch Elder Bingham in the act of coming down from his perch.

Nick also tried to spot Elder Steven. He figured he would be somewhere among sectioned-off group of elders in attendance, but couldn't identify him from his distance. Nick also tried to identify the students he was friendly with, and tried to listen for their names when Elder Bingham announced their names from memory, but Elder Bingham's voice rattled through the trees and was intelligible.

Nick then wondered if anyone could identify him as he felt that fleeting sensation of being watched. Nick tried to direct his eyes where he thought theses sensations were coming from to maybe make eye contact with someone looking at him. But the faces were vague, and even the ones that looked as if they could be looking at him could not be verified because their eyes were too sunken in the distance.

Then Nick realized Elder Bingham was no longer on the stand. He missed him again.

From the top of the bridge the way back to the laundromat, Nick saw Pedro's Malibu in the parking lot. No doubt, this wasn't a replica.

Chapter Seventeen

Sure enough, Alyce and Pedro were back in town—if they had ever left. Apparently, they had little use for the academy's dress code. Alyce, who looked good no matter what code she was under, wore a burgundy T-shirt with the "Nike" swoosh boldly displayed across her chest. Talk about free advertising. But what really stirred Nick were Alyce's blue jeans. Nick had never seen her in such garments, and how they enviably hugged her lower body all the way down to her small white boots. Alyce wasn't wearing her pendant.

As for Pedro, he was also dressed in jeans, but his hung more loosely and his bell bottoms were frayed at ends and only covered the top laces of his gym shoes, which were Nikes by the way. Yet Pedro wasn't wearing a Nike shirt, rather a standard black-based rock-and-roll T-shirt which glorified Tesla. Nick always assumed Pedro listened to rock and roll music, and he even had a CD player in his Malibu. But Pedro never played CD's or even turned on the radio during the times Nick was a passenger. And Nick wondered if Pedro was really a Tesla fan, and if his clothing and that of Alyce were really theirs.

When Nick entered the laundry mat, both Alyce and Pedro seemed happily surprised the second they saw him. But Nick got the impression that they both saw him several moments earlier through the glass double-doors when he approached it straight on from the parking lot. Alyce was the first to greet Nick as she pranced over gleefully to give Nick a firm hug. Nick enjoyed the feeling of her body up against him, but when he tried to return a hug of his own with the same firmness, Alyced released much of her grip and gently pushed herself away to attain conversation distance.

"I didn't know if we would ever see you again," Alyce said while beaming her captivating smile. "Where have you been?"

Nick was happy that Alyce expressed concern about his whereabouts. But a troubling thought crept into Nick's mind as Alyce indicated that she, and probably Pedro, too, already knew about Nick's expulsion and, perhaps, the reasons for it.

Pedro eventually came over and shook Nick's hand with about the same firmness of Alyce's hug. The Tesla shirt fitted Pedro pretty well. His arms tightly filled the short sleeves, and the shape of his triangular torso was more defined with the shirt tucked neatly inside the jeans.

"What's up?" he said to Nick.

"I'm just doing my laundry," Nick said. "I just came back from the graduation ceremony at the academy."

"You mean they let you in?" Alyce exclaimed rather loudly. Now Nick was alarmed—they must know about his expulsion and, perhaps, the reasons for it.

"Yeah," Pedro said. "When we came back, they were real assholes to us."

Nick was dreading the thought of Alyce and Pedro knowing the details of his expulsion, yet quickly seized the opportunity to direct the subject to their plight.

"Why did you come back?" he asked. "And when?"

"Oh, it's kind of funny," Alyce said while looking about ready to blush. At the moment, Nick thought she was going start by relating the incident on the lake. "We decided to drive west into the setting sun—"

"Yeah," Pedro interrupted. "You know? To run and run to catch up with the sun."

Nick didn't really believe that the two were ignorant enough to think they could drive into the sun to prevent it from sinking. Then again for Nick to realize such an attempt was impossible was not from common sense alone, rather from his numerous trips back home from the academy. Neither Alyce's nor Pedro's families lived west of the academy. Alyce lived out east, and Pedro supposedly lived near in the southern part of the state.

But why weren't they with their families now?

"Of course, we couldn't catch up to it," Alyce said while smiling at Pedro as if to ridicule a preposterous idea—maybe her own. "But later we came back to get our stuff out of storage—" Alyce continued before Nick blurted an interruption of his own.

"You mean you have a place to stay?" he said.

"Yeah, yeah—but we'll get to that later," Alyce said. "But anyway, I realized I didn't have my pack of cards."

"Pack of cards?" Nick said.

"Yeah, don't you remember them from that game we played?" Alyce said. "They weren't in my dresser."

"Oh, them," Nick said. "I didn't know you were so fond of them."

"But they're BICYCLE cards! LIMITED EDITION!" Pedro said while mocking the implied importance of the pack. "I said, 'Jesus, we could buy a pack of cards anywhere.' But she kept insisting that they were a special edition, and that they were a special gift from some special relative."

Didn't Alyce feel the same about her now absent heart-shaped pendant? Nick wondered.

"So we went back to see if they had them. But they—"

"They kicked us out, and threatened to call the police if we didn't leave immediately."

"Yeah," Alyce said. "Can you believe that?"

As Alyce and Pedro folded their clothes—which were more abundant and colorful than the loads they used to wash, making Nick further wonder where they got them from—and Nick transferred his more-modest load to the dryer, they continued to catch up on things, although Nick deftly was able to keep the focus primarily on them. Nick learned that some time before being turned away without Alyce's pack of Bicycle cards, like himself they thought of seeking shelter at Elder Steven's apartment.

"But I said 'Fuck that,'" Pedro candidly remarked as he cast a long stare out into the parking lot. Alyce appeared to give a condescending look to Pedro, as if to accuse him of making something out of nothing.

"Yeah, 'Fuck that'—that's what he said," Alyce said, mocking Pedro. "But where could we go?"

Nick was compelled to ask them about why they didn't return to their families, or at least to one of their families. An answer from either would clear up a mystery, but Alyce continued the story.

"So we decided to look for a place," Alyce said. "But we didn't have much money for rent." Nick was compelled to clear up that mystery, too—where they got their money.

"But we came across this ad in the paper," Pedro said. "It simply stated that a guy was looking for tenants who could live rent free if they were willing to do maintenance and general work around his mansion, as well as…" Nick noticed Pedro's eyes momentarily rolling back into his head "…a few chores here and there."

"Mansion?" Nick queried.

"Yes, mansion," Alyce said. "You know, the one about five or so miles west up the road?"

Nick was familiar with the mansion, known by locals as "Kover Castle," perhaps after the surname of the person who built it, or bought it after it was built. It loomed over "The Great Highway" from its high-hill perch. It was barely visible from the road during the summer months with the full foliage from the property's hundred-year-old oak trees engulfing the entire structure, except for its turret and the turret's spire on the building's west side. During the winter or late fall, a portion of the mansion's face was visible from the road as the bare limbs offered a see-through screen while giving the building a gothic character.

Such character didn't go untapped. During Nick's first semester at the academy, several underclassmen on his dorm floor decided to visit the mansion when it was being rented out and dressed up as a haunted house for some sort of Halloween fund-raiser. Nick thought he was too old for such nonsense—he had since abandoned "trick-or-treating" before he was even in middle school—but went along anyway for camaraderie's sake. He didn't think any production consisting of cardboard decorations and settings complemented with actors in tacky makeup and costumes could ever get a jolt out of him. Even the times when five or six years old when he was taken to these haunted houses, Nick never got remotely scared.

That was the case for most of the tour through the mansion. Several youths about Nick's age at the time dressed as zombies, ghosts and monsters and rambled about the place, coming out of dark hiding places to make threatening and strange noises and momentarily grab people as they went by. Tours through the house went in foursomes with a hokey guide—Nick guessed the guy couldn't have been more than a junior in high school—dressed as a vampire with fake blood dripping out of his mouth leading the way.

Near the end of the tour, Nick's guide led the Nick's foursome into a small room. It was a graveyard setting with a prominent headstone in the middle with "Lucifer" scripted on it. There was no date of birth and death on the headstone, yet Nick didn't think that would be appropriate, let alone suggesting that Lucifer could even be buried in a grave. The room, or gravesite, was illuminated with a strobe light. A strobe light had been the staple and overused effect at the other haunted houses Nick had visited, but this was the only part of the tour where it was being employed.

There seemed to be something wrong, like the actor working in the room had missed his queue. The vampire guide stopped the tour and seemed to wait extra long for this Lucifer to emerge, no doubt, from the grave. Nick also waited while fixing his eyes on the Lucifer's headstone. Finally, Lucifer emerged. He, or she, was like your typical devil but with an element all of its own. Yeah, there were the horns and the spaded tail. Yeah, there were the fangs and the bat-like wings. Yeah, there were the goat-like feet and the talon-like claws. But this devil was green, an Earthly green illuminated brightly by the flickering strobe light. And when it approached Nick, the strobe light made it jump forward in seemingly unnatural increments, like it was being transported from one space to the next about five feet or so ahead a split second later. At first it seemed like it was moving in slow-motion, but before Nick knew it the creature was right in front of him hissing at him while displaying its pointed tongue through its fangs. Even the tongue was green.

Nick was terrified, but tried to keep his cool in front of his peers. But when he realized his peers and the guide had moved on to another part of the tour leaving him alone with Lucifer, Nick lost his cool. While letting a puppy-like yelp slip through mouth, Nick rushed toward where he thought the exit was, but encountered a wall and fumbled with his hands along the wall for an opening amid the flashing darkness and light. Nick heard Lucifer laugh in the background—a deep stock horror laugh, like the ones heard in B-movies of the past—before falling clumsily through a black-curtain opening. Nick saw his group several yards ahead about ready to be led into another setting, and hurried to rejoin it.

"His name is Leon Eldridge," Alyce said of the mansion's owner. "Isn't that a neat name?"

Leon Eldridge? Nick thought he may have heard that name before. But where?

"Yeah," Pedro said. "This guy is a total Jesus freak."

"Pedro!" Alyce chided, while playfully punching Pedro's thick arm. "He's not a freak. He's just an—an eccentric—an eccentric type, who is—"

"Really into Jesus," Pedro finished.

"So what's wrong with that?" Alyce said. "Aren't we all into Jesus?"

"But not like this guy," Pedro said. "But he's cool, I guess."

"What do you mean, 'you guess'?" Alyce said again while attempting another punch, but this time missing as Pedro was ready for it and took a step back. "And he's letting us stay at his mansion," Alyce said. "And all we have to do is several chores, but really not much."

Nick needed a place to stay, but didn't quite yet want to inquire if this Leon Eldridge was taking in more tenants. Instead, Nick asked, "How many people live there, besides you two and the owner?"

"Well, there's this one guy who has been there since we've been there," Pedro said. "That guy's a freak, too."

"Pedro!" Alyce exclaimed.

"I mean freak in a nice way," Pedro said while shaking his head. "I mean, they're nice people, of course, just in a freak kind of way."

"Pedro!"

Pedro smiled as if to admit that he shouldn't be taken too seriously.

"And there are a couple of other people," Pedro continued. "They seem to come and go. People our age, maybe a little younger. I suspect they are the type that gotten into fall-outs with their parents, and need a place to stay."

Nick definitely fit that bill.

"But we're pretty much moved in," Alyce said. "We've got the whole basement to ourselves." Alyce then cast a look out of the corner of her eye at Pedro. "But there are other rooms, much better and cleaner in the place, but he insists on sleeping in the basement."

Nick thought Pedro might take time to explain his preference, but he didn't.

"By the way, where are you staying?" Alyce asked Nick.

Nick had to think momentarily before attempting to answer. "Really—eh—nowhere."

"Nowhere?" Alyce and Pedro said in unison.

"Well, I've been staying at a hotel," Nick said.

"Uptown?" Alyce asked.

"Yeah, uptown," Nick said. "But I'm still looking—

"Why don't you move in with us?" Alyce said. Like when Elder Steven made a similar offer to Nick, it was music to his ears.

"Oh, but I don't know," said Nick while trying to conjure up some fake resistance, like he wasn't as desperate as he really was. "Are you sure this guy wants another stranger living in his house?"

"Hell, there's a different stranger every week, or at least that's what it seems," Pedro said.

"Come on, Nick," Alyce said. It pleased Nick the way she was pleading for him to come with them. "Everything is going to be all right with Leon, or Mr. Eldridge. I like to call him Leon, though."

Nick agreed to come to the mansion in the prospect of becoming a rent-free tenant. But he sensed that he had better address the owner as "Mr. Eldridge" upon their first encounter.

Once again, Nick was relegated to the back seat of Pedro's Malibu. But he wasn't alone. Apparently, Alyce and Pedro did some shopping beforehand—one of those required chores?—and packed the goods in the trunk. Their laundry loads were stacked on the seat and floorboard next to Nick, and Nick had his load in his lap. As usual, Pedro aggressively weaved in and out of traffic at a high speed just to be the first car stopped at the red light at the intersection most tenants in Elder Steven's apartment complex use to go in and out of the place. The delay at the light visibly irked Pedro, who remarked "Come on!" twice as if he had a tight schedule to keep.

"Say, why didn't you look up Elder Steven for a place to stay?" said Alyce, who may have been prompted to ask the question by the complex's vicinity.

"I…I… " Nick started to answer "I did," but caught himself just in time. "I thought about that, but I…I didn't want to impose myself on him."

It was a goofy explanation, and Nick knew it, especially when he was on the verge of imposing himself on a complete stranger, whoever this Leon Eldridge was.

Finally, the light changed and Pedro gave praise in his own special way— "Jesus Christ!" When he was the first one at line at the next red light, Nick had a chance to inquire more about Leon Eldridge without contending with a fuel-pumped engine.

"So this guy owns a mansion," Nick said. "What does he do?"

"For a living? Who knows?" Pedro said and offered no further explanation.

Alyce shed a little more light. "He's an artist," she said. Pedro let out a "guffaw," as to dispute such a claim.

"He is," Alyce said to Pedro before turning back to Nick. "And he's a good one, too. I don't know if that's what he does for a living, but you should see some of his work.

The light turned green. And Pedro's luck changed dramatically as he got every green light en route to the mansion's arched entrance just off the crossroads. The trees were filling out, but there was still enough gaps between the leaves to make out most of the mansion's face from the road. The mansion was still graced with a gothic foreground, but now with bold strokes of green.

If everything went as smoothly as suggested, this was going to be Nick's new home.

Chapter Eighteen

Pedro drove the Malibu through the entrance and up the property's pathway. The engine turned quiet enough to resume conversation. Still not too sure, Nick again queried about this total stranger who would no doubt take him in, no problem.

"You're as good as already moved in," Pedro said before glancing back at Nick. "Really. He'll take in a mass murderer if he's willing to cut the grass."

"Pedro!"

The winding pathway deteriorated as it ascended. What was solid asphalt at the entrance became broken and more broken before transforming to gravel and then just plain dirt and mud the higher Pedro's Malibu chugged up the grade.

Through the trees, Nick studied the looming mansion as the pathway approached it from the east. Now at closer range, the mansion reminded Nick of eccentrically designed houses that were typical in various affluent neighborhoods he was familiar with back in and around his hometown, except this was a scaled-up version. The front of the varied stone-cut exterior mansion mainly consisted of three gigantic triangular dormers reaching out from the marooned-shingled gable roof. *Is this Leon Eldridge another flawed triangle subscriber?* Nick thought. The two on the sides were smaller than the one they flanked, and both had big double-paned windows that rounded off at the top while completing semicircles. Same-shaped shutters accompanied windows, and with their solid black color, stood out prominently against the light-brown stones in the bright sunlight, as both sets were open.

The middle dormer had a giant rose window near the top. Nick tried to better study the design but couldn't get a good look as the car continued up the hill while passing a cluster of oak trees that obscured the view. Through various openings, Nick saw how with protruding thrusts, the middle dormer maintained its shape down to the mansion's entrance, which consisted of two mammoth doors shaped liked the double-paned windows and, from Nick's vantage point, appeared to made out of solid wood with long handles a big-levered knockers on each side that appeared to be made out of brass, or something of the sort.

On the sides of the doors there were long strips of glass, which appeared to be stained, but Nick couldn't tell from the distance. There were other strips of window on the mansion's broad face, ten of them about a foot wide and about a foot and a half apart on each side of the giant triangle. The pair of five outer strips were about eight feet long, and the five inner strips on both sides tapered from the bottom in accordance to the protruding triangle. These windows looked like they had standard glass, but perhaps darker than normal, as if they were smoked or had shades covering them from the inside.

Nick took note of the mansion's front porch, which appeared to be out of the same type of various stones. All these stones, of course, could be fake. Nick was able to get a look at the impressive winged griffins perched at the top of the porch's stairs about 10 feet in front of the doors. The porch didn't have any railings, but appeared to have some at one time, as indicated by the series of brick posts with concrete spheres the size of medicine balls on the tops and urn-shaped balusters in between, but nothing connecting them.

As the path leveled off and continued past the mansion, Nick saw the huge base of its chimney that could only indicate a huge fireplace inside. The chimney itself rose about 10 feet above the highest point of the roof, and the porch appeared to encircle the building. But Nick was unable to track the porch's extent as the pathway veered further away from the mansion and deeper into the trees before making a long loop toward the back of the house.

Nick couldn't remember if this was the way his freshmen acquaintances took en route to the mansion when it was a haunted house. In fact, Nick couldn't remember much about that night other than his encounter with Lucifer.

"You should see the big painting he made," Alyce said while looking back at Nick. "It's the first thing you see once inside the front entrance—that is if you could enter through the front entrance. But anyway, it's an awesome painting of him and Jesus."

Him and Jesus? Awesome? Nick noticed Pedro roll his eyes.

Soon they were at the back of the mansion. The dirt road returned to gravel and ended in what looked like a makeshift parking lot ten yards from the building. Stationed there was a 1969 Chevelle that could have been any color at one time but now donned a permanent shade of rust. There were several other cars, much newer models with their body paint intact, but looked about as reliable.

While looking at the mansion's backside and scanning the backyard, Nick could see that there was a lot of work to be done as well as the grass needing to be cut. This side of the mansion seemed non-visible from any part outside the general property, and that was probably a good thing. There was a hip dormer at the top with two square windows. Directly below were a boarded-up door and two boarded-up windows looking out at a balcony, which had the same unconnected urn-shaped balusters except some were broken in half and others seemed to be missing altogether.

Below and to the left was a glass-encased room. Nick could see one glass plate was cracked and the room's tattered screen door appeared to be the only back entrance other than the balcony door. Nick also noticed a garden hose that snaked into the glass room through the ajar screen door.

The porch almost did encircle the mansion before steps on both sides came down to a peanut-shaped in-ground pool and its orange-tiled deck. Though summer was fast approaching, there was no water in the pool. And from the black grime of aged algae that draped down its faded-blue sides, Nick got the impression that there hadn't been water in it for some time, nor was there going to be in the near future.

Just before Nick exited the car—he waited for Alyce and Pedro to exit first—he saw who he thought had to be this Leon Eldridge. Yet he didn't really imagine him to look this way. The man was tall, well over six foot and perhaps even closer to seven, and bone thin. He wore dark blue jeans and had a work shirt that matched their color. He looked like he could be in his 40's, or maybe even in his 50's. There were speckles of gray in his dark hair, but his beard seemed to have retained much of its original color. And the beard was the most striking feature about this man other than his height in Nick's eyes, as it nearly engulfed his entire face before stopping more than halfway up his cheeks. A little higher and he could have passed for a giant wolf man. The man was using a sledgehammer to break up the orange tiling around the pool. Either it was a renovation project or a demolition one. Whatever, the man appeared focused on what he was doing as he repeatedly slung the hammer as high as possible over his head before violently pounding it on the crumbling surface. He seemed to pay little attention to the return of Alyce and Pedro, but when Alyce greeted him while taking a laundry basket inside the mansion, the man stopped to acknowledge her with a brief smile before continuing his work.

Just then, Nick noticed that Alyce brought his sack, which she placed on top of a laundry basket, into the house. That just made him more uncomfortable. Nick thought at least Alyce would introduce him to this Leon Eldridge before helping him move in. Nick was hoping Alyce would soon emerge from the house to do what she should have done earlier, or that Pedro would introduce him. But while still waiting for Alyce to return and seeing that Pedro had popped the hood of his Malibu to check his engine for some reason, Nick realized that he probably should introduce himself.

"Excuse me, excuse me," Nick said while cautiously approaching the man. The man stopped his assault on the tiling to let Nick continue his introduction.

"Hello. My name is Nick. And I'm a friend of Alyce and Pedro. I was told that you need some help around here, and I'm willing to do whatever that you deem fit to be done. I…I…I promise you that I'm not a free-loader."

The man took a long look at Nick as if he was weighing the proposition. Then his reached out his right hand.

"Pleased to meet you, Nick," the man said with a deep and virtuous tone, like a voice-over from a Cecil B. Deville movie. Nick could sense by the firmness of his handshake that he had great strength in his bone-thin body. "My name is Jack. But I believe the man whom you are looking for is Mr. Eldridge. And Mr. Eldridge is inside."

Jack then resumed his work.

Nick took a few steps back to give Jack more room than he needed and tried to look inside while waiting for Alyce to return. He thought about going over to Pedro is see if he needed any help, but it would have been a fruitless act because Nick didn't know squat about cars, as well as barely knowing how to drive them. Instead, Nick continued to survey the backyard and the surrounding property, and he thought he saw a young man and woman frolic amid the trees in the distance.

Finally, Nick saw Alyce emerge from another door leading into the glass room. Using both of her hands, Alyce tugged in a playful manner a man's arm to bring him outside. When they both emerged, Nick saw that this guy was about Pedro's size, except a little chunkier, and had an unusual hairdo— although nowadays it was hard to tag any hairstyle as unusual. But Nick never saw this design: a shaved head complemented four thick dread locked strands which started from points on the top and the sides of his head and draped down to his shoulders. They made this guy's classically handsome square-shaped face seem even squarer, and more classically handsome.

He looked as if he could be still in his 20's, or maybe into his 30's. And he wore a scripted black T-shirt. The script was encircled with a slash running through it. He obviously was protesting something, but Nick didn't take immediate note of what it was as he and Alyce approached him. *This must be Leon Eldridge*, Nick thought.

"This is my close personal friend, Nick," Alyce said while releasing the man's arm. The man then offered his freed arm to shake Nick's hand. Like Jack's, the firmness of his handshake indicated great strength.

"Any friend of Alyce is a friend of mine," he said with a slight drawl, the type Pedro should have had if he really came from where he said he came from. "I've heard a lot about you."

"Hello," Nick said. "You—you must be Mr. Eldridge."

The man smiled, indicating that Nick did address the right man this time around.

"You—you do go by that name, don't you?"

"To tell you the truth, I prefer to go by my full name," Leon Eldridge said. "But I let some people, like Alyce here, just call me Leon. Jack over there tends to call me Mr. Eldridge"

"Well, I'll call you Mr. Leon Eldridge," Nick said. Leon Eldridge and Alyce both laughed.

"Nick will be staying here for a while," Alyce casually said. Nick was stunned at the nerve of Alyce inviting someone into someone else's house, but Leon Eldridge relieved his tensions.

"Good, good, good," Leon Eldridge said. That was more music to Nick's ears. "We need more people like you around here. We really do."

Leon Eldridge smiled while showing his teeth. Like Alyce's, they seemed perfect except for one of middle incisors appeared to be made out of diamond. Leon Eldridge's eyes were dark blue, which didn't seem to match his hair which, with closer inspection of the stubble—Nick wasn't sure that the dark-colored dreadlocks were real—appeared to be brunette, or at least a very dark shade of brown. Leon Eldridge's eyes had a distinct quality about them. They were inviting, yet penetrating. Nick got the feeling the deeper he was drawn into them, the deeper they looked into him.

"Thank you, oh thank you," Nick gushed, even though he initially tried to keep his gratitude subdued. "I...I..."

"I'm sure you'll like it here," Leon Eldridge said with his open smile still intact. Leon Eldridge had indicated that he was somewhat familiar with Nick, and expressed confidence that their pending relationship would be a good one.

But Nick got the feeling this Leon Eldridge was still trying to look deep into him while coaxing Nick to do the same to him.

"You don't know what this means to me," Nick said. "It's that I'm in a, eh…" Nick lowered his eyes to read the slashed wording on the shirt, which made him stop in mid stutter. "Dark Matter" was being slashed. A protest of its existence? *How strange*, Nick thought.

Nick also noticed Leon Eldridge's small but distinctive crucifix, which was made up of two miniature spikes fused together.

"We all get into binds," Leon Eldridge said. "I understand."

Nick smiled, but remained focused on the slashed "Dark Matter."

"Well," Nick said. "I guess I should help Alyce and Pedro unload."

Nick then walked over to the car where Alyce had already resumed taking in the loads of laundry. Pedro had stopped looking at his engine and was unloading the bag of groceries out of the trunk. On the way inside with two bags in his hands, Pedro stopped to say something to Leon Eldridge.

"Sorry Chief, but you may find this hard to believe," Pedro said. "The Sunday edition of the paper you wanted was already sold out. And it's still Saturday."

Leon Eldridge laughed a little before, as if needed time to contemplate what Pedro had just told him, breaking out into a hysterical laugh that seemed to come deep from the groin and was loud enough to echo off the glass room and the surrounding trees. It was enough to grab anyone's attention within cannon shot, except maybe Jack who seemed not to notice as he continued to smash the tiling. Then Leon Eldridge abruptly stopped his laughter and looked at Nick, now carrying one of the laundry baskets, with that diamond-tooth smile.

How strange, Nick thought.

Chapter Nineteen

There were no eccentricities amid the mansion's back portion, just mainly abandoned dust in the wake of an unfinished project. Indeed, there was work to be done.

The project had yet to reach the mansion's kitchen, modest in size with no stove or refrigerator. The glass room door led into it. Piss-colored sections on the kitchen's white-tiled floor indicated the former presence of appliances. The only visible items that could be used for cooking were a small microwave oven—maybe good for heating ravioli—and a two-pan hot plate—maybe good for cooking ravioli—stationed next to each other in the middle of a long black countertop. Neither heating nor cooking appeared to have been done recently as the kitchen looked unused. If there were any pots and pans, or forks, spoons and knives, they were in the white-color-tile-matching drawers and cabinets, which were all closed.

Alyce was leading Nick to his room, which was on the same floor as the kitchen and located on the opposite side of the house's back portion. On the way, Nick took note of the loose wiring and unfastened light switches that branched out from some of the partially demolished walls, and even from several non-demolished ones. While they walked, Nick's dress shoes and Alyce's small sexy boots made echo sounds with every step on the wooden floor. On the way—Alyce started leading Nick the same way she brought Leon Eldridge outside, by tugging his arm, but had since set Nick free and walked briskly several feet in front of him—Nick stopped at a window he didn't note from the outside. It would have looked out at the same floor level of the porch, that is if the porch had completely circled the mansion. Instead, it provided an overhead view of the pool, further revealing its sordid state. Dead oak leaves adopting the same color as the aged algae, forming a thick black carpet on the pool's graded bottom. Near the rim, Jack had stopped his sledgehammer and was engaged in what seemed to be a serious conversation with Leon Eldridge. Jack was doing most of the talking as Leon Eldridge nodded his head several times in response. Then suddenly as if he knew they were being watched, Leon Eldridge looked up at Nick and again displayed that smile. Nick smiled back, then quickly went to find Alyce, who continued her lead despite Nick's pause at the window.

Several walls that still stood impeded a would-be straight path to the other side of the house. As Nick looked around corners for Alyce, he noticed several tool boxes and their contents strewn around one room which, before having a wall knocked out, must have been two rooms. He also noticed the overhead lights fixtures were removed. Light bulbs in their bases descended to eye level from wires that dangled from crude holes in the ceiling.

Soon, Nick heard Alyce call out his name and they found each other again.

"Where did you go?" she asked.

"I don't know," Nick said. "You could really lose yourself in this maze. You probably shouldn't have let go."

Nick had hoped she would take his arm again. Instead, she turned to go through an already opened door to a room that still had all of its walls intact.

"This is where I wanted to stay," Alyce said. "But Pedro insisted on sleeping in the basement."

Apparently, the two were still sleeping together.

"So I guess you're the lucky one."

Yeah, right.

Nick thought the room was rather small and cozy considering it was in a mansion. Like the twisted path that led to it, there was no carpeting in the room. But there was evidence it was carpeted at one time as Nick noticed several bent U-shaped nails sticking out of the wooden floor. And like the remaining walls Nick saw on the way, the room appeared to have been wall-papered at one time as white patches and strips of torn but still pasted on paper remained — all the coloring and decorations were apparently peeled away. Like the other and former rooms on the way, there was no furniture, excluding a wooden framed bed with a wooden headboard adorned with flower-shaped carvings. The bed's mattress had a purple covering, and there was an un-sleeved pillow and a neatly folded brown blanket on top. Also neatly folded on the mattress were Nick's clean laundry as well as his trusty sack, which still had several of Nick's personal items, including his wallet and money inside.

There were no light bulbs hanging from the crude holes in the ceiling, but an expensive-looking lamp with an emerald-colored shade was on the floor near the outlet it was plugged in. The outlet was bare and emerged from a crude hole in the wall.

There was also another window that Nick didn't note from the outside—he couldn't have due to the obstructing trees—that looked east and faced the bed located on the opposite wall. There were no curtains on the window, and that concerned Nick. Anyone walking outside on the porch could look inside and directly at the bed. And someone facing up in the bed could look directly outside. Nick looked outside the window to scan the wooded view beyond the porch before turning back to notice that Alyce had departed.

That day Nick found no proof that the mansion was haunted. But it sure was infested—with a horde of intimidating wasps. They were nested somewhere within the structure of the building, and they remained active at night. Whenever a light was turned on in one of the rooms, they congregated around it after emerging through one of the crude holes. Nick always had a slight phobia of flying insects that sting, and had hoped that they wouldn't find away into his bedroom at night if he decided leave the lamp on.

But at least it was better than shacking up in a junkyard.

Later that night, the wasps, Nick, Alyce, Leon Eldridge and several of whom Nick thought were the other occupants in the mansion convened in the glass room. Seated in folding chairs and lawn furniture, Nick, Alyce, Leon Eldridge and three other people formed a semicircle around a small electric-filament heater. It was an unseasonably cool night. Jack wasn't among the group. Either he was inside the mansion somewhere, or he lived off campus, so to speak. Nick still didn't know much of the setup of the place and its people.

As for the three strangers, to Nick they didn't look like mass murderers. Nor did they resemble Jesus freaks, rather burnt-out and ambitionless teenagers. Leon Eldridge introduced Nick by name to the group, but didn't tell Nick their names. Maybe he was expecting them to do that themselves, but none of them bothered. Granted, they weren't entirely uncivil. Each of them looked up from their slouched positions and acknowledged Nick with thin smiles, but with no words or handshakes. They gave such brief glances in his direction that Nick didn't get a chance to learn the colors of their eyes. But that would have been difficult anyway because—unlike Leon Eldridge's captivating stare—all their eyes seemed to be sunk well back into their sockets.

Even while wearing his parka that covered his standard academy garb, Nick immediately got the feeling that the strangers thought he was a square.

As for the whereabouts of Pedro, Nick thought he saw him working on his car with the aide of a floodlight near the makeshift parking lot. But Nick couldn't tell for sure as condensation blanketed the glass room. Maybe Pedro just didn't want to hang out. Maybe he thought the strangers themselves were squares.

One was a somewhat attractive but compact girl with frizzy black hair and wearing a blue and white-designed flannel shirt. Nick thought he may have seen her earlier that day in the woods, but he was conscious he may again be filling gaps in his memory. She was seated between Leon Eldridge and the guy Nick thought he saw her with. He had long red hair, longer than the girl's, and had thin arms accentuated by a black tanktop vest he wore. Apparently, the cool weather didn't bother him. Nick assumed the two were girlfriend-boyfriend. Then again, maybe the girl was Leon Eldridge's girlfriend, since she positioned her folding chair closer to Leon Eldridge's reclinable lawn chair.

Alyce was on the other side of Leon Eldridge, and Nick was seated next to Alyce.

As for the other person, Nick was certain he never saw him before. He looked a bit older than the other two, as indicated by his short balding blond hair and his roundish figure. He seemed more aware of the cold as he wore a shining royal jacket that commemorated a team's adult league championship of some sort. The Brewster Boys was the name of the team. Whether they were a softball, baseball or bowling team, the jacket—at least its front side—didn't indicate.

The guy in the jacket served two purposes at this mini-party. He manned the cooler filled with green-bottled Moosehead beer while distributing them to the two other strangers when needed. All three also smoked cigarettes and used emptied green bottles for ashtrays, although much of the ashes ended up on the porch's stone-designed surface where the room was built over. Leon Eldridge and Alyce were not drinking or smoking, and of course neither was Nick, who never understood how anyone could bear the rancid taste of beer, or could inhale cigarette smoke. Yet Nick still remembered the pleasurable experience when he smoked that joint, despite the eventual consequence.

The guy in the jacket's other purpose was to operate a boom box, which he did in an irritating fashion. He was constantly changing stations while searching for songs to fit his, and his only, fancy. Even when he finally settled on a tune, the guy's attention span seemed limited as he rarely let the song finish before hastily feeling the knob for another. The red-headed guy eventually took issue with this.

"Why can't you stay on one fuckin' station? And what the fuck's the matter with your CD player?" he asked.

"I don't fuckin' know," he answered. "It's the fuckin' change in the weather, going from fuckin' hot to fuckin' cold all of a fuckin' sudden. It must have made it all fucked it up inside for some fuckin' reason."

Nick thought the strangers' salty language made that of Pedro's seem like, well, like that of a soul-winning missionary—a more stereotypical one, that is.

"And all the shit on the radio, especially the new fuckin' shit, is, you know, fuckin' shit."

Just then, a radio DJ announced an exclusive new release.

"See what I mean?" the guy in the jacket said while turning the station before a note was aired.

"But don't you like at least some new music?" the girl asked. "Like your CD collection has a lot of new bands in it."

"Yeah, but good new bands."

"But how did you find out about these new bands?" the girl continued. "I mean, you have to had given them some chance at one time. You have to had listened to them for the first time."

The guy working the boom box seemed perplexed and fumbled for a response in the same manner he fumbled for songs.

"I have never liked a song the first time I fuckin' heard it," he said, prompting laughter from the two other strangers. Even Nick thought the explanation was amusing.

"That doesn't make any sense. Then what makes you go out an buy new music?" the other guy asked.

"I don't fuckin' know," the boom box guy said, now laughing at himself. "It's like a hear a band, or hear a fuckin' song, and if I like it, it's because I heard it before somewhere from some place, but I can never pin down when or where. It's like deja fuckin' vu."

The other two strangers laughed again, and Nick laughed with them because what was proposed seemed so absurd. Then Leon Eldridge spoke.

"You're right," he said. "It is deja vu." Leon Eldridge's evaluation sparked silence instead of laughter, until Alyce spoke.

"But how can that be?" she asked. "If you like a new song, it's because you either like it immediately, or you like it later after it grows on you."

"And if even if you don't know when or where you first heard the song," the other girl said while seeming to compete for Leon Eldridge's attention, "you probably remember its beat or tune subconsciously in your head, and when you hear it again you instantly remember it even though if you still don't know exactly when or where you first hear it."

"So you believe things like deja vu simply come from our subconscious?" Leon Eldridge responded.

"Yes," Alyce and the girl said in unison, but the subsequent expressions on both their faces didn't display much conviction. "At least I think so," the girl opposite Alyce meekly added.

Leon Eldridge eased back deeper in his reclined chair. He was wearing a blue jacket that was halfway buttoned down revealing a shirt that featured an angled and partial closeup of Saturn and its magnificent multicolored rings. The shirt had a black but starless base, and Nick became drawn to it because Saturn was his favorite planet ever since the academy set up a telescope in the middle of the lake for students to view it at an opportune time. While looking through the telescope for the first time, Nick saw Saturn's rings as a straight line dissecting a sphere.

The shirt provided a better view. Nick took note of the depictions of the planet's moons Prometheus and Pandora serving as inter and outer shepherds for the F-Ring. How they weren't a part of the ring itself Nick could never figure out. And while studying Leon Eldridge's shirt for a possible answer, Nick realized it was a holographic image, except an inverted one that made that portion of Leon Eldridge's chest collapse in on itself.

Leon Eldridge looked at Nick and said, "What's your take on this?"

"W-W-What?" said Nick, while snapping out of his trance. At first he thought Leon Eldridge asked him about the moons and the rings, but remembered the topic of conversation. "I don't know much about music. But you say deja vu is not a product of our subconscious?"

"I didn't say that," Leon Eldridge said. "But does it always have to be?"

Leon Eldridge then smiled at Nick in the same way he had done numerous times before. Nick mulled his mind for a proper way to continue the conversation, but he was drawing blanks. So instead he changed the subject.

"I'm sorry, I don't want to get personal or anything, but where did you get that diamond tooth?" Nick said.

Leon Eldridge leaned up in his recliner to get closer to Nick and curled back his upper lip for Nick and all to see. "It's not a diamond, it's a sapphire," he said as his curled-up lip slightly altered his accent.

"A sapphire?" the girl opposite Alyce said. "But it's clear like a diamond. I thought sapphires were supposed to be like colored, like the rings on that strange shirt of yours."

"Strange shirt?" Leon Eldridge said. "It took us a lot work to make this."

Nick instantly wondered who 'us' were. "But no, sapphires can be virtually any color, even a non-color like this one it, except red."

"But why a sapphire?" Alyce asked.

"Because it's such a fascinating and mysterious stone," Leon Eldridge said. "Do you know they're on the verge of making a living computer, one that is actually a sentient being? And you know what the chips and circuitry are going to be made out of when they do?"

"Sapphires," Leon Eldridge answered himself rather loudly. "They possess the quality and complexity of life."

Then Leon Eldridge got up from his lawn chair. For the first time, Nick noticed that he was wearing sandals. Leon Eldridge walked over to a section of glass where most of the wasps gathered. Nick marveled at his fearlessness when Leon Eldridge positioned his face several inches from one climbing to the top. He seemed to study the insect as it moved upward.

"Don't you find it peculiar the way they can walk up a surface, a surface that is slippery and wet, the same way we can walk on the Earth?" Leon Eldridge asked out loud.

The group again had a bout of silence. However, the boom box still played, now finally fixed on a song. It was from Tesla, and Nick—perhaps realizing it for the first time—liked the song.

Chapter Twenty

 Speaking of Tesla, for church the following morning Pedro wore that same shirt, still smeared with jet-black grease especially visible on the artwork and lettering. Didn't Pedro have a fresh load of clean laundry? Maybe Pedro was planning to do more mechanic work that day. Maybe that's why they chose to ride with Jack, the owner of that rusty Chevelle.

 Alyce, for one, was back in uniform with her blue overall dress and white shirt. As for Nick, all that was missing was his tie—he didn't pack any. Jack wore one that, like the Pedro's grease smears, was jet-black and barely noticeable from a distance as it blended in with Jack's deep-blue denim shirt, which was paired with his deep-blue Dockers. His hair and beard were combed. He still almost looked like a giant wolfman.

 Nick got up early that morning. Shortly after the gathering dissipated the night before, Nick retired to his room. The feel of the firm mattress after the night in the burned-out minivan soothed Nick upon falling back on it. He turned off the lamp when, to his dismay, it did attract wasps to his room. A low-hanging full moon managed to beam through the crevices of the oak leaves and into the room, providing plenty of light for Nick to scan the pasty walls and ceiling, and to see the nails in the floor, but not enough for the wasps who left for other parts of the mansion—though for awhile several miniature hour-shaped silhouettes trekked the window the same way that earlier caught the interest of Leon Eldridge.

 Even with enough ambiance to read large type, Nick fell asleep within minutes. Whether he stayed asleep until morning was something Nick wasn't sure of when morning came.

 Sometime during the night, Nick thought he saw a figure on the porch staring at him through the window. For some reason, it didn't alarm Nick the way he thought it would, and he kind of expected it. Also, Nick found himself in a relaxed state of mind, so much so that the setting seemed surreal to him. Nonetheless, the vision prompted Nick to go to the window when it disappeared the split second Nick thought he saw it. Nick looked out at the porch and into the trees in the background to spot the figure, or at least signs of movement, with the aide of the full moon and the property's other pole-elevated floodlight located northeast of the mansion and angled to illuminate the mansion's face, but saw nothing. Later that night, Nick thought he saw the figure again, which again instantly disappeared like a phantom. Still not too alarmed, Nick wanted to investigate again, but the extra sleep under his belt discouraged him from leaving the bed, although his nerves weren't as relaxed as before.

Just then it occurred to Nick that his first vision may have been a dream, as well as his act of investigating it. Yet this second vision, despite its fleeting presence, seemed more vivid in comparison, and Nick's state of awareness seemed more weighted with gravity. Going to the window this time around surely would not be a dream and could possibly reveal the intruder, who surely must be real. So Nick, managing to conjure enough energy to arise, crept up to the window, this time much slower than before, to possibly catch this figure by surprise. As he got closer, Nick crouched down to keep his head lower than window. Then he got right under the window, and on a mental count of three, popped up only not to see anyone or anything. Nick could hear his heart beat at an excited rate.

The next time Nick woke up, it was caused from the rising sun making its way to the window. The sunlight was sprinkled in small blotches that, while dancing with the shadows molded by the swaying oak leaves, resembled animated diamonds—or animated sapphires—when the window's glass caught and enhanced the bits of brightness. Nick wondered about his visitor, yet noticed the blanket and his laundry were still folded on top of the bed and under his prone body, indicating that he slept on them all night. And Nick's trusty sack was at the foot of the bed. Nick then began to suspect that both visions at the window as well as Nick's motions afterwards were dreams, figuring he would have taken time on either occasion to remove the items, or at least unfold the blanket, before lying down again.

Alyce was in the front seat with Jack, who had to hunch his neck forward slightly to give himself enough headroom. Pedro was in the back with Nick. It was unusual to see Pedro in the back seat—at least while traveling. As for the car, despite its exterior and interior—its vinyl bench seats were torn in the front and especially in the back where its crumbling spongy foam insides spilled out—the car seemed perfectly operable by the sound of its engine, which purred like a well-maintained sewing machine.

Nick asked Alyce if Leon Eldridge was coming with them. Jack answered for her when he said, "Mr. Eldridge prefers to worship the Lord in his own way."

Alyce asked Nick about his first night at the mansion. At first, Nick was going to mention his visions at the window, but thought better of it. After all, he wasn't sure they were real, and if they were—who knows? Jack could have been the culprit. It didn't look like he lived off campus as Nick "remembered" seeing his rusty Chevelle still parked in the lot the night before. Instead, Nick related his sobering shower experience earlier that morning.

As far as Nick knew, there was only one working bathroom in the entire mansion. It was located adjacent to the kitchen, and was rather small with a shower stall instead of a tub. There was no running water inside the building, hence the garden hose, which went through the kitchen—where it probably sometimes was used—and into the bathroom—where it probably often was used. For water to flush the toilet, it was placed in tank. To take his shower, Nick hung it over the shower curtain and used its spay gun. The water was cold, and it didn't help that a steady outdoor breeze, still nippy for that time of the year, found its way through the crack in the door that made way for the hose.

"If you want warmer water," Jack said, "you might want to take a shower late in the afternoon, like I do."

Like I do? Nick hoped Jack preferred to take showers alone.

"With water still in it, you roll up the entire hose in its coil out back…" Nick instantly "remembered" seeing the coil, which consisted of an upright big wheel drum with a handle to rotate it, near the pool the day before. "… if the day's conditions are right, put it out in the sunlight so the coiled hose and the dormant water inside of the coiled hose will heat up," Jack said.

Jack didn't look back at Nick while he was talking, or even into his rearview mirror. Instead, his remained focused on the road in a trance-like stare. It was like he didn't want to deter from total concentration for concern of making even the slightest driving mistake.

"Of course, this won't work if someone needs water for the kitchen or cleaning, or for urination or defecation."

Pedro chuckled, apparently amused by the use of the word "defecation."

"You know that Jack here used to work for NASA?" Pedro said to Nick.

Nick's was initially impressed. "Ain't that right, Chief."

Nick heard Pedro call Leon Eldridge "Chief" several times the day before. Nick had a passing thought of there possibly being too many chiefs and not enough Indians—or make that American aborigines—at the mansion, but he was more interested in Jack's alleged work at NASA.

"Really?" Nick said. Jack seemed to pay no attention as he was still focused on the road.

"I was meaning to ask you, what did you do at NASA?" Alyce said.

"Oh, just a lot of math," Jack said. He did deter his forward stare to take a glance at Alyce.

"Was it, eh, hard?" Nick said, knowing instantly that he just asked a stupid question.

"I imagine you have to take a lot of schooling to get into NASA," asked Alyce, whose question wasn't much brighter.

"You need to have acquired plenty of knowledge, that's for sure, and be willing and able to acquire more," Jack said. "But you've got to be careful. Sometimes the knowledge they try to put in your head is not always correct. And if you don't have the discipline needed to unearth the inherit truths of right and wrong, this so-called knowledge can lead you astray, tormented by the flames of ignorance."

Near the end of his explanation, Jack raised his deep voice an octave, like he was no longer in a movie but in a theater play that required characters to project themselves. Nick noticed Pedro rolling his eyes.

Aside from its reliance on a garden hose, another unique thing about the mansion's mini-bathroom was its two mirrors. One naturally was located over the sink. The other was on the wall directly across from the sink's mirror. It was as wide as the former, but longer, starting from about foot from the floor and reaching the same height level. And it wasn't flush to the wall, rather extending out at an angle of less than 10 degrees. It was a deliberate angle as Nick noticed the thin wooden triangles that were fastened to the wall and mounted the mirror at the top and bottom.

What purpose was this setup? Nick didn't try to guess. But he was slightly intrigued and surprised by catching an un-reversed and non-staring-back image of himself in the background while trying to shave with cold water. He also noticed to his amusement how his image was copied and scaled down as it traveled back to, presumably, infinity. Yet, due to the angle, Nick only saw six scaled-down images of his himself before the lineage was cut off from view.

Because Nick couldn't see the continuation, he wondered if that disqualified infinity as a destination.

The church was painted bright white with a small steeple. It was some sort of "reformed" institution, as advertised on the heading of its marquee, which message walked the fine line between clever and lame—"Seven days without prayer makes one weak." To Nick, these reformed churches seemed to be in vogue for the last two decades, or at least since the time he was born. Other than the Stars and Stripes draped from the ceiling right of the altar and about the same size of the replica Jesus on the cross, the church resembled the one Nick and his family often showed up late for back home.

Yet the replica Jesus was portrayed a little different. Blood streamed from his wounds—Nick's family's church had a Jesus with wounds but no blood. And Jesus' face was grotesquely contorted in agony with his tongue hanging from his mouth.

But no triangles in sight, thank God.

The foursome were seated in their wooden pew a couple rows back from the front a good 15 minutes before mass started. Pedro had the aisle seat with Alyce next to him. Nick was on the opposite side of Alyce, and Jack was seated next to Nick.

While looking over the congregation, Nick realized that Pedro wasn't really all that underdressed. More than several of the parishioners, mostly the younger ones, donned blue jeans, athletic shoes and casual shirts and sweaters—some of which glorified various sport teams and others that were (enough already!) scripted with snappy sayings and boasts. One guy who was probably 13 or 14 years old had a shirt that featured a foreboding and muscular basketball player with a head but no face. Granted, it wasn't entirely out of place because the script that complimented the figure advised, "Go to church and pray you don't have to guard me."

As for the mass itself, it didn't seem much more reformed than a typical Catholic mass Nick's family used to go to. The first part consisted of relating scriptures from the New Testament, but the second part went right into the standard group prayers and rituals that, in a normal Catholic setting, take place after the priest's sermon. It was only until those two parts were concluded that the priest gave his sermon, which was considerably longer than the ones the Catholic priests at Nick's family's church used to give.

Maybe that's what made this church a reformed church.

As for the priest, he reminded Nick of Dom. He was about Dom's size, except for his black hair, and about Dom's age, give or take a couple of years—

most likely "take"—if Dom were still alive.

Was this his church? Nick thought while being reminded of Dom's ultimate goal before his untimely death. Or was he one of several priests on staff? Nick's family's church had more than one priest.

Before his sermon, the priest walked down the aisle and greeted several parishioners with handshakes and small talk. One of the first people the priest encountered was Pedro, who seemed at first not wanting to shake the priest's hand only to give in when the priest didn't withdraw his offer.

"Glad you could come here today," the priest said to Pedro. "Nice shirt." Either the priest was being sarcastic, or he got into Tesla.

The priest continued such banter with other parishioners for a while offering several jokes that all got a good laugh out of the audience. That's the thing about priests or other revered religious figures: they could always get a favorable response no matter how corny their efforts were. Elder Steven's Moses-Jesus joke may have been the only exception.

Nick assumed the priest was the author of the message on the marquee.

After the social hour concluded—it wasn't really an hour, but to Nick it felt like one—the priest positioned himself in front of the altar and finally began his sermon.

"Can you believe the weather today?" he said. Nick thought the priest was still caught in a small-talk rut, but soon learned that it was his introduction. "I thought, with a little precipitation, I could build snowman out front."

The audience laughed. As for the weather, it was still unseasonably cold, although the day was picturesque and the sun shined brightly with no clouds to obstruct it. Nick didn't notice much of the cold despite not bringing a jacket. After his bone-chilling shower, Nick's skin and nerves must have toughened up. But Pedro at least seemed bothered by the weather as he folded his arms tightly to seemingly fend off the slight current that drifted through the building.

"It just goes to show you how inexact and unpredictable our world really is," the priest continued. "All this science and technology, and I didn't hear one weatherman or one extended forecast that said it was going to be 48 degrees today, or even during this time of the year.

"When I was young—well, it isn't like I'm quite ready for the retirement home [group laughter]—I used to sometimes dream of it snowing this time of the year. And you know, these dreams used to always disturb me. They were my worst nightmares. Of course, many of you are probably thinking that I used to get spooked pretty easily since snow in June shouldn't be something to get too worked up over. But the thought of such a thing happening really terrified me, no lie."

During his sermon, the priest paced back and forth, about the length of the altar, which was on a platform about three feet above where the priest was pacing. He stopped momentarily while pausing after admitting that the possibility of snow in June terrified him. Then he continued pacing and talking.

"Why did it terrify me? Because during my dream I felt something was out of order. Something was terribly wrong."

Another pause.

"Rest assured, I don't think it's going to snow today, or for at least another four or five months. I can't guarantee it, but let's just say I have great faith that it won't. I'm sure these weatherman and meteorologists could provide you with more concrete and scientific reasons for this. But really, do they really know what they're talking about?

Another pause, then the priest answered himself. "Of course they do, at least in the context of what you and I know about the weather. They understand the general order of weather, although they will be the first to state it's still very unpredictable, it's still very chaotic when it wants to be.

"Chaos," the priest continued. "We live in a very chaotic world. In fact we came from a very chaotic beginning, that's where I will agree with all these experts."

Nick glanced over at Jack, who stared at the priest intensely, much the same way he stared at the road while driving. But Nick thought he caught him nodding his head slightly.

"Yet somehow order tends to prevail," the priest said before pausing. "The question is, of course, where does this order come from? Some experts have come up with some fairly plausible explanations, and they could be on to something. Who knows? I'm not one to say they're wrong. I don't have the knowledge they possess. But I have to admit that I'm a little skeptical about these subsequent theories that often pop up, or these added buttresses, so to speak, that are almost required to support their previous theories.

"But what about this dynamics of order emerging from chaos? And what about the order that sometimes graces our lives? Where does it come from? What is its origin? Could it be eternal love?" Pause. "Of course, I'm just throwing it out there. Yet I get the feeling there are some skeptics in this audience who think I'm off my rocker claiming that this dynamic principle could be based in love. Just let me give you an example."

The priest called to a young male parishioner in the front row who was wearing a Dallas Cowboys sweatshirt.

"I take it you're a Deion Sanders fan," the priest said.

"Sanders doesn't play for the Cowboys anymore," the kid said while sparking some laughter from the audience.

"He doesn't?" the priest said. "That's why I don't do so well in football pools."

More laughter, even Nick laughed a little. Pedro and Jack had remained stoic through the schtick. Alyce sometimes smiled, but never laughed.

"I don't know if you saw this, or read about it," the priest said while addressing the youth in the Cowboys sweatshirt. "You may not care since Neon Deion…" the priest raised two pairs of fingers to represent quotes around "Neon Deion," "… no longer plays for your team, but from what I understand he recently went through a major transformation. I think some you, with the possible exception of this young Cowboys fan, may know what I'm talking about."

Instead of laughter, Nick heard a muffled grumble amid the pews. Apparently, not everyone—if they were familiar with "Neon Deion"—were convinced of this major transformation.

"Neon Deion lived the good life, or what he thought was the good life. He was rich, he was famous, he was good-looking, and he took advantage of such traits by being an unapologetic adulterer. In other words he led a chaotic lifestyle. But, as some of you well know, something happened. Something unexpected, yet, if you're familiar with the plight of man and woman, you could say was expected.

"He surrendered himself to Jesus," the priest said before pausing. There was some more grumbling, but more muffled.

"I get the feeling that some of you take a somewhat cynical approach to this story. Maybe time will tell how committed Deion Sanders is to Jesus and His Father, and his—Neon, that is—new way of life. But these stories are not uncommon. They happen everyday, to people like me and you, not just superstar quarter—what position does Sanders play?"

"He plays several positions," the youth in the Cowboys sweatshirt said.

"You see, that's why I don't do well in football pools," the priest said sparking what had become predictable laughter.

"But adulterers, alcoholics, drug addicts, those afflicted with depression—those whose lives are in complete chaos either have one of two things happen to them. Either they self-destruct or somehow order comes to their lives. And this just doesn't afflict the reckless, but the mild-mannered as well. Take Sanders' former coach Tom Landry–

"Landry wasn't the Cowboys' coach when Sanders played for them," the youth boldly interrupted. Of course, the laugh-in continued.

The priest looked up in the air while gyrating his upward palms near his ears. "Let me guess—it's baseball season, right? At least I think I know that. It just feels like football season."

Now even Pedro was laughing. Not Jack, though, nor the tongue-waggin' Jesus.

"But these people are continuously saved from despair and self-destruction by these abrupt collisions with clarity, with order, with eternal love that derives from something all these just-the-facts experts seem to have great difficulty grasping or defining. It happens too often for there to be nothing to it. Yet it has to be accepted and surrendered to for it to be truly experienced.

"You just have to believe that no matter how crazy this world gets with the unpredictable predicaments it throws at us, love will find a way."

Hey, maybe the priest did get into Tesla.

The priest went on and on for about another ten minutes on this theme, often reiterating points he previously made. Nick's attention began to fade, and he sensed Alyce and Pedro were also starting to drift. When the priest gave another example of a celebrity who achieved clarity after chaos, Nick saw Pedro roll his eyes. Yet Jack remained upright and focused.

Finally, it was time for communion. Nick was familiar with the ritual from his hometown church. There wasn't such a ritual at the conclusion of Elder Bingham's so-called Sunday masses at the academy, and that was probably a good thing. Nothing could have been more daunting than to approach Elder Bingham to receive the body of Christ, if you so happened to be in his dog house at the time. Who know? He could decide to deny the wafer if he felt you weren't worthy of it. No doubt, Elder Bingham was more than capable of inflicting such humiliation.

When one of the church's valets came to the foursome's pew, Nick, Jack and those right of Jack got up to enter one of two lines to the priest and his big golden grail of wafers. All in the pew participating in communion had to negotiate past Alyce and Pedro, who both remained seated. Nick wondered if Alyce and Pedro knew of the ritual. They may not have if Elder Bingham's masses were the only ones they ever attended, yet Nick assumed they were repeat visitors to this church. When Nick got outside the pew, he looked back and asked if they were going, which they apparently weren't going to do. Alyce looked straight ahead as if she didn't hear the question. Nick stayed back a little longer while letting Jack go ahead of him to ask the question again. Pedro then answered, "I don't know where that guy's hands have been."

As was the case at Nick's church and the church that truck driver formerly went to, there were two ways to accept wafers from the priest. You could either allow the priest to place the wafer on your extended tongue, or you could accept the wafer in your hands and then put it in your mouth yourself. Jack, who was now ahead of Nick, preferred the former. Then, instead of looping around the pews and re-entering from the opposite side, which all the communion-accepting parishioners were doing on both sides, Jack took couple of steps opposite to where he was supposed to go and ascended halfway up the series of stairs leading up to the altar's platform. Jack took a knee on one of the stairs and crossed himself, and then in a rather ostentatious manner, doubled back down the aisle between the two rows of parishioners and out the doors. The priest took note of this as indicated by the wry grin he gave Nick before he gave him his wafer. Nick took it with his cupped hands and fed it to himself.

After communion, the priest called on a Cub Scout in full uniform to lead a standing recital of the Pledge of Allegiance.

While on the way to Jack's car, Nick asked why Jack left early. Neither Alyce, who ignored the question like the previous one, nor Pedro answered. Nick decided that he shouldn't press the issue, but when Jack pulled out of the parking lot, Pedro said to Jack, "Hey, Chief, Nick here wants to know why you leave church early."

Nick fumed and he glared contemptuously at Pedro.

"I chose not to honor a symbol of an standing entity that brazenly rips life from the womb of its mother," Jack said, sounding again like a theater actor. After Jack's dramatic explanation, Pedro rolled his eyes—he seemed to do a lot of that lately.

While pulling into the parking lot in back of the mansion, Nick saw that Leon Eldridge—who supposedly was worshipping the Lord in his own way—was doing his laundry and was in the process of hanging it out to dry on a line that extended from two trees. During the course of the mass, the weather had righted itself as much of its seasonal warmth (or order) had been restored just in time for Leon Eldridge to dry his laundry. Nick saw the inward-dimension jacket/sweater as well as the slashed dark matter shirt, and another scripted shirt in the same vein that stated "Dark Matter is Dead."

And among those on the line was another shirt with an illustrated slashed circle, except there was no script inside. Instead, it was the face of Albert Einstein.

Now Nick rolled his eyes.

Chapter Twenty-one

The following day was stormy with rain-driven gusts. Nick had planned to cut the property's overgrown grass, but that would have to wait.

Nick was conscientious of earning his keep, though no requirements were outlined. Not only was Nick living rent free, but also eating for free. In the kitchen coverts was a well-stocked supply of microwave-ready soups and canned foods—yes, there was ravioli—and Nick first helped himself after returning from church Sunday and being coaxed by Alyce, who insisted that he shouldn't be bashful. The times Nick fed himself, he made sure he thoroughly cleaned up, although washing the pans, bowls and utensils was done with the cold water from the hose and without any dish soap—Nick couldn't find any—so Nick wondered how effective his efforts really were.

That Sunday after his first free meal, Nick thought best to help Jack with his work around the pool. No one asked him to, but Nick was eager to show his worth. He shoveled the smashed tile into a large wheelbarrow which, when full, Jack wheeled it down a small ramp leading to a double-wooden-door basement entrance on the west side of the mansion. Nick didn't know where this smashed-up tile was going, or even if it was going to have another use. He was just content that he was doing something and that Leon Eldridge, who was in and out tending to his peculiar laundry on the line, noticed he was doing something.

When he saw Nick with a shovel in hand, Leon Eldridge smiled that smile, and Nick smiled back, this time with an authentic gesture. Nick was starting feel comfortable at his new "home."

The job didn't last long. Even with some broken tile remaining, Jack eventually didn't return from the basement. He didn't tell Nick he was done.

In fact he didn't say much during the task, except "Thank you" when Nick offered to help, and a little exchange afterward. When Jack was busting up the last intact section of tiles with his sledgehammer, Nick noticed small sparks emerging and immediately disappearing upon impact.

"Why does it spark like that?" Nick asked, assuming Jack should know the answer.

"It's a matter of matter turning to energy and back to matter again," Jack said. Even while talking, Jack never abated from breaking up tiles and producing sparks.

"I didn't know that was possible," Nick said right before he looked over at the Leon Eldridge's laundry line and saw the back side of the scripted and illustrated shirts with the white-based "Dark Matter is Dead" shirt being transparent enough while waving in the daylight to read in reverse.

"It happens all the time," Jack said.

After Jack left for the last time, Nick stayed in place for a good 20 minutes waiting for what he thought would be at least one more return. He even had a shovel full of tile already scooped up and ready to be deposited.

While waiting, he studied Pedro who was working on his car. He thought if Jack failed to return, which seemed imminent after over ten minutes, he might lend Pedro a hand. But as stated before, Nick knew little about cars and he soon sensed that Pedro didn't want to be bothered or helped. Nick thought he saw the tiny hairs on the back of Pedro's neck stand up, like the back hairs of a dog warning not to approach it. There seemed to be something else on Pedro's mind other than car woes.

Now, even with no outside work possibly on the agenda, there was definitely plenty of interior work to be done. Nick was equally as anxious to help out with that, even though he knew as much about carpentry as about cars. Still, he could be a "gofer," as in "Go for this." Yet for some reason there was no one doing any interior work that day, at least on the main floor. Moreover, the mansion seemed deserted, although Nick knew it couldn't be as the cars parked in the driveway indicated there were people somewhere in the house, probably including Leon Eldridge, though Nick didn't know what car he drove, or even if he owned one.

Not content to stay in his room and read the Bible which he inadvertently packed in his sack while leaving the hotel, Nick decided to venture to other parts of the mansion he hadn't previously. Heading due north from his southeast corner room, Nick at first came across more of what he saw before—stripped down rooms with several walls, lighting and electrical fixtures missing. Eventually, Nick made his way to the front part of the mansion and came upon a giant room that appeared to be fully renovated. There was no furniture in the room, but it seemed like it didn't need any, like it was supposed to be a big open ballroom that could accommodate nearly 100 guests with enough room to gracefully move around. The walls on all sides were painted white in the same brightness that graced the church Nick had just gone to, and the wall's brightness of the walls and the storm-diluted daylight coming through the thin-stripped front windows reflected off the impressive finish of a brown parquet floor.

Hanging from the middle of the room's high ceiling was a spectacular chandelier emblazoned in what had to be crystals, or diamonds (or even sapphires). There were three levels of candle-designed bulbs resting in a multi-scalloped bobache. Looping around and within the structure were numerous strands of flickering and linked diamonds (or sapphires). The way the strands intersected each other made them appear to be tangled in some spots. But to Nick, perhaps influenced by the previous day's sermon, there appeared to be "order" amid the arrangement.

The chandelier was something most would expect to be in a house as grand as this. And so was the fireplace. That was adorned with gold-colored andirons and a Victorian grate—who know? Maybe they are gold. Contrasting the gold were upright black iron tools, and a white cast stone mantel and its overmantel that blended into the wall. After checking his shoes, Nick walked over to the fireplace and noticed that it had been used as indicated by the charred ashes inside. It also looked as if it was recently used with ash-outlined footprints near the grate. Maybe Leon Eldridge used it to heat up the water to do his laundry the day before.

While leaving the ballroom, Nick noticed how by walking by the strips of window gave them the illusion of a being a drapeless picture window, a similar effect of a observer in motion looking through a slim-slitted shadowbox or picket fence.

Funny, Nick thought, how the strips gave him a whole yet water-blurred view of the outside from the inside, yet greatly shielded the inside from the outside. And the glass, at least from the inside, wasn't smoked. However, the true weather outside was obscured as Nick didn't realize how violent it was until he came upon the mansion's front doors. As Alyce had told him before, you couldn't use the doors because their brass indoor handles, which resembled the ones outside, were tied together with a thick-linked chain that appeared to have no lock but was tied together in such a firm and tangled mesh that it probably didn't need one.

There was enough slack to allow the doors to buckle inward in a manner that gauged the power of the storm's wind. It seemed as if some desperate intruder of was trying to break in. Nick felt portions of the storm's water and wind that filtered through the slight opening and closing of the buckling doors.

Nick almost continued past the doors, but something caught the corner of his eye. It was something he was curious about the moments before entering the house for the first time, but had since slipped his interest. It was the painting Alyce had told him about.

It faced the double doors on a wall that made up the width and length of the rather small foyer (about 12-by-12 feet) and extended to the top of the mansion's giant dormered roof. The painting traveled with it, all the way up from the floor to the tip of the triangle. There was no electric lighting in the foyer, at least none that Nick could see, as the only light source came from that which spilled over from the ballroom and the other adjacent parts of the mansion, and that provided from the giant rose window above the double doors and the slitted windows next to the doors. Nick assumed on fair days sunlight would shine through the rose window and slitted windows to better illuminate the painting.

The storm's dreariness didn't do much help, but there was still enough light for Nick to study the painting. Much like commissioned paintings for the wealthy during the Middle Ages, this one had Jesus and the mansion's alleged owner Leon Eldridge—both at about half life size—together and linked with the right-hand grips. The setting appeared to be somewhere east of the mansion and near the bottom of the property's hill as indicated by the dark shape of the mansion upward in the distance. It looked like the setting was at night, but Nick noticed no stars or moon near the top of the painting above the trees.

Nick saw that Jesus was helping Leon Eldridge up the hill's steep grade. Jesus was depicted as a stereotypical Jesus with his long hair and beard, and robe and sandals. Leon Eldridge, from what Nick was able to see despite the lack of light, was wearing a similar robe. The four-corner dreadlocks were also in place.

From what Nick could see, it appeared that Leon Eldridge had some artistic talent, but the painting didn't enrapture Nick the way it apparently did Alyce. Perhaps that was because Alyce may have first viewed it with the sunlight of the beautiful day beaming through the rose window. Nick could imagine how those beams would be refracted from the window's glass, and outline magnificently the borne particles in the air. That would probably give it a more of a spiritual quality. To possibly experience that, Nick figured he would have to view the painting again with better incoming sunlight.

Nick soon came across another painting project, but this appeared to be more practical. While leaving the foyer and heading toward the western front part of the mansion, Nick couldn't help but notice a narrow hallway right of the painting. One side of the wall was painted a light shade of green, an odd color especially with the white brightness of the ballroom nearby. The other wall, the one perpendicular to the painting, was unpainted and stripped except for blotches of yellow paste and white paper, like most other walls Nick encountered in the mansion.

Judging from what he saw in the hallway, Nick assumed the wall had been painted recently. Covering the hallway the floor was a stained canvas anchored by a pair of black cylinder containers on each end of the hallway floor. Also on each end of the floor were two high-powered lights. Nick initially thought the lights were being used to make the paint dry faster, as the smell of fresh paint indicated that it was recently applied. But upon further review, the lights didn't look like what Nick thought paint-drying lights should look like. Rather they resembled footlights from of a theater stage. And the lights were focused near the center of the wall with about the half of their circular projections overlapping each other.

Maybe that part of the wall was where the newest paint was applied, Nick thought, although that wouldn't have been a logical sequence for the project.

Across from where the projections overlapped was a door-less entrance to a room. Nick tried to angle his neck to see what was inside this room, but only saw darkness. Just then something entered Nick's mind. Nick had since realized that any effort to retrace the steps he and his associates took through the mansion while it still was a "haunted house" would likely be a waste of time. So far, Nick recognized nothing from that outing, and expected not to. But somehow Nick got the feeling that inside that room was where his confrontation with Lucifer took place. Nick had a slight temptation to investigate what was inside, but the canvas on the floor indicating a project still in progress gave Nick of an excuse to hold that off for another day.

Yet from the outside Nick could see that the room didn't take a full rectangular shape. At the other end of the hall, the unpainted wall tapered downward with the wooded rails and steps of the mansion's main stairway.

Soon Nick came across the mansion's elevator while continuing his looping tour of the house. It was located along the western wall, or what seemed to be the western wall, and at first Nick wasn't sure what it actually was. Thick stainless steel borders surrounded and extended slightly from it double doors, which were black. On the right-hand side, there were two buttons with arrows pointing up and down. Overhead was a red rectangular light. It sure looked like standard elevator, but something you would see in an office building, not in a house or even a mansion. Heck, there weren't any elevators at the academy despite some of its dorms being four stories high with basements.

Partially thinking that elevators couldn't exist in a house, even a mansion, Nick thought it could be an elaborate entrance to another room. But taking a second look at the arrowed buttons, Nick realized that it couldn't be anything else other than an elevator. Surely though, it couldn't be operable, especially in a place with no inside running water. Yet Nick had to find out for himself, and when he pushed the arrow pointing up, he was surprised to see it light up. A few seconds later, the red rectangular light above turned on while being heralded with a bell, which also surprised Nick. Then the doors opened, and Nick, somewhat bravely, walked in.

Just inside the door there was another pair of arrow buttons. Nick waited for the doors to close, but it came apparent that they would only do so if he pressed a button again. Nick was going to go with his original choice—up—but decided to change it to down when he remembered that he had yet to see where Alyce and Pedro were sleeping together, and there was a good chance that both of them were down there.

The doors closed the second Nick pushed the down button. Then he could feel the slight tug of his innards when the elevator started to descend. During his brief trip, Nick noted how well the elevator was maintained, at least from the inside. Overhead, there were a pair of fluorescent lights shielded by a white plastic covering. Nick noticed several wasp silhouettes in motion on the other side of the covering and wondered how long they would survive while being baked by the fluorescent lights.

Just then the doors opened. Nick instantly saw that the basement was probably the most dilapidated floor in the mansion. Puddles of standing water formed in spots along the uneven concrete surface, and along the northern wall where it appeared to be several inches deep. Nick was also enveloped by a strong moldy smell that immediately besieged him when the doors opened.

To Nick's right and several feet from the elevator, there was a wall about 15 feet long with scaffolding sections leaning up against it. Nick assumed the scaffolding probably was used for the giant painting in the foyer.

Unlike the dead silence above, the basement was filled with sounds of people and activity. Nearby, Nick could hear a jumble of quick conversation consisting of bits of laughter and cursing, and the impact and echo of an object smashing into other objects. People were bowling in the basement.

Despite the sound, Nick didn't discover the activity until emerging beyond the wall on his right to get a full view of the basement. It was cavernous, but aside from those from the room next to the elevator, there were no walls. Instead, thick-rounded beams all placed within 20 square feet of each other provided the support. But even with the thick beams all about, the basement seemed wide-open and virtually empty which gave Nick a queasy feeling that there wasn't enough support to keep the mansion from collapsing in on itself.

Making the setting even more foreboding was the light arrangement that, in Nick's imagination, seemed the type that illuminates dangerous coal mines. It consisted of an array of standard light bulbs inside upside down silver saucers. These saucer lights were fastened on four-by-eight wooden boards that ran north to south on the basement's ceiling and were in the center of each four-beam square. About a third of the lights were either burned out or simply not working. And giving it more of a cave-like feel, the basement had no windows.

Nick didn't notice any duct work for central heating. Before even walking into the place, Nick had an inclination that the mansion had no air conditioning. Now he had good reason to believe it was not equipped for heat other than portable electric elements and the fireplace. But winter was well off, and Nick was confident that either he wouldn't be still living there by then or, if he were still around, a sufficient heating system would be installed by then with help from fellow rent-free tenants.

As for Alyce and Pedro's room, it was more like a tent and was located along the east wall. For the room's other three walls, bedsheets were nailed to the ceiling boards near the back wall and tied to the top of two nearby beams, and another sheet went from beam to beam completing the square. From an opening between two sheets, Nick could see Alyce's cherry-wooded amoire and a large plastic cooler. It was becoming obvious to Nick that if you wanted to keep edible and drinkable things cold while residing at the mansion, you'd need a personal cooler.

The people down there were Pedro, Alyce and the two male strangers Nick sort of met his first night at the mansion. They were bowling—the males were, that is—on a pair of lanes starting from near the southeast corner of the basement, several yards away from Alyce and Pedro's room. The wooden lanes as well as the wooden approaches were raised about a foot from the concrete floor by what appeared to be six or seven layers of wood. Also on the elevated base were a scorer's table and two anchored seats. There were no other seats, except an old couch behind the scorer's table and just off the elevated base.

From the bulky contraption with tangled and broken belts off to the side of the lanes' back pit, Nick imagined at one time these lanes operated the same way at local alleys—felled pins automatically getting scooped up and placed in a triangle-shaped steel rack before lowering down to the pin deck for the next bowler. But now it was all manual. The system they employed was to have the bowler who had just finished his frame go down to the other end and man the pit and rack. When a 10-pin rack was ready to go, a lever was rigged to lower it in place and then raise it. The person also had to return the ball by rolling it down a small but steep grooved slope that flattened out between the gutters of the two lanes. The ball then would have enough momentum to ascend up another steep slope and onto a holding tray near the scorer's table.

The pit consisted simply of a black tarp wedged under the end of the lanes and raised to a two-foot level by a U-shaped rail embedded into the floor about five feet behind the lanes. There were no outside gutters, unless you considered the puddled basement floor the gutter.

As for the lanes, only the one furthest from the wall was being used. The other lane seemed beyond repair. Its center boards were worn white and formed a noticeable bowed channel from the spot arrows several feet in front of the foul line all the way to the pins. The other lane was much better preserved as the ample helping of oil made the lights overhead reflect brilliantly off its tanned boards.

Pedro, with his blue jeans and white T-shirt, looked like a taller version of James Dean. The red-headed guy was dressed in a dingy flannel shirt unbuttoned near the top uncovering a black-based shirt with some art and/or script on it—probably another rock and roll shirt. The balding blond guy was more conservatively dressed with a light-blue collared shirt that looked about a size or two too small, and loose-hanging dress pants.

Alyce, of course, was the one who stood out. She wore a dark-blue jersey with white circles around the shoulder. It was a size of two too big, probably someone else's jersey, but when Alyce, who wasn't bowling yet served as the official scorekeeper, reached up near the top of the table from her seated position to record a score, it stretched out the jersey in front while gripping her bosom. There was no number on the front of the jersey, but there was one on the back: Pi. Amusing, Nick thought, yet not entirely original as Nick had seen examples of pi jerseys before.

When Nick approached the foursome, they appeared to give him little notice other than slight nods of the head. Even Alyce seemed reticent, yet showed some surprise when her eyes grew wider for a split second after first seeing Nick. She may have wondered how Nick found his way to the basement without any guidance. While glancing at the scorer's table, which had a half-used stack of tear-away score sheets, Nick was hoping to discover the names of the two strangers. But all Nick could tell was that the balding blond guy went by "Rock N' Roller," and the red-hair guy's moniker was "Sugar Daddy." Pedro, who was listed third on the sheet, went by "Pedro"—not "Peter" of course

Nick sat on the couch with Pedro. Nick could tell by its pungent smell that the couch endured considerable water damage. While glancing back at the makeshift tent bedroom, Nick wondered if Alyce's armoire was safe in the basement

Rock N' Roller and Sugar Daddy didn't rest on the couch between turns and pit shifts. Rather, they hovered around Alyce at the scoring table while instructing Alyce how to add up the pinfalls. Rock N' Roller was especially "helpful," although Nick was suspicious of other motives. If Pedro was also suspicious, Nick couldn't tell as he just looked forward at the pins in the distance while drinking from a bottle of Moosehead. Rock N' Roller, with his personal cooler, was again supplying the drinks, although he didn't have his boom box with him.

"The scoring system in bowling is probably the most perfect in sports," Rock N' Roller said while explaining how to add up strikes and spares to Alyce, who seemed attentive yet confused. Her neat handwriting was evident, but because she used an eraser-less pencil the frame boxes were littered with crossed-out numbers and corrections.

Rock N' Roller appeared to be the best bowler among the trio. He was a left-hander with an efficient pendulum backswing and follow through. His ball had a custom finger-tip grip that enabled him to put enough lift and angular rotation to get it to hook toward the headpin after banking the gutter. And he apparently took the game seriously, as he not only had his own ball and accompanying double-ball bag, but also his own bowling shoes. Pedro and Sugar Daddy simply wore gym shoes, which were a great detriment as they would often stumble at the foul line after releasing their shots when their front feet stuck instead of gracefully sliding like that of Rock N' Roller.

As for Rock N' Roller's ball, it was a piece of art. Its outer shell was made of some light orange transparent substance revealing an inner core that was shaped like a spiky star. The star was bright red and sparkled when in motion. While traveling down the lane, the ball's inner star gave the illusion of tumbling back from where it came.

In addition to bowling in gym shoes, Pedro and Sugar Daddy also had to share the same ball, which was black and had noticeable scuffs and gouges on its surface. It also fitted their hands at the second knuckle of their middle and ring fingers. It apparently was a "house" ball. Nonetheless, Sugar Daddy, a right-hander, was able to make the ball hook to some extent. Pedro, also a right-hander, threw a straight ball with a slight reverse rotation.

All three were able to hit the headpin on most of their first balls, but strikes were infrequent and many of their leaves were nearly impossible to convert. Rock N' Roller was having the best success, but he wasn't without reservations. He was having a hard time keeping his ball from hooking away from his intended target, the 1-2 pocket, and when it once got too much of the headpin he only managed to knock down four pins. That even amazed Nick, who had remote knowledge of the dynamics of the sport.

But Rock N' Roller had since diagnosed the problem and took it upon himself to fix it. While heading back to man the pit, he took a can of oil and paint brush located on the side of the inactive lane and, while kneeling in the two inside gutters, began applying oil to the spot where his ball usually began its break. Rock N' Roller applied it with long back-and-forth strokes using nearly the same pendulum motion he used while bowling. Nick wondered if he was involved in painting project upstairs.

Sugar Daddy, who was the next bowler, was pissed by the delay.

"Come on! That's the second fuckin' time this game," he said while maintaining his "gutter" language.

"You want this lane to end up like that lane?" Rock N' Roller said while pointing to the respective examples.

"There's already plenty of oil out there," Sugar Daddy said. "And if you don't agree, real fuckin' bowlers adjust."

"Quit your fuckin' bitchin'," Rock N' Roller said. "This only affects my side of the lane."

"The hell it does," Sugar Daddy said. "The motion of your ball moves it to our side."

"Then like you said, real bowlers should adjust."

When Rock N' Roller came back, he leaned over the scorer's table to check Alyce's scoring which again was flawed.

"You see after a strike, you've got to add the sum of both balls," he said with his blond hair nearly touching Alyce's.

Now Alyce was pissed. She bolted from the chair and exclaimed, "I'm sorry, I'm sorry. I tried to do my best, but I just can't please everybody." And then she said that she was going upstairs and headed toward the elevator while not looking back. All four watched her leave before Pedro got up from the couch and threw what seemed to be a sure strike ball only to leave the pin in left corner—the seven pin.

"Don't worry, that's why you get two chances in this game," said Rock N' Roller, who now was keeping score.

When the ball did come back, Pedro quickly snatched it before it reached the top of the returning slope and, without hesitation, fired a spare attempt with placement and speed being virtually the same as his first ball, thus not coming close to the seven pin.

Nick could tell by the scoresheet that the threesome were nearing the end of their game. Nick thought about asking if he could bowl if there was going to be another game, but wasn't too sure because bowling—like playing basketball—had always been a humbling experience for him. To beat the heat during the summer, Nick and Dom and sometimes Dom's girlfriend at the time would go bowling. Nick could never break 100, but usually carried on like he didn't take the game too seriously while quelling any mounting frustration. Dom, on the other hand, seemed to be a natural. Once Dom bowled a perfect game, a feat made more impressive by the fact that Dom used a "house" ball.

"I've seen Leon Eldridge bowl three perfect games down here," Sugar Daddy said while Rock N' Roller was wiping oil off his ball with a towel—he even had his own bowling towel and rosin bag.

"So," Rock N' Roller said. "Big fuckin' deal. Perfect games now happen about ten times more than holes-in-one, and everyone even gets those at one time or another."

"Yeah, but I've only seen him bowl four times."

By the way Rock N' Roller's eyebrows raised, he seemed more impressed, but maybe not.

"Well duh! What do you expect from someone bowling in his own house?"

"Yeah, but even while bowling in your own house it's still something to string together a perfect game on this lane," Sugar Daddy said. "There are no walls on the side of the deck so you don't get the added action of pins bouncing back to take out those still standing. That's why it's hard to score down here."

Sugar Daddy appeared to have a point. Nick saw on most first-ball attempts, several pins flew off the side of the pin deck and onto the floor or into the empty deck next to it. The only added action came when pins deflected off the top of the steel rack overhead.

"That's just slop," Rock N' Roller said. "To knock down 10 pins, the ball only needs to make contact with four pins, walls or no walls."

Just then Nick decided to speak up.

"You know to hit all the balls in on a break in pool the cue ball only needs to hit one ball," he said.

Rock N' Roller and Sugar Daddy both looked at Nick with incredulous expressions on their faces. If before they treated Nick with indifference, they now seemed settling closer to indignation. Nick felt stupid of what he said, and couldn't even remember where he heard of such a theory.

Soon, Rock N' Roller delivered a perfect hook that drove all 10 pins into the pit. There were no strays this time around.

"See what I mean," he said with a proud smirk.

"Yeah, that's why you'll need three more of those just to break 150."

Pedro returned from the pit to score for Sugar Daddy's pending frame. Before Sugar Daddy was ready to roll, Pedro asked, "Where's the woman? I haven't seen her around the last couple days."

The queried appeared to touch a nerve with Sugar Daddy and Nick could see his mouth get line tight and his eyes sink deeper into their sockets.

"Ah, I don't really fuckin' know and I don't really fuckin' care," he answered with his back to the scorer's table. "She only hung around here for one fuckin' reason anyway."

Pedro looked intently at Sugar Daddy's back and opened his mouth slightly as if to ask a follow-up question, but didn't. Sugar Daddy then unleashed a shot with considerable extra speed on it. When it reached the pins, the ball acted like an exploding grenade scattering pins everywhere. Only three ended up in the pit, and one nearly hit Rock N' Roller, who was standing behind the raised tarp, a seemingly safe spot until then.

"Jesus fuckin' H Christ," Rock N' Roller said. "Three more of those and you just might break 120."

Chapter Twenty-two

Watching all that bowling made Nick hungry for another meal. So he left the threesome and ascended up the elevator to where he had hoped it would stop at the main floor. Nick felt that the upward motion was longer than its previous descent, so when the doors opened he wasn't surprised to find that he wasn't on the main floor.

When Nick left the elevator to look for the staircase so he could get to the main floor on his own, he realized he wasn't on a complete floor—or at least other parts of the floor seemed inaccessible from where he was. A wall faced the elevator from about eight feet, and another wall several feet to the south of the elevator joined it. The wall facing the elevator continued until reaching a northern wall about 20 feet down the hall. The northern wall led way to a west-bound-only passage to another part of the mansion. Nick figured it had to lead to the turret. Where else could it go? As for going anywhere else, that appeared impossible because none of the walls had visible doors or openings

As for the walls, they were painted beige and were illuminated directly and indirectly by a pair of movable track lights that hung from opposite ends of the hallway. Similar to the footlights that shined on the green wall, these were focused near the middle of the wall facing the elevator with their circular spotlights overlapping each other. They illuminated a large framed portrait photo of a man accompanied by another same-size frame next to it. The latter frame didn't encase a photo, rather a series of indecipherable notations, illustrated with white print on a black base, which appeared to be of algebraic and/or geometrical in substance, and complemented with a crude drawing near the bottom which seemed to depict light beams going through and reflecting off stacked layers of glass.

As for the photo, it was of a middle-aged man with horn-rimmed glasses and balding at top. He looked as if he was peering down a microscope, but the photo didn't reveal for sure. His name was revealed in an engraved golden plate under the photo: Dr. Dennis Gabor — 1900-1979. There was another engraved golden plate under the other frame: "An experiment in serendipity."

Though Nick still wanted to get back to the main floor, he was impelled to investigate what had to be the turret, which had to offer a magnificent overhead view of "The Great Highway." But while approaching the passage way, a strange and slight vibration crept through Nick's nervous system as if to tell him that there were places in the mansion he should not invade unannounced, and this could be one of them. Nick stopped short of the passage way. He felt a fresh sample of the cold wet air, probably coming through an open window in the turret.

Nick returned to the elevator, which still had its doors open as if was waiting for him.

The following day would have been ideal for mowing the lawn if it wasn't for all the standing water left from the storm the day before. But with clear skies and the temperature in the 80s, Nick seized the opportunity make some outside work for himself.

To prepare to cut the grass the next day or sometime that week if the weather could hold, Nick decided to clear the property of debris, and there was plenty of that. With the wheelbarrow Jack used to cart away the smashed tile, Nick encircled the mansion while collecting anything that could be a menace to a lawn mower. Much of what Nick picked out the grass, which had grown to nearly a foot and a half, were those Moosehead beer bottles. They were strewn everywhere: the back, front and the sides of the mansion. Nick figured that Rock N' Roller and the rest of crew must have little regard of tidiness, but what really irritated him was that they couldn't keep their waste confined to one section. The culprits also left evidence who they were as several bottles had cigarette butts soaking up the backwash in them. Nick couldn't tell those that came from Rock N' Roller or Sugar Daddy because Nick didn't note what type of brands they smoked, but he had good reason to suspect the much-thinner cigarette butts, some with lipstick on them, came from Sugar Daddy's "girlfriend," unless there were other girls that frequented the mansion who also smoked thin cigarettes.

Nick knew Alyce didn't smoke. She wasn't that type of girl.

Although they were everywhere, it was hard to spot the green bottles that blended so well with the grass. Nick made numerous circuits around the mansion to be thorough and continued to come across another bottle or two he missed. It was as if they were weeds that grew miraculously fast. With a wheelbarrow full of empty green bottles as well as pop cans, empty cigarette packs and other types of litter, Nick leaned up on Jack's rust-colored Chevelle to rest a bit and ponder of what else he could do to keep himself busy. While casting his eyes down the western grade, Nick managed to catch the reflection of what appeared to be another Moosehead bottle in a clearing beyond the trees. Nick didn't think he would be expected to mow down there, or even amid the trees where the grass' growth was smothered by a blanket of un-raked oak leaves from autumns past.

Yet already in motion to rid the area of any garbage, although it would probably be replaced to some extent in a matter of weeks or days, Nick ventured down the hill to retrieve it.

After picking it up and—believe it or not—collecting another bottle down there, Nick was startled when he saw Leon Eldridge standing in front of him when he turned back to head up the hill. It was like he materialized out of thin air. Nick didn't notice him outside at the time, nor did he hear him ascend down the hill after him. He appeared to be wearing that same robe depicted in the painting in the foyer. The robe had enough cleavage at the top to reveal a healthy portion of Leon Eldridge's hairless chest and his spike-fused cruxifix. He engaged Nick briefly with his now-familiar sapphire smile before looking away and fixing his stare to the northwest. Nick sensed that Leon Eldridge wanted him to look where he was looking at, and Nick did while trying to align his sight with Leon Eldridge's. But Nick saw nothing, or at least nothing worthy of much attention.

"There are certain days when you can see it from here," Leon Eldridge said while still staring in the distance.

Nick looked again to where he thought Leon Eldridge was looking, but still didn't know what he was referring to. "See what?" Nick had to ask.

"It's over there," Leon Eldridge said while pointing to help guide him.

Nick looked again with more concentration. He started to suspect that Leon Eldridge was playing a mind game with him, but then Nick saw it, or he thought he saw something that looked like it. It had the same erect shape that Nick and many people even outside the Midwest were familiar with. Nick heard of students and elders even from the academy located several miles down the road seeing it on clear days. But how could it be it?

By Nick's estimation, the structure in question would be about 40 miles away. It stood alone, which mystified Nick. *If that in fact was what it appeared to be,* Nick thought, *other structures, although not as tall, should also be visible by its side. But what else could it be?*

Nick only visited "The City" three times during his life, and only once did he view the world from the top of that structure. It was during a rare academy field trip that stopped at various parts of "The City" with the advanced students saving souls along the way. One stop was the structure's observation deck. Though it was the highlight of the trip, Nick was somewhat underwhelmed. He thought the view looking straight down would be much higher, and that he could peer almost limitlessly into the distance. But even while using the deck's coin-operated binoculars, Nick couldn't even spot the academy's man-made lake and its fountain, something he had planned to look for.

"Why can't we see it on every clear day?" Nick asked while still not being convinced of what they were really looking at.

"Maybe the reason why we can see it today is because someone up there is looking in our direction," Leon Eldridge said.

At first Nick thought such a theory was absurd. But while looking at the structure he felt with another one of those strange vibrations that someone up there was looking in their direction. The thought of people exchanging glances from about 40 miles away began to stir Nick's imagination, though he still didn't accept it as possible. Eventually he looked away to notice that Leon Eldridge had vanished much the same way he had appeared.

Nick made one more loop around the mansion and, alas, found another bottle. That would have to be the last one because the wheelbarrow was over-filled and too cumbersome to move without spilling its contents. Nick didn't know what to do with all the collected debris. There wasn't a trash receptacle in sight. He imagined Leon Eldridge was the type who would prefer to have the bottles separated from the unrecycliable items, but that would have to be another job for another day.

In what started as such a fine day was now spoiled by the stench of cigarettes mixed with beer and spit which Nick could now smell on himself, especially on his hands. So he decided to go inside and wash up. The water was warm, just like Jack said it would be under the right conditions.

Soon after, Nick retreated to the basement by way of the elevator. He had hoped to see Alyce and Pedro down there, but the basement was deserted. Nick wondered where they could be. He thought he saw Pedro's Malibu in the parking lot. What he did find down there was no surprise: about a 12-pack worth of those Moosehead bottles which were left by the scorer's table and the couch, as well as several upended ones behind the pit. In addition to cigarette butts and backwash, Nick could see wasps in several of them foraging for food.

Nick decided to throw a frame or two.

First Nick had to set up the pins. That was a little harder than he thought from watching the threesome do it without a glitch the day before. Eventually, Nick was able to get a rack-full of pin upright in their correct spots. Now it was time to knock them down.

The scuffed-up house ball was left on the ball-return rack, and after picking it up Nick knew that knocking the pins down was going to be as difficult, if not more, as setting them up. Whenever Nick went bowling with Dom, he always had trouble finding the right ball. Often, they were too heavy or the finger or thumb holes were never the right fit for a comfortable grip. This ball was both: a pound or two too heavy, and the finger and thumb holes all a size or two too big. Also, inside the holes were greasy, probably from all that extra oil "painted" on the lane.

Nick held the ball with both hands up by his chin and targeting the headpin with his left eye squinted as if there was a scope on top of the ball. Dom once suggested that he should "spot bowl," meaning aiming for something close on the lane, like the arrows. But Nick never got the hang of spot bowling, nor bowling in general. While approaching the lane, Nick began to lose control of the ball during his backswing before stopping and recovering in time before it slipped out of his hand. During his second try, Nick was able to hold the ball long enough to release it onto the lane, but it didn't even make it halfway down before it rolled off the edge to where the right gutter would have been and onto the concrete floor.

Nick watched the wayward ball make a track through a section of moisture left from a puddle the day before and toward the door of the room next to the elevator. When the ball hit the door, which was made of some sort metallic composition as indicated by the rust near the bottom, it made a booming sound which surprised Nick. It was louder than any sound made from the more skillfully thrown balls the day before. The ball also opened the door, which was slightly ajar before impact, and the rolled into the room.

Nick went to retrieve it, but while peeking into the room he saw other items on the floor and couldn't decipher what they were in the darkness. So Nick felt along the walls inside near the door for a light switch — probably not a safe thing to do in a mansion plagued with crude electrical wiring and mixing fixtures. Yet Nick managed to find it and turned it on without getting shocked.

There were several "coal mining" lights on the ceiling, but they weren't activated by the switch. Instead, it turned on those same type of tracking lights Nick saw upstairs—or more like "upelevator"—which had their tracks fastened along the wooden planks on the ceiling and about four feet in from three of the walls, also painted beige. Like "upelevator," these lights—four or five to a track—illuminated framed photos all about 8-by-11 inches in size, though were not focused on the frames, rather where the ground and the walls met. It was the expanded light that illuminated the parallel photos, which were in black-and-white and in color lined up in two rows along the walls.

Due to the direction of the lights, the middle of the room remained dark though not completely. Nick was able to make out some shapes in the middle as the room — sets of shovels and rakes and other items stacked in a semi-upright position which Nick couldn't fully see in the darkness — as the room apparently was some sort of tool and storage shed. Amid the shadowy shapes, Nick recognized a manual lawn mower, the kind with a circular series of twisted blades that rotate on the axis of the pushed big wheels. And although the back wall wasn't illuminated, Nick noticed the double wooden doors where Jack entered with the wheelbarrow. And Nick discovered where he put the smashed title.

Near the room's northern wall was a double line of tall black buckets, the same type that anchored the canvas to the hallway near the foyer. Filled to the brim were the contents from Jack's sledgehammer project. While looking for the bowling ball, which he thought ended up around the buckets, Nick noticed how the contents in the buckets grew smaller and smaller down the line. At one end, the tiles in the buckets were nearly intact. At the other end, which Nick assumed were the final entries, much of the contents were powderized. Nick also surmised that one of the two buckets on the powderized end was the last one filled, since its contents spilled over the edge.

Maybe that's why Jack didn't return that day—there wasn't another bucket to fill.

But was there a designed reason for the increased degrees of pulverization from one end to the other? After thinking awhile, Nick came up with a reason: maybe the increased pulverization was the result of non-targeted tiles cracking up before direct impact due to transmitted energy, and when those tiles felt the brunt of the sledgehammer, they broke into smaller and more fine "particles." Plus, the dust that topped the final few buckets probably accumulated on the bottom of the wheelbarrow.

While looking around the buckets, Nick couldn't find the ball and feared that it may have ended up amid intertwined items in the darkness. However, Nick avoided going there in favor of continuing his search along the better-lit areas near the walls. Eventually, the framed photographs diverted his attention.

At first Nick thought the arrangement had all black-and-white photos on the top row and all color ones on the lower. That was because the first five pairs he saw were that way. But Nick soon found out that there was no apparent set pattern as black-and-white and color photos were mixed rather evenly amid the top and bottom rows for much of the rest of the display.

Nick did know a little about photography. One of the things he didn't pack before running away was his 35 millimeter Pentax camera that he had gotten from a wealthy uncle for Christmas when he was 10. Nick now had no use for photography and hadn't taken a picture since Dom's death—before, Nick did plan to take photos of Dom's church, the construction and completion.

Shortly after receiving the gift, Nick took a photography class provided at his school. There, Nick became familiar with "composition" and what distinguishes "taking a photograph" in respect of the art from just simply "taking a picture," like a tourist trying to use up all his or her film. And Nick's knowledge about the subject, though limited, enabled him to critique these featured photos.

Nick couldn't find or decipher composition in any of them. They all had human subjects in various settings, mostly public. Yet it seemed that most of these subjects were not cooperating as indicated by the scowls and surprised looks on their faces. They were like celebrities shunning the parrazzi. There was little in the photograph to suggest why these people were being photoed, and aside from the lack of composition there were glaring technical flaws. Some subject's faces were muddied by back light. Other subjects' faces were bleached out due to being over flashed. Other flashed subjects in several color photographs had red beady eyes. Some blurred subjects seemed to be moving too fast for the shutter speed to capture. And others appeared to be captured at high speed but the photo was so grainy that the subjects probably wouldn't be recognized by people they knew.

One photo was of a nude woman—or nude girl—looking down into the camera in the middle of what appeared to be—or what was simulated to be—a sex act. She had dark hair, and Nick thought it could be Sugar Daddy's girlfriend, except this girl appeared to be thinner and her skin a shade darker. But who could really tell? She was too out of focus and the photo was too grainy.

Under each photo was a strip of silver duct tape with notations written in thick graphite. Nick was able to make out the meanings of most of them. Like the one that noted "1/125 SP 5.6 AP 400 FM" Nick knew it meant the shutter speed was set at 125th of the second, the lens aperture (the opening that admits light) was set at 5.6 and the type of film was 400 speed.

Then just like earlier that day, Leon Eldridge suddenly materialized. He was standing in the doorway of the room, and he had the wayward bowling ball in his hand.

"I see you have come across one of my great mistakes," Leon Eldridge said.

This time Nick wasn't that startled by the materialization. But he did wonder where the ball was and how Leon Eldridge was able to find it instantly—maybe it was behind the door where Nick neglected to look.

"Einstein once said that he made a great mistake only to have people say after his death that he was right all along," Nick said, who was reminded of the T-shirt on the laundry line.

Leon Eldridge's face lightened after Nick's comment, and he seemed amused by it.

"It's kind of like the guy who thought for once in his life that he was wrong only to later admit he was mistaken," Leon Eldridge said. "But maybe I'm mistaken in referring to my mistake as a mistake. A better definition is probably a false assumption."

"So what was your false assumption?" Nick said.

Leon Eldridge walked over to where Nick was and looked at the photographs in a manner like he was studying them for the first time.

"I once was enchanted by the idea of capturing moments in time," Leon Eldridge said. "I thought I could capture the essence of the present tense—the essence of now."

"So I take it that you took these photos?" Nick said.

Leon Eldridge nodded his head. Nick re-examined some of the photos, yet couldn't fathom the assumption, false or not.

"Wha—what were you trying to do with, eh, this?" Nick asked while trying to be careful. He didn't want to bluntly torch Leon Eldridge's photography talents, or lack thereof.

"I was convinced that I could prove, with these photos, that universes spawn other universes," Leon Eldridge said. "And that we pass through one universe to another and to another linearly and seamlessly."

Leon Eldridge got up close to one of the photographs and motioned Nick to come closer, too. It was taken on some urban street, perhaps from "The City" or "The Heart of Darkness," and showed several people walking in both directions. Unlike others, the black-and-white photo was well-lit and all the subjects were in focus, yet it was not level due, no doubt, to the camera not being held in a level position.

"Look at that guy," Leon Eldridge said of a Caucasian man positioned closest to the eye of the lens. He was the only one looking directly at the camera, and by the frown on his face, he didn't appear too happy that he was being photographed. "What do you think was going through this guy's mind at that precise moment?" Leon Eldridge asked.

Nick took time to look deeply into the man's seemingly raging demeanor. "To say the least, it doesn't look like he's in a very friendly mood."

"Mood?" Leon Eldridge said. "You talk about his mood? You have to understand, if I wanted to photograph someone's mood, I would have been better off using a video camera with sound. What I'm asking is what was going through his mind at this moment in time, meaning," Leon Eldridge pointed to the notation written under the photo, "at that 125th of a second?"

Nick didn't quite know the answer, but responded anyway. "Actually, I don't think you can define what's going through someone's mind during a such brief moment in time," Nick said. "It would just be a sample of what he was thinking before and what was going to think immediately after."

"Exactly!" Leon Eldridge said exuberantly. "So why can't this snapshot taken at 125th of a second depict a universe within itself?"

Nick took a little time to think about the question. "Because nothing living consciously exists in such a short period of time alone," Nick said.

"Exactly!" Leon Eldridge said with even more exuberance. "But I tell you what, the effort wasn't a complete waste of time. It did lead to some interesting observations."

Another case of "serendipity," Nick thought as Leon Eldridge led him to a group of photos along the long wall.

"You see this photo," Leon Eldridge said. It was another un-level street scene with several people whose moments were greatly blurred. "This was a road race, meaning a long-distance run."

Good thing Nick was told that, since most long-distance race photos he was familiar with had groups of runners together or one runner alone. This photo had several subjects on both ends of the frame, yet none in the middle.

"This was shot at 60th of a second, and you can see it wasn't fast enough to capture sharp images," Leon Eldridge said. "But look at this photo."

It was the photo under it, apparently from the same spot during the same race. But the runners were much better lit and were sharper, their movements better captured.

"This was shot at the same speed, but I used a flash synched at 60th of a second," Leon Eldridge said. "It's like the flash slowed down time. Isn't that amazing? And look at this one."

It was another photo taken during the race, but Nick didn't realize it at first because it was in color and level. Also, a single runner dominated the frame. He was flashed and his eyes, which were looking directly at the camera as he was running by, were beady red.

"You notice here and even in the other flashed photo, but it shows up better here," Leon Eldridge said while pointing to the back edges of the runner in the color photo. Though the runner was sharp and in focus, he seemed to leave a bright and slightly colorized six-inch layer of his backside behind him. It reminded Nick of what the edges of images in 3-D photos look like without being viewed through special glasses.

"You know what these are called?" Leon Eldridge asked. Even with his slight knowledge of photography, Nick didn't know the answer and shrugged his shoulders.

"These," Leon Eldridge said while pointing to the edges of runners in both flashed photos, "are ghosts." Leon Eldridge paused a bit while Nick remained silent. "And you probably thought ghosts didn't exist, but here they are caught on film."

Nick squinted his eyes to get a better look at these ghosts before Leon Eldridge motioned him to view another photo on the wall near the buckets. While walking over there, Leon Eldridge's robe got snagged by one upright item in the middle of the room.

"It's funny how clutter can build up," he said while freeing his robe. "It's like it comes together from a force much greater than magneticism. But anyway, this is my most interesting photo."

It was another black-and-white race photo. Except it had different halves separated vertically. One half was much more dimly lit from under exposure than any of the under-exposed photos Nick noted in the collection, and there wasn't much contrast as the dark grayness of the blurred runners blended with the buildings of near the same shade in the background. Yet the other half was bright and alive with runners and their ghosts trailing close behind.

"Now how do you think that happened?" Leon Eldridge said.

Nick looked at the notations under the photo and took an educated guess.

"It's because you set the shutter at 125th of the second while the flash was synched at 60th of a second."

"Exactly!" Leon Eldridge said. "Isn't it funny how that does that?"

Soon, Nick and Leon Eldridge left the room and boarded the elevator and ascended up to the floor that Nick was certain was adjacent to the turret. Leon Eldridge left the elevator while still carrying that bowling ball which he never put down even while pointing out and explaining his failed photo exhibit. He looked back at Nick and said, "Thanks for cleaning up the yard."

Nick smiled, and just as the doors were closing quickly returned a pleasantry, "Thanks for letting me use your ball"—although Leon Eldridge was taking it with him.

With the foul stench long since washed away, Nick had a renewed urge to return outdoors. He went to the place where he and Leon Eldridge had earlier viewed the structure from a great distance. Yet for some reason Nick couldn't spot it even after an extended survey. Granted, the sun was in a different position, but the skies were as clear as before.

It is almost needless to note, however, Nick did find two more Mooseheads.

Chapter Twenty-three

The following day, Nick entered the storage room by way of the wooden doors. Still morning with the sun broadly cast on the mansion's east, muddied light traveled down the slope for a better view of what was inside. One thing Nick knew for sure wasn't there the day before was the wheelbarrow, now coupled next to the manual lawnmower. Empty though. Nick wondered about the Mooseheads.

Nick tried to free the lawnmower from the clutter, which actually was held together by something other than magneticism. Rakes, shovels, gardening tools and Jack's mighty sledgehammer were placed on top and/or leaning on the sides of the lawnmower. There were several long, iron-shafted tools piercing the open areas between the blades. The lawnmower's handles were also hooked with the wheelbarrow's. When Nick tried to untangle things, several iron-shafted tools fell to the floor, shaking off rust filaments that outline the impacts.

While Nick struggled the light in the room suddenly dimmed. It was a spanning thin boundary-blurred shadow, a shadow inverted to the mansion's massive shadow outside. Jack made it.

Without saying a word, Jack grabbed the wheelbarrow handles and instantly freed it . Then he grabbed the coal shovel Nick used in assisting him days earlier, put it in the wheelbarrow and started up the slope. The lawnmower was also free.

"You guys ought to get with the 21st century and get a gas-powered lawnmower," Nick said to the back of Jack

For a moment it looked like Jack was going to depart without a reply, but turned and said, "Gas to cut the grass? That would be a wasteful."

"Don't you use gas for your car?"

"That I do, but I only drive to church."

"You could always walk to church."

Jack pursed his lips with his eyes cast upward. "I guess I could to that."

Nick had figured mowing the lawn would be difficult, but not this difficult. Even two days after the hard rain, the tall grass was still moist. And the rusted blades were not sharp. Nick had to continuously retrace tracks to mow down erect blades that survived previous passes. Also, Nick couldn't mow much more than 15 square feet without using the garden hose to clean off the caked-up mulch in between the blades.

Throughout the process, Nick found four more Mooseheads, yet was somewhat surprised he didn't find more. Nick didn't know where to put them because Jack had the wheelbarrow. Eventually, Nick decided to place them on the back porch ledge near the pool. While there, Nick saw Jack at the bottom of the pool shoveling the disgusting black sludge into the wheelbarrow.

It took Nick over four hours to mow the property's lawn. Halfway through the task, Nick shed his white-buttoned shirt, which was drenched with sweat and had grass stains—probably un-removable—on it. While shirtless, Nick felt his skin soak up the sun as its former paleness shifted to shades of red. Other than on his face, Nick hadn't had a real sunburn for quite some time, and for the most part forgot how one felt.

Even after that arduous task, Nick determined there was more work to be done: raking the clippings. For some reason Pedro, who was milling around outside, had decided on his own to rake the clippings around the mansion's northwest corner, yet his efforts seemed unfocused. Pedro was making little mounds with just two or three rake motions before going to another row to do about the same. Pedro didn't take time to combine them into one big mound to make a clearing. At least he was doing something, though.

Nick grabbed a rake from the storage room and started raking the backyard. Like the debris collected the day before, he didn't know where he would put the clippings. But Nick barely got started before Jack approached him from behind.

"Don't rake the grass," he said.

"Why not?" responded Nick, who though the lawn was aesthetically worse than before being thickly covered with light-green clippings, like the grass's color instantly faded upon being felled. "The grass will die if I don't."

"On the contrary," said Jack, raising his gangly index finger to the side of his hairy mug. "The grass will be reborn."

So Nick returned to the storage room to put the rake away. That's when Pedro entered in a huff.

"So let the place look like shit! What do I care?" Pedro said while flinging his rake violently onto the concrete floor, dislodging more rust filaments. "Just trying to help out around here, but if he doesn't want us to, so be it. Fuck 'em."

Pedro's voice was loud and, although it was inside the storage room, Nick could feel it slip outdoors where it probably was well within Jack's earshot.

"Who the fuck is that guy anyway?" Pedro exclaimed. "NASA scientist? My ass."

"Pedro," Nick said while patting his palms in front of him, conveying to Pedro to keep his voice down. "It's no big deal."

"No big deal? Yeah, you're right. No big deal, then don't—ah, fuck 'em," Pedro said in a still loud voice, though he did lower the volume when continuing, "Like I was saying, who is that guy? He's like a vampire in reverse. You never see him at night, though his car is still here. Where does he stay? Where does he fuckin' sleep? I haven't figured that out yet. It's real creepy, if you ask me."

Pedro took a deep breath and scanned the bizarre photo gallery, prompting a contorted visage. "And who is this Leon Eldridge? I mean, come on, what kind of name is Leon Eldridge? I bet he has a fuckin' cousin named Lee Harvey Roswell."

"Pedro," Nick said patting his palms. Pedro's voice was getting loud and profane again, and Nick worried that during such a rant Leon Eldridge would suddenly appear out of nowhere as was his habit. "He's letting us stay here for practically nothing," Nick said in a near whisper. "So he's an...ah..." Nick was going to say eccentric, but opted for something more polite, "...renegade of sorts, so is Jack. So what? They're harmless."

Though it came from his mouth, Nick wasn't too sure of what he said at the end. He had only been there for a half of week. Pedro and Alyce, from Nick's estimation, probably were there for at least week or two before, thus Pedro's reservations about the "landlord" and his "assistant" could be better scouted. Yet during Nick's association with him, Pedro developed reservations about a lot of people.

Pedro shook his head and said, "I don't know. I've about had it with this place."

"What's the matter? What's wrong?" Nick asked.

Pedro put his hands in the air and said, "Everything." Nick pressed for an elaboration, but got none. Though Pedro did cast light on his future plans. "I think I'm going to blow this place. You want to come with?"

"But Pedro, where are you going to go?" Nick asked.

"I don't know, just away from here," Pedro said. "You want to come with?"

"What about Alyce?"

"Like I said, do you want to come with? Anyone who wants to leave with me can leave with me."

With that, Pedro stormed into the basement while flinging open the door in a way where it banged loudly against one of the tile-filled buckets. Nick obviously was concerned about Pedro's state of mind, and hoped that a little time by himself might cool his head. But if Pedro's attitude didn't get any better, Nick figured it would probably be best for him to leave before making trouble. Of course Nick wouldn't want Pedro to take Alyce with him. And Pedro's wheels would no longer be a convenience—*We could all walk to church, then.*

After washing up, Nick located the stairway from the south and climbed it to the second floor. Maybe this was where Jack stayed during the night, Nick thought while trying to solve the mystery that perplexed Pedro and even a little himself. But there was no evidence any rooms were being used as living quarters. Much like the ballroom, the second floor appeared to be completely renovated. The walls shined of wet white, and the fresh smell of paint – like that of the green hallway — permeated the entire floor. The floor itself, like that of the main floor, was wooden, yet it was clean and dustless, and had no nails sticking out. And even the lighting fixtures were all in place. The level looked liked that from newly built house still waiting for its first tenants.

Nick eventually found the way to the attic—a trap in the ceiling on the eastern portion of the floor. A rope through a wooden tube handle hung from the door low enough for Nick to pull. When he did, the door opened and a stair-step ladder on a wheeled track rolled down and nearly took Nick out. Aside from being startled by the ladder, Nick was alarmed by a platoon of wasps circling around the opening. As quickly as he could, Nick pushed the ladder back up and heaved the door upward hoping that it would catch and close, which it did with the aide of some sort of built-in spring action. Nick could hear the swarm buzzing in agitation.

On the way downstairs, Nick saw Leon Eldridge and Jack staring into the room under the staircase. Instead of looking directly into the doorway, both men were looking into the room from an angle closer to the mansion's face. The canvas had been removed from the hallway revealing the same parquet floor and finish of the ballroom. The canvas may have been gone when Nick ascended up the stairs, but the stairs' impressive floral-carved wooden railings caught his attention then.

Nick smiled at the two and Leon Eldridge smiled back briefly with closed lips without flashing his sapphire tooth before resuming his former attention. Leon Eldridge's right hand pinched his chin and his left hand held his right elbow in place. Jack's arms were folded.

Nick spent most of the remaining daylight hours in his room reading his Bible, or trying to read it. For some reason, Nick had great difficulty absorbing the randomly opened-to passages even after re-reading them. No one had ever taught him how to read the Bible... Nick's parents gave a few post pre-school lessons, but they didn't know shit. After a while, he decided to go see what in that room had demanded the concentration of Leon Eldridge and Jack. Maybe that would be easier to comprehend.

Feeling certain that Leon Eldridge and Jack had called it a night, Nick went inside to investigate. Where the room should have gave way to the staircase, Nick saw something that seemed to violate laws of space and gravity. A large mesh of green-glowing interlocked rings, loops and spirals was suspended in mid air. It appeared to be the only light source in the mostly dark room. Upon further review, Nick realized a giant mirror was fastened to the inverted slope and the mesh hung in the middle of it. That caused two illusions: one the room had a full rectangular shape, and that the mesh—half reality, half reflection— was floating in the middle of this volume.

Interesting, Nick thought, but not entirely original. Nick once owned a hand-held cube-shaped coin bank that had a "floating" cube displayed in its small window. Inside the bank, like the room, was an inverted-sloped mirror. The other side of the mirror was where the coins were stored and hidden.

The rings, loops and spirals varied in size. Most of the rings and loops were bracelet size, yet several deep inside the mesh were about the size of basketball hoops, and one the size of a hula-hoop. Most bigger hoops were half hoops completed with reflections.

They also varied in thickness, thinnest being that of electrical wire, and the thickest being that of a lawn hose.

As for the loops and spirals that intertwined with each other, Nick couldn't determine if they formed knots or not. (That was another thing about "Parables and Possibilities" class: they went through a half of a week discussing knots and non-knots—What was up with that?)

A thin spiral wrapped around one of the basketball hoops, which together snared Nick's attention for more than a moment.

As for the mesh, it was asymmetrical. From its thick base at the mirror's plane (corpus callosum again reared from Nick's subliminal mind), the mesh draped and narrowed more as it descended along the slope to single bracelet-sized ring at the tip, which hung about three feet from the floor. With the upper half naturally being the reflection of the other, they resembled wings, perhaps those from an angel soaring sideways and downward, like heading for a crash landing—at least from Nick's angle.

Not all of the suspended display was connected together. There were several independent spirals that took form of bent slinkies in zero gravity on the mesh's sides. Two spirals on one side intertwined together to form a double helix. Another spiral was connected to the top part of the mesh's middle base at the mirror's plane and hung freely, parallel to the wing tips on both sides of the mirror.

The mesh's radiance reminded Nick of the glow-in-the-dark toys he would dig out of cereal boxes from youth's past, but the mesh's glow appeared to be waning, just like those toys when darkness started to take over. Yet the source for the mesh's glow was constant, and Nick soon discovered it came from outside the doorway—the two overlapping spotlights on the wall. When Nick looked back at the spotlights, he noticed that there had been some alterations. Instead of being focused in the middle of the wall and directly in front of the room's doorway, they were moved closer to the front of the mansion in effort, Nick concluded, to align them with the "floating mesh" through the doorway.

Such a correction, if that's what it was, didn't come without consequence. The spotlights were no longer symmetrical as the closer cast spotlight was smaller and brighter, and the other was bigger and dimmer.

Amid the mesh and spirals was a configuration of stars. Looking up while seeing his mostly obscured overhead reflection peering back from inside of the mesh, Nick's sunburned face reflected the green glow. Finally figuring it out, Nick noticed that the stars and the midnight blue sky were reflections of what was painted on the floor and the walls. The man-made midnight reminded Nick of the man-made lake.

The way depicted, some stars were bright, others were dim—all were white despite being, in strange probability, brought out by the green glow— gave the sky a three-dimensional quality. Peering up at his glowing self, Nick saw that he also seemed to be floating. Then a prone-position silhouette appeared the prone-position doorway. Nick got a whiff of vertigo when he turned in the actual direction.

"I... I... didn't touch it," Nick professed.

"Don't worry," Leon Eldridge said as he walked into the room. His easy

Southern accent revealed the identity of his silhouette before the mesh's glow illuminated it. "It doesn't bite."

Leon Eldridge stood next to Nick and joined the study of the mesh. Assuming this was another one of Leon Eldridge's art projects, Nick was worried that he was going to be asked of this thoughts. Nick believed that it was a rude gesture for an artist to request a review while burdening one's civil sensibilities. Yet Leon Eldridge remained silent.

"What's it called?" Nick asked to break the pause.

"A name is not appropriate," Leon Eldridge said while cocking his head as if he saw something wrong.

"How long did it take to make it?"

"Very long," Leon Eldridge said. "Almost a lifetime."

Nick turned to look at Leon Eldridge, who was still looking up at the rings, loops and spirals. He couldn't fathom how something like this required a lifetime to make.

"Of course making this itself didn't take too long," Leon Eldridge said as he pointed upward with an open palm at the mesh. "Don't get me wrong, this was a project. But to come to understand it, to visualize it, to compose a meaning…that, my friend, is a life's work—still in progress, I might add."

Nick almost laughed at the thought of the trick coin bank inventor exerting as much effort.

"And it's still not done," Leon Eldridge said. "There are still things that need to be tweaked." His accent resonated with the word "tweaked."

"Like what?" Nick asked.

"It needs to be more bright," Leon Eldridge said. "We should be able to fix that."

Nick thought more bright would make it Lucifer.

"What is it?" Nick asked. Though no name, Nick thought it at least had to represent something worthy of composing a meaning to.

"Everything."

"Everything?"

"Everything."

"Everything great and small?"

"Everything great and small," Leon Eldridge said, turning to stare intensely at Nick. "That's what it is."

Nick was mystified by the explanation, and was slightly taken aback by the intensity. "Everything great and small, huh?" he eventually said. "Does that mean the universe?"

"The universe is just a minuscule part," Leon Eldridge answered.

Though Nick was far from understanding what this was all about, he was growing troubled by his budding perception of pretentious idolatry. After a moment of silence where Leon Eldridge remained fixed on his creation, Nick conjured up enough nerve to ask a bold question.

"Mr. Eldridge—"

"Leon Eldridge, please."

"Leon Eldridge, uh, I …I… I hope you don't take this the wrong way, but I think I have to ask you this." Nick waited for a queue from Leon Eldridge, who didn't deter his stare. Nothing.

Nick then took a deep breath seeking better composure. "Mr. Eldridge, I…I mean I'm sorry—Leon Eldridge. Ah, do…do… eh… do you believe in God?"

Leon Eldridge remained transfixed, and then cracked a smile.

"I hope you're not offended or anything," Nick said as the smile gave him more confidence to proceed. "And I know you're really into Jesus, just like Alyce said. But I know that there are some people, believe it or not, who actually claimed to have surrendered their lives to Jesus yet still fancy themselves as atheists or agnostics for some strange reason. I'm not saying you're like that but—well—what I am saying is, or asking is—"

"Do I believe in God?" Leon Eldridge said, this time including his sapphire in his smile.

"Yes. That's what I'm saying—or asking."

Leon Eldridge folded his arms and said, "Funny you ask me that in this room."

"Funny I ask? What's so funny about it?"

Still smiling, Leon Eldridge shook his head and said, "May I ask you a question?"

"No, uh, I mean yes, but after you answer my question, please," Nick said. "I asked first."

The smile left Leon Eldridge's face, and Nick sensed that he may have painted Leon Eldridge into corner.

"Well then," Leon Eldridge said. "Like I said before, it's funny you ask me that question in this room. To alleviate any doubts on the subject, do you want me to prove to you that there is a God?"

"You don't need to prove to me there's a God," Nick said. "But I'm glad you at least answered my question. I hope you're not mad about my inquiry. It's just you were going on about everything great and small and I just wondered if God fit into the equation."

Leon Eldridge's smooth brow crumpled. "I think you may be letting me off the hook too easily. Don't you want me to prove to you that God exists?"

"Like I said, you don't need to."

"Well, then, but what evidence of God's existence can you provide?"

Nick let out a big sigh. "Well, that's a toughie—one, mind you, that I didn't require you to solve. I don't know if I, or you or anyone else can do it scientifically." Nick raised his voice. "And I don't think it's right for other people to try to prove God's existence scientifically, or through some scientific theory. In a way, that's what they tried to do at that…" Nick caught himself before saying "damn" "… academy."

"So scientific proof is unnecessary?" Leon Eldridge asked.

"Yes," Nick answered loudly. "I admit, science is part of God's world, but it's not needed to bolster or reveal the already faithful who already see God everywhere."

"But if you see God everywhere, why exclude the scientific world?" Leon Eldridge asked.

Nick felt Leon Eldridge was using blatant debate tactics on him, and lashed out angrily, "I said I don't need a scientific explanation!" Just then another back portion of Nick's mind surfaced and he was reminded of Elder Steven's DNA-empowered-by-clay notion, but he never considered that a scientific explanation, rather just playful fun with a myth. Then Nick's eyes involuntarily moved to catch another glance of the glowing double helix.

"I don't mean to get you upset, Nick," Leon Eldridge said. "I, myself, have a problem with contemporary science, at least how it's theorized. Now Nick, I bet you have some of the same beefs that I have."

"And what is that—or what are those?"

"Tell me yours and maybe we could compare notes."

Nick didn't know where this was going, and he didn't really have such protests on the forefront of his mind. But after thinking for several moments while staring up at the mesh, Nick was able to come up with something.

"Okay. This is my big beef with the elitist scientific community and all its atheistic underwriters. First of all, these sponsors, also elitists I should add, always go out of their way to ridicule the history of God. They go off on this and saying that God couldn't have been around forever nor will be around forever, that it violates the fundamentals of time, and how there had to be something before God because something had to make Him. Then they claim that making the planets, stars and universe in six days all by Himself is pure fantasy. But here's the kicker: Yeah, okay, all this seems impossible, but you tell me this, or they should tell me, which is more fantastic? God making everything 'great and small,'" Nick made a pair of peace signs for "great and small," "… in six days, or some 'big bang,' "more peace signs, "… where everything, I mean everything came from something the size of a pinpoint? Now that's pure fantasy."

Nick noticed Leon Eldridge sapphire smiling again. Maybe they did have common beefs.

"Imagine if Genesis had such a passage," Nick continued before utilizing Cecil B's voice-over, "'And God snapped his fingers and all the universe came forth from a size of a pinpoint.' These same people who support such an absurd notion would be wiping their butts with it if it were in the Bible."

Leon Eldridge laughed out loud. Nick laughed with him.

"Well, is that a beef of yours, too?" Nick asked.

Still laughing a little, Leon Eldridge paced a bit around the star-struck floor floating in outer space. "This is how it all came to be," said Leon Eldridge, coming to a stop and lifting his index finger much the same way Jack did while claiming the grass would be reborn. "In the beginning, there was one."

"One?" Nick said after Leon Eldridge issued a deliberate pause. "You mean God, right? That's what or whom you mean as one?"

"In the beginning, there was one," Leon Eldridge said, index finger still on display. "Let's just think of the numeral. One."

"One. Okay. So it's the beginning of time, and God was —"

"No, no, no," Leon Eldridge interrupted. "Let's just forget about time —"

"And God, too?" Nick said.

"Nick," Leon Eldridge said, "may you please give your inhibitions a rest and just listen without interrupting. What I'm explaining probably seems complicated to many people, but it's really quite shockingly simple."

Nick lowered his eyes and softened his focus. "Okay, I won't interrupt anymore," he said before looking back at Leon Eldridge. "But I get the feeling you're trying to prove to me that God exists, and I already told you that was unnecessary."

"Inhibitions, sleep!" Leon Eldridge gestured Svengali-like with open and pointed hand-claws near Nick's face. "But the rest of you stay awake and just hear me through. In the beginning, there was one. One. Number one."

Leon Eldridge paused again like he was badgering Nick to interrupt even after instructing him not to.

"Now, let's say this one becomes two," Leon Eldridge continued. "Now you probably want to know how this one became two. Maybe one spawned another. Or maybe one got split in half. But aside how one became two, now with two, things have changed dramatically. You know why?"

Nick was perturbed. Leon Eldridge had told him to keep his trap shut during his presentation, now he wanted interaction. "I don't know. One is now two," Nick hastily answered.

"Yes, that is true," Leon Eldridge said. "But think about it, if all there was in the beginning was one, and another comes making two, even if they seem to be the same, or exact replicas, the mathematics before when there was just one is now far more advanced. When there was just one, addition did not exist because there was nothing to add. Now with one and another one, you can add them together making two."

Nick was still foggy. "When you refer to one and two, you're referring to universes, right?"

"Again, let's just think of numerals," Leon Eldridge said. "Now let's say one of the two spawns or splits making three. Then all three split in half, making six. And so on and so on. Every time something like that happens, numbers become more numerous and mathematics becomes more and more complex. Soon, fragments will appear—if in essence they didn't form already with the aforementioned splits—and common denominators, and square roots, and higher forms of algebra and trigonometry, integer relations and so on as mathematics, with more numbers and equations at its disposal, grows exponentially. You still look confused."

"Well, shouldn't I be?" Nick confessed. "And I don't think it's because of my inhibitions. So what you're saying, I think, is that there was a mathematics evolution."

Leon Eldridge put his hand on his chin and paused a bit before saying, "You may be getting it, but I don't know for sure."

"Are you saying that everything came from one plus one equals two, and so on?" Nick asked.

"Nick, let's say that this 'mathematics evolution,' so to speak, reached an apex of complexity, to where even the most-revered mathematicians and the most-advanced computers couldn't solve its ultimate riddle. And that's where we stand today."

Now more than ever, Leon Eldridge was floating in outer space.

"That's where we stand today?" Nick said. "We're already coding DNA and making clones, and you're saying there are aspects of mathematics that we still don't understand?"

"Yes, there are — or make that 'Yes, there is.'"

"What can it be? The non-solvency of Social Security?"

"Pi."

"Pie?"

"Pi, as defined as denoting the ratio of the circumference of a circle to its diameter," Leon Eldridge said. "A fascinating number."

"Pi, huh?" demurred Nick, who remembered Alyce's jersey. "What makes it so fascinating?"

"Oh, you had to have heard of scientists and mathematicians becoming born again while trying to unlock its mystery," Leon Eldridge said.

"Yeah, but I don't know what the fuss is all about," Nick said. "I mean, they found out where it ends after the decimal point."

"No, they haven't," Leon Eldridge corrected.

"They haven't?" Nick wasn't too sure on the subject, yet added, "Well, it has to end somewhere."

"Who said?" Leon Eldridge asked.

"I don't know, but I'm willing to bet it ends somewhere. And if pi is such a fascinating symbol or number, how come it's not listed as one of the six most important numbers in the universe?" Nick was referring to Sir Martin Rees' *Just Six Numbers*. He never read the book, but he had leafed through Elder Steven's copy enough to remember that pi wasn't among the six.

"An interesting omission," said Leon Eldridge, who, for all Nick knew, may have read the book. "Then again, maybe pi should stand by itself."

Leon Eldridge walked up closer to his floating mesh and said, "Granted, if the radiation of the sun was just a little bit more or less, we wouldn't be having this conversation. But pi had to come to be for matter, energy and consciousness to exist."

"What about God?"

"For God to exist, too."

"Now that's just blasphemy!" Nick shrieked. He wanted to leave Leon Eldridge, his suspended display and his mansion at that moment. Leon Eldridge obviously was a heretic with nonsensical beliefs. But Nick hesitated, as he didn't really know where to go, although he was earlier offered a ride out. And Nick wanted to see Leon Eldridge's reaction to his forceful rebuke. Yet Leon Eldridge didn't appear to react at all as he still looked placidly up at his creation. Nick wasn't going to bolt before aggressively confronting this idiocy.

"I mean how can you say pi had to come to be for God to exist?" Nick asked while walking up close to Leon Eldridge. "Then who made pi?"

"I just went over that with you," Leon Eldridge calmly said. "You obviously weren't listening."

"I was listening!" Nick shouted as he felt his agitated blood heat up his face and tears well in his eyes. "From what you're spewing, pi simply came about from this goofy numbers game you propose, yet God came from pi. What kind of…" Nick was now sobbing "… bullshit is that?"

"Nick," Leon Eldridge said while reaching out, but Nick quickly backed away from pending contact, "there's no reason to get upset."

"What do you mean there's no reason?" said Nick, still backing away.

"Nick, please. Don't cry. Maybe I'm going too fast for —"

"Don't patronize me," warned Nick, now stepping forward in anger. "I can handle any bullshit you deliver. And just because I don't accept it doesn't mean I don't understand it."

"So you don't accept pi being the primary force in the grand matrix of things?" Leon Eldridge asked.

"I don't see how. But it's not because I don't understand," Nick answered, maintaining his disposition.

Leon Eldridge turned to the floating mesh. "This is what this is all about. I'd like to explain further, but I don't want you to get more upset."

"I said I can handle it."

"Good, good," Leon Eldridge said. "Now please, come a little closer."

Nick shuffled pensively closer.

"You see all these rings, loops and spirals," Leon Eldridge said.

"Yes, and don't tell me they all came from pi," Nick tartly retorted.

"Yes, they did."

"Yeah," Nick said. "And how come they're all tangled together? And another thing, if pi is the result of a perfect circle—or make that a perfect circle is the result of pi, and pi plays such a big part in the universe, how come most orbits in outer space are not perfect circles? Most of them are, eh —"

"Elliptical," Leon Eldridge answered.

"Yeah, elliptical. That right there eliminates pi."

Leon Eldridge reached up to grab one of the rings in the mesh. As he pulled it toward him, Nick heard the gentle clicking of parts indicating that is was mostly made out of hard plastic, or hard something. "It's because these obits affect and intersect others."

"I don't know about that," said Nick, who was reminded of that twisted Earth-moon dance postulation. "Has anything like that been proven?"

"It's been documented that you could change the course of an electron by just looking at it," answered Leon Eldridge, whose beaming eyes seemed to support the claim.

"Now take this ring," Leon Eldridge continued while holding an interlocked "bracelet" about five inches in diameter. "As depicted, it represents a path of sorts. And you're traveling along this path and you start here…" Leon Eldridge pointed to one side of the ring "… with the hopes, or better word ambitions of ending here," he pointed to the other side. "But let's say another path intersects your intended path…" with his other hand, Leon Eldridge held one of the other interlocking rings that was a little smaller than a bracelet "…and sends you along its path. And then another intersects it, and then another." Leon Eldridge switched to other interlocking rings. "But somehow you get to the intended other side or even back where you started. The original path was a perfect circle, or perfect semi-circle, and even though you didn't travel one, you found your way back."

Nick didn't understand, but wasn't going to admit it. Though he had to ask, "Where are all these pi-related paths?"

"Everywhere."

"I knew you were going to say that, but where…where is everywhere"

"You may not see them, but you feel them."

"I do?" Nick said.

"Sure you do. They hold you together, and even hold you in place."

"They do?" Nick said. "What are they? Particle beams. Electric forces? I do know a little about strong and weak forces, but…but…are they that?"

"Vibrations," Leon Eldridge answered. "That's what they are. And, like I just said, you feel them without really knowing it. Now I know this has happened to you at one time or another: You're sitting or standing somewhere minding your own business and keeping to yourself, and suddenly, for some involuntary reason, you turn your head and make immediate eye contact with someone who was staring at you. Now tell me, has that happened to you?"

Nick, of course, was familiar with the phenomenon. But instead of confirmation, he reiterated, "Again, I say, where does God fit into all this? We can talk all day about vibrations and electro weak forces and how pi holds together atoms, the solar system and us to it. But where is God in this matrix?"

"You told me already that you didn't want me to prove to you that He exists," Leon Eldridge said. "And I don't want you to get upset again."

"Go ahead, you win," Nick said while flailing his arms over his head. "You were going there, anyway."

Leon Eldridge smiled and said, "First of all, one of my greatest faiths is that wisdom will triumph over vices."

"With the help of God," Nick quickly added.

"And Jesus."

"Well, at least we can somewhat agree on that," said Nick, now folding his arms. "Anyway, continue."

"A moment ago you noted the overwhelming presence of elliptical orbits in outer space," Leon Eldridge said. "Now would you qualify Earth's orbit around the sun as elliptical?"

"Maybe, I don't know for sure," Nick said. "Could be, or could be a perfect circle. Like I said, I don't know for sure."

"But its path in no way completes a perfect circle, meaning it ends exactly where it started," Leon Eldridge said. "Even if the universe doesn't expand the way they say, and everything is fixed in place despite overwhelming evidence to the contrary, theoretically the Earth doesn't return to the same place it was 12 months before."

Nick unfolded his arms and tilted his head...like that was going to help him better comprehend.

"You see, the Earth goes around the sun over and over again," Leon Eldridge said while making circles in front of him with his finger. "But every time it comes back, things are different. One year, this team won the World Series, the next year, someone else. One year, a so-called civilized nation embraces slavery. A hundred or so revolutions later, such a practice is universally deemed unacceptable. So, an optimistic way to perceive Earth's and humankind's progress is to imagine it spiraling upward. Like here is slavery..." Leon Eldridge leaned down to start an index-outlined spiral near his knees before ascending it over his head "... and here is freedom."

Leon Eldridge then took a hold of the spiral that was parallel to the tips and unbent it with its reflection. Nick saw that it was elastic.

"The reason why God is such a factor in our lives is because He probably exists in our future," Leon Eldridge said.

"What?" Nick gawked. He wasn't going to accept that. "First you said you're going to prove to me that God exists. But now you're talking probably."

"We will continue up the spiral," Leon Eldridge said while pointing up to the reflection of himself, which was holding the "other" end of the spiral. "Unimaginable greatness awaits in the future."

"And that's where God awaits, right?" Nick asked in a surly manner before noticing that Leon Eldridge's spike-fused crucifix best adopted the mesh's green glow.

Nick looked up and away and addressed Leon Eldridge's reflection where unimaginable greatness and God supposedly await. "That's preposterous. If He exists in our future, how the hell, eh, excuse me, but how the hell does He affect us today?"

Leon Eldridge then took the lowest ring of the mesh and held it to the free spiral with his two hands. The other side of the mesh naturally bowed in the same direction, forming a crescent moon, but more pregnant in the middle— at least from Nick's angle

"Let's say this end here is the beginning of time," Leon Eldridge said. "And let's say up there is —"

"God. I already got that," Nick sarcastically interrupted.

Leon Eldridge smiled and continued, "And in the middle…" referring to where the spiral touched the moon's expanded belly "… is where we are. And this…" Leon Eldridge shook the mesh "…is another orbit—"

"From another dimension, I assume," Nick blurted in.

"Good, you seem to be catching on," Leon Eldridge said. "This other orbit intersects the beginning, middle and end."

Leon Eldridge held the moon in place for a moment or two as if he wanted Nick to take time to study it.

"You see Nick, this illustrates how we are always connected with our origins as well as our potential," Leon Eldridge said before letting the mesh drop away from the spiral and return to its original shape.

"I…I…I don't quite understand. Okay, I admit it," Nick said. "I mean if God is in our future as you claim He is, how can He guide us today? I know I just asked you that, and you sort of answered with this crazed idea that signals can pass up and down this bizarre spiral timeline by this even more bizarre pi-made portal, but I still don't get it. It's almost like all those mediocre movies and television shows that have people going back into the past and screwing around with this or that and then coming back to see that everything in the present has changed. It's a worn-out script, but they use it all the time even though the real world tells us it's impossible. But what you claim is even more impossible. You're saying something in the future, or probable future, is already affecting the present with information and intervention, though that something doesn't exist yet. I just don't get it."

Leon Eldridge put his hand on Nick's shoulder, and with the rest of his arm, gently turned Nick toward the green hallway. As they walked out of the room with hand and arm still draped on Nick's shoulder, Leon Eldridge said, "It happens all the time."

Just then, Nick experienced deja vu. And when he looked back at the rings, loops, spirals and stars, Nick's experience was still in effect. He didn't understand that, either, but his memory was jogged for a better recollection of that former missionary's T-shirt.

"God does not equal $(+/-)(pi/2)$...something else."

Chapter Twenty-four

Nick went back to his room and lamented. He was concerned with Leon Eldridge's prevailing opinion of him, and how it may have been affected by Nick's emotion instability. Nick had a history of such outbursts.

Then again, maybe the tiff wasn't that bad—nothing more than firm and assertive stand against what he perceived as blasphemy. Yet Nick's scathing review of Leon Eldridge's life's work had to have left some scars. Nick felt that any critique of his own life work, that is if he had one, would be disheartening.

It was evening, but not late enough to call it a day. Nick, who hadn't ate since morning before cutting the grass, planned to go down to the kitchen for another bite. Nick decided to limit his meals to at most two a day. But be it the yard work or grappling with Leon Eldridge's grand-unified orientation, Nick felt like laying down for a little rest before eating. When Nick woke up, although it seemed he had just laid down 10 or 15 minutes ago, Nick had a feeling much more time had passed. He hoped it wasn't too late to still get a bite to eat. Nick's mother often said it was unhealthy to eat after midnight, and Nick always took that as the gospel truth.

However, Nick's hunger wasn't as pressing as it was before he had lain down. Instead, he wanted to revisit Leon Eldridge's glowing creation for perhaps a better understanding.

When he returned, Nick saw that things were a little different. The spotlights still favored the north side of the wall, but Nick could see the footlight on the far side had a black shade with a hole in the middle to focus the beam, making the overlapping spotlights more equal in size, though the closer spotlight was still brighter. As for the display, from what Nick remembered earlier, it appeared the alterations resulted in a brighter green glow.

Nick went inside for a closer look. While looking at the rings, loops and spirals, Nick determined there was far more open space within the mesh than matter itself, though it didn't seem so during his initial study. Nick also saw designs inside the mesh he didn't see before, which were probably always there but you had to notice them for them to exist. From one particular angle a design emerged that resembled a point—actually a long ring shaft coming forward—serving as the center of rings of increased sizes, like radio waves transmitting from an antenna as visualized from above.

And some of the smaller rings deeper inside the mesh now appeared to take bubble-like dimensions.

Intersecting and interlocking rings and spirals representing vibrations and beams, and vibrations that are beams and vice-versa, and bubbles...*THAT IS EVERYTHING GREAT AND SMALL?*

Then, at the mesh's planed middle, Nick was able to make out one of those damned equilateral triangles that fanned out with the wings. The more Nick looked at it, the more it took a three-dimensional shape before finally evolving into a pyramid. The color of the space taken up by this pyramid was, of course, glowing green. But it also seemed to emit other more obscured colors that changed and danced up and down the spectrum as Nick moved closer for inspection.

Nick then attempted to recreate the crescent moon. But when he grabbed the mesh's lower ring, another ring from somewhere inside the mesh somehow got dislodged and fell to the star-struck floor, breaking perfectly in half. Nick was startled. He didn't know if he should leave the broken halves on the floor, or to pocket them to hide the evidence. For many, the missing ring could go unnoticed, but if Leon Eldridge put as much effort into this as he had indicated, it probably would not. Nick picked up the two halves, which, like the felled grass, seemed to have lost much of their glowing color. Nick hung both of them on the lower ring. Nick decided he would confess some time the following day.

Then it finally all came back to him. That's it, Nick remembered: "God does not equal (+/-)(pi/2)(sort (3))."

Nick left the scene to visit Alyce and Pedro in the basement. When Nick first came aboard, he wouldn't dare to visit Alyce and Pedro unannounced during the evening for fear of catching them in the act. But for some reason Nick felt that wouldn't be the case. From what Nick was able to gather as of late, it appeared their relationship had cooled down, or at least matured, like they were a married couple well after the honeymoon. They were probably watching Alyce's TV, and Nick could join them to complete the same comfortable and seemingly platonic threesome of days before.

When Nick entered the basement from the elevator, he didn't hear a TV, bowling or any noise that would come from torrid activity. *They could be asleep,* Nick thought, though the mine-like lights in the basement were still on. Thank God for that. It would no doubt be a harrowing experience to feel one's way through a pitch-black basement while negotiating the beams.

When Nick got to their makeshift room, he was apprehensive in pulling back one of the sheets for fear of surprising its occupants. Maybe they slept with the lights on. But while catching a glimpse of their bed through an opening in between the sheets, Nick could see they weren't there. Nick then pulled back the sheets to further confirm their absence.

Something else was missing: Alyce's amoire.

Alyce's TV was there. It was placed on a standard dresser, presumably Pedro's. Also on the dresser was a LED-display clock displaying 3:15. *It's past three-o'clock in the morning? Nah,* Nick thought. *Can't be. If it were that late, Alyce and Pedro would surely be here sleeping—or at least in bed doing something.*

Just then, Nick heard a noise in the storage room. Maybe Alyce and Pedro were returning from a late night on the town. The noise was very loud and violent as Nick heard the crashing of tools being dislodged from the clutter. Negotiating one's way through the storage room in pitch-black darkness would probably be just as difficult. And indicated by the continual crashing heard inside, whoever it was having an especially difficult time. Then a scary thought came to Nick—could it be a burglar or a dangerous intruder? Even in pitch-black darkness, those familiar with the storage room shouldn't be having that much trouble.

Nick heard a voice— "God dammit!" He instantly recognized it as Pedro's. Nick's heart slowed down several beats. Eventually, Pedro emerged through the rusted door—but no Alyce. Where was Alyce?

As for Pedro, it didn't take Nick long to know why he was having so much trouble getting through the storage room. In one of his hands was a bottle of Moosehead, which appeared half full. And when Pedro wavered forward, Nick got an indication he had consumed far more than a half bottle of beer.

About his third step out of the door—Pedro didn't bother to close it, and apparently he didn't bother to close the wooden doors as Nick felt and smelt the night air waft into the basement bringing the fragrance of wet grass and alcohol with it—Pedro stumbled into one of the beams while hitting his forehead hard against it.

"Get out of my way, motherfucker!" Pedro barked at the inanimate object, yet he still had to wrap one of his arms around it to hold himself up. The beer bottle remained in his other hand and hung a foot from the floor. Then strange convulsions started to take over Pedro's upper-body before he lowered his head while he still clung to the beam and spewed out a seemingly inhuman amount of puke onto the uneven concrete floor. It didn't take long for Nick to get a whiff of that fragrance, too.

"I guess that's-s-s s-s-supposed to makes me feel —" Pedro threw up again, but not as much, before continuing his slurred statement, "better." Pedro wiped off his mouth with his back of this forearm. "But I s-sure in the hell don't."

Pedro started forward again before stumbling into another beam, yet not as hard as before. Nick could see a reddish bump growing on Pedro's forehead, and rushed to his aide to prevent him from further injuring himself.

"Get away from me, motherfucker," Pedro said while flailing his free arm at Nick when he approached. "I fuckin' can make it on my own."

Nick was offended by being called a "motherfucker" by Pedro. It was the first time Pedro had ever addressed him that way. Then again, it was probably the first time he addressed a basement beam that way.

Pedro stumbled ahead of Nick, as it appeared he was heading toward his room. But Pedro started to veer off in the direction of the bowling alley, and once again Nick tried to help him only to be, once again, harshly spurned.

"I said leave me alone, dammit," Pedro said as he pushed himself away from Nick, who tried to grab him at the arm. The act of pushing made Pedro further imbalanced as he tripped on the alley's raised approach, falling on his side while sliding a little on the smooth finish. Amazingly, he was able to hold his beer upright without spilling it.

Pedro slowly positioned himself to sit on the approach with his right foot under his left thigh. Nick looked at his face, which drooped noticeably from under the eyes and along the sides of the cheeks. It was like all of Pedro's facial muscles were in a sleeplike state while the rest of his person hung on to consciousness. Pedro raised the bottle and peered at it with one open eye, as if he was checking to see if there still was beer left in it, then took a strong swig. Nick couldn't understand how someone who had just puked his guts out could continue to drink.

Then this came gasping out of his mouth: "I'm going to hell."

"Pedro!" Nick said while walking up onto the approach. "Please don't say that."

"Well," Pedro said while his upright body swayed a bit, "if I don't say it, does that means-s I'm not going? Bullshit! I'm going to hell if you like it or not."

Nick crouched down next to Pedro and tried to look in his eyes. "Pedro, please. You're drunk. It doesn't mean you're going to hell."

"The hell I'm not," Pedro said. "I'm going straight to hell…" Pedro started to sob "…straight to hell!"

"Pedro!" said Nick, who never saw Pedro cry before, nor drunk. "What's the matter? Please talk to me."

"What's the matter?" Pedro said forcefully as the tears, though dripping from his bloodshot eyes, appeared to be drained from his voice. But when he repeated "What's the matter?" his voice was crying again. "I'm going to hell, that's-s what's-s the matter."

"Pedro, I said don't say that."

"And I said leave me alone," Pedro said. "Unless you want to go to hell with me."

"Oh Pedro," Nick said while lifting himself up and walking a little further away. "Now you're just being silly—and very sinful."

"S-s-sinful, huh," Pedro said while looking down at the wooden boards. Then he turned his body slightly to face Nick. "What do you know about s-sin except you don't—it bothers the fuck out you?"

Nick didn't respond as he took a seat on the smelly couch and eyed his sorry friend. Pedro remained seated on the approach with his head slouched. After a minute of silence, Nick asked, "Where's Alyce?" Pedro didn't respond as his head slouched even further down. Nick asked again but Pedro still didn't answer. Then Nick got off the coach and angrily demanded to know "What did you do to Alyce?"

"I didn't do fuckin' anything," Pedro said. "And she's going to hell, too."

"Pedro! Don't say that! That's evil speak."

Pedro shook his head and slowly got to his feet after using his bottle as a miniature cane. "You don't understand," he softly said while almost falling backwards. Pedro walked forward and appeared for a moment that he had enough balance to remain on upright. But when Pedro reached the end of the approach, the drop caught him off guard and he stumbled forward. Nick attempted to grab him, but Pedro had too much forward momentum and passed him before landing headfirst into the couch. Thankfully, it was a hard landing on a soft surface and Pedro was able to maneuver himself in a semi-reclined position. Again, Pedro was able to prevent his beer from spilling, although all he had left in the bottle was probably mostly backwash with remnants of his disgusting vomit.

Pedro leaned his head back and put his free palm over his brow like he was shielding the mine-like lights from his eyes, or feeling the bump on his forehead, or both. Nick sat on the opposite end of the couch, which musty smell was overtaken by the stench of what Pedro consumed and exhumed. Silence ensued, this time for more than a minute. Nick thought Pedro was on the verge of falling asleep, if he wasn't asleep already. But then Pedro spoke in a clear unslurred tone that suggested he suddenly regained his sobriety.

"I suppose you want to know what happened."

"I guess you could talk about it in the morning, when you feel a little better," said Nick, whose knowledge of hangovers was virtually nil, despite enduring the exploits of his father. "Maybe you should just get some rest and—wait a minute, where's Alyce?"

Pedro looked at Nick through his squinted eyes before raising the bottle to his lips for another drink. What Pedro tasted made his face grimace—maybe his vomit did find its way into the bottle. Then Pedro leaned back and covered his brow the same way before.

"She's here," Pedro said.

"No she's not."

"Yes she is," Pedro said while shaking his head in a negative motion, as if he was contradicting what he was saying.

"Then where is she?"

"Where is she?" Pedro said while leaning forward and closer to Nick. "I'll tell you where she is."

"Please do."

"Please do— please do," Pedro said mockingly. "I'll tell you what you don't want to know—please do—okay, I'll start from the fuckin' beginning."

Pedro pause for a moment and looked down at the floor at the foot of the couch, then leaned back and began talking upward at the ceiling, "Me and Jeff and whats-his-face—I don't know what the fuck his name is—but you know them…" Nick assumed they were Pedro's bowling buddies "…we decided to go, you know?—out. I asked Alyce if she wanted to go, but she said no, which was all right with me, at least at the time. I was even going to ask if you wanted to go, but you were asleep, or I mean you must have been asleep, because I knocked on your door and you didn't answer and I couldn't find you anywhere, unless you were up there with…" Pedro's face grimaced again "… him. But anyway we went to the bar down the street. But for some reason, they wouldn't let us in. Fuckers. They kicked us out. Damn them!"

It sounded like Pedro was on the verge of sobbing again before the same type of convulsions began to affect his upper body again. Pedro managed to hold it down, and then leaned back and became silent again.

"Okay, so they wouldn't let you stay," said Nick, who imagined they might have gone to the tavern next to the laundromat. Pedro may not have known about the ban the owner imposed on them. "What does that have to do with Alyce?"

"God dammit," Pedro snapped as he lurched forward. "Are you going to let me tell you what happened, or what?"

"Please do," Nick responded.

"Okay, " Pedro started again before pausing to look indignantly at Nick, a delayed response to the "please do." "Me and Jeff and whoever that motherfucker is…" Nick could see that Pedro had downgraded his language to that of his new friends—unless Pedro always talked that way when he was drunk "…we went and got some beers. But they wanted to go to this party somewhere, but I said 'Fuck that.' So they took their share of their beers and went on their…" a sigh and long pause, as if Pedro was groping to for something to finish his sentence "…merry way. But I stayed here. But I…" he raised his voice suddenly "… STAYED HERE!"

Pedro leaned back with his hand over his brow again. His eyes were closed, and Nick could see tears emerge from the eyelid slits. And again, Pedro became silent. Nick waited for about a half-minute. He was now leery of trying to jumpstart Pedro's dialogue, so he continued to wait. Eventually, Pedro leaned forward and faced Nick and continued where he left off.

"So I stayed here," Pedro said. "I came down here. It was—I don't know what the fuck time it was—but Alyce wasn't down here." Pedro then moved closer to Nick as if he had a secret to tell, and lowered his voice "But I had a good idea where she was."

Until that spring, Nick was—to say the least—woefully ignorant of affairs of the heart. That's why Alyce's fling with Pedro blind-sided him in such a way, although in retrospect the telltale signs were in front of his face. Now, from seeing Pedro's state of mind and recalling recent events and words, Nick had a good indication of what Pedro was going to reveal. But he wasn't quite ready to hear it.

"Now, now wait a minute Pedro," Nick said. "You're going to fast."

"Going to fast!" Pedro shouted. "Please do, please do—where's Alyce? Tell me what the fuck happened. A minute ago you couldn't wait to hear what happened."

"Yeah, I know. But—"

"But what?" Pedro said. "This is where she was…" Nick put his hands in front of him to signal Pedro to stop, but to no avail "… she was upstairs fuckin' that motherfucker."

Nick's heart almost stopped, like a sledgehammer to the chest knocked it out of rhythm and almost arrested it.

"And that's not even half of it," Pedro said. "When I walked in on them, they both seemed surprised at first, but then they just kept on going at it."

Nick was instantly reminded of the first time he saw Alyce and Pedro going at it in the alley. If they noticed Nick watching them, they would have probably kept going at it then, too.

"I was standing right in the doorway, looking at them," Pedro said while starting to sob again. "And they just kept going at it, going at it, going at it."

Every time Pedro repeated "going at it," it stung Nick's ears yet livened up his groin.

"So what—" Nick started to say before swallowing the excess saliva that accumulated in his mouth, "w-w-what did you do?"

Pedro let his bottle drop on the couch and put both of his hands over his face. He rubbed his fingers near his excreting tear ducts before revealing his face again. "This is why I'm going to hell."

Nick eyes widened. He feared the worst.

"I just stood there watching them go at it, and I didn't know what to do," Pedro said shaking his head. "I mean, what would you do? Hell, what the fuck would Jesus do?" Pedro opened up his mouth as wide as if he had to for what he had to say next. "I didn't want to lose her. I wanted to somehow make her still be mine. But she was with him, fuckin' him right in front of my eyes. So I only had one choice as far as I was concerned."

"Pedro," said Nick, who could feel nerves tingle under his skin, "what did you do?"

Pedro looked at Nick and then looked downward and away before answering, "I joined them."

Nick jumped up from the couch and screamed, "You what? You didn't."

"Now you still say I'm not going to hell?" Pedro said and then looked up to face Nick. "But I only wanted to fuck Alyce. That was my intention. I was only willing to share her. I was only —"

"I don't believe you," said Nick, who was starting to sob himself. "How dare you."

"What do you mean how dare me," Pedro said. "How dare him. Like I said,

I only wanted to fu—share Alyce. I didn't want to be a faggot. But—oh God…" Pedro buried his face in his hands as his next words were muffled by his palms "…he started to fuck in the ass."

"Whaaat?" Nick said as he moved closer to where he was looking down over Pedro.

"He started to fuck me up the ass," Pedro said more clearly while looking straight up at Nick.

"You mean he raped you?"

"No, he just—" Pedro bowed his head and covered his face. "I don't know. It seemed so unreal like it was some sort of nightmare. I didn't know what was happening."

Nick sat down close to Pedro and said, "Pedro. That's what it was. It was a bad dream. That's what it was. Right? You've been drinking, and you passed out —"

"No, no, no, no, NO! " Pedro said. "You don't fuckin' understand. The reason why I'm so drunk is because of what happened. And what happened was real. I was perfectly sober when it did. Well, not perfectly. But it happened."

Pedro leaned back on the couch. Nick slouched forward and gazed unfocusedly along the approach. He whispered to himself, "This can't be true," which was audible enough for Pedro to hear, who leaped onto the approach in a rage and threw his bottle down the lane. The bottle skipped along the surface while its contents spilled onto lane. Then near the rack of pins, which presumably where the same pins Nick set up days earlier, the bottle bounced up striking the top part of the head pin, which fell back to knock down one of the pins behind it, which fell back to knock down another pin, and that pin knocked down another. Meanwhile the bottle ended in the pit, which, until then, was probably the only place in and around the mansion a Moosehead bottle didn't find its way to. Then Pedro turned to face Nick. His formerly droopy face was now alive and ruddy.

"You've got to get your head out of your ass," Pedro shouted while thrusting both of his clenched fists downward below his hips. "Alyce was never the fuckin' angel you made her out to be. There was a reason why she was sent here, or there. It's the same fuckin' reason I was sent there—because we were on a one-way path to hell. Huh…" Pedro opened his fists and put his hands on his sides "… a lot of good that did."

Pedro then looked up in the direction of the turret. He curled back his lips and displayed his teeth like a rapid dog. "And him," said Pedro, thrusting his index finger where he was snarling at. "What makes him so special—so perfect?" Pedro stepped toward where his was pointing and snarling and stumbled when he accidentally stepped off the approach. Pedro was able to keep his footing, but he appeared to be disoriented as now, though he was still pointing upward, it was in the opposite direction of the turret.

"What makes him so holier than thou? Who put him in control? Who? WHO?"

Pedro bent down with both hands on his knees. He looked up at Nick, whose mouth was open. "I'll tell you what," Pedro said. "If I'm already going to hell, I have nothing to lose." When Pedro said "nothing to lose," he motioned with his hands like an umpire signaling a safe call. Then, while seemingly to have regained his balance and agility, Pedro made great and quick strides toward his room and disappeared behind the sheets. Nick couldn't see what Pedro was doing, but he heard him fumbling for something in what had to be his dresser. Then he heard Pedro curse, "Dammit, it better be here." Sounds of one drawer being slammed shut and another one being open made Nick even more curious. Then the other drawer shut, and Pedro emerged from behind the sheets. He had a gun in his hand.

Nick couldn't believe he was about to be a witness to an attempted murder. From his remote knowledge of firearms, he could tell it was a clip-loaded nine-millimeter. Pedro pulled back the top the cock it, and then started to move toward the elevator.

Nick attempted to stop him, but Pedro overpowered him and threw him to the floor. Yet while doing so, Pedro lost control of the gun, which also fell to the floor, but didn't go off, thank God. After it hit the floor, the gun slid about 10 feet on the concrete surface. It stopped closer to Pedro, but Nick was able to pull himself up and grab it just out of Pedro's grasp.

"Give it to me," Pedro said while his motioned toward Nick. Nick, who held the gun by its barrel, was able to quickly elude Pedro while using several beams as interference.

"Pedro, what's the matter with you?" Nick said as he had enough distance to get a better look at the gun, which had SIG SAUER engraved near its hammer. "Are you crazy?"

"Give me the God damn gun," said Pedro while still trying to corral Nick, who remained a moving target. Eventually, perhaps realizing he didn't have the faculties to catch or corner Nick, Pedro seemed to opt for another ploy.

"Come on, Nick," Pedro said, trying to sound more reasonable, or less insane. "Give me the gun. You're going to hurt someone with it."

"No! You're going to hurt someone with it," Nick said. "Where did you get this?"

Pedro bent down to put his hands on his knees and threw up just about where he first puked. "I've always had it," he said while still looking at his growing mess. "You think I went that s-s-shithole to save niggers' s-s-souls without it?"

Pedro straightened up and slowly walked in Nick's direction. By the nonchalant way Pedro moved and the way his bloodshot eyes appeared to be unfocused, Nick felt that he gave up in retrieving the gun. But when Pedro got within five feet of him, he slyly lunged forward only to have Nick elude him again.

"Go ahead, keep the damn thing," Pedro said. "If you had any balls, you would shoot me with it."

"Nobody is shooting nobody," Nick said.

"Huh," Pedro said while sniffing up the fluids—be it vomit or tears, or both—that found their way to his nose. He sauntered toward his room with his head down and walked in the middle of the broadside sheet. He tried to fling it out of his way only to get tangled up in it and tearing it down as he spun and fell backward on the bed. After taking a deep breath, Pedro raised his head and torso high enough to address Nick.

"You probably think I'm one evil son of a bitch," Pedro said. "But if you want to know who is the epitome of evil…" Pedro pointed at the ceiling, but not in the direction of the turret "…go upstairs and check out that fuckin' painting Alyce is so much in love with. I mean really…" Pedro now pointed at Nick "…take a gooood look at it."

Pedro laid himself back down with the sheet still wrapped around his lower body. And that was the last Nick heard of him. Nick still had the gun, which was much heavier than what he imagined a handgun would weigh. The only other type of gun Nick handled was a water pistol. He definitely wanted to keep it away from Pedro, but he didn't know what he would do with it himself. He was afraid if he took it to his bedroom, he might actually hurt someone with it, mainly himself. Nick didn't even know if the safety was off or on, or even if it had a safety. He figured the more he handled it, the more dangerous it would become.

While making sure Pedro wasn't looking and satisfied by the way his breathing made his prone body expand and recede, that he was asleep, Nick lifted one of the couch cushions and buried the gun under it. Nick then sat down on it, and eventually laid himself down. He took another glance at Pedro. After witnessing him in his drunken murderous state, Nick wondered if he really knew Pedro. He had always considered him a friend despite his transgressions and sometimes contemptuous attitude. But those collectively tended to cast an enduring light than a troublesome one. He was a rebel, but never a criminal, or so Nick thought. Pedro's latest transgression was real troublesome, and real criminal.

And how did Pedro view Nick? As a friend, or as a middleman to pave the way to Alyce? And who was Alyce? Nick also wondered if he really knew her.

Eventually, Nick fell asleep, even with the lurid images described to him by Pedro and Pedro's frightening actions still roaring. Nick didn't dream, or he didn't think he did. And when he woke up, it was his head that was spinning like it was he who had a hangover.

When he turned to the makeshift bedroom, Nick saw that Pedro was gone. The top drawer of the dresser was also missing, as well as the LED clock. The lower drawers were still there, but they were opened and appeared to be empty. Alyce's TV was still there.

By the diluted light that trickled through the storage room's open rusted door, Nick saw that it was still morning. Nick ventured outside and saw that Pedro's Malibu was gone. Nick then noticed the bed sheet Pedro inadvertently tore down folded and placed in the wheelbarrow. Nick could see by the stains as well as the putrid smell that Pedro used it to clean up his mess. At least he showed a little scruples before leaving.

Nick was then reminded of something. He rushed to the couch and pulled back the cushion to reveal—thank God—that the gun was still there. Nick put the cushion back on the gun and sat down while breathing a sign of relief. Though Pedro appeared to have taken his valued belongings, Nick had a good feeling he was not going to return to get his gun, or at least anytime soon. If he did, maybe Nick in the interim could find a better place to hide it.

As for Nick's future residence at the mansion, he still didn't know what he was going to do as he began to weigh his options contingent on what really happened. If what Pedro described was 100-percent true, he would definitely leave immediately, even with no place to go. If it was 50-percent true—i.e. Leon Eldridge and Alyce being unapologetic lovers, yet no sodomy involve— Nick may stay out of convenience yet with deep heartfelt reservations.

But Nick had to find out for himself. And after mustering up enough courage, Nick headed toward the elevator, which was stationed in the basement and already open, like it was waiting for him.

Chapter Twenty-five

Nick's stringy muscles stiffened in his arms, legs and sides of his neck as he exited the elevator. Even his heart muscles were affected. His stride was mechanical and gimpy, like the tin man in *The Wizard of Oz*. As he passed Dr. Dennis Gabor and his experiment, Nick sneered as if he was somehow the cause for this mess. Upon reaching the end of the hallway, Nick felt an outdoor breeze. Nick took a deep breath and walked into it, which streamed through his red locks that had grown longer than usual.

As expected, the short hallway led way to the turret, which, again as expected, appeared was Leon Eldridge's room. And Leon Eldridge was present. He was exercising on a stair-climbing machine while facing the middle of three big windows. Nick remembered the turret having only one window. Perhaps only one window was what he saw and remembered from various vantage points outside, and never put them together.

One window faced due north, another due west, and the third in between—northwest. They all had door-like hinges. The one Leon Eldridge faced was wide open, and Nick could see by the clearness of the stirring oak leaves outside that it had no screen. The other two were partially opened, each by about a foot and a half. From the door-less threshold, Nick felt half the breeze escape down the hallway, and the other half circulate around the turret.

The turret walls of the turret were the same attractive stone-and-mortar masonry that made up the mansion's outside identity—maybe it wasn't a façade with the mansion actually being made of stone. The carpet was artificial grass, not the retro baseball park type, but two-inch-high artificial grass. Nick also took note of the king-sized bed near the doorway and its leopard-designed bedspread. Nick assumed the bedspread was artificial, too. The bed was neatly made, possibly hiding evidence.

Nick was surprised there were no banners or posters with banal and trite statements tacked up. He looked for Leon Eldridge's themed T-shirts, but saw none. Maybe they were in his quadruple-door closet along the north side of the turret next to the north window.

A computer hard drive, keyboard and monitor on a desk were located near the entrance. The computer was hooked to what looked like a printer, but Nick couldn't see a phone jack. Nick had yet to see a phone jack anywhere in the mansion. The system, as well as the stair-climber, were powered from a multi-outlet extension in the middle of the room and half-buried by the artificial grass. Nick couldn't see where the extension cord led to due to the high grass. *A grass-fire hazard?* Nick thought.

In front of the desk was an S-shaped piece of furniture, either a sculpture or an ergonomic-designed chair—probably the latter but you could never tell in this place. And next to the closet was Alyce's armoire. On top of it was a 35-mm camera with a flash head on top. The camera was angled toward the armoire's mirror, and its reflection was pointed directly at Nick.

"Come in," said Leon Eldridge, somehow aware of Nick's presence although he never looked back as his legs steadily climbed upward yet remained in the same place. He had his hands raised to ear level, as if a gunman was holding him up. He was wearing black shorts, athletic shoes, white socks, and a gray tank top. The backside of the tank top was drenched with sweat. The sweat also draped on Leon Eldridge's broad shoulders and mostly bald head, making them both shine with help from the sliver of sunlight sneaking in from the north-facing window. A white towel covered the top of the machine, which had to be its control board and/or timer.

"My door is always open."

Therein lies the problem, Nick thought as he stepped onto the long artificial grass. It actually felt real, though Nick wasn't barefoot to truly experience it.

Leon Eldridge continued to climb while facing forward. Even from where Nick stood, the view outside the windows was magnificent. "The Great Highway" was partially visible through the foliage of the oak trees. Winter time would probably provide even a better view. Leon Eldridge lifted the towel from the control board and announced that he had three minutes to go. Nick waited anxiously as he scanned the room some more. Lying on the grass near the closet and the armoire was Leon Eldridge's bowling ball. A billiard ball—the 8 Ball—was half-obscured in the grass next to the bowling ball. Nick didn't see a billiard table anywhere in the mansion, so where did that 8 Ball come from?

Somehow, Nick got the intuition that Alyce stole the 8 Ball came from the tavern. After all, she wasn't an angel anymore.

Just then, a low-flying, southeast-bound airplane buzzed near the mansion. The tops of the trees swirled and Nick could feel the extra turbulence circle the turret as the plane passed by.

"That reminds me," Leon Eldridge said slightly winded, "we've come a long way since the Wright Brothers. We can land shuttles from outer space. If we live long enough, we might even see the first man or woman set foot on Mars. But only until recently have we started to find out why a plane really flies."

Nick didn't come up there to talk about airplanes, but that wasn't going to stop Leon Eldridge, who turned to face Nick while walking up the stairs backwards.

"For years they thought it was the high air pressure under the wing coupled with the low pressure above the wing that pushed the plane up," Leon Eldridge said before taking a deep breath. "Variances of air pressure do have a lot to do with an airplane flying. But it's the downward direction of the air as the wing alters it while passing through it that really gives the plane the lift. And we're just finding that out."

Leon Eldridge turned to face the window and raised his hands again.

Soon, the machine stopped. Leon Eldridge stood on the top step and wiped the shiny sweat off his shoulders while being lowered down.

"Time is relative, that I agree," said Leon Eldridge, hanging the towel on one of the handrails. "Compare 45 minutes on that to waking up to discover that you have 45 minutes to sleep in before your alarm clock goes off.

"Though I do dispute other observations."

Leon Eldridge went over to pick up the bowling ball and 8 Ball, walked over to the bed and dropped the bowling ball in the middle, revealing that it was a waterbed.

"That is our sun. And this," Leon Eldridge held up the 8 Ball, "is our planet." Leon Eldridge then dropped the 8 Ball inside the indentation and, naturally, the 8 Ball rolled down before coming to rest on the side of the "sun."

"And what's wrong with this picture?"

Nick had enough.

"What's wrong with this picture, huh?!!" Nick shouted belligerently at his host. "I'll tell you what's wrong. I didn't come up here for one of your theoretical exhibitions!"

Leon Eldridge's eyes widened upon hearing Nick's vociferous rebuke.

"Nick, why are you upset?"

"Yeah, and go ahead and act like nothing that happens here could ever upset me," Nick said.

"Nick, I would never try to upset a guest to my —"

"Spare me your holier-than-thou hospitality," Nick said as a droplet of spit flew out of his mouth. "In case you didn't know, Pedro just left here for good."

Leon Eldridge's face became expressionless. "He did? Why, he didn't even say goodbye."

Nick took that as sarcasm. "No, he didn't. I suppose that really breaks your heart."

"Alyce is still here," Leon Eldridge said.

"I bet she still is," Nick said while looking at the armoire, which was proof positive that Alyce didn't leave with Pedro. "Where is she?"

"I believe she's downstairs taking a shower," Leon Eldridge said.

"Oh yeah," Nick said before motioning with his face toward the armoire. "And why is that up here?"

"Because it's a family heirloom," Leon Eldridge said, giving Nick information he already knew. "It would have probably suffered water damage if left down in the basement."

"Water damage, huh," Nick said theatrically, shaking his head up and down. "Okay. Let me just ask you one more question, and I want an honest answer. No bullshit. Okay. You ready?"

Leon Eldridge squinted as if he really did have no idea what was bothering Nick.

"Here goes," Nick said before taking a deep breath. "Why are you having sex with Alyce?"

Leon Eldridge's face recoiled from the squint and went expressionless. "Isn't that what males and females tend to do on occasion?"

Nick's blood raced to his head and tears welled up in his eyes. "Okay, that's a good one. Good answer. Gooood answer," Nick said, bobbing his head up and down, increasing the flow of blood and tears. "Ya got me on that one, I've got to admit. Of course... natural procreation of the species, just your typical Discovery Channel stuff.

"But if that's the case..." Nick had to swallow the tears that seeped into his throat, "let me ask you another question."

"I thought you were going to ask just one more," Leon Eldridge said.

"Don't get fuckin' smart with me," said Nick with a thrusting index. "Fuckin' Alyce is natural, you say. But answer this: did you sodomize Pedro?"

"You mean did I have sex with Pedro?"

Nick took that as a yes, and the stone walls seemed to close in on him. "My GAWWD!" he cried out as loud. "You are the spawn of Satan! You are hideously evil. How could you do such an ungodly act? You, you Satan!"

The outburst made Nick light-headed. He was not ready to flee, although the conditions for flight were realized, Nick sat down on the bed making his own indentation. The bowling ball and billiard ball came to rest on the side of his leg provoking Nick to violently push the bowling ball away, but not far enough as it rolled back to his side. No longer paying attention, Nick slumped his head forward, buried his face in his hands and started to weep.

Leon Eldridge took off his tank top, catching the slight attention of Nick's uncovered black-and-white vision. Leon Eldridge placed his tank top on the "S" furniture and sat down on the bed several feet away from Nick.

"Get the fuck away from me you, you Satan," said Nick, moving further away. Leon Eldridge's indentation attracted the two balls, which he placed on the floor.

"Nick, if you want me to stay away from you, my bed is the worst place to stay."

"You've got that right," Nick said before removing his face from his hands to address Leon Eldridge eye-to-eye. "I don't know why I fuckin' even came here. You're evil! Evil!"

Nick got a better glimpse of Leon Eldridge's uncovered and muscularly cut torso and the prominent two tattoos placed on each pec. Sapphire tooth, dreadlocks but bald hairstyle, bisexual lifestyle—tattoos should have been expected. They were either oriental caricatures, Arabic letters, or examples of both, Nick couldn't tell, nor wanted to spend more than a second studying them. Instead, he buried his face in his hands again and unleashed muffled admonishment.

"You're so fuckin's evil. And you're so full of fuckin' bullshit," said Nick who, now hearing more of what was coming out of his mouth, felt that he involuntary adopted the language of Pedro and his bowling and drinking buddies, like there was a contagious strain of Tourette's Syndrome going around. But he didn't care.

"Nick, if I have hurt you or made you confused…" Leon Eldridge cordial accent made him seemingly immune from the strain, "…all I can ask is for your forgiveness."

"I'm not going to accept a contingent apology."

"Contingent apology?"

"Yes, contingent apology as in 'if I hurt you, then I'm sorry,' " Nick said. "If I was some sort of immoral schlock who didn't give a damn about all this, then I guess according to you there's no reason to apologize even if God is watching, which He is no doubt is? And I'm not confused!"

Nick got up from the bed and breathed hard to replenish the wind he had blown. Leon Eldridge got up, walked over to his computer and punched a couple of keys. From his angle, Nick couldn't see what was on the computer's screen. Whatever it was seemed to have been transferred to the printer as, several seconds later, it was activated. Nick watched a letter-sized piece of paper slowly emerge from the printer, half-inch by half-inch. He couldn't quite see what was being printed, yet his brief interest faded and he resumed his tirade—this time in a mean-spirited whisper.

"You're going to hell, that's all I got to say. That's what being an atheist will do to you."

After showing little or no reaction to being called evil and even Satan himself, Leon Eldridge's demeanor displayed offense with the atheist accusation. "I am not an atheist, I assure you of that," he said in defense.

"The bullshit you aren't," Nick said. "In fact, you told me so yesterday."

Leon Eldridge looked mystifyingly at Nick while handling on the paper coming out of the printer. "In fact I told you so yesterday? I don't think you've got your facts straight."

"Oh, I've got my facts straight all right," Nick said. "You're the one who hasn't got his facts straight, pal."

"Well," said Leon Eldridge, looking at the now freed piece of paper, "I'm glad we're still friends."

"The hell we are," Nick said. "Sodomizing atheists are no friends of mine."

"That's not very Christian, Nick."

"I never was a Christian. You're the only Christian around here, you atheist!"

"Why do you insist I'm an atheist?" said Leon Eldridge, now irritability oozing from his voice. "I never told you that."

"Did so. Yesterday, like I just said, by that damn contraption, or whatever that damn thing you conceived," Nick said. "It's all based on bullshit, and atheism. And you're going to pay dearly for it, believe me."

"I told you so yesterday?" Leon Eldridge walked toward Nick while holding both sides of the printed paper in his hand. "From what I remember, I proved to you that I did believe in God."

"No! You went on to prove to me that you don't," said Nick, stepping toward the approaching Leon Eldridge before both stopped within a foot of each other. "I don't quite remember all that you said because it was full of so much convoluted bullshit that it didn't all stick in my mind. But whatever it was, and whatever your hackneyed project represented—pi-fueled vibrating paths, or neutrino beams or whatever intersecting and crossing to form particles or whatever and spiraling all over the fuckin' place—bullshit—all at the same time ensuring the cockamamie fact—no, not fact, bullshit, that true wisdom and God will emerge in the future. Our future? Some other quantum or parallel universe's future? Who knows? You didn't go that far, from what I remember. But wait! I do remember—that's it—God will materialize in our probable future, according to your evil and absurd theory. And that makes you the quintessential atheist. There you go. I answered your question."

Leon Eldridge held the piece of paper close to his chest, as if he was hiding his hand in a poker game. "Intersections serving as particles? I can't believe I never articulated it in my mind that way."

"Yeah, and you also never articulated dark matter or God—or nor God— Oh, what the hell am I correcting myself for you, you, you piece of shit!"

That got a stir out of Leon Eldridge, whose lips tightened together. Nick had vented his frustration with no-holds-barred vindication, but now he felt he just uttered fighting words, pushing Leon Eldridge to the brink of responding to them.

"That's no way to talk to anybody," said Leon Eldridge, flipping the piece of paper on the bed with the unprinted side showing. Nick was nervous with Leon Eldridge's hands now free.

"You've got a lot to learn about people and life in general," said Leon Eldridge, while raising his index finger and then his middle finger, respectively representing people and life. Then he pointed this "peace sign" at Nick's eyes. "Is that the only way you know how to respond to conflicts of the heart and mind...with filthy and immature insults?"

Leon Eldridge paused for a while. Nick put his hand on his forehead and circled away, relieved just a lecture was Leon Eldridge's immediate response.

"I'm sorry," said Nick who, shortly after saying it, couldn't believe he had just apologized. He couldn't turn it around, though. "I...I...I just woke up with this splitting headache and—maybe I'm not thinking with a clear head."

"Why don't you sit down?"

Nick sat down on the bed. Leon Eldridge sat down, too.

"I mean, I'm sorry about what—"Nick caught himself almost apologizing for Leon Eldridge's actions again before changing direction, "I mean I can't change what has happened but—I don't know. It's all confusing."

"Why is it so confusing?"

Trying to stay clear from sexual escapades for fear it draw hell fire again, Nick instead was willing to address Leon Eldridge's probable God proposal in a more civil manner. "I mean, I still don't get it. You claim, or I think you claim that God is something that we will eventually evolve to, right?"

Leon Eldridge was silent.

"So that indicates that He is in our future, as I was saying. But that also means He doesn't exist now. So now, as in right now, we presently live in a Godless world."

"That doesn't mean we live in a Godless world."

"How can it mean otherwise?" Nick said. "What is now is now. We cannot travel to another point in time to affect the past. Even God can't do that."

"I thought with God anything is possible," Leon Eldridge said. "But I do see what you're saying: Real things from the past, present and future cannot exist simultaneously along different points of a timeline. Even in a short period of time. We, and you're probably right with me on this one, cannot go back in a time machine five or ten minutes from now and introduce ourselves to slightly younger versions of ourselves."

"Yes," Nick said, but he wasn't quite sure of his confirmation. Then reflowing the explanation in his head, he repeated with more conviction. "Yes. Yeah. We can't do that. And, like I was saying all along, believing God is in our future is not believing God exists in our universe timeline—or whatever you just said."

"But that applies to real entities. What I'm referring to is probable entities."

"There you go again," said Nick, shaking his head. "How could something in our probable future have any affect on us now. I mean, yeah, I'm starting to understand that connection of the past, present and future theory you showed me the other day, or yesterday. Yet still I don't see how could work, or apply, in the real or even probable world."

"You know what you should try to do," Leon Eldridge said. "Write a book."

"Like I really have such time," answered Nick, who actually had all kinds of time on his hands aside from his self-appointed chores. "Plus, I'm not a writer. And neither was Jesus."

"And neither was Socrates. But you should try it anyway. It doesn't have to be long, yet you should start with an ending in mind and work from beginning to end without jumping ahead or going back while making you first draft. And after arriving at this ending, which may be a little or substantially different from what you originally had in mind, go back through your draft and see how many changes you end up making."

"For your information, some of the greatest authors of all time never made revisions," Nick said.

"I'm not talking about them, I'm talking about you."

"Yeah, yeah, yeah," said Nick, waving by hands by his ears to convey his half-ass frustration. His movements caused small ripple waves in the waterbed. "Regardless, we're talking about making fiction. Fiction is fiction. Obviously, it can be changed. Even after it's printed. But you can't change what has already happened in a non-fictional world. Unless of course you're saying the past is probable, too."

"Of course it is."

Nick let out a guffaw. "When is this going to end? Then I guess taking that into consideration, the present is probable, too? Right?"

"Really, what constitutes the present?"

"Jesus Christ," said Nick, flailing his hands up in the air. "Look, you made me say the Lord's son's name in vain. You and you're rhetorical questions: What makes a plane fly? What constitutes the present? But I'm not getting upset again. I'm not going to let you this time. Because, I'm sorry I have say this, but I'm a servant of God and my ultimate goal is to lead others who are astray to be servants, too, but it's you who are confused, and that's what I'm really sorry about. It's not that I don't understand what you're saying anymore. I understand it perfectly. It's just not right, or correct. There's no way it can be."

Leon Eldridge sapphire smiled as if he knew Nick had more to say.

"Okay, I'll accept the theory that the future is probable—"

"It's not a theory, it's the real thing," Leon Eldridge interrupted.

"The real thing?" Nick said. "A second ago you indicated the present is not really real. But anyway, the future is probable, there I'm willing to agree with you. But God is surely not probable, and surely neither is the past. And like I said yesterday, we cannot go back into the past and change things likes we're in a science fiction movie."

"But we do it all the time."

"Yeah, and like when and how?"

"I'm sure you have seen documentaries or read books about historical events. Like *The First Americans* or *What Really Happened at Little Big Horn* or other research productions that systematically change history right before our eyes."

The examples reminded Nick about Elder Steven's buffalo and "American aborigine" painting and its subsequent disappearance.

"Again," Nick said, "that's where I think you're very confused on matters of basic reality. They didn't change history. They have either have done the digging and research to provide a more accurate account, or non-accurate account depending on how competent the researchers. But revisionist history, at least in regards to our history, is going to go the way of the, eh, dodo bird because just about every significant thing nowadays is being electronically, or digitally recorded to a point where there will always be a tangible and true record of it."

"The assassination of John F. Kennedy was recorded," Leon Eldridge said. "Is there an undisputed record of that?"

"There you go with those rhetorical questions again," Nick said.

"You seem not to like them, though I don't classify them as rhetorical," Leon Eldridge said. "And I don't seem to remember asking you an airplane question."

"You did," Nick insisted. "You asked me what makes an airplane fly."

"I told you what makes an airplane fly, but I didn't ask you why," Leon Eldridge said. "And that was only about five minutes ago, but that past had already changed in your mind."

Nick paused to recall the recent exchange. "Okay, you're right. But of course if you never corrected me, it doesn't make my version the right version."

The waterbed grew still during the ensuing seconds of silence. Then Leon Eldridge spoke. "I heard your brother died recently."

Nick straightened up. He was surprised that Leon Eldridge brought up the subject. "Who told you?" he asked.

"Alyce."

"What else did she say about me?"

"She told me that you and her are real close."

"She did?" Nick said. "And what did she say about Pedro?"

"Nick, I don't know if we should delve into that with neither party present."

"But you two no had trouble delving into my life when I wasn't present," said Nick, who immediately regretted being too sensitive. "I'm sorry. I didn't mean to be an asshole. Yes, he died two years ago."

There was more still silence before Leon Eldridge spoke again. "She told me he died from a snakebite."

Nick straightened up again. "Leon, if you will—"

"Leon Eldridge, please."

"Okay, if I'm going to make concessions about calling you by your full name, you're going to have to make concessions by at least trying to abide by my emotional state. Now I told you I'm going to try not to get upset again, at least not today. So I ask you that we should talk about this when I want to talk about it, if ever."

"So he died from a snakebite. Is that what really happened?" Leon Eldridge asked as if oblivious of the request.

"Unfortunately, yes," Nick reluctantly confirmed. "Alyce probably told you the whole story, so I don't know why I should repeat it to you."

"A deadly snakebite in this part of the country?"

"It wasn't an indigenous snake," said Nick, who got the indication Leon Eldridge didn't know the whole story. Then again, he could be tanking. "It was a green mamba. It was raised by some kid who lived nearby. It got loose, and it killed my brother during a walk we took near the site of the church he was going to build. I saw the whole thing. It was terrible. There's your story."

"But Nick, was that really the whole story?"

"You just don't give up, do you?" Nick said. "I think you like seeing me get upset. Like it gets you off or something."

"Nick, you know there was more to it than that, at least at that time," Leon Eldridge said.

"What do you mean more to it than that? I mean, it was a freak chance of nature, or not even that because nature dictates that such creatures don't belong in that part of the world. It was just bizarre bad luck and it..." Nick stopped as he felt more tears coming, but he was able to fight them back "...shouldn't have happened."

"What I mean by it being more to it than that was how you perceived the event at that time," Leon Eldridge said.

"How I perceive it? I don't know of any —"

"No. How you perceived it at that time," Leon Eldridge said. Nick saw by his intense stare that he was driving at something. Maybe he did get off stirring up Nick's emotions.

"What you're asking me to do is relate a memory of a memory, and a very, very, very bad memory at that," said Nick, trying to return an intense stare of his own. "Yes, it was bad. Immediately after was bad, but not the worst. I mean, during the wake and funeral you're in God's world then. Of course you're in God's world all the time. But his presence is felt better during that time. But afterwards, that's when it seemed He left us for good."

Leon Eldridge nodded his head as if was coaxing Nick to continue.

"I mean before, God and even Jesus were firmly planted with my family. But when Dom died, there was so much grief and vengeful hatred, especially from my parents. You could almost see the grime building on their souls. And they started to return to their, uh, evil ways. And it wasn't only like evil was coming from within, but all around us, and it was closing in."

"Explain that, the closing in," Leon Eldridge queried.

Nick looked angrily at Leon Eldridge. Nonetheless, he abided. "You see, there was all this controversy that came out in the aftermath. Not sex-with-intern type controversy, but it still was disheartening and very disrespectful, like people didn't think twice to spit on Dom's grave. And it all started from these, these…" Nick's voice grew louder and more agitated "…freedom-from-religion bastards. Bastards! That's what I call them. Freedom of religion and separation of church and state, that's what they fly under. Freedom from religion, that's what they're really all about. They're all damned cynical atheists, maybe not like you, but the kind who go out of their way to stick their noses in other people's and God's business. They started raising a fuss on how Dom, eh, procured, I think that's the word, an arrangement to build a church in a forest preserve, and how the money was raised and stuff like that. I mean it's easy to attack someone when he's dead and unable to defend himself. And the damn local newspapers followed their lead, and only printed their side of the story. It was terrible. It was like —"

Nick bit his lower lip in effort to prevent what he was about to say, but Leon Eldridge said it for him.

"Like the devil destroyed your brother."

Nick shook his head solemnly, then softly said it himself, "Yes, it was like the devil killed my brother and his good name."

Nick closed his eyes and put his hands his nose and mouth like he was praying while trying not to inhale poisonous fumes. "But what made it really seem like that, at least at the time, was they never found the snake."

"So it must have been the devil."

"Well, no. It wasn't the devil. But it seemed to be at that time."

"When did it seem not to be?"

"I don't know for sure. But later someone, I forget who, told me they found the snake."

"So it couldn't have been the devil."

"No it couldn't, even though they never found it."

"But you just said they found it."

"No, now you're changing the very recent past," Nick said with a winsome smile that dissipated in a split-second. "I was told they found it. Either it was relayed misinformation or someone thought I would feel better if I thought they did. But later I overheard a conversation my mom was having on the phone that revealed that they never found it."

Nick vividly remembered his mom saying to an unknown party, "And that son of a bitch never spent a night in jail. I hope it bites someone else. That will make hell even hotter for him."

"So it was the devil after all?"

"No, no, no, no, NO!" said Nick, shouting the last NO! "Satan did not kill my brother. I don't know where you got such a sick idea."

"I got it from you," Leon Eldridge answered.

"Jesus Christ! See, you made me say it again," scolded Nick, who almost got up from the bed to leave for good, but refrained. "Either you have a terrible memory, something you just accused me of, or you just don't listen well. I told you what you asked me to tell you, about how I perceived the death during its aftermath. And yes, at one time I thought Satan did intervene. But I was in a state of despair, and so were my parents. But I managed to grow from the experience. I managed to understand that although this was a freak occurrence and they didn't find the snake—it probably didn't last long out of its natural environment and its body got eaten up by a squirrel or something—that the devil, or Satan, is incapable of doing such a thing, that is take a human life."

"What makes him incapable?"

"God, of course. He's far more powerful, and wouldn't allow such a thing."

"But you do agree that the devil is capable of taking a human soul?"

"No, no, NO! You're wrong again. He can only take our souls if we let him."

"So from what I understand, and I am trying to listen, that you were able to get beyond the grief and accept your brother's death as something that came about from natural, although strange and unlucky, means."

"Well first of all, I don't think 'accepting'..." Nick used his fingers to symbolize quote marks "...my brother's death is the right term. And second of all, you can never really get beyond a loved one's demise. If you had ever lost someone close, especially in an unexpected death, you would know that there are two types, or make that three types of grief. The first is the shocking type of grief that hits you right after the death. Then, after the deceased is honored and buried, you begin to suffer another type of grief, the type I just told you about that comes in the weeks when you try to get on with your regular life. But even when you move beyond that, another type of grief rears its head. It comes at various times of the following year, like Thanksgiving and Christmas, or times during the spring and summer where you are reminded of what you were doing about the same time the year before with someone who's no longer…" Nick sucked back some building tears "…there. When I returned to the academy, even though the year before was the first year I wasn't accompanied by Dom, I began to go through that dark period. But that's when Alyce came to my…" Nick took a deep breath while sucking back the remaining tears he didn't get before "… rescue. She helped bring me back."

"I take it that's when you and her became close."

"Very close," Nick said with a sigh. "When I returned home for summer break that year, during dinner my mother asked me how I was doing, and I believed she was trying to find out handling things in regards to Dom. And I wanted to tell her and my father that I was doing all right. Then I mentioned Alyce, and how she helped me cope, and how through it all we became inseparable, and how beautiful she was, and how I may have found that special someone to spend the rest of my life with and how I couldn't wait for next fall to see her again. Then I said something stupid, something very stupid. I said something like—I can't remember the exact words—maybe certain things were meant to be, that there's good that comes from bad. That's when my father exploded. He pounded his fist on the table and said—and I can remember his exact words—'Don't you ever say Dom's death is a blessing in disguise!' I thought he was going to hit me. He had struck me before for much lesser offenses, and even at times, many times, for no reason. He didn't this time, though it was one time maybe he should have."

Then Nick looked Leon Eldridge straight in the eye, "But I was in love with Alyce. I hope you know that."

Leon Eldridge stared back and waited several seconds before asking, "Do you still love Alyce?"

Nick looked down at the fake grass. "I don't know."

Leon Eldridge then asked another question, "How do you perceive Dom's death, now?"

Nick was still looking down in a state of melancholy. He heard Leon Eldridge's last question, but it had yet to seep in. But when Nick played the question over again in his head, the intentions of the inquiry became clear. Nick's blood again began to churn and he leaped from the bed.

"Satan did not kill my brother!" Nick screamed while waving his finger at

Leon Eldridge. "Satan did not kill my brother. Don't say that about my Satan! Don't say that about my brother!"

Nick thought about turning to leave for good, but had to reiterate his point even further while demanding for a retraction

"Satan did not kill my brother! Satan did not kill my brother! Say Satan did not kill my brother! Say it, God damn you, say it! Take it back!"

Leon Eldridge got up and approached Nick. Nick didn't recoil as Leon Eldridge got closer, but continued to shout belligerently, "Say he didn't kill him! Say it! Say it!"

Leon Eldridge put his hand on the back of Nick's neck and gently pulled his face toward his tattooed pec. At first, Nick offered slight resistance but gave in and buried his tears in Leon Eldridge's body. The fight was out of Nick. He just wanted to be comforted now. The smell of Leon Eldridge's sweat soothed him.

"Why does it hurt so bad?" Nick sobbed with his tears returning to the original conflict. "Why do people you love hurt you so bad?"

Leon Eldridge said in a whisper, "Because the pain is part of the solution."

Nick didn't understand, but his queries, like his body and soul, were exhausted Leon Eldridge continue to talk, no longer in a whisper, but in a soft and clear Southern accent.

"The pain comes from trying to experience the present, the true essence of now. We're rarely there because our consciousness is a mesh of what we remembered, what probably happened in the past and what will probably happen in the future. What is truly now is always fleeting, always escaping our grasp. But we need to experience it, and we need to experience it with others— imagined or real. Because the experience of what is truly now links us simultaneously with our true beginning and our true potential. And we must go there. And do you know how we get there? Do you know how we make that connection?"

Nick looked up.

"When we have an orgasm," said Leon Eldridge, answering his own rhetorical question.

Before Nick knew what was going on, Leon Eldridge was nibbling gently on his ear while speaking into it.

"While seeking that connection, we often neglect the ones around us, the ones who also want to make that connection. We don't always feel their pain, but we always feel our own pain when it's our time to suffer. And we all suffer, but we also inflict. All of us do. You mocked me when I offered that contingent apology as you call it. But what else can I do? I must live. I must make and feel that connection. That's the ultimate prove of life, the ultimate proof of God. I fear to expose myself as a simpleton when I consider any unbeknownst pain I cause during my connection quests as collateral damage. Collateral damage is a statistic, but it exists and guilt is its natural consequence. Guilt is hard to discard because we can never forgive ourselves for the pain we cause to others. We must however forgive those who cause us pain. That's the only hope they have. That's the only hope we have. And hope derives from the pain…the key to our salvation."

Leon Eldridge walked Nick over to the waterbed. While being led, Nick felt he was floating instead of walking, like he was in a dream and aware of it. Nick allowed Leon Eldridge to kiss him on the cheek as they laid down together, making one big indentation. Then Leon Eldridge started kissing Nick on the lips, and Nick turned away and got up on his hands and knees. But he didn't leave, like he was trapped inside the indentation. From behind, Leon Eldridge began to unbutton Nick's white shirt and rub his chest. Then, still from behind, his unfastened and unzipped Nick's pants. It had to be a dream, Nick wanted to believe while striving to further attain a dream-like awareness.

After Leon Eldridge pulled Nick's pants and underwear down, he stopped momentarily. Nick couldn't see what he was doing, but he could tell from the ripples of the bed that he was retrieving something at the other end. Soon Leon Eldridge returned to his former position right up against Nick's backside. Leon Eldridge reached around Nick to place in front of him the piece of paper he just printed.

It was a black-and-white photo of Alyce, nude and in the throes of sex, though from her familiar on-top position you couldn't see what was under her hips—no doubt it was the photographer. The shape of her irises, not blue in the colorless photo, were that of a crescent moon on one side and a partial eclipse on the other—a flash effect perhaps. And the expression on her face and the blurred motion of her breasts indicated that she was experiencing the true essence of now and the photo, unlike the ones displayed in the storage room, was able to capture that fleeting moment. Nick's penis grew hard, but when Leon Eldridge started playing and tugging on it from behind, his cold sweating hands made it shrivel up.

But Leon Eldridge himself wasn't shriveled, and Nick found that out when Leon Eldridge started to thrust his erect member into his anus. The feeling was so unique, so intrusive that Nick, to his horror, realized this could not be a dream. And as Leon Eldridge continue to fuck Nick like a dog, Nick didn't feel himself rushing toward the ultimate connection that binds what is truly now with what was/is the true beginning and the true potential. Yet the sensation did warp his sense of time.

It was like he was shitting in reverse.

Chapter Twenty-six

Nick threw up the first step into his room.

It wasn't en mass as Pedro's—Nick didn't have much to regurgitate, just the 24-hour-old ravioli remnants, now pinkish-white, and a light-green slice of slime, which slicked through the chunky mess as if Nick also ate the grass he mowed.

Maybe it wasn't alcohol that made Pedro sick. Maybe this was common for those who had just taken it up the ass for the first time.

Nick closed the door but still needed more privacy. After using his bed sheet to sop up the vomit, Nick took it to the window. With no drape rod at his disposal, Nick was going to wedge the sheet in place at the top-half of the window. But just as he was trying to lower the top-half, a wasp stung Nick on the knuckle, and before he knew it three or four others were circling menacingly around him. Nick briefly used his sheet as a shield before dropping it when a wasp attached itself to it near his fingers. Nick then juked, shuffled and bobbed across the room with the insects in pursuit.

Eventually, they left him alone, but Nick knew nature was against him. Nick sat on the bed, which felt like its was carved out of a stone quarry. His ass also hurt. Nick wondered if he sustained severe damage down there and/or contracted a deadly disease.

Nick reached down for the Bible on the floor near the bed. He could see a small portion of his vomit splattered on the black cover. But he didn't see the wasp resting on it, and Nick got stung again on the same hand.

Now God was against him.

Nick vengefully squashed the wasp and then picked up the Bible and threw it overhand at the window, shattering the top half while taking a few wasps with it.

"Fuck you all!" Nick shouted. He then sat back on the bed, buried his head in his cupped hands, and started to sob.

After he had cried himself dry, Nick looked up and studied the broken window. He thought the opening would encourage the wasps to flee. Instead, more wasps from the outside were drawn inside. It was time for Nick to leave. But where?

Didn't matter. Nick hastily packed his belongings in his trusty sack. He could smell his soiled wardrobe through the sack when he threw it over his shoulder. Nick sensed what he was wearing had the same stench. Nick made way to the back door while trying to be as quiet as possible. He didn't want to alert anyone of his departure.

As hoped, Nick didn't encounter anyone while existing the mansion, and no one was in the back yard. Nick headed west through the open field before finding his way down the treacherous grade to "The Great Highway." When he got to level ground, Nick stopped and lowered the sack from his shoulder. He tried to spot "The Great Structure" from afar, but today—like his subsequent return—it wasn't there. Nick turned to the turret clearly visible through an opening amid the trees. Sure enough, it had three windows even from the outside. He couldn't make out any figures through the windows, but Nick didn't gander too long. He picked up his sack and continued his departure. There was no sidewalk accompanying this portion of "The Great Highway."

But where? Nick still hadn't decided though he was cognizant that he was heading toward his parent's house in the great distance. But to Nick, it seemed involuntary—like he was being led by some unseen force.

And though Nick didn't retrieve the Bible he threw through the window, one of its stories came to mind: The Prodigal Son.

During the few occasions when Bible passages were displayed for academy students outside the "Real Jesus" package, they usually mixed liberal interpretation with conservative fundamentals. During one of Nick's freshman classes, the Prodigal Son was played from a vinyl record with use of an old-fashioned, single-speaker turntable. The record was produced in the '60s, and somehow preserved enough clarity through the scratchy and worn sound. The Prodigal Son was portrayed as an unapologetic "playa" (though a post-'60s term) who squandered his money on alcohol, drugs, gambling and—cleverly suggested—sex. Upon returning home, he was greeted with open arms by his father, much to the chagrin of the other brother, whose previous overtures of faithfulness and restraint made him sound like a comically patronizing Eddie Haskell, which got a repeated laugh out of the class.

"Your brother was lost, now he is found," the father said to Eddie Haskell. Nick thought of that as he continued westward. But did the parable really apply to the current situation? For one, Nick no longer had a brother.

At a roadside diner a mile or so from the border, Nick grabbed a bite to eat and pondered. He didn't have much money left, though it was the same he had before taking residence at the mansion. Funny how far money could go without paying for rent or food. Nick stirred a french fry in some catsup. French fries and catsup, that's all he ordered—the ice water was free.

The inevitable unhappy resolution of his return began to plague Nick as he tried to make the fries last as long as possible. Then he thought about Alyce.

It pained Nick that his last vision of Alyce was that climatic photo placed in front of him during Leon Eldridge's sex act with him. Nick didn't want it to be that way. When he finally finished his fries and water Nick decided to retrace his steps to bid Alyce adieu.

But he was not returning for good. He was not going to allow himself to be Leon Eldridge's Prodigal Son. He was going to say goodbye to Alyce knowing (and hopefully she too) that they would never see each other again. Then maybe exchange a handshakes or hugs or a goodbye kisses on the cheeks. Nick would force himself not to cry. But how about Alyce? If not in Nick's presence, maybe in the days to come.

Did Nick still love her? Leon Eldridge's question earlier that morning echoed in Nick's mind. Eventually, Nick came to believe that he still did so. If not, why was he adding miles to humping a smelly sack?

Maybe spurred by the swollen irritation of his twice-stung hand still needed to grasp the retractable string for better control of the sack, but resentment began to rage in Nick's soul toward Alyce and her new lover. And how many new lovers had Leon Eldridge procured in his young lifetime? Well, Nick for one.

"Ah, fuck, fuck, fuck!" Even the voice in Nick's head seemed afflicted with Tourette's. Nick then sneered upward over his shoulder at the sun. With it no doubt serving as God's eyes and ears, Nick knew He was aware of his malignant thoughts.

When Nick reached the mansion, the sun was still high in the sky, but it was obscured by the looming oaks and cast cavernous shadows. It seemed later that it really was. But even with it really being late afternoon—or early evening, depending on how you separate the two—Nick wondered how the walk to the diner and back, about five or six miles combined, could take up so much time. Maybe Nick's pensive French fry meal accounted for the gap.

Nick didn't enter the same way he exited. Instead, Nick opted to go up the driveway along the east side of the property. Remembering that the driveway slithered slightly to the southwest after the entrance, Nick took a little shortcut up the hill. Just before Nick reached the driveway, he found himself in a familiar spot though—he at least thought—he had never stood there before. Nick looked up at the mansion's silhouette lording the black back-lit oaks.

Nick trekked his way up the driveway, now gravel. Like his departure, Nick encountered no one in the back yard, auxiliary room, kitchen or that level of the house. Nick returned to his former bedroom to momentarily to leave his sack and to rehearse his farewell. Leon Eldridge wasn't going to be a part of the script.

When Nick got to his room, the wasps were gone but the vomit stench had multiplied. Reasonably fatigued, Nick sat on the bed, which wasn't as hard as before. Nick's ass still hurt, though. Soon, Nick laid prone on his side to rest even more. He wondered where he would sleep that night, or if he would sleep at all. Eventually, Nick fell asleep right where he was.

Nick dreamed self-aware that he was dreaming. His dream, or dreams were ripe with violence though Nick couldn't decipher the fleeting abstract images that flittered like a film made entirely of subliminal frames.

Then Pedro showed up. Nick didn't see him, but knew he was there. He seemed placed in-between each subliminal frame, hidden but pervasively present. Yet Pedro wasn't just on film as Nick could feel Pedro passing through him like a ghost seeping into his person. And though this ghost didn't speak, it reminded Nick of the last thing its host said to him.

"Take a good look at that painting."

Nick awoke. His upper-body rose perpendicular from the bed like Dracula rising from his coffin or the Frankenstein monster coming to life from his gurney. The sun was down. The evening had become black, but not completely. Enough light escaped from the ballroom, guiding Nick's path. The moonlight was the main source, multiplied by traveling through each of the slitted windows. The wax floor shined and the dormant chandelier sparkled. Nick made his way to the foyer and looked up at the full moon nearly full, filling the rose window. It offered Nick a better study of what it spotlighted.

Nick strained his eyes as if it was a puzzle Pedro troubled him to solve. Nick instantly remembered his initial familiarity of the spot just up the hill and near the entrance. Finally, he realized that something had changed—or rather had been stored in his memory as reversed: Leon Eldridge was helping Jesus up the hill, not the other way around.

In the spirit of the great Dutch painters, the two figures had glowing qualities emanating from within. It was like they were painted over a bright ball of white light just under the surface. And a fanned beam from this bright ball blazed an upward path through the baroque-brushed wooded hill to the mansion.

Leon Eldridge was not original, but Nick conceded that he at least displayed a considerable amount of dexterity in his proper depiction of the figures' hands, arms, legs and body at work and in motion. Leon Eldridge's grip of Jesus' hand was an example, and that's when Nick saw it: Leon Eldridge's right hand was rotated more to the top as it pulled Jesus up, and middle and index fingers were placed on Jesus' big wrist veins.

Leon Eldridge was seducing Jesus.

Nick elevated down to the basement and retrieved the 9-millimeter from inside the couch. Back near the elevator, Nick first noticed the basement's probable light switch. It was located near the northwest corner. Again, it was always there. It was red and, within a steel box with a flexible pipe up to the ceiling, looked more like a circuit breaker. The red switch was up.

For some reason, the elevator didn't wait for him this time. Nick pressed its button and walked over to the red switch. After pausing for a moment, Nick flicked it down and was immediately enveloped in complete darkness. Nick thought it could have been the main circuit breaker shutting off power to the entire mansion because the elevator still hadn't arrived. And that's when he remembered the pole-propped power lines just west of the mansion in the painting and, thus, in reality, too. In the painting, it was likely referenced from a photo, a technique borrowed (or stolen) from the renowned cartoonist Crumb. And, of course, it always had to be there. How else did the mansion get electricity?

The elevator doors opened, and Nick stepped into the light.

The doors remained open and the electric light seeped into the basement, unimpeded from any shadow from Nick, who leaned his shoulders at the back of the elevator. Nick was able to see three beams into the basement. Funny, a quick thought came to Nick while waiting for the doors to close, that if he stared long enough he would be able see all the way to the east wall and Alyce and Pedro's makeshift bedroom, as if his eyes' ability to adjust their aperture affected the light's reach.

The doors closed. It was now in God's hands. If the elevator stopped at the main floor, Nick would head directly to his former bedroom, grab his sack and leave, this time for good. Maybe the walk back wouldn't be a total waste as Nick planned to keep the gun. He may need it for some reason, and it started to feel comfortable in his un-stung hand.

Nick estimated the upward movement passed the main floor, so when the beige walls appeared through the crack of the opening doors, Nick wasn't surprised or dismayed. It was God's decision.

Nick briskly walked by Dr. Dennis Gabor with the intention of not looking. But as he passed, Gabor's eyes followed him, or so thought Nick, who quickly turned in hopes of catching him in the act. Nick continued and turned at the wall. Leon Eldridge's bedroom wasn't visible, but as Nick moved forward, they emerged: Alyce and Leon Eldridge were porning on the waterbed.

Nick moved closer. The encased water slosh so violently with the physical action that the bed seemed to be on the verge of exploding. The lovers were in flux—top, bottom, from the side. Nick was caught in a sensual time warp, unable to determine a second from a minute. A thin layer of perspiration made both of their bodies shine, much the same way Leon Eldridge shined earlier that morning.

When Nick first saw Alyce and Pedro fornicate, Nick got as close as he could. The back of the Malibu separated him from them at the time. Now, Nick could actually feel the waves as the sloshing grew more torrid. They were facing away from the turret's doorway, but not completely away from the slowly approaching Nick, 9-milimeter still in hand. At least one of them had to see Nick—or maybe not.

Nick stepped to the threshold. Alyce assumed her familiar cowgirl position using Leon Eldridge's bloated balls for extra bounce. Nick had an urge. But though Nick's concealed cock was achieving maximum growth, the gun in his hand pulsated even more, like another organ begging to be emptied.

Nick stepped into the room and now was at bedside, though Alyce continued to ride Leon Eldridge's cock as if he wasn't there. Nick was tempted to shout something like "Hey!" but that would have been rude. Instead, he continued to gape before taking a couple of steps back from the bed, using his twice-stung hand as a guide. The fucking continued.

Before pulling the trigger, Nick put things in God's hands again. Nick didn't know if the gun's safety was locked or unlocked, or even where the safety was located, or even if there were bullets in the clip. If the gun didn't fire, Nick would leave immediately and never look back. If the gun did fire, well then, it's God's decision.

Aiming at a general target rather than a specific one, Nick pulled the trigger and the gun fired. The shot was much louder than Nick had anticipated and the bullet penetrated the leopard-designed covering on the side of them, creating a miniature waterspout. Alyce let out a scream. Her eyes were so darkened by widened pupils that they looked like those from an old-fashioned doll. Leon Eldridge seemed unfazed, except now he was being drenched in water. The fucking stopped.

But not for long. Alyce restarted her ride wetter than ever, and Leon Eldridge began to time his upward thrusts with Alyce's descent. They started to yelp repeatedly, prompting Nick to fire the gun again, this time drawing blood as the bullet ripped into Leon Eldridge's far shoulder. Yet that didn't stop a thing as the pace picked up. Nick fired again, this shot more lethal, tearing into the Leon Eldridge's profile just under his ear. Now Alyce was in overdrive. The next bullet would be for her.

Nick took specific aim at Alyce. In gross inestimation, Nick planned to fire and then close his eyes to avoid seeing Alyce sustain the hit. Of course when Nick fired, he was able to see the bullet pierce Alyce's inward belly button — a perfect shot if he was actually aiming for it—as well as the clunk of blood and flesh exiting her backside just off the spine. Amazingly, that still didn't stop Alyce as the impact altered her movement, making her hips swirl even more. Nick fired again and the bullet entered and exited the hardened tip of her nearest tit before entering her body again in between her breasts. But her body was still pumping. Nick fired again, this time right between Alyce's doll-like eyes—a perfect shot, and maybe he was aiming for it. Alyce's head snapped back and then slumped forward, bringing her whole being body down on Leon Eldridge. Their blood mingled with the spouting water.

Nick looked at the finally still bodies and then at the armoire's mirror and caught himself staring at himself. He saw blood splattered on his white shirt as well as the gun in his hand. He was now a murderer—a mass murderer at that, but Nick was surprised how therapeutic such a splurge of violence can be. He felt relieved. Maybe he could live through this.

Then they came back to life, at least their lower parts did resuming their swan-song fuck. Horror and panic descended on Nick, who pointed the gun and pulled the trigger again and again while screaming, "Stop! Stop!" But they didn't stop, and the gun didn't fire. Although it was a 9-millimeter, apparently it was loaded with a revolver-amount of bullets.

Nick fled the room, and as he passed Dr. Dennis Gabor, he threw the gun at him but hit the experiment instead, shattering the frame's glass. The elevator again didn't wait for him—who can be using it? Nick frantically pushed the button over and over as he could still hear what was quite literally dead people fucking on a murdered bed.

Finally, the doors opened and Nick pressed the down button once inside. But the doors didn't immediately close, prompting Nick to scream "Come on! Come on!" before they finally did. In the elevator, Nick anxiously hopped up and down in place ready to bolt from the scene in record time. When the doors opened, Nick saw he was in the basement. The light from the elevator only traveled to the first beam, like eternal darkness was closing in. Nick didn't want to brave it, and frantically and repeatedly pushed the up button. When the elevator doors opened again, Nick let out a shrill scream seeing that he was back on the turret floor again. Sound waves from the fucking zombies echoed through the halls.

The elevator opened on the main floor. Nick ran toward the front entrance, and as he approached the foyer, he caught a fleeting glimpse of Leon Eldridge's floating creation. Its green glow seemed greater than ever before—but how could Nick really tell from the corner of his eye?

When he got to the doors, Nick "remembered" they were tied shut with the thick chain. Was it a knot or non-knot? Nick violently tugged at the tangled mesh to no avail before foolishly trying to open the doors anyway. Nick was able to find the end of the chain and, remembering again that there was no padlock to deal with, began to un-loop the chain from the doors' handles. But being in such a hurry to escape, Nick undid only a couple of loops before trying to open the doors, then undid a couple of more before trying again. The effort wasn't entirely futile. Every time Nick tried to open the doors, the gap got a little bigger due to the extra slack.

Nick felt that the "illuminated" figures in the painting behind him were observing his actions. But Nick didn't dare to turn back for fear of what forms they now took.

When Nick got to the final loop—which he could have undone and freed the doors for good—the gap was big enough for Nick to duck under and squeeze himself while popping off the steel fastener of his pants and ripping them at the zipper. Nick's erect groin was also compressed.

Nick leaped off the porch but didn't clear the final step and fell hard while twisting his ankle again. Nick didn't feel the pain and got up to run down the hill, taking another shortcut. But his unfastened and torn pants lowered down to Nick's thighs, making him lose balance just before he got to the bottom of the hill. Nick fell hard again, and rolled a few times before finding himself face-to-face with the driveway's asphalt.

Nick pulled himself up. Now his pants were nearly torn in half and were a useless hindrance, so he tried to discard them. Nick also discarded his shoes when they became obstacles in the removal of his pants.

Now with only his shirt, socks and erection-concealing underwear on his person, Nick ran, faster than he had ever ran before. He was heading east—but not toward the academy or Elder Stephen. Nick planned to run well past that, all the way to the next state. And with his legs free of pants and shoes, Nick actually believed he could make it without stopping.

No longer settling for the shoulder, Nick took to the road. Cars swerved and changed lanes to avoid Nick, as the motorists couldn't help but gawk at the sight, prompting several incredulous insults. Nick's bright-white-leg trek eventually caught the attention of a civilian on patrol, who slowed down to pull along side of Nick.

"Get off the road!" the officer shouted through the rolled-down passenger window—his strobes were activated. Nick kept on running. The officer angled his vehicle about 30 feet in front of Nick's lane, then with nightstick in hand, got out of his car. Nick didn't try to elude him. Instead, he laid himself on "The Great Highway," pried his erection out of the leg opening of his underwear, and started to masturbate.

The officer was taken aback by this exhibition, giving Nick a chance to get in a good beat. Finally, he grabbed Nick while keeping Nick's hands and arms away from his cock, rolled him over on his stomach—Nick's groin was compressed again—and handcuffed him. Then he lifted Nick off the street and began to forcefully escort Nick to the squad car. Nick's penis and balls were still hanging out of his underwear. While escorting him, the officer did Nick—who desperately wanted to finish what he started—a favor. The officer pulled hard on Nick's right bicep, which in turn moved Nick's cuffed right hand forward enough where he could grab his hard-on, which was conveniently exposed on that side of Nick's body.

When Nick got a hold of it near the knob, the officer pulled on Nick's right bicep again. The aided action caused Nick to shoot the mother of all loads on the front of the officer's uniform. Some of it even soiled his badge.

"Jesus Christ!" the officer said in disgust.

Chapter Twenty-seven

For Nick, things could have been worse. Really.

He could have been placed in the bowels of the government center with the newly-incarcerated "population." The jail, bowels and all, was the hub of the center, surrounded and insulated by the other county government offices. It was a stop for the local felons, sometimes for the full sentence.

Pedro, from the population alumni he encountered during his ventures into "The Heart of Darkness," knew and told about the bowel's frightening conditions and its frightening "blatnye-brute" occupants numbering well into the hundreds and placed into sections so cramped that they could appall the likes of Solzhenitsyn. The sections were simply outlined with streaks of paint on the floor, which begged to be breached, thus spoiling any desired separation between rival gangs and ethnic groups. When fights and riots broke out, they lasted terrifyingly long, with understaffed guards standing back only wading into the fray when the violence had mostly bled itself dry.

Nick wasn't placed in the bowels. Instead—suicide watch. It was for his own safety, they explained to Nick, and the safety of others.

Nick made a statement the night the semen-sprayed officer took him in. Authorities at first didn't know what to make of Nick dressed only with socks, underwear and a blood-splattered shirt. He had to be on drugs. And when Nick offered to make the report more comprehensive, he had to go through his rambling testimony three times before being taken seriously enough to be officially recorded.

After the murder scene had been checked out, verifying much of what Nick said, he was transferred to the government center where he made a more coherent statement. Later, Nick was informed that he was being charged with two counts of first-degree murder, resisting arrest and assaulting an officer. Nick couldn't help but chuckle at the assaulting-officer charge. Those present may have thought it to be amusing, too, but their faces remained stoic—apparently experienced with the follies of the indigent.

"I just want to remind you," one of them told Nick, now cleaned up and dressed in blue denim jumpsuit with matching slippers—they took his shirt for evidence, but they let him keep and wear his cum-crusted underwear, which probably could have been used as evidence for the assaulting-officer charge, "that your statement is not a confession."

Nick, who had grown weary and detached during the passing hours, suddenly perked up. "What do you mean I'm not making a confession?"

"We're not accepting one until you have been counseled."

"I don't need to be counseled to make a confession."

"You do if we want it to stand up in court."

Nick didn't want to go to court. He just wanted to be locked up for life, or better yet, be put to death. But he realized that he might not have a choice in the matter.

Then they took Nick to his cell. It was one of three side-by-side connected rooms encased on three sides by Plexiglas so thick that a stinger missile probably couldn't penetrate it. The back wall for all three was pink drywall. The entrance to each cell opened and closed like a door, and had shelf trays similar to those at gas stations in crime-ridden areas. The cells each had a plastic table and chair, a cot and a stainless steel toilet coming out of the pink drywall.

They didn't seem entirely suicide proof. For one, the cots had pillows, something to smother oneself with. And there was no padding on the walls to prevent one from bashing his head against them. But there was a watchman, a black man in uniform who had to weigh over 400 pounds. He sat in the middle of three sets of chairs and desks in front of the middle cell, Nick's new home for now.

He seemed to pay little attention to Nick. He had his feet propped up on the desk and was watching a miniature TV and reading a newspaper at the same time. But every once in a while, the watchman caught Nick staring at him. Apparently, even stinger-proof Plexiglas couldn't shield vibrations.

A series of inappropriate open-sea and sailboat-based paintings were tacked on to brown, plywood-covered wall facing the cells from about 15 feet. There was a wide doorway in the middle of the wall, which partially revealed a big office behind it. After three or four hours, Nick, who remained seated upright in front of the table as—although he was tired he didn't feel like sleeping—saw the office fill up with government employees, some in uniform, some not. This concerned Nick because knew he would eventually have to use the toilet, and he didn't want to shit in staff view.

Later that morning, Nick met in private with his appointed defender. He was a young man with slick combed-back, black hair. Though dressed professionally, he looked somewhat disheveled and Nick suspected this wasn't his only case for the day.

He greeted Nick with a cordial hello, but he didn't offer a handshake nor make much eye contact with Nick. He was more occupied with the contents contained within the brown folder apparently just prepared and handed to him.

"I see you made two separate statements," he said to Nick while perusing the papers.

Nick didn't answer.

"Before we go any further, may I ask you a question?" he said as if giving Nick an option to refuse before asking it anyway. "Were you under the influence of drugs or medication?"

Nick was surprised by such audacity. "I don't do drugs," he said firmly, before meekly adding, "Or a...a...at least not anymore."

The public defender's eyebrows rose. "Listen, if there ever was a time to admit to doing drugs, this is it."

He continued to ask other questions, and Nick began to fade. The defender's voice plodded along with excruciating condescension. At one point he said, "You don't look like a killer to me," and Nick just nodded his head, like that splattered person staring back at him in the armoire's mirror wasn't really him.

Several hours later, Nick and his defender stood in a courtroom, where, as a pre-trial formality, were asked for a plea.

"Not guilty," the public defender answered before Nick had a chance to open his mouth.

Not guilty? Then again if the past is probable, maybe Hitler is not guilty.

After lunch—ravioli incidentally—and dinner—some meat-like substance and cold mashed potatoes—Nick had to defecate. He waited until the office was empty, but the black watchman remained. He must be working triple shift. Nick had to ask him for toilet paper, and he obliged by slipping a half roll under the tray's glass.

"Bring it back when you're done."

After his movement, Nick went to sleep. He dreamt that he was walking toward his parents' house after he finished his french fries at the diner. It was a more enjoyable journey, as Nick barely felt the weight of his sack. He was so relieved that he decided to continue westward instead of turning back to murder Alyce and Leon Eldridge in their erotic throes. The dream had to be real. How could the other events be anything but a nightmare?

Then Nick heard his full name being called out. And again, more louder than before. It woke Nick, now back in suicide watch.

"You have a visitor," said a new watchman, this one a Caucasian but with about the same girth.

Who could it be, and was he ready for a visitor. A meeting with Pedro would be unpredictable. A meeting with Elder Steven, probably Nick's most-able confidant, would be too painful. As for Elder Bingham or Nick's parents—go to hell!

Nick tried to look into the partially concealed office to possibly get a glance of who it was before saying, "I don't want to talk to anybody."

"Fine," the watchman said. "You'll be eating those words."

Later that day, they transferred Nick out of suicide watch. They escorted him to a floor that resembled that of a hospital lined with semi-private rooms. Nick anticipated rows of iron-bar cells with inmates in clear view. Instead, the cells had standard-looking steel doors with one-by-two steel-mesh windows at eye level. All of them were closed—Nick arrived during lock-down.

When Nick's cell was opened, he discovered he had a cellmate. Nick tried not to look at him, who was seated on the far end of the lower bunk bed. *I wonder who gets top and bottom*, Nick dreadfully thought. Nick's cellmate was reading some sort of literature. Nick didn't acknowledge the man's size or skin color as he just kept him in the corner of his eye while he sat himself on a protruding bench near the cell door. Nick knew interaction was inevitable.

Nick's cellmate moved closer to the other side of the bed. Now they were only several feet apart, but Nick still didn't know his skin color or dimensions.

"Hey," Nick's cellmate said, making Nick flinch on the inside. "I know you."

Nick then faced him, and he did know him, or he at least knew who he was: the slight balding, goateed man Nick was about to approach at the tavern before being brutally beaten. But he never got to him. He must have remembered the thrashing.

"Yeah, I remember you," the man said smiling—the left side of his upper bridge was missing. "You're one of those—I don't know what they call you guys—soul winners...is that it? But you should have been a comedienne. That joke you told me about the holes in Jesus' feet nearly killed me."

What? Nick thought as he tried to recheck his flawed memory. Was this that "back-from-the-dead" guy who smoked that fateful joint with me?

"I never laughed so hard in my life," he said, confirming that he wasn't. But where did he hear that joke?

"But seriously, what you said later sure set me on course."

What?

"And it's funny how two people traveling such different paths end up in the same place from time to time," the man said before pointing both of his thumbs upward. "Though what matters most is where we end up in the end."

A smile then crept over Nick's face. He somehow believed him.

The End

To Mike,

Hope you like it
If you ever have time
to read it.

John Brady

Printed in the United States
41544LVS00003B/619-639